MONEY IS LOVE

RICHARD CONDON

MONEY IS LOVE

The Dial Press New York 1975

Manufactured in the United States of America

First printing

Library of Congress Cataloging in Publication Data

Condon, Richard.

  Money is love.

  I. Title.
PZ4.C7460Mo   [PS3553.0487]   813'.5'4   75–5556
ISBN 0–8037–5752–2

For My Darling Evelyn

Special appreciation is gratefully expressed for the scholarship and poetic insight of Gustave Davidson in his **A Dictionary of Angels** *(The Free Press, New York; Collier-Macmillan, London) and to James Bailey for his brilliant invocation of ancient history in his* **The God-Kings and the Titans** *(Hodder and Stoughton, London) from which this author drew inspiration and information.*

MONEY IS LOVE

Money, money, always money,
Is money a new kind of language of love?
Would you talk about money to the Easter bunny?
Does a dove coo money to another dove?

> *Fill up nine canoesful,*
> *Money is baroque—*
> *The only time it's useful,*
> *Is when you're broke.*
>
> —*The Keeners' Manual*

PART ONE

One

Eugene Quebaro, homeowner and husband, sat with the wife of another man in a restaurant on East 60th Street run by a canny Filipino who carried a $127,000 retirement policy sold him by Gene. Quebaro would have stood out in a blur of rich politicians or senior Mafiosi like a great opal in a coal bin. His clothing seemed to have been painted on him by that Power which had invented butterflies.

The birdcage motif of the restaurant was so successful that many of the luncheon patrons seemed to have a tongue tic, as if they were tasting for feathers in the food. Golden conures and emerald touracos perched or flew behind the lighted glass walls and the glass ceiling overhead. Ticless, Gene was eating an argotic *Pancit Guisado* with long, slow, sideways chews.

He was euphoric. That morning, he and Carlotta had decided to liquidate their Australian nickel mine shares. The mine was sound but the management hadn't yet been able to get a road to it. They were going to put what was left of their investment in forward Thai *baht*. The *baht* had closed at nineteen to the dollar and they could get a guarantee of sixteen, collectable in nine months, yet still earn interest, so they would have to be crazy, Carlotta had explained, to hold on to the nickel mine stock.

Carlotta was brilliant. She just had the instinct. She was also very pretty and sensual but what Gene loved about her, after her being just Carlotta, was her complete peace with money in any form.

Mrs. Garvish, the woman across the table from him today, was having waffles à la mode with a very tall glass of iced tea. Her hat was made out of two viridescent

3

straw hands held palm upward in the form of a cup from which tropical flowers were growing. Gene had taken care to admire the hat extravagantly because it was such a heinous mistake.

"Say—are you Italian or something?" she asked as softly as she could and still be heard over the din of the restaurant.

Gene shrugged lightly. "My grandmother was a Swede and my grandfather was a Filipino."

"Is this a Swedish restaurant?"

"Filipino."

"My God. No kidding? How come they have Jewish waiters?"

"Mrs. Garvish, my grandparents had nineteen children in the Islands. Only one, my father, came to the States. My mother is a New Yorker of Polish descent. She went to Julia Richman High School."

"My God. I went to Julia Richman."

"Consequently, I look Filipino, like my grandfather, but I am very tall, like my grandmother."

Mrs. Garvish stared at the printed menu. "So that is Filipino."

"Spanish," Gene said. He took her hands in his, across the table. He said, "If you really want Ronnie to have a chance at finding his place in ballet, and little Frieda to become a CPA, then you'll have to make it happen yourself."

"I hate to tamper."

"With your own kids?"

"I hate to get involved."

"That doesn't sound like a mother talking."

"What am I supposed to do?"

He stared at her hard so she couldn't escape the truth. "You have to buy the future," he said slowly. "There are all kinds of money, all kinds of currencies. Money isn't what you spend, it's what you buy. You will be buying happiness and security for two wonderful kids. That is called Mother's Gold and there is no higher form of money."

"You don't know my kids. Frieda only says

she wants to be a CPA. My husband is determined that she is going to be a dentist."

"Either or both are honorable professions."

"But what am I supposed to do? Frieda is only seven. My husband thinks it's his choice. I'm all mixed up."

"You'll have to convince your husband tonight."

"Tonight? His parents are coming tonight. He'll be in a terrible mood."

"You will start on him after the parents leave. Keep at him until he runs out of bed and locks himself in the bathroom."

"I don't know if I can do it. We don't have that kind of a relationship. He gets so frustrated he tries to set fire to the towels." This was a white lie. It was Mrs. Garvish who got that frustrated and, as she knew, charred towels are no cinch to dispose of on a regular basis.

Gene went on inexorably. "Then, tomorrow morning, as soon as you see his eyes are open, you begin again with the same thing. And you keep it up while he tries to eat his breakfast. Then you let him rush out of the house. You wait an hour—" Gene made implacable gestures with his hands to instruct Mrs. Garvish that she was not to interrupt"—and you begin to call him at the office. You keep demanding to know if he has made an appointment to see me. And remember—you have the easy part."

"I know. I know."

"Frieda is seven. Ronnie is five. In about a dozen years you've got to be ready to give them your dreams."

She looked away from him, bit her lower lip, and nodded.

"The process takes time," Gene said. "It's the only reliable way for capital to accumulate. You've got to think for your babies."

Her eyes got misty. She blinked the moisture away and it spattered on the palomino mink car coat that her

mother had bought her for giving up cigarettes and switch-
ing to pot.

"Today and tomorrow are nothing," Gene
said gently. "Everything that counts is ten or fifteen years
from now. That is what made America great." Whenever
Gene thought of his own years ahead, he saw himself with
Carlotta at one of those terrific Rockresorts, playing scratch
golf on an absolutely empty course while grinning black
caddies adored them. Carlotta had shown him projections of
what they'd have ten, then sixteen, then twenty-nine years
from now. They lived together in the future as though it
were a motel.

His huge hand enveloped Mrs. Garvish's as
the pod envelops a tiny pea. Gene was neither small nor
quick but his face had a ferally pretty Filipino cast and a dash
of intelligence. His teeth were almost always laid out across
his face like an African trader's ivory samples, in a salesman's
lifetime grimace of reassurance. His teeth were made all the
whiter by his perpetual tan and his shining straight black hair
which reflected light like a polished steel helmet. The entire
portrait contrasted with his rooted New York speech.

"Your husband is young and healthy, Mrs.
Garvish. The premiums will be so low that it will be like
finding the money when those two wonderful youngsters
need it. And—which is out of the question—if your husband
should have an accident and pass on, all of you would be
sitting pretty."

Mrs. Garvish's chin got firm. "Sylvan will call
you, Mr. Quebaro," she said. "But I wish you hadn't let me
order waffles in a Filipino restaurant."

"It looked like a great waffle, Mrs. Garvish."

"It wasn't bad."

o

Eugene Quebaro was an outstanding life insurance and retirement plan salesman. He had been voted
the Best Dressed Man at the Million Dollar Round Table for
eight consecutive years while nobody, not even his father,
knew that Carlotta made his suits, shirts, ties, handkerchiefs,
and underwear. When they had been first married she had

also loomed the material for his suitings and overcoats but now she bought them direct (at cost) from her father, who was in the woolens trade at Leeds, England. Carlotta had attended the Merchant Tailors School in London because she was determined to be married someday to a very sharp dresser and, feeling the way she did about money, she was equally determined that they were not going to pay any fancy prices to dress him well. Carlotta also made her own wine, soap, bread, sauerkraut, and the candles used in electrical power emergencies.

Also, she was a wildly keen hobbyist with a genuine knack for electronics. She had fitted out a little hobby workshop in the cellar at home where she designed and built Gene's little electronic pocket calculators, the color television sets they had built into every room, the hi-fi of course, and the two-way conversation gadget to Gene's car wherever it might be within a 227-mile radius. Everything mechanical they owned had been transistorized by Carlotta. She could turn on her stove or turn off her washing machine from New York to Connecticut. Gene's pride was that she had managed to do the whole thing for just over $370 (and that included six color TV sets with twenty-four-inch screens) with quite a bite of that represented by sales tax.

Carlotta was a natural ash blonde and so pretty, so elementally sensual, that she had once been pinched all over her behind by a native Italian priest who was visiting New York on the Papal Nuncio's staff. Carlotta had dragged him off the Madison Avenue bus and tried to have him arrested but the young Irish-American cop had refused to believe her. The priest, who couldn't speak English, had gone free. Carlotta was really liberated. She had run after him, giving him cruelly severe pinches on *his* behind. A militant Catholic woman had leapt out of a taxi and whacked Carlotta with her handbag. In the ensuing fight, Carlotta had decked the woman while she kept a firm grip on the priest. A big crowd gathered, which attracted a mobile unit of *The Daily News,* so Carlotta got her picture in the paper, which brought in two marriage proposals and over two hundred indecent offers. The caption overlooked the priest in the

7

picture, even though he was struggling to get away.

Overall, Carlotta concentrated on three things in her life: (1) Gene, (2) the fact that Gene earned $85,000 a year, coming up from $10,000 the year they had been married, and (3) the sure knowledge that, working closely together the way they did, they could raise Gene's income as high as $150,000 a year. Gene and Carlotta loved each other deeply and knew they were each other's true money. They knew that, as long as they had each other, they would never want for anything. Gene spent his wife's cunning every day. Carlotta spent Gene's animal magnetism and his stamina. Combined, it was one of the great American fortunes.

Carlotta understood money. She knew that a great first baseman was really a beautifully cut Siam ruby with a specific gravity of 4.05 and a hardness registering 667 on the Brinell scale because, when the beautiful young mistress of the aging owner of the baseball club said she could not live without a ruby of that specific gravity and hardness, the baseball magnate sold his first baseman in order to be able to acquire the ruby which the mistress would then purchase from the aging owner with *her* money: i.e., a superior bottom, two planetary-pointing boobs, and a mouth having the softness of .00003 on the Pablum scale. Money was money wherever you found it, Carlotta understood.

Also, Carlotta knew what to do with money after she got it; i.e., to use it to generate more money in many different forms. It was just that she did not have the necessary creative knack to attract money to herself in the first instance. Gene had that gift. Gene's sales concept alone was why he was sitting at the Million Dollar Round Table earning $85,000 a year. How did he do it? What was his sales secret? He never sold directly.

Gene believed that female beneficiaries should sell insurance for him. They had been trained by the man, who had been guaranteed that he would die first, to believe that they would need protection. If women were to become, suddenly, the people who bought and paid for all the insurance, the statistics would soon show that women die sooner than men. He believed that, to sell insurance on a sure-fire basis, he had to press down hard on the women to sell the men to buy it.

He had been timid about going up against his company's tested sales systems at first. "After all," he said to Carlotta, "the company has worked out its selling techniques in a really scientific way."

"Bullshit," Carlotta said. "It's only a scientific way to produce a lot of sure-fire ten-thousand-dollar-a-year men. Give me seven hundred thousand salesmen all sure to knock down ten thousand in commissions and I'll show you a healthy business. Your way, this new way, contains the wisdom of the ages, so let the company knock off with their scientific selling techniques."

"What do you mean?"

"About what?"

"The wisdom of the ages."

"It's right there in all the homely sayings, isn't it? The hand that rocks the cradle rules the world. That's Instant Wisdom? Isn't that what life insurance is all about?"

Carlotta's simple maxim became Eugene Quebaro's prime article of sales faith. He and Carlotta worked tirelessly to test his theories and prove them right.

"Children are the money a wife has to spend," Carlotta explained. "They are the only sound currency she can buy the husband with."

Together, she and Gene shaped their sales methods to make friends with the children to buy the attention of the mother who could be guided to sell the husband to buy the insurance. There could be nothing careless about this stage.

Once Gene got well into it, he found himself working on many levels. In some cases, he would be closing the sale with the husband. With others, he would be starting anew, meeting the children. He could be on as many as eleven cases at one time at different stages of development. For fifty-six dollars a month Carlotta bought a specialized list of young executives who earned not less than thirty thousand dollars a year. Anyone who earned less couldn't afford rent, much less insurance. Any young fellows who earned more might have the arrogance to think they didn't need life insurance. Carlotta photographed every prospect's child through a hole in the panel of a Volkswagen delivery truck which Gene's dad, a Volkswagen dealer, had let them have at cost. She worked in front of each family's apartment building for a dollar bribe to the doorman who thought she was looking for a place to park. Carlotta developed and printed the pictures herself and, with the flash of another dollar and a forged *Daily News* card, the doorman would identify each child in the pictures. After that everything moved semi-automatically. The children would be followed to their schools. During outdoor playground periods, Carlotta's uncle, a retired English midget dressed as a boy of twelve, would enter the playground and beat up the prospect's children as Gene came running in from the street, shouting in Spanish, driving Carlotta's uncle away. Then he would bundle the weeping children into a cab, take them home, and instant contact would have been made.

Next came the brush with death for the mother: the big sales key. This was no television commercial. This was the real thing. It placed the problem squarely in the woman's terrain. It established that death was at everyone's elbow.

Carlotta would know where the mother shopped. Gene rented a dog on a leash—preferably a small active dog—and would be passing the supermarket as the woman emerged, laden with bundles. They would nearly collide. The woman would recognize Gene as the wonderful man who had saved her children from a Puerto Rican monster because *Gene's* yelling in Spanish would have convinced the confused children and, naturally, the mother wanted to believe that anyway. The little dog would pull and dart and get himself entangled in their legs.

Carlotta would follow Gene and the mother home, driving a new orange Volkswagen station wagon. She had been a winning stock car driver in the Ladies' Day Races on the Big Dixie Wheel for eleven months before she met Gene, and was a superb driver under any conditions. Her eyes were as pale as ball bearings: as she glared out of the car, leaning over the wheel with a black cigarillo dangling from the corner of her mouth, the effect, as she flashed by and was gone, was terrifying. Carlotta could make a car do anything. She came roaring around the corner and just missed hitting the mother, but clipped the little dog and sent it flying. The bundles scattered. The mother's legs turned to water and she collapsed on the pavement. Gene positioned her sitting against a lamppost so that, when she could focus again, she would be looking at the dead dog. Once, Gene had been lucky enough to have a mother with a slight coronary condition. As a result of Carlotta's great driving, he had closed with her husband the next afternoon at the hospital.

Gene would remain as steady as a rock until he got the mother home. Then his own legs would give way and he would be invited upstairs to recover. They would share a joint or a Coke or something. Gene would stare at her glassily and say, "I can always get another little dog, I guess, but we can't shop around for another life, can we?"

"It was a Connecticut car. My God, that woman's eyes!"

"They drive special jobs. That was a very kicky kind of a car—"

"My God, that little dog!"

"My whole life passed in front of me," Gene said dully. "Worse—I saw my family defenseless and I thanked God we had sacrificed to buy a plan."

"What kind of a plan?"

"So my family would be safe."

"It must cost a fortune."

"I wasn't spending. I was saving my own money which my family gets all back—*plus.*"

"Where did you get it, the plan?"

Gene took an in-put from the joint, setting his face grimly. "I am now in the business of plans." He leaned toward her: earnest and clean-cut. "I was within ten hours of signing for a fried chicken franchise. Which is money in the pan. Then my wife asked me to sit down and talk it all over with her."

"The franchise?"

"The plan. Her sister had invested in a plan and her sister's husband wasn't nearly in the income bracket

11

I was. I humored her. I read the plan through. I read all the fine print. I was absolutely knocked out by it. I mean—so much so that I turned my back on a fried chicken franchise and put on my hat and went downtown and had a long talk with the people who developed that plan." He stood up as if that were all there was to say. He walked to the hall table and picked up his hat.

"Where are you going?"

"It's running late. I know we both have a million things to do."

"But what about the plan?"

"Not today. I am too humbled by that brush with death to talk about anything as arrogant as business."

"Business? But you said—"

"Tonight, just know a little togetherness with your husband," he said in a wistful way. "Remember what it is to be alive. Tell him—if you can remember it—about my little dog. Tonight just celebrate being alive." Then he would leave her alone.

o

It was late spring. He felt euphoric. He squeezed Mrs. Garvish's hand across the table in the Filipino restaurant on 60th Street, paid the bill, and left her there. He turned the corner into Lexington and started downtown to the pet shop on 56th Street to pick up the next dog rental. He crossed to the east side of Lexington, walked past Bloomingdale's, never noticing a tall Afro hairdo who was standing in the bright sun wearing mirror shades and popping caps into his mouth like they were peanuts. As Gene passed him, the man with the naps, black three hundred and sixty degrees, began to walk heavy behind him. To buy some fun, he took Gene around the throat with his left forearm and, with a tricky twist he had picked up in Nam, broke Gene's neck, held Gene over his own chest and stabbed him all over the rib cage with a seven-inch hunting knife. Gene never made a sound, never knew what happened. If he had known, he would have died happily, knowing that he had bought a plan for Carlotta before the clink nixed him out, all the way.

12

Two

The clerk recorded the closing of the first session of the Ninth Convention of the Joint (⚕) Commission for the Evaluation of Sin, in New York, in June 1975, simultaneously with the death of Eugene Quebaro. The meeting was the first to be called by the J(⚕)CES since the marvelous convention held in Copenhagen in November 1814, ten years after the invention of power printing by Koenig, on the day the first machine-printed copy of *The Times* appeared in London.

There had been agitations to force other conclaves in the interim. When the first needle addict, Mrs. Alexander Wood, wife of the late, great Dr. Wood, prime developer of the modern hypodermic, had become hopelessly hooked, a move was made to convene, but not until the Germans produced the first heroin in 1898 did the leaders agree to another summit confrontation, "in the near future." At short last, seventy-seven years later, an agenda had been worked out.

Petitions to call a new meeting were, in fact, always coming up, but both sides hated the idea because of the old guilt. Every time they sat to set new codes of right and wrong for the human beings who had invented them, they all felt themselves teetering at the edge of the possibility that what Lucifer™ had done might not have been all that bad. Yet the convention also knew its work was important. Man had created them as divinities to administer the morals which Man himself did not understand but vaguely felt were useful because by and large they were good for business, for "social progress," and for status control. Each time the J(⚕)CES was forced to call one more convention to draft yet

13

another moral code—a readily evaluable system for sinning by points—it was because mankind had lapsed *again* into too great a familiarity with the former moral system arranged at the previous convention. A new set of specific rules was required so that both Heaven and Hell could administer the required morality. Man evaded any explanation that sin, therefore, must be a relative thing, a negotiated rules system which both Heaven and Hell could agree upon as being their common policing goals for the tenure of the new moral code established by the previous convention. As long as "good" and "evil" were apparent, in regulatory form, they did not have to be real. They only had to *seem* constant. They had to suit the whims and tastes of the Client who was Man the creator of God and all other things divine. Many, many other deities had been invented by many, many other geographical and cultural constituencies but they everywhere existed in only two basic accepted groupings: Establishment religion and Pagan religion, each of these being further sub-divided into work parties of divinity, representing "good" on the one hand and "evil" on the other. The Joint (⇅) Commission for the Evaluation of Sin, for instance, was separated into equal forces representing Good↑ and Evil↓, but the essence of the Being of both sides was the collective Godhead of the most conservative sort of Establishment religion.

The divinities of this Establishment were, of course, wholly controlled by the humans who had invented them. God® and his angels, Satan™ and his fiends had been denied free will. However, over the millennia they had accrued a vast histrionic ability and no small number of illusions so that, relying on the lack of interest of all Men in passing down total truth from one generation to the next, they managed, through the manipulation of partial truths, and the knowledge of various arcane systems, to maintain the illusion of an upper hand over the gigantic constituency they served.

Within three thousand years of the moment the first lung fish had sauntered out of the oceans, the first J(⇅)CES convention had been summoned. Until then no reexamination of sin had been necessary. Fish are a fundamental sort of religious group, a stolid lot who seemed more than willing to remain with the moral code they had demanded be provided for them to insure that size alone did not fix the submarine social structure. However on dry land this was the case no longer, due to the stimulation of oxygen and sunshine and, later, of eating all that meat.

The second convention of the Commission was called in 39,000 B.C. at the time of the enormous industry for the mining of haematite, the trading currency for the Boskops and Florisbads of South Africa with the European trading capital, La-Chapelle-aux-Saintes, in France. As this mining industry with its camp followers and appetites undertook its peri-global spread across the 5500 miles between Swaziland and France, the entire moral atmosphere became disorganized and therefore far less useful to mankind than it should have been until the Joint Commission, newly hired for that purpose, could look the other way no longer. Morals, in this neanderthal period of the Middle Stone Age, were being bent out of all recognition. They had been invented to serve a bigger and better haematite mining industry and a cohesively profitable travel agency business to link the two, but gambling was rife and wasteful; dance halls and dance-hall women were tiring the labor force before their time. Certain business leaders were conspiring to get much, much more than their share. The Commission knew its duty and it did it well. It acted to set down a wholly new, improved schedule for acceptable sin. More than any other religious group of divines, the Establishment group, representing Heaven↑ and Hell↓, understood that they were to hand down codes capable of being adapted to modern human requirements for convenience sinning.

The third J(⤧)CES rally was called in 818 B.C. in Acapulco, in late February, just after the Phoenicians had established their steamy Mexican colonies, and 2100 years after the discovery of America by promoters from the Sumerian city-states in Mesopotamia. The Sumerians had been entirely satisfied to set up their capital at Lake Titicaca in Peru, to trade with Asia, to invent the Incas, to take their profit and return home, but the Phoenicians were a pack of drunken sailors who couldn't get enough of carousing, ignored all thrift programs and, in the course of loud-mouth-

15

ing everything, broke up a lot of nice, middle-class homes. This Joint(⇕) Commission met on Faro Point where John Wayne was to settle briefly 2783 years later. They enjoyed Acapulco a lot. The moral code they were able to hammer out at that convention was long-lasting and really useful to the Cretan, Greek, Scandinavian, Portuguese, Italian, and Spanish discoverers of America who followed in the next 2200 years.

○

Of course, just because the members of the Commission were divine didn't mean that they would not have many moments of *great* difficulty in solving human problems creatively with attractive, acceptable sins. On March 18, 3953 B.C., for example, when a Sumerian named Keifetz announced through the various trade media that he had perfected his invention, the first system of writing, done in cuneiform, the plain fact was that the Joint(⇕) Commission simply underestimated it. Sumerian was an agglutinative language and, frankly, the Commission never expected anybody to even try to invent the first writing to get sounds like that down on paper. But Keifetz did it, achieving polyphones and homophones in a remarkable system which his wife said (fourteen years later) he should have patented. "This could have been bigger than the tea bag," she told him.

The Commission awoke with a jolt when the Proto-Semitic alphabet came at them out of nowhere in the second quarter of the second millennium B.C.—that is, in the Hyksos period now commonly dated as 1730–1580 B.C. The Commission was so upset by the founding of the alphabet that would, in only 3500 years, grow into that wild babble of the greatest overcommunications industry conceivable by the most convoluted minds of the Firmament, that nobody wanted to take credit for inspiring the invention. Raziel[†], a great and learned angel, was able to narrow it down to the Hebrews, Hurrians, Hittites, and Indo-Iranians who had participated in the vast Hyksos movement but even a very, very brilliant angel like Raziel could not draw a tighter indictment than that, not even after the fourth Joint(⇕) Commission convention.

That was a scared convention. This alphabet stuff was not just a bunch of signs. It was a system that denoted each sound by one sign only. The alphabet revolution required a terrific overhaul for the moral code and a tremendous job for the entire conclave.

But the plain facts were that the Permanent Secretariat of the J(⇕)CES had been improvising about the ethics of these lung fish for well over a million and a half years and they were experienced. They kept impeccable records. They did their homework. And so it was generally realized that the time had come for actual field studies of a (more or less) controlled nature among the lung fish themselves, to get the "inside" client viewpoint. Example: from the outset no information had been sought by anyone at the J(⇕)CES concerning what the lung fish themselves thought of their moral health *before* radical new codes were voted and adopted. How well or badly adjusted did the lung fish consider themselves to be? Were they happy or unhappy; worried or unworried; optimistic or pessimistic? The subjective findings of past Commissions had been that (essentially) the lung fish did nothing about their troubles and, most often, demanded the right to diminish their joys. They would not (or could not) solve their moral problems for themselves, preferring rented solutions from astrologers, bartenders, priests, cab drivers, psychoanalysts, politicians, pushers, and the dangerous overcommunications industry.

As moral codes were developed for test areas —Las Vegas, Washington, Peking, Johannesburg, New York, et cetera—then modified and frozen as being "generally acceptable for adults," each new program would be almost immediately confounded by the lung fish for whom this carefully planned convenience sinning had been drawn. As each congress of angels of the Permanent Secretariat attempted to construct a code of morals that would be more elastic, the lung fish would cause these to be outmoded: a little indecent exposure would proliferate into mass streaking, the five-cent schooner of beer would become a five-dollar bag of tecana, coitus interruptus would grab at The Pill, the chastity belt, in the angels' view of time, was instantly replaced by panty hose. The more relaxed the Commission's moral codes became, the less the lung fish seemed capable of living with them. Not that the angelic blocs within the Commission were entirely blame-free. Each bloc wanted larger constituencies. Each sub-committee leader wanted a bigger "problem" to govern. Therefore excessive populations of lung fish were encouraged even though it was apparent that increased populations addled the poor fish and great multiplications of populations crazed them.

o

      At the first convention, the delegate Metatron↑, the greatest of all heavenly hierarchs, the link between human and divine (whose *assistant* was Gabriel), the Chancellor of Heaven and Chief of Ministering Angels, whose name is said to be pure Jewish invention but whose nickname was "Little Yhwh," took the keynote speech.
      "They can now breathe," he proclaimed grimly, "so soon they will start to talk. This is not going to be any easy job for us to keep up with, believe me. Let them talk and they will start up with political parties. As soon as they have politicians, they'll invent hypocrisy and they'll make war upon the weak. Therefore, to help them, which our basic contract with them calls for, and to separate them in our own minds from decent, right-living fish, we must begin by re-classifying them. I move, therefore, that we stop calling them lung fish and start calling them people."
      "Spelling, please," a backbencher yelled.
      Metatron glared. "P-e-e-p-u-l."
      "It doesn't sound right."
      "The clerk is instructed to improvise spelling along those guidelines," the Upper Chair↑ ruled. The Lower Chair↓ nodded agreement.
      At the fifth convention contracts were let to the theological establishment for the manufacture of Adam and Eve and considerable begatting began. Shortly thereafter, the eating of unrefrigerated pork was banned and

a draft of seventeen* commandments was proposed and approved.

There was much irritability about the demand for a sixth assembly when bagpipes were invented by the Greeks in A.D. 51, almost on the heels of the birth of Christ December 25, 0000, when the delegate Kavod↓ took the keynote.

"December twenty-fifth, zero zero zero zero," he orated, "was a day which will live long in infamy."

There were outcries.

"Hear, hear!"

Or, "Shame, sir!"

Or, "Stand down, sir!"

Kavod was indignant. He was a stocky angel with twenty-six wings and a pair of eyebrows on him like twin salamis. "An alibi for self-righteousness has been delivered unto them," he boomed. "The human fuzziness resulting from this single birth will sustain hypocrisy unto the apocalypse. Sins more devious, more difficult to evaluate than we could ever anticipate will be fashioned. Also—and this is no little also—this one happening will create an officer corps of clergy which will one day exceed the population of the present world—an army of smarmy layabouts, foursquare against honest work and beyond hope of rehabilitation."

No other Joint(↓↑) Commission session was called until 1794, on the afternoon the patent was issued to James Watt for his raised-pressure steam engine. The meeting was held in a pasture behind the house of a Mrs. Sis Ryan at Kilmoganny, County Kilkenny, Ireland, the commission knowing that the industrial revolution about to follow would never disturb this place. A delegate named Tzadiquel†, an archangel who ruled (rules) the planet Jupiter on Thursdays, held down the keynote with a sheaf of graph projections that were boring, but the debate on the coming moral transmogrification had begun. His keynote theme was: "The lung fish invented us because they needed us to behave well for them. Let us therefore set them our example."

*Subsequently reduced to ten by the client.

The people, formerly lung fish, were slippery, themselves morally inventive to an almost preposterous degree. What required moral mapping next, therefore, simply could not be anticipated. What the preposterous lung fish could think of to do wrongly was staggering. In the innocence of their greed for each other's attention they would produce triumphs of "the human spirit" (or "free will") which would quickly become obsolete. Last year's witches were next year's martyrs. A glorious empire upon which the sun could never set became, so shortly, a heinous exploitation. France continued to produce the French blandly as if there were absolutely nothing wrong with that. A dollar earned and invested at 11 per cent became a force for pollution and corruption. The Russians discovered the profit motive at the same instant the Chinese discovered a Dr. Kissinger.

No one, divine or mortal, could figure out what they were going to do next. The *lung fish* could *corrupt* anything. Even their invention of medicines had eventuated, almost in the twinkling of an eye, into the creation of a wholly chemical society. The J($^{↓↑}$)CES did their level best to sweep up after their clients and to provide the objectivity about sins and sinning that their clients could not be expected to maintain. Not that the lung fish were beyond redemption. Factually, the successive series of moral codes developed for them by the J($^{↓↑}$)CES had most certainly improved their ethical conduct enormously, at least for a time, the angels assured themselves. There was no question of the J($^{↓↑}$)CES *controlling* the lung fish but there was a hearty need for the J($^{↓↑}$)CES to *understand* them. If angels started to control the very clients who had invented them, given the willfulness of those clients, it was entirely possible that the lung fish would set about disinventing them, go about their world wailing "Is God dead? Or is he alive and well and living in Fairfield County?"

It was the lung fish themselves who began to suggest that money might be the cause of their burgeoning amorality—a condition which they proved time and time and again that they were capable of recognizing. But they did nothing to *understand* money, even while they complained (which was typical). Certainly nothing had been done to banish either money or the oil companies and other political systems which it had caused. The sudden identification of money as the villain made the angels blink. The scholarly inclined among them ran to their books. The others took a "wait-and-see" attitude. With the exception of seven out of more than 7,400,000 angels, none of them even knew what money was. If being created by Man as an angel didn't mean not needing to have the faintest idea about money, then what was the big advantage of being an angel?

Surely, after the 1814 meeting, considering the evolving Victorian duplicities, the development of the German compounded noun, the river of wars, the introduction of television, and the price of beef, one might have thought that any number of further J(⚕)CES meetings would have been called, but it was not until the vivid, vertical descent of all morality in the 1965–1975 decade, the ten terrible years when lung fish had more food and shared it less fairly than at any other time in history, that such a decision to meet once again was taken.

The Terrible Decade had been an excrement of time. These were peak years in the human struggle toward mass psychosis: the murder of the ecology by the creatures permitted to share the planet with eight thousand other dependent species; the universal use of mind-tunneling narcotics; violence, crime, and corruption as instruments of politics; and the total pollution of leadership.

The Money Congress (as it came to be called) met on the upper floors of the old Liederkranz Society Building in East 58th Street between Park and Lexington. The Liederkranz Society Building no longer existed; that is, not on the "level" or in "the other place" wherein the lung fish lived. The J(⚕)CES could not have operated effectively or controlled those social phenomena they were capable of controlling, if they operated among the lung fish in the same world as the lung fish. There had been nine J(⚕)CES conventions; therefore there were ten "worlds" or "levels" or "other places" that were more or less precise duplicates of the original place called variously "the world," "the earth," or "my home town." These were piled on top of each other in the Firmament, all sort of willy-nilly, no attempt being made at symmetry because the engineering angels almost always got dimensions wrong and the "worlds" or "levels" were of every which size. Still, it was a good system and it worked because, while it permitted the lung fish to believe that the angels and executive deities were directly above them, in heaven, at all times, it allowed the angels—by reason of total separation through *psychic* distance—complete adjacency to the lung fish and the use of their lives and bodies *in duplicate form.* Due to the nine conventions, every human now existed in multiples of ten. No one was aware of this, of course. Once the "cross-over" duplication was accomplished, no one remembered previous worlds. It would have been terribly confusing to have been doing the identical thing in ten places at once—if one *knew* that, that is.

The Liederkranz Society Building had been re-created in this tenth world because a Heavenly eastern district ward leader, one of the Gibborim[†] boys, of the order of song-uttering angels or cantors, said the Liederkranz Society represented "the good, old days"—before population densities had pushed all lung fish backs to the wall of mass insanity, due to money or its lack.

The fact that the J(⇕)CES could fit comfortably into the old Liederkranz Hall certainly smashes for all time the "positive count" of fallen angels made by the Cardinal Bishop of Tasculum in 1273, who said that 133,306,668 had fallen from heaven in a nine-day period; a mistake repeated by Alphonso de Spina in 1488. Enoch, who was much closer to the whole falling out, *claims* two hundred angels fell, but *names* only nineteen. The truth is, nineteen is the correct figure. That includes The Adversary™ himself.

However, neither of the Chief Executives— The Fallen™ nor The Power On High®—attended the convention sessions, with the exception of momentary flashing by Satan™. Head Office sent eighteen delegates plus a Chief of Mission, which matched the nineteen from the Lower House. Each mission was supported by its advisers, experts, researchers, translators, contact people, coordinators, secretaries, Xerox key operators, fixers, masseurs, finance officers, MC–82 typists, floral arrangements people, musicians, administrative aides, statisticians, relatives, communications and maintenance men, transportation and entertainment bureau chiefs, public relations units, cultural affairs experts, union leaders, camp followers, and the always essential security people. In all, the number of delegates plus administrative personnel who served the Money Meeting came to 133,306,668 angels, in and out, over the nineteen-day period of the convention.

The essence of the rules the meeting set down for field study procedures established that "the subjects for these objective field study tests will be one or more lung fish made available due to dying in 'the basic other place' (but otherwise in excellent health and of acceptable age) at points within the Borough of Manhattan, City of New York, which will be nearest to the meeting site of this convention at the micro-millisecond at which this convention will recess for lunch on the first day of assembly" and that "a sufficient number of observers" would be assigned to supervise and conduct field tests "representing Upper and Lower jurisdictions." These observers would "write and cause to be printed" a joint report on these investigations into the nature of money so that the Commission might prescribe a new morals program for the lung fish.

"What kind of a bunch are these lung fish?" cried out N'Zuriel Yhwh†, one of the eight highest ranking princes of the Merkabah, all of whom, it seemed, occupied stations superior to Metatron. "There is even a gap between the men and the women for the balance of hair and the distribution of testicles. Money, whatever it is—and I am very, very sorry it didn't come to my attention sooner because, after all, if I can help I want to help—has called up a terrible indifference by youth to any form of hope or by their elders to any form of despair."

He sat down abruptly, very red at the wing-tips but controlling his agitation. There was an enormous applause.

When it subsided, Raziel, whose nickname was "Secret of God" and "Angel of Mysteries," an intellectual-looking angel who wore bi-focals made of Umbramatic glass—a German product which made the eyeglasses darker as the light got brighter—got to his feet with ineffable dignity. He was the best-selling author of *The Book of the Angel Raziel* wherein "all celestial and earthly knowledge is set down." If it had not been for this book, Noah would never have known how to go about building The Ark. One of the reasons the book was such an all-time best-seller was its explanation of the 1500 keys to the mystery of the world, which were not revealed even to the holy angels.

"Upper Chairman, Lower Chairman," Raziel began with his deep, stuffed voice, "God, if He is listening this morning, Fellow Conventioneers: As a specialist on earthly knowledge, as one of the few angels qualified to interpret the theme of this convention to you, let me say that this money about which our esteemed colleague N'Zuriel Yhwh has just spoken to us has brought about one real mess for the lung fish. Personally, but without recriminations, I think we made a big mistake in 703 B.C. when we agreed to let them know about barter even as a temporary expedient. But when we went further and put them wise to currencies such as furs, salt, opium pills, cowrie shells, rice, knives, and tea as measures of value, we opened the door to money and now look what has happened! In came the middleman. In came the businessman, that dope of dopes. Furs weren't durable enough, he said. Salt is a storage problem, he said. Rice and tea aren't portable, he said. How can you make change for a knife? he said. One opium pill isn't as strong as another, and there are too many sea shells, he said. Enow! Enow!" Raziel clapped his hand to his forehead and staggered backward two little steps to make an effect. "He demanded a common standard so—like boobs—we tipped them off to precious metals and that wise guy among us who told them 'Don't take any wooden nickels' is responsible for the entire mess these lung fish have got themselves in today. They would actually have you believe that what is good for general gloaters is good for the country."

"So begin at the beginning," N'Zuriel Yhwh thundered. "This money business is a whole new idea to a lot of us here."

"You don't know yet what money is?" Raziel

asked sardonically, setting up a joke which was older than Croesus.

"No. Would I kid you?"

"Then you must be an economist." It got the same old big laugh. Grinning, Raziel continued. "Listen, carefully. Barter is an exchange of possessions. That's all. Beyond barter it gets confusing. Nobody, not even me, knows what money means or how it works—only where and how the lung fish use it. There are no general laws of money. There is no understanding of it—not by even the wisest of their bankers. They only know it has to be portable, durable, divisible, and recognizable. They know it can get them anything. It is more mystical and desirable to them than any person, any flag, themselves, or any religion. But there is an intangible essential which is more important than those qualities and harder to define. The intangible essential is value acquired by reputation, or association, or by use— which is what luck is among lung fish. Luck makes objects so desirable that they pass for money. But that is *all* we know about money."

Raziel's utter wemlessness took the sting out of what they wanted to feel about this ideological enemy, money, which had taken them away from more important work.

"Why are you sitting down?" N'Zuriel Yhwh asked Raziel across the floor. "I am just beginning to get the drift."

"What should I do?" Raziel asked him with a shrug which caused his wings to bang against the Liederkranz Hall ceiling, "Repeat myself?"

"But you are the expert. You know all the answers to lung fish. What are we supposed to talk about for the rest of the convention?"

"So," Raziel said, "you'll do what I had to do. You'll improvise."

o

Before his fall, Lucifer™ had been a member of these committees: Seraphim, Cherubim, Powers, and

Archangels. Lucifer™'s Field Study Team would be represented by Miss Phyllis Stein↓ and Mr. Palmer Mahan↓ (both cover names). Miss Stein was a former librarian from Archangels who had defected with her satanic peer group. Mahan was a thermal engineer from Furnaces Maintenance, which was run by the Powers Committee.

Miss Stein's opposite number had been assigned the name Alice Trudy Kehoe↑. She was a harpist from Virtues. Mahan's opposite number, Justin Case↑, was from Dominions; a top security agent. He was a dark, romantic-looking angel whose work demanded that he think of himself as a policeman.

In charge of the unit operations in the field, as monitor-regulator for both Chiefs of Mission, was an extremely valuable and experienced Cherub-on-Loan from Thrones called Victoria Saxe-Coburg↓↑. It must be pointed out that whereas the "women" on the field study teams were not exactly ♀, and while the men were not precisely ♂, in that angels were not designed by their client to employ sex (a shameful thing *as Man understands that usage*), the necessary adjustments had been made in their basic equipment to accommodate various demands which could be made upon them during field study tests. They were all, after all, *agents provocateurs*. That a certain amount of sex, among other things, was involved in their work should, by no means, come under any criticism. The published White Paper* shows the Field Study Groups to have been enormously helpful.

*God's Stationery Office. Frs. 5.95

Three

In a big city, people do not look into each other's faces because that could be too depressing. Eugene Quebaro, during his life, and Doris Neriades, during hers, were not aware of ever having been anywhere near each other, but they had once had a shouting match over the possession of a taxi. And they had once ridden almost opposite each other on the Lexington Avenue bus.

Doris Neriades was an orphan of Greek descent. She lived in an apartment on West 54th Street between Fifth and Sixth Avenues. The Quebaros lived in Stamford, on Long Ridge Road, just beyond the pale of the tantalizingly fashionable Rockrimmon Road of the Connecticut elite, not because they couldn't afford Rockrimmon Road but because they hated to tie up the money.

Considering the wide range of possibilities for human imperfection, Doris Neriades really had only one flaw: a left branch bundle block which caused ischemia, which is to say coronary insufficiency with angina pectoris. A heart disease like that was as rare among women as Doris herself. Otherwise, perhaps aside from a determination to do what she thought was right and not live by other people's rules, she was a gentle, inordinately pretty girl of twenty-four, nine years younger than Eugene Quebaro. She was single. She lived (mainly) alone and earned $850 a week working for a psychiatrist who earned $2,385 a week (net) and owned a chain of very popular dehydrated meat shops called The Eternal Steak.

Doris had glossy black hair. She had soft, khaki-colored skin which appeared to have been dusted with cinnamon around the cheek bones. She had large brown eyes with violet centers. She was a smashing-looking girl who had enough energy to fill a power hose. With some of that energy Doris was presently enjoying the body of a twenty-six-year-old opinion sampler, a sturdy man who was employed by a very rich man who wanted to be President of the United States but who could not make the necessary overt decisions to declare his candidacy because the opinion polls he subsidized offered too many options. The young opinion sampler was out of town a lot but even though Doris enjoyed his body while he was in town, she never let him stay overnight because, in her experience, other men whose bodies she enjoyed always asked dopy questions the next morning such as, "How can you eat soup for breakfast?" (Coffee was a vegetable which was cooked into a broth which became a *potage* when cream and sugar were added to it, but have yourself a bowl of delicious, unbitter black bean soup for breakfast made from beans almost identical in color and shape, and charges that you are eccentric are flung at you.)

Doris was a rare specialist in the field of psychiatry. She worked with one of the four great American leaders in the field, Dr. Abraham Weiler, as a total "clearfield" clairvoyant. She was Dr. Weiler's sole staff and (despite the breathtaking number of his degrees and professional associations) was the only source of therapy for his patients. Her gifts had made him the great psychiatric figure he had become. Dr. Weiler used Doris's honed powers the way a different sort of businessman might employ on-line computers.

Throughout her working day, Doris sat in an air-conditioned cubicle behind a two-way mirror which was framed behind Dr. Weiler's desk. Concentrating on the thought/emotion feedback from the patients, Doris would deliver this transmitted psychic information to Dr. Weiler through a compact tight-circuit intercom system. Dr. Weiler received the information through his eyeglass frames, in stereo. A typical patient manipulation worked something like this, just to show how much and how far Doris carried the ball.

A stout, white-bearded man with eyebags as heavy and as black as the velvet swags of papal mourning faces Dr. Weiler in his exquisitely furnished consulting rooms. Looking out through the mirror from her cubicle, Doris has Dr. Weiler's bald spot in her foreground and a clear view of the patient, a Mr. F.M. Heller, in the background. She speaks into the headset microphone: *"Mr. Heller is fulminating, both deep down and on the surface, in his unconscious and his conscious mind, about the Port of New York Authority, while he is actually talking to you about his grandaughter, little Heather, Doctor."*

Dr. Weiler immediately interrupts Mr. Heller. He is direct and forceful. "Mr. Heller," he says, "I want you to tell me again about your resentment of the Port of New York Authority."

"What?" Heller is startled.

"Why are you always thinking about the Port of New York Authority?"

"Why do you say that?" The question is fearful, off-balance.

"Come, come, Mr. Heller."

"How do you know what I'm thinking?"

There is a long-suffering sigh from the doctor: "Mr. Heller, it is both my business and my art to know the things which disrupt your adjustment. The key word in the title of what you resent is 'authority.' Is that correct?"

"Yes, I think so, but—"

"He is thinking of his beard, doctor, and—in his subconscious—he is taking his beard off and putting it on a very stolid, stubborn-looking, elderly, German-seeming lady."

"Did you grow your beard because of the Port of New York Authority, Mr. Heller?"

"Yes, I think so, but—"

"Did you resent your grandmother?"

"Yes, I think so, but—"

"What was your grandmother's name?"

"He can't make himself say her name, Doctor. But he is thinking it. Her name was Portia."

"I put it to you, Mr. Heller, that your grandmother's name may have been something like Portia. And that you resented her because she exercised such authority over you."

"How do you know these things, Dr. Weiler?"

"I put it to you, Mr. Heller, that you live in Connecticut because you resent New York, even though your work is in New York. Why do you resent New York, Mr. Heller?"

"I—I thought I loved New York. How could anyone not love the fun of New York? I thought I lived in Connecticut because, like everyone else, I enjoy riding on the New Haven railroad."

"He resents New York because the Korean waiters in Chinese restaurants giggle at his pronounciation of Eggs Foo Yong— which he pronounces quite correctly but with more of a Nanking than a Peking accent. Right now—because of your question—he is thinking of not being able to use chopsticks well. Wait a sec! He is associating chopsticks with piano music. The tune of Chopsticks is dancing through his head. The legs on the piano are reminding him of his grandmother's legs . . ."

"Did I ever tell you that I had spent much time in China, Mr. Heller? That I speak Chinese rather well?"

"No. As a matter of fact you—"

"Say these words for me, Mr. Heller, please." Dr. Weiler wrote rapidly on a slip of paper and slid it across the desk.

Heller read the words aloud. "Eggs Foo Yong," he said.

"You have a superb Nanking accent. Did you know that, Mr. Heller?"

"I do?"

"Did you know that most of the waiters in the Chinese restaurants of New York are Korean?"

"They are?"

"I shall put a circle of words to you, Mr. Heller—a circle of words which are pressing on you like a steel ring which makes you hostile even though you know that hostility is the worst possible thing for your asthma. Now hear this: Portia—Port. Eggs Foo Yong—New York. Chopsticks—Piano legs. Piano Legs—Portia. Portia—Port. Portia has your Beard—Authority. Portia, Chopsticks, Piano,

Portia, Beard, Authority—Port of New York Authority. Am I reaching your cores, Mr. Heller?"

Mr. Heller began to weep with relief and with new friendliness to himself. "Yes," he sobbed, "I think so, but—"

"But—what?"

"But why am I so fixated on my granddaughter?"

"Because a granddaughter may, most certainly, become a grandmother and you fear for her. As long as you carry that terrible fear you will carry the fixation. To be free of that fixation you must forgive your grandmother."

"*No! No!*" Doris warns instantly into the microphone. "*His mind is filling with black steam! He just snatched the beard from his grandmother's face and is attaching it to his face with padlocks! You must eradicate the grandmother now.*"

"When I say *forgive*, Mr. Heller," Dr. Weiler added rapidly, "I am speaking psychiatrically. In those terms, forgive means to wipe out, to eradicate. Eliminate your grandmother, Mr. Heller. Rub her out of existence everywhere you know."

"*He is rubbing a blackboard eraser across his memory, vigorously and rapidly. He laughs like a jolly Santa as he wipes out his grandmother. She is going—she is aaaalmost gone. Only the legs remain. My—she did have legs like a grand piano. The legs are gone. The shoes are going. She's gone. Aaaaalll gone.*"

"You have erased your grandmother, but are your hostilities erased, Mr. Heller?" Dr. Weiler asked.

"Yes! Yes! Portia faces death. Accentuate the positive beard. Chinese food is a put-on."

Dr. Weiler stood up abruptly. "That is all for now," he said. "We have accomplished a great deal today." Mr. Heller snuffled gratefully and left the consulting room. Dr. Weiler sat down, wheeled in his chair and spoke to the mirror. "Did we go too far, Miss Neriades? Did we kill the goose?"

"It doesn't seem possible that he can stay cured," Doris reassured the doctor falsely, knowing that Mr. Heller was free and cured. "Just trying to be able to afford a taxi, or trying to get a table in a restaurant, or a seat on the train home will bring his grandmother back to him, snatching at his beard. If we can keep it from him that nobody has authority any more, he'll soon snap back to his old hositilities."

Dr. Weiler was mollified but not convinced. "Thank you, Miss Neriades. Who is next?"

"Miss Ross is in the waiting room, doctor. She is thinking about abstract, violent sex."

Dr. Weiler rubbed his sable-dyed moustache with the backs of his hands. He rose, flaring his nostrils, adjusting his clothing, with his back to the mirror.

"You are thinking that it is about time that I left for lunch, Dr. Weiler."

"Am I, Miss Neriades? Well, then, perhaps you should." He strode across the room and opened the door to the waiting room.

o

Doris read her own future every morning in the solid fillers of the different kinds of soup she had for breakfast just as other women might, with far less basis for belief, consult the astrology columns of the daily newspapers. The implacable thing she had discovered about these daily readings, over the years, was that they were not refutable.

Before she left for work on the morning of the day she and Dr. Weiler cured Mr. Heller, she read her own fortune in the dregs of some Cyrillic alphabet soup which her present beau, Warren Hutch, had given her the previous Russian Easter, in dehydrated form. She had bathed, dressed, brushed her teeth, hair, and shoes while the soup was warming. She ate most of it with much pleasure before she settled down to read the coming events of the day in the last of it.

The prediction started out quite pleasurably: "(1) A young male will call you for a quickie before you leave for the office. The quickie will be successful beyond any previous sexual apogees." Doris felt a frisson which continued to oscillate wondrously. "You will fall as madly in love with him as he is (presently) with you and will make a firm,

32

crypto-fanatical arrangement to repeat the same sexual experience this evening—a longie. (2) The lasting effects of the
matutinal quickie will leave you euphoric throughout the
morning and you will die happy. (3) Bye-bye now. Over, for
you, and out."

Doris stared into the Cyrillic pasta with horror. The telephone rang. Still staring at her doom she
reached out and picked up. "Good morning, Warren," she
said.

"How did you know it was me?" the young
man said irritably. "You always seem to know it's me.
Doesn't anybody else ever call? Not even a wrong number?"

"Where are you, Warren?" She knew where
he was, but what was the use?

"I just got in at La Guardia."

"Do you have time for a quickie?"

"Jesus, Doris. That's just what I called to ask
you. Do I? You should see what I'm carrying around."

"Then you'd better hurry right on over and
show it to me," she said with mortal tristeness. She hung up
sadly. Her last bang was coming up. The last of the fun she
loved so well; her last li'l ole hunka poontang. Well, if this
were to be the last one she just had to make it good. She had
to make it good enough to last through all eternity. Since she
could not take Warren's enormous pants package with her,
she was determined to appreciate it while it was here. She
floated off, undressing as she went, toward a tube of miracle
whip lubricant. She used what was left of a bottle of *Jolie
Madame,* put three tablespoons of lecithin into a glass of
ginseng, stirring well. When the doorbell rang she was
sprawled lewdly and nudely across the bed, pinkly and pre-
paredly. She sent a pornographic telepathic summons into
Warren's consciousness. He kicked open the front door and
ran through the rooms toward her.

It was indeed the greatest, most callid cou-
pling of her sweet life. She paid him her entire fortune of all
the orgasms it would have taken her fifty-two years more of
a normal life-span to realize. These crashed upon him like
tidal waves, battering great lunch-whistle shrieks out of both
of them, changing totally the personality of Warren Hutch

who had never remotely suspected that he was the lover he had suddenly become. They lay gasping like live bagpipes in a pool of sweat and sperm, vowing brokenly to meet again at six fifteen that evening, causing Doris to weep, Warren to exult.

She took her thrumming orifice to the office, clitoris ticking in thlocking excitement—but edged in black. After she had helped to cure Mr. Heller, she slipped out to Park Avenue while Dr. Weiler undressed Miss Ross with four lightning-like gestures. Doris went to the Finast supermarket on East 58th Street, across from where the Liederkranz Hall had been long years before, to stock up on nourishments that would keep Warren going while he waited for her, not knowing he would never see her again. Cooperating with the President's Phase Nine Policy, the noon food prices had gone up 11 per cent over the opening prices at nine that morning. The cost of the six items that Doris bought had soared to $61.87 when she reached the cashier. Doris stared down at the cash register slip, clutched at her chest and died upon a pyramided stack of TODAY's SPECIAL at the identical instant that life departed from Eugene Quebaro just around the corner.

Four

. At the Thessaly Restaurant, 28th Street and Eighth Avenue, presiding over an extraordinary session of the pantheon of the gods of ancient Greece, Zeus accepted a message written on the back of a menu from young Hermes, the gay god, who was dressed characteristically (if wearing only a *petasos,* sandals, and a cane can be considered dressed). Zeus, forty-two feet tall, slipped on his glasses, read the message, slipped off his glasses, stood up, and shook his aegis for attention, a gesture which caused such a rainstorm in the metropolitan area that bar and taxi business and the unit sales of *The Joy of Sex* went up 18.3 per cent.

"Your attention, please," Zeus thundered, getting the instant attention of his sacred congregation.

The founder-members of the pantheon sat on the dais facing the assembly of the fourteen children of Eris and the fourteen children of Nyx, and two or three hundred assorted naiads, demi-gods, nymphs, heros, dryads, and satyrs plus a prime oil shipper named George Pappadakis (who had wandered into the meeting room from the public bar), and the Olympus Permanent Secretariat.

Zeus stared down at them all with the terrible seriousness of the near-sighted public figure. "I think you should know," he said, "that I have just received confirmation of the news that the Judeo-Christian opposition movement has opened its convention here in Fun City on the site of the old Liederkranz Hall on East 58th Street." He paused for effect. "As you know there are only two basic religions in this world—the Orthodox-Established Church and the pagan religions. Now, we have been worshipped for a long, long time. My grandma, bless her, who was in on the beginning of the entire movement, started out with my grandad, Uranus, four thousand years before that bunch of pagans over at Liederkranz were even thought of by church-going people. *We are the Established Church.* Remember that. We don't take a back seat to anyone."

A sustained hubba-hubba broke out from the awesome throats of Typhon, Berberus, Chimaera, Hydra and Othrus; the fifty beautiful, more beautiful, most beautiful daughters of Nereus and Doris; the fifteen principal Giants; all the Furies; the hundred-handed Hecoatobchrires; Cronus himself, still around but ailing; and the noisy, disorderly Phrygian Corybantes (who may have discovered iron, which is all well and good, but who were nonetheless as vulgar a set of three girls as had ever been invited out). Most of the convention was already tipsy and it was only 14:55 o'clock.

"Furthermore," Zeus said, "I have learned that the Opposition is here to organize a field study which could possibly be the same thing we had in mind but I doubt it because they already got a very good thing for them going here with two hundred thousand full-time churches in such a rich market. So there is a spy in the oinkment, as Circe used to say."

An even worse rhubarb of sound spattered against the walls of the room. Zeus quieted them. "It is perfectly all right," he reassured them. "There will be no conflict of interest. After five thousand years the Opposition has apparently—from what we hear—decided they should find out something about money and we can only hope it isn't too late. However, I think you ought to know that they will be using a nice Greek girl in their research—she happens to be a Neriades—and you can be sure I will keep an eye on her welfare."

Knowing that Zeus liked a little appreciation as much as the next fellow, four foul harpies, utterly horrible-looking birds with the heads of maidens (and, most certainly, one-hundred-per cent sure, maidenheads)—the same girls who were described by Aeschylus, the gossip writer who covered their debut, as "with breathings unapproachable they snore and forth from their eyes drippeth a loathsome rheum"—shrieked so dissonantly that Athena gave the nearest one a good smack on the head with a copy of *Women's Wear Daily* and said, "It is impossible to believe you are sisters of that nice Iris."

"Anyway," Zeus continued, "here's to this big, new market where they need a state religion that isn't always carping about this sin and that sin. I never could understand how the Opposition ever established itself, the way they are always blaming the people for what they do. Everything is a sin with them—anything that's pleasurable or satisfying. Therefore, naturally, people aren't going to church the way they used to. All right. So Greece and Rome aren't what they used to be either. But I have told you I am going to lead you to a big, new congregation, and that is why we are here. This is a country that spends more on pleasure and leisure than any country in the history of the world. We are absolutely the natural gods for them. We are going to research this right down to the bone, then we're going to make them an offer that will bring us back as the national establishment church like we never were even in the very, very best days in the old country."

The applause was tumultuous. Over the din, Zeus proposed that they try some of the ahinoi and mithia yemista, which, in his humble opinion, were sheer ambrosia. The members of the pantheon could eat only ambrosia and drink only nectar so a considerable amount of Zeus's time was spent endorsing booze and alimentary products as either one or the other. Real ambrosia was hard to come by once you were eight miles past Mount Olympus on either the Athens or the Salonika road.

Zeus sat at the head table behind piles of dolmathes, bourekia, and pink olives, in the company of his eldest boy, Apollo, whom he called Sunny, born as a result of an out-of-town trip on which Zeus met Leto Coeus (not his wife); and his eldest girl, Athena, whom he had had all by himself (and therefore also not with his wife) as the result of a splitting headache followed by a knock on the head with a rock flung by Prometheus, which in no way constitutes a love affair, although it should be stated that, to get the head-ache in the first place, Zeus had swallowed his pregnant first wife in a tantrum, a fairly neurotic gesture. Another son, Hephaestus, was also on the dais, a boy whom Zeus had actually had with his own wife, Hera, who was not at the convention because Zeus was a god who had become relatively famous for not believing in taking his wife on business trips.

"If this Doris Neriades who just dropped dead in the Finast outlet is related to Nereus Neriades and his wife, she must be some looker," Zeus said. He chewed an olive thoughtfully. "That man has fifty daughters and each one is better looking than the next." He tried some of the dolmathes. "I had a big thing going once with his daughter Glauconome."

"You also had a big thing going with the wife," Athena reminded him.

"What do you have in mind about working with the Opposition, Dad?" Apollo asked.

Zeus, the lecher, vanished. Zeus, the statesman, stood in his place. "It is entirely a matter for negotiation," he said. "They will be gathering vital information about this religious market; otherwise they wouldn't be wasting their time here. Dumb they are not. We have our duty and we will do it. The duty is to confuse them. That is what religion is all about, but let's get one thing clear. I want that gorgeous Lincoln Memorial in Washington as one of my temples."

"Is that what we're after? Information they are able to dig up? To find out what they find out . . . then mix them up?"

"First we will bargain to plant observers with their field study groups."

"Why should they okay that?"

"Because they need us. They are studying money and don't know the first thing about it. At least we know the first thing. We invented money. Croesus was almost a Greek, after all. We will tell them we want to help them."

"Why?"

"Are you some kind of a dumbie, Sunny? So we can find out all about money before they find out, but if they find out before we find out, we can kidnap whoever finds out so they can't find out."

"I see."

"And all the while we'll be spreading our doctrines of fun, games, sex, and happiness plus a quick, new, easy weight-reducing diet. We will blow the Opposition out of the water. We are selling pleasure. They are selling damnation—and I mean *eternal* damnation—in return for something they call sin. How can we miss in this market?"

"Hozzabot a copple more pitchers of nectar on this end of the table, Zeus?" someone yelled from across the room. Zeus snapped his fingers and sent the waiters running. "Try the retsina nectar," he yelled back. "It's good for tired ichor."

An ethereal fluid called ichor flowed in their veins, keeping them immortal. They enjoyed their immortality very much. They were molded in their original human form with all the correctly corresponding parts and costumes—Zeus in a handsome chalk-stripe, double-breasted brown suit, for instance. Especially did Zeus's daughter, Aphrodite, who was just then having it off with two waiters in a telephone booth, correspond to her human form today. The Greek gods were, however, subject to certain limitations of energy and judgment. They were highly sensitive to corporeal needs and human affections, which made them, possibly, not the best analysts, all around, to undertake a human field study. Zeus's appetites, particularly, for absolutely anything from thunderbolt throwing to wife-weaseling were overweening. Besides, he was such a poor executive that he kept interfering from the moment he delegated authority.

"But, Dad," Apollo said (such a handsome kid, his father thought dotingly, like a regular Greek god), "why don't we want the Opposition to find out what nobody seems to know anyway?"

"Because," his father answered, "if we can find out, we can make a comeback for Spiro. And while we are finding out, we'll be getting inside information on what makes this whole market tick. If this money stuff is strong enough to break the backs of such a proud people as these . . ." he checked his notes, "ah, Americans, in such a short time, then the same thing must be going on all over the whole world. America is just a microcosm. If we get the secret that makes them tick, then we are going to make ours the comeback of comebacks. That is our whole goal, the comeback to the very tippy-top of big-time religion. That is the entire reason for our convention. The trouble is our people like a little drink, a little sex, a lot of good food—so okay maybe they don't make the best researchers in the world. But the Opposition lives on The Work Ethic. They will work their asses off and when they come up with the secret ingredient we will grab it and run with it. Then, naturally, we'll need someone very big in politics to make our arrangements. And with a solid Greek-American like Spiro to lead them, there can be a whole religious renaissance in this market, and as a result of the gratitude Spiro will feel for our delivering *his* big comeback, he will see that the government sets up temples to you and your sister, plus a couple of hundred to me and on every other street corner in the entire world our names will be up in lights again."

His voice rose as he built his answer. He had the attention of the entire room once again. The convention put down their wine glasses and broke into spontaneous applause.

o

Hermes arranged with the Permanent Secretariat of the Joint (⚕) Commission to agree to a meeting between Athena and Apollo of the Olympian Party and Raziel and Dagon↓ of the other crowd. Dagon, a fallen angel in *Paradise Lost* (I,457) who just happened (also) to be the national god of the ancient Phoenicians and later on, of the Philistines, was a good-looking bearded angel who ordinarily wore the lower body of a fish.

Zeus became enraged because he was prevented from attending the meeting. Since no one of his equivalent rank in the Opposition was even attending this sitting of the J(⚕)CES, Athena told him flatly that nothing could be accomplished if he attended, because the opposite numbers simply would not be in a position to discuss with him. Rank was rank. Second lieutenants do not treat with field marshals. Zeus sulked but he had to agree. "They are so *unsound* in their theology," he groused. "Their whole take-off point, the Adam and Eve anecdote, is nothing but gossip about a Sumerian working-class revolt which their clergy, entirely in character, called Original Sin. They are such Johnny-Come-*Late*lies! All right. Go ahead and meet them. Just see how far you can get without my generalship."

The meeting was held in the bar of the old Knickerbocker Hotel which had once, long before, stood at 42nd Street and Broadway, a wonderfully comfortable place in its time, with the city's outstanding free lunch. The meeting was conducted in Greek, the "in" language after Chaldean. To Zeus it was a test to see if the Judeo-Christian gang could even speak Greek. The word barbarian in Greek applies only to people who cannot speak Greek.

Being mental types, Athena and Raziel got along well. While the real ice was being broken, Apollo and Dagon talked about chariot race results, archery scores, cattle prices, and women they had known. When Athena felt the time was right, she murmured to Raziel, "My father was hopeful that we could help you."

"How very kind," Raziel said.

"It had come to my father's attention that you were holding your convention to learn about money, setting down the guidelines for field study groups, and so forth, and, since I am sure you know about Croesus, you'll know our people actually in*vent*ed money."

"By you a shekel is something to eat?" Dagon asked.

"I thought Croesus was a Lydian, not a Greek," Raziel said.

"Well, his people were our people. I mean in a religious sense. They were in our temples all the time," Apollo said. "Why I remember—"

A choked sound from Athena stopped him. Athena was staring into the eyes of Zeus disguised as a waiter. Zeus was really rotten at disguises. He had never fooled his wife, nor anyone else. Leto was overcome with laughter when she tried to describe Zeus as a swan. Europa dined out on her description of Zeus masquerading as a bull. Luckily, neither Raziel nor Dagon had ever seen Zeus before, or maybe they were the sort who never looked at a waiter.

Having the gift, Athena read her father's mind and passed along what she saw. "Anyway, my father was wondering if money might not be much different since Croesus."

"It has come to *our* attention," Raziel said, "that your father is so interested in that topic that he called a party convention here."

"A convention, yes." Athena said truthfully. "But not about money. Ours is strictly a missionary meeting."

The waiter hovered around the table ready to clang a silver tray on each side of his head for having sent Apollo instead of Aphrodite. He started off to telephone her when he stopped, realizing with revulsion that he did not know whether angels do not practice sex as Greek gods and humans know it. He reversed his course and got back to the table to hear Raziel saying, ". . . and, after all, we don't have the budgets you people have. You are rich and powerful. What are we? Richer in spirit perhaps, but not in the resources and wit that you people command."

The waiter basked under the words. He went hot with amazement as he listened to Athena and Apollo treat such truth with contempt.

"Don't give us that," Apollo said.

"You have all of Europe, North America, and South America going for you," Athena said. "You have Australia and South Africa and all those paintings in all those churches in Italy. All we have is one scrubby, mountainous country and one tiny wine-dark sea."

The waiter gaped at her. Scrubby! Olympus?

"Tell us a little more about how you are going to operate," Raziel said, "then we'll probably tell you a little more about how we'll operate."

The waiter seemed ready to interrupt so Athena said quickly, "Waiter, bring a bottle of Pommery '28, please. Quickly, please." Zeus had to go off to the service bar, looking backward over his shoulder, while both sides exchanged information as openly as could be expected under the circumstances.

"We are using an updated Unknown Soldier system to find our lab humans for the field tests," Raziel said. "What are you people doing?"

"We are setting up a series of old-time revival meetings where we hope millions will come forward to declare for Zeus," Athena said.

"We were lucky enough to come up with two healthy specimens right out of the box."

"Here comes the champagne," Apollo warned his sister. Zeus rushed in with a bottle in an ice bucket. Athena lifted the bottle out of the ice. "What is *this?*" she asked indignantly. "Who asked for Texas champagne?" She stood up abruptly. "This is out*land*ish." She swept away from the table. Her brother, then the two angels, followed. Outside they got into a cab, which Dagon directed to take them to Reisenweber's. "If we're gunna be in this era," he said, "we might as well have the best."

"No wonder they didn't have a twenty-eight," Raziel said. "It is already only about nineteen-oh-one."

At once, Athena spotted that the cab driver was her father wearing as ill-fitting a red wig and as silly a red moustache as she had ever seen. "Forget Reisenweber's, please!" she said. "Driver! Take us to the rowboat pier in Central Park."

While Dagon paid the cab in the park and Apollo engaged a boat, Raziel made sure the area was authentically 1903, when naked maidens could stroll there without fear of mashers.

The four negotiators sat in a boat, Athena rowing. The discussions were held without the possibility of any eavesdropping, except by a small mosquito that hovered above them—or at least someone or something trying to disguise itself as a mosquito, since its tiny head was the replica of an airedale terrier, making it anomalous if not anopheles.

Agreement was reached and a treaty was hammered out before dawn the following day. One point of the treaty stated tersely that no Chief Executive of either The Firmament or The Pantheon could assume any formal or informal place in the field study. Athena considered that as the masterstroke. They had been saved from Zeus's executive help.

Five

Carlotta did not yet know that she had become a widow.

She was wearing a sweet butter-yellow house dress that plopped her figure out nicely at plateau after plateau. Her hair was fetching. Her eyes were clear white surrounding delft blue. She was looking as pretty and as clean as a bar of twelve-dollar soap for Gene's arrival home in about fifteen minutes.

Jeremiah Mason, the Community Relations vice-president of the insurance company in whose service Gene had been murdered that afternoon, rang the doorbell. Carlotta kept the door on the taut chain and opened the door just a crack.

"I am Jeremiah Mason, vice-president of Protective," the extraordinarily somber man wearing the six-button suit jacket said. "May I come in?"

Carlotta led the way into the split-level, helped him down into the conversation pit, then asked graciously whether he would prefer a drink or a joint.

"I would greatly appreciate a joint," Mason said.

"You must have had a hard day," Carlotta said, sliding the stainless-steel joint box across the table to him.

"Maybe the worst in my life," he answered. He got the joint lighted shakily.

"Would you like a downer?" Carlotta asked solicitously. Mason shook his head, exhaling from his toes.

"What's on?" Carlotta asked.

"Give me a couple more swallows of this," Mason pleaded.

"It's not good if you take grass that big, Mr. Mason," Carlotta told him. "No kidding. You may be the one in sixty who segues because of a personality quirk."

"No. It's okay. May I explain my work, Mrs. Quebaro?"

"Why not? So long as you don't try to sell me a policy." She laughed. "Gene does all the selling around here."

"*Did*, Mrs. Quebaro. That's the whole thing, right there. Gene *was* the best salesman but—"

"Are you trying to say Gene was fired? Impossible."

"Mrs. Quebaro . . ." Mason's voice broke. "You see . . ."

"What is it?"

Mason took in enough cannabis smoke to allow a Lipan Apache manipulating a blanket over it to transmit the complete works of Tennyson. He swallowed hard. He held it down until his eyes watered, then he blew it out slowly. He grinned at her broadly. "Your husband was murdered in front of Bloomingdale's at two ten this afternoon," he said.

"Murdered?"

"Yes." Each of his eyes seemed to roll in a different direction. "I am very sorry, Mrs. Quebaro. I had the greatest respect and affection for Gene."

Carlotta was wondering what kind of an angle Gene could have stumbled upon to have spread a rumor like that. But there couldn't be any angle. This twit had it wrong. "You have to be crazy, Mr. Mason," she said equably. "Gene wouldn't do a thing like that."

"Gene is dead, Mrs. Quebaro."

"I don't believe it."

"Nonetheless—"

"Can you prove what you are saying?"

"I was required to identify Gene's body at the city morgue. The company wanted to spare you that. I have come here directly from the morgue."

"Is that where Gene is now?"

"Yes."

She was seated directly across the conversation pit. She stared into him; not so much into his eyes as into him. "This is a rotten trick," she said. "I don't ask you to understand it but it could comfort you to know why I am not falling about with shrieks of grief. You see, Gene may be in the morgue, Mr. Mason, but he is not dead."

Mason's eyes got shifty. He had gained total control over his grin. He *felt* he looked somber but he couldn't be sure.

"I am putting you through all this, Mr. Mason," Carlotta said, "because if what you say is true, I intend to get Gene back and I want every assurance from the company that his place will be waiting for him, untarnished, and that his quotas will be frozen at the productivity levels he had reached when—when this nonsense happened to him. Will you guarantee that?"

"I don't know as we can, Mrs. Quebaro. There just is no precedent." He knew grief took many different forms. This woman wasn't insane, he told himself, she was just coping.

"I am afraid I'll have to have the company's assurance in writing, Mr. Mason. And I mean direct from Dr. Hanly, the national sales vice-prexy."

"I'll convey that, Mrs. Quebaro. I will. My job is to give you all possible support. I want you to lean on me until the funeral is behind you and as long as you need to after that."

"Thank you. You *can* help me. Gene is insured by The Plan for five hundred thousand dollars in the straight life clauses and, of course, in that you say he was murdered, that means the payment will need to respect the double-indemnity clause. I shall sue the City of New York. Protective must protect me by providing attorneys who are experienced in these things. Also, the company, under its own benevolent plan, had insured Gene in my favor for fifty thousand, which must also respect double-indemnity. My question is this: when may I expect to receive Protective's check in the amount of one million one hundred thousand dollars?"

Grief? Mason asked himself. This wasn't grief. This woman was insane with greed. A wonderful young man lay dead with a broken neck and fourteen stab wounds and this woman was blandly dictating the terms of a claims settlement. She was a monster! What kind of a life had the two of them led together?

"There will be forms to be signed," he said tersely.

"Very well. Then these are your tasks as I see them: one, the arrangement for Gene's transfer to a suitable funeral factory; two, obtaining copies of the so-called death certificate and filling in the forms you mention; three, retaining for me a really wild-eyed lawyer. I suggest that we meet at the funeral factory tomorrow morning at ten. You can telephone tonight to tell me where to go."

"Yes, Mrs. Quebaro," Mason answered coldly.

"Please instruct the coffin jockeys that I want the funeral finished and out of the way by this time tomorrow. I want to be returned to this house at not later than five peeyem so that I can get to work to get Gene back here from wherever they are holding him."

"They? Who are they, Mrs. Quebaro?"

"It is too abstruse to explain. I don't suppose more than four people in the world could follow my thinking. But Gene must be given back to me."

This woman may be insane, Mason told himself, but she was driven insane by grief. He pulled heavily on the joint. He saw suddenly that he had never looked upon a purer or more beautiful effigy of elegy. She was the timeless widow, defying the cruelties of time by rationalizing them into some grotty retributive game. Why—he would do *any*thing for this woman! In fact, he discovered he would very much like to kiss her. Right now. Right in this conversation pit with its broad velvet banquettes. He sidled around the table between them until he was sitting beside her. He put his right arm untentatively along the back of the seat directly behind her. He faced her with baked eyes and shallow breathing. She leaned toward him.

"If you would like to find yourself upside-down in that fireplace, Jack, just make the next move," she said.

"Pardon?"

"Look, Mr. Mason, you're all in little knots. The only way you're ever going to get them all untied is to sign up for classes in Tantric Yoga, the ancient path toward enlightenment through the use of sexual energy. You can go to the Zen monastery in Okinawa or you can pay two hundred and fifty-four eighty-five to a Madame Schrader in Washington Heights. She gives you the whole thing: massage, movement, chanting, choreography, and intense visualization techniques. What do you say?"

"I'd like Madame Schrader's address, please."

Carlotta walked up the nineteen steps out of the conversation pit. She jotted down the Tantra facts on a telephone pad. "I'll look forward to seeing you at ten tomorrow, Mr. Mason."

He took the slip of paper, shook her hand, and left the house. Carlotta went into the bedroom, stretched out on the bed, and stared blankly at the ceiling until it got dark at about a quarter to ten. Then she washed her face with ice water, poured a tall glass of Chiaretto wine over ice, and took the drink down to the cellar to her little electronics workshop.

o

The first time Carlotta saw Eugene Quebaro she had been feeling his thighs as part of the routine for GUESS YOUR WEIGHT, a concession she had been operating at the Rockrimmon Fair for Lou Perry who had had to rush away to establish a new hat concession at Disneyland Hawaii. Gene stepped forward into the circle. She touched his calves. She patted his thighs, sides, and behind. She looked upward and—*wham!*—she was staring into his big, black eyes and that was it for Carlotta. She was hunkering close to the ground on her haunches and she felt her legs turn to water. Nothing like this reaction to a man had ever happened to her before. She had always been able to maintain a balance of power with men. She shook her head vigorously to knock out the sudden dizziness, then stood up and continued to pat him lightly around the arms and chest.

"One hundred and eighty-four pounds," she chanted. Gene backed in and sat down on the scale seat surrounded by the thicket of people which the carnies called a tip. The arrow on the scale swept to its verdict. It read 184 pounds. The tip broke into applause. Carlotta grinned, directly at Gene. He got off the scale seat and paid his fifty-cent fee. "I don't see how you do it," he said admiringly. Then he walked out of her life and disappeared into the crowd.

Carlotta didn't know what she was going to do. She had her duty to Lou Perry but she also knew she had a duty to her own life. Furthermore, she was experiencing a growing sense of duty to Gene. So she compromised. She told herself she would work two more hours, average the income out for five night hours, then pay Lou his share out of her own pocket for the three hours she wasn't going to work. She had to take the chance that the 184-pound dark-eyes would still be around when she went looking for him. But she knew she wasn't taking any chance. He was marked as hers. It had all been settled somewhere else.

At nine o'clock she told the tip she had to break to grab a sandwich. She had taken in $136 since six o'clock. She hung the OUT TO LUNCH sign over the weighing seat and knifed into the crowd, her head turning like a turret, her eyes combing through the bodies. He was so tall and oriental-looking it was easy. She found him in the second row of a tip staring up at the Ferris wheel while Crummy Steinett did his gimmick to bring in business. Steinett ran the Ferris wheel. When business wasn't booming enough he would get into a gondola with some lone woman or kid, have his operator stop the wheel when the gondola got to the top, then stand up and rock the flimsy little boat until the woman or the kid had hysterics. A woman was up there now yelling her head off. The crowd and Steinett were having a helluva time. Carlotta was standing next to Gene when he said, "What is that guy doing?"

Carlotta told Gene (and the man with him, who turned out to be Gene's father) about Crummy. "It's just sales promotion," Carlotta explained.

Gene went through the crowd to the wheel operator. "Bring them down," he said. Carlotta moved in right behind him.

"Get outta here," the operator said.

Gene lifted him off his chair and just threw him away.

"I can run it," Carlotta said. "But Crummy is a rough cat."

"Bring them down," Gene said.

Carlotta threw the gears and the wheel began to move slowly. Bewildered faces swooped down from above, went past them and started up again, until the gondola with Steinett and the weeping woman came level with the ground. Gene dragged Steinett out of the gondola and, by dint of whacking him about the head, soon had him fast asleep. Carlotta passed the girl into the crowd. Gene dumped Steinett into the empty gondola and Carlotta sent it aloft again.

o

It was a beautiful night. Someone had screwed hundreds of electric light bulbs into the sky. The carousel music was moving. Carlotta took Gene's arm. The three of them had hot dogs and beer. Gene's father said Carlotta was the best-looking girl he'd ever seen. Then he said good night and left them alone together.

Gene helped her dismantle the scales and stow all the gear.

"Do you travel all over the country guessing people's weight?" he asked her.

"It's not my regular work. I was helping out a friend."

"What's your regular work?"

"I sort of help out friends at things."

51

"Like what?"

"Oh—you know. This spring I had a friend who was in a flying act who was going to have a baby—so I filled in. I race stock cars. I've done some house painting."

"Some spread," Gene said.

"I am finding out what I am meant to be doing. What do you do?"

"Salesman. Are you English?"

"Yes. What do you sell?"

"Volkswagens. For my father."

"Do you fit it?"

"I sell the most cars on the lot."

"You think that is what you were meant to be doing?"

"I like selling cars all right."

"How much does it make you in a year?"

"About ten thousand."

"A man who makes decisions the way you do —a fellow as direct as you about going straight to the point of anything—you could be making a lot more than that. Where do you live?" she asked.

"Stamford. Out on Long Ridge Road."

"I'd like to live in Stamford. The show is finished tonight. I'll look for a place tomorrow."

"What about tonight?"

"Oh, any hotel."

He leaned down and kissed her lightly on her lips. His lips touched her and were gone but in that soft brush Carlotta knew what she was meant to be.

Mr. Quebaro was awake drinking beer and watching the crud when they got to Gene's house. Gene told his father they had a boarder. Mr. Quebaro seemed to have taken that for granted. "Do you cook?" he asked Carlotta.

"I never tried."

"Good. We'll be able to turn you into a good Swedish-Filipina cook because you won't have anything to unlearn."

Carlotta just puddled around the Quebaro house for the next two months. She picked up about nineteen hundred a month making color television sets in the hobby workshop Dad Quebaro set up for her. The housework took her twenty-seven minutes a day because she did it all electronically. The house sparkled. She had plenty of time to study cooking as Dad Quebaro taught it to her. He had his own sweet potato vines and flowering pumpkins. He grew squash in the summertime. He had accumulated a cellar store of cans of tamarind, green mangoes, and green guavas. He taught her how to make *bagoong*, a flavoring made from shrimp and small fish mixed with salt and allowed to ferment for three days to three months. It was used the way Italians use Parmiesan cheese—a touch to add tang—a little like Japanese *dashi*. She learned to make *lumpia*, the Filipino answer to Chinese egg rolls; chicken, beef, or fish *en adobe* and every kind of *pancit* using her own home-made *miti*, those wide, yellow noodles. She learned to cook so well, so quickly that the doctor said her *Flårnata med glas*, a Swedish almond wafer cake with ice cream, had cured Dad's sprained ankle. It did more than that. It inflamed Gene.

She sat with her feet up on his bed, sipping cold, dry Orvieto wine and flipping through the pages of the new *Scientific American*, and sort of watching over Gene who was supposed to be sleeping off a cold when she heard him say, "When shall we get married?"

She didn't look up from the magazine. "You don't have to think I think marriage is everything."

"Christmas Eve?"

"Dad would like that."

"You think we ought to sleep together first?"

"*Sleep?*"

"You know what I mean."

"I think we should have slept together the first night we met, but serious men have different ideas on that."

They were married on Christmas Eve, 1965. They never left the Fifth Avenue Apartments in Aspen, Colorado, on their honeymoon. It wasn't only the pleasure of each other that kept them indoors. Carlotta was laying out a new career for Gene.

"Sell in*surance*?" Gene cried out, aghast. "That has to be the most competitive business in the world."

53

"Not actually," she said intently. "Writing popular songs is more competitive. Insurance comes in at around third."

They talked about it until she convinced him.

o

The insurance company forms covering the claims made for Eugene Quebaro's death were signed. In twenty-four hours the company's check was paid over.

The J($\downarrow$)CES camera team covered the event as a matter of record. It was so puzzlingly interesting that they suggested that an Executive Committee look the footage over. Raziel, N'Zuriel Yhwh, and Dagon attended the screening during lunch hour. They were baffled.

"Look here," N'Zuriel Yhwh said after the screening. "The wife had a very, very high regard for the husband, according to his file. The wife *loved* the husband. Am I right on that?"

"Devoted to the husband," Dagon said. "A very tragically sad woman underneath."

"So—the husband dies. He's gone from her for good—right?"

"That is correct," Dagon said.

"So a stranger comes in and pays her one million one hundred thousand dollars because he is dead and gone. Therefore, it must signify that money takes the place of the husband, could even be preferred to the husband. If I am wrong, please correct me."

"I don't see how that can be the way with them. I mean he was no king or shah, he was a salesman. She had nothing to do with his dying—so why should she be paid? This is a very screwy set-up here." Raziel said.

"But you saw the forms!" N'Zuriel Yhwh put in excitedly. "It was a regular ritual, a traditional thing. They have the death certificate. They sign papers. They tell the wife what a sad thing it all is, and it certainly must have been if it was their million one they paid out. It was an absolutely tribal thing."

"We gotta watch it closely," Dagon said.

o

The wild-eyed lawyer known in the profession as an Underdog Specialist, found by Protective for the suit against the City of New York, was a passionately aggressive man who looked as if he had given over his life to the smashing of adversaries' glass-topped desks. He said there would be an open-and-shut $250,000 settlement.

"We take care of our own," Dr. Hanly told the sales executives grimly.

Gene looked very good indeed in the silk-lined, half-couch casket due to an application of Executive Tan lotion, but his head tilted wistfully. More than two hundred friends, associates, clients who wished to ask Carlotta if Gene had protected her with a Plan, and the necrobuffs who hang out in funeral parlors paid their last respects. The sister and brother-in-law of Chester Frank Heimer, the man who had aced Gene out, attended this last farewell.

"We wanted you to know that my brother has *never* killed anyone before this, Mrs. Quebaro," the sister, Mrs. Lewis, said. "That talk is all a lot of newspaper and police surmisal. Chester had many, many money worries. Chester had job worries, too, and a very expensive habit to support."

"The Salvation Army doesn't give methadrine away," her husband said. "They don't just hand it out like soup. Please understand that Chester is gunna be very sorry about all this because that is his nature. He is a sweet person."

Tears flooded Mrs. Lewis's eyes. Carlotta put an arm around her shoulders. "Please don't be upset," Carlotta said. "It was very nice of you to come to pay your respects."

"He hardly ever goes downtown!" Mrs. Lewis said.

Mr. Mason got Carlotta away and introduced her to a beefy, tweedy, bearded, prematurely resigned man who was Dr. Hanly, Gene's big boss. Hanly went right to the point impatiently because he just had to get out of there.

Gene's corpse represented a million one loss and he was a committed company man.

"Although at first," he said to Carlotta, "I found your request to freeze Gene's quotas to be unusual, I soon came around to the memento mori aspect of the requirement and, of course, in that sense, understand it fully. You wish time to stand still in terms of your husband's real achievement as an insurance representative. So be it. Here is our official letter on it."

○

Carlotta allowed the funeral director only one mourner's car to follow the hearse across the city to the Brooklyn crematorium. Dad Quebaro rode with her. His eyes were red-rimmed. His head hung on his chest. "Whoever thought I would have survived Gene," he said for the sixth time.

"Dad, you blubbered like that before and you heard my answer," Carlotta said. "I am going to say it once more, then we will never mention it again. Okay?"

"All right, Carlotta."

"You did NOT survive Gene nor will you. Gene is coming back. Now, you don't understand it so please let it go. Have I ever given you wrong information before?"

"Not deliberately wrong information, no."

"Then just accept one fact. Gene may be dead, but it's a mistake. I am going to make them give me Gene back because they have no idea how much I love Gene and how we have not yet achieved what we set out to achieve together. That is real currency, Dad, and I am going to use it to buy Gene back. They simply have to show respect."

"Carlotta?"

"Yes, Dad?"

"Who is *they?*"

"Dad, for heaven's sake! If you live for fifty more years you'll never be able to understand it. It concerns a relationship between a man, his wife, and God—whoever that may be. It is entirely a problem of communications and semantics. Now, please, light up a joint and sit back and enjoy the ride. It takes at least forty minutes to get to this bloody crematorium."

Six

Each J($\Uparrow$)CES Chief of Mission addressed his teams separately, away from the convention hall. The Chiefs seemed more concerned that their people maintain their fixed regional styles and attitudes, i.e., $\uparrow$ or $\downarrow$, the Hell people to remain their imponderably evil selves under all circumstances regardless of temptation, and the Heaven team to operate constantly and indefatigably for good. These considerations seemed far more paramount than any philosophical field objectives or any lofty directives issued by the Executive Committee. In fact, at this Operations level, to listen to the Chiefs of Mission, the lung fish were only things to be manipulated. It could even be said that they spoke cynically.

The Chief$^\uparrow$ was a *very* devious Avenging Angel from the Michael Brigade, an elite corps. He was much the gentleman-ruffian of the Churchill school, a crypto-capitalist who affected a vastly useful self-appreciating manner. His name was Af$^\uparrow$. He was one of the Angels of Destruction, an over-subscribed volunteer battalion. He held the title of Prince of Wrath, ruler over the deaths of mortals. At home, he stood five hundred parasangs tall and was forged out of chains of black and red fire. At the 53rd Street YWCA, where the briefing took place, he wore a billycock bowler and a black stumpy-making suit. Standing in a modish, round-shouldered manner, he seemed a shortish man.

"You must return with the ekshull scientific formula for the meaning of money, you see, my dears," he explained avuncularly to the team: Alice Trudy Kehoe and Justin Case. "Money has wrought some damned nasty conditions, you see. On your shoulders, for instance, will rest an explanation for the disappearance of the three-dollar novel and the ten-cent loaf. But, above all else, money quite to one side, you must protect Quebaro and the Neriades woman from the monsters of Hell↓ who oppose us in this anophysial crusade."

"Must we do it *all* with words and example?" Alice asked.

"How do you mean?"

"Well, sir," Justin put in. "Hell *will* have unlimited money to bribe and corrupt. They always do have, don't they?"

"Bribery and corruption is their metier," Af said blandly. "But they have restrictions. They are forbidden to try to bring down the subjects with bad advice, whereas you two may help your charges with all the good advice you have."

In a back booth of a Third Avenue saloon called McCrory's, Haurus,↓ a great duke of Hell, Chief of Mission, instructed Miss Phyllis Stein and Mr. Palmer Mahan without moving his lips. He had every look and gesture of a television casting director's idea of a hit man. No light reflected from his eyes. His teeth badly needed scaling, which was going to lead to a rotten gum condition. He wore tennis shoes, slacks, a loose V-necked sweater, and an eight-piece tweed cap which was held together on top by a large tweedy button. He was making one of his rare appearances in human form. Usually it was his conceit to show himself as a sort of zooid leopard.

Stein and Mahan, although seated, held themselves at full attention. This was real brass they faced.

"It's very big, kids," Haurus said. "Don't fool around. You wanna make it wit' us, you gotta bring to Poppa what Poppa gotta have—dig? The Man™ wants to know about money. I don't care what you do, who you hit, how you spend. This is the biggest. Don't disapernt Haurus and Haurus don't disapernt you. But revayse it—and, kids, you got yourself baaaad trouble."

Mahan shuddered. Miss Stein leaned weakly against the wall of the booth, nickering involuntarily.

"All right," Haurus said. "Here it is. There will be two Ups† and two Greeks on the contract. Clear everything with Vickie Saxe-Coburg, coordinator. Remember—I picked you. My judgment is on the line. You are about the two rottenest angels in Hell and you know I gotta have razzults—right? Never forget it, kids.''

o

Zeus gave a short talk to his assembly which lasted three hours, four nine zero seven minutes. In the main, he repeated what he had told them before but made references to atochthons, the Golden Age, the Silver Age, Pandora, and the Brazen Age. He quoted from Ovid. He mentioned Astrea, the Goddess of Innocence. He confided to them that, if they were successful in bringing Spiro back, they would move to the United States. He closed with: "They have terrific shopping here."

o

Alice Trudy Kehoe[†], Justin Case[†], Phyllis Stein[↓], Palmer Mahan[↓], and Hermes[☿] materialized before Miss Victoria Saxe-Coburg[⇵] at the same instant. "My instructions," Miss Saxe-Coburg told them all tranquilly, "are those of any case officer who is running agents in the field. You will be visible, out in the field. I will remain inside, invisible. My job is to insure that your actions advance the objectives of this operation, that none of your actions hinder the winning of those objectives. This clearly requires that I dominate you but, more importantly, that, when you need help I see that you get it. Hermes, whom you have all met, will act as a Cut-Out whenever I deem it necessary; that is, Hermes will act as intermediary between me, as case officer, and you as agents, when and if I deem that necessary. He will also act as Cut-Out, in extraordinary circumstances, as intermediary between our Executive Committee[⇵] and you as agents. I tell you this so you will understand that he is authorized.

"Angels[†] may influence Quebaro and Neriades only for the good. Angels[↓] may influence them only for evil. The contrast, in terms of information about money, will produce interesting results, we think. There may be no deviation from this rule. Please feel free to freeze any action, or to replay it, if that will provide you with more detailed support. Do concentrate on turning in your finished reports just as soon as possible upon completion of your field research so that I may combine them editorially, cross-reference, and footnote them, so that the total report, our final White Paper, may be read at the closing session of the convention.

"There is just one final thing. As you will soon discover, humans place a great deal of stress, not to say value, upon sex, a body contact sport in continual play, in one form or another, among them, which the Greeks fully understand. It was, indeed, the Greeks who threw in the impurities of Original Sex which led to lung fish corruption which, almost as directly as a thrown spear, led to the unfathomable puzzlements of lung fish money morals. I know sex will baffle you, but I am depending on all of you to read the several insurance company sex instruction booklets which have been included in your Fact Kits. If you have further questions, do contact Pharzuph↓, genius of fornication, angel of lust. I am ordered to assure you that a little sex will not—repeat NOT—hurt you, and may even be pleasant. If murder should become necessary anywhere along the line of studies please refer it to Miss Stein or Mr. Mahan. When in doubt about anything, consult me. Any questions?"

"I have these tennis match tickets . . ." Palmer Mahan began.

"Not to worry. Flash me and we will freeze time and action." She looked into all of their faces in turn. "Good show, then. I think you will find this a comfortable, even frequently interesting assignment. Good luck to all of you."

Seven

Eugene Quebaro awoke in a large double bed beside his wife, Doris Neriades Quebaro, in their two-and-a-half-room apartment (on which they owed $31,900) on the fifty-second floor of the condominium, Fortress East. This apartment complex was named for the American architect and financier, Anne Knauerhase Fortress, who had designed and built the ninety-seven-storey building, standing between Third Avenue and the East River, and between 21st Street and 89th Street—one long, wide, continuous housing development. It was a safe and solid block of flats, offices, parking spaces, cinemas, department stores, hospitals, nightclubs, libraries, greeting-card shops, firehouses, banks, jails, bowling alleys, undertaking parlors, swimming pools, churches, consulates, and embassies—in short a country within a city, all with 16,004 miles of piped rock music and PORN-CATV. Nine hundred and sixty eight thousand families, averaging 3.7 persons each, lived in Fortress East and, if any one of them peed in the elevators—*out!* If any one of them wrote Fuck U on the walls—*out!* If any one assaulted or shot a neighbor—*out!*

No one wanted to be *out!* because they could get killed out there—except in the jewelcase part of the city between Lexington Avenue and the Avenue of the Americas, from 49th Street to 59th Street, the glamorous New York which the world knew so well from airline calendars. Here elegance swaggered through the thousands of merchandise museums which sold amazements in silk, electronics, flowers, flesh, precious stones and the more costly wines. Here were the bespoke hotels for the fortunate visitors who were rushed from the airports through the cordons of slums in

sealed trains. Here were the eight thousand troops in plain-
clothes who made sure that everything purred along to
maintain the ineffable dignity of man; never a junkie unless
he was a rich junkie; hardly ever a mugger; no pushy street
whores until after one in the morning (although then by the
thousands); rarely an indecent exposure although many a
decent one, for it was given to the rich to streak, not the
poor. And there were never more than three daily homicides
in the magic circle.

There were other Anne Knauerhase Fortress
developments. Most of the affluent city had been replanned
for multiples of her apartment blocks. Fortress East, where
the Quebaros were fortunate enough to hold a mortgage,
was the oldest and smallest but, being on the east side,
having a view of beautiful Queens, it was considered the
most desirable.

The real residential problem for New Yorkers
was where and how a family lived when it was—*out!* Not that
they were denied. There was Harlem and Washington
Heights; the south and east Bronx; the Lower East Side;
Bedford-Stuyvesant, and all of lovely Brooklyn; in fact, just
about everywhere was available outside the Fortress developments but living out there wasn't as much fun: the rats
kept running off with the baby and, with the new viruses the
guys had picked up in Nam, a tenant could get paresis just
from shaking hands. So, to an optimum degree, the resi-
dents did their best to observe all the rules. Every one of
them, whether in or *out!* believed astounding luck had been
painted on them to be privileged to be living in exciting,
stimulating, thrilling New York, the absolute center of the
planet.

The *out!* people hustled frantically to support
the people in the Fortresses, who broke *their* hearts to be
allowed to support the people in the jewelcase, who in turn
sold *their* hopes to maintain a belch of politicians who would
kill at the drop, all for a much, *much* smaller group who
preferred not to be identified just now, but who were known
generally as "the stockholders."

o

Doris Quebaro looked as adorable and fitting under Gene Quebaro as she had such a short time earlier under Warren Hutch, before her fatal heart attack. She smiled sleepily at her husband.

"Happy anniversary," she said.

"You always remember."

"Three years isn't just a sneeze, Gene." She rolled him off and got out of bed. "Gene?"

"Wha'?" He hated to awaken.

"Please let me lend you twenty dollars."

"No."

"But, honey, we'll starve to death while I have a hundred and ninety-two dollars in the bank."

"No."

"For God's *sake*, Gene! We've had spaghetti with margarine sauce for dinner every night for eight nights."

"I have a client coming in today."

"Gene!"

He got out of bed wearily and shuffled to the bathroom. "Our third anniversary," he mumbled, "and I can't even get together enough money to buy you a greeting card."

"Never you mind," Doris said cheerily. "We'll celebrate just the same at Elaine Shubagger's shower after the bowling finals." She began to dress rapidly.

"Do you think your stepfather would lend me twenty-three hundred dollars?"

"No."

"Why not?"

"Because you already owe him over fifteen hundred dollars. Also he went co-maker for you."

"We. *We* owe him."

"That isn't the way he feels about it, Gene. He is still terribly upset about your stock tip."

"How was I supposed to know they wouldn't be able to get a road to the mine?"

"He is very bitter about it, Gene."

"I still think Reggie got mixed up about the name of the stock."

"Then why did he flee to Rhodesia?"

Gene clambered into the tub and stood under the shower head. "If we don't get twenty-three hundred dollars from somewhere by Friday, they will foreclose the mortgage and we won't have any place to live." By mistake he turned on the hot water instead of the cold. He screamed. Doris leaped across the room and turned the cold water on.

"That was very self-destructive," she said. But she tempered her disapproval instantly. "But everything is going to change with this client today. I can feel it."

Doris had certain clairvoyant powers which were, in themselves, absolutely amazing, but they only worked effectively when she was locked in her office where she was employed under the euphemistic title of "Chief Statistician" for the nation's largest and most influential bookmaker. Locked in her small room, Doris was able to divine which horses were going to win, place, show, and lose at all the race tracks in the United States, enabling her employer to lay off the wrong bets on other bookmakers, thus making him the nation's most powerful and influential in his field. Outside the locked office, she had occasional vague flashes about herself and Gene, but these had one drawback: they were always wrong.

"I can see the client," she said. "This is a big thing. It is a wonderful, wonderful opportunity for you. He is a marvelous man. He is a very rich man and he is going to bring you action beyond your wildest dreams."

Gene stood limply under the shower. He couldn't find the strength to soap himself. "If your stepfather would only look at my figures," he said. "If he would just go over the Dinner Plate Portfolio I've been playing with trading—just on paper—over the past ten months, he would see how real money can be made. Dermatologists have to be the world's dumbest people."

Doris had left the room to make breakfast. She couldn't hear Gene because of the shower noise.

"Even if we traded over-the-counter," Gene yelled, "I can show him how to avoid dealers who handle only a few lines of plates. He could get murdered in a situation like that and I would make sure he watched the five per cent mark-up which the NADPSD allows. That's complicated stuff for a dummy like your stepfather." He turned off the shower and got out of the tub. "Were you listening to me?" he yelled.

"You were talking about trading dinner plates, right?"

"Yes."

"So why should I listen? It's a fantasy. Give me permission to break into my savings account so I can bring home a steak and, believe me, I'll listen. Meanwhile, *please* let's forget about getting anything out of my stepfather."

Gene manipulated an electric toothbrush and a Waterpik in his mouth simultaneously, coordinating the crossovers beautifully. When he finished, he still wanted to cry, but he felt better around the teeth. He had eight dollars and thirty cents to his name. His secretary hadn't been paid for four months. His wife had had to take up bowling just to get out of the apartment once in a while. Thank God for sex. It gave them something to do together. It made up for the shows they hadn't seen and the dinners in restaurants that they had missed. What a wonderful girl. Lately, he always felt like crying.

He sat on the edge of the bed and dragged his socks on. The room was decorated with artifacts by Australian aboriginals, mostly from the Rirejjingu linguistic group (so the man said from whom Doris had been able to get them indirectly). There were representations of human figures with ostentatious genitals against red-ochred backgrounds, painted in black, yellow, and white. Gene saw them as his bad luck pieces.

He tottered into the living room, which was done in imitation pot-bellied Louis Quinze. The kitchenette unfolded out of a wall in the living room. As soon as he got there Doris carried their breakfast into the bedroom. He followed her. They lay down on the bed, fully dressed. Doris passed coffee and toast to Gene. "I love having breakfast in bed," she said. "Gosh, having a real client must be so *exciting* for you, Gene. Gee, we may even be able to see a movie again. And yesterday I saw the most marvelous pair of bar-ber-pole pantyhose—oh, Gene!"

Tears filled his eyes. "Let's not count our chickens."

"Will you ask Miss Kehoe to listen in and call me as soon as she knows what it is all about?"

"Sure."

"And wear your lucky tie."

o

As always, walking across town to his office, Gene began to recover from the stark terror of waking up. He was beginning to feel almost reassured.

He had seen only three clients this year and it was the third week in June. Gene Quebaro was a member of the New York Bar. He had practiced law for eight years, working his way up to his present earning capacity: approximately ninety-seven cents a day, including barter. Raziel had personally programmed his past with great care. Gene knew that there was no reason whatever for thinking that the visitor he expected today would be any more than a lawbook salesman, no client at all. And in fact, out of the three clients who had come in so far this year, two had been deadbeats. One was a butcher in trouble with the Department of Weights and Measures. He had paid Gene with poultry and lambs' liver. One was a city fireman who wanted to sue his Lieutenant for causing him a hernia by throwing him at a fire pole while sleeping. Gene had had to secure a garnishment on the man's salary before he could collect the rotten fifty-dollar fee. The third client had been a woman who had fallen off a 49th Street crosstown bus almost at his door. It turned out, bitterly, that she fell off city buses for a living through lawsuit settlements.

But hundreds of people knew he was practic-ing law. Sooner or later *someone* would have to recommend him. As there were more and more people because of the population multiplication, they needed more and more law-yers, although, even so, it was possible that 609,000 lawyers were too many for a city of New York's size.

Gene was practicing law because his Uncle Raimundo, a Filipino, had provided in his last will that if Gene would practice law for a period of "not less than ten years," he would inherit an estate which had, at his death, amounted to approximately $846,000 and was growing all the time. The estate was not only cash. There were three underground parking lots and a fabulous collection of beer-bottle labels.

It had been a terrible eight years. That it would probably be the most oppressive ten years of his life was all the more poignant because, the way Raziel had programmed him to believe in his own past and in his dreams for the future, Gene knew what he should be doing with his life. Given proper access to the exercise of his free will, he would have taken his accredited representative exams immediately and become a licensed dinner-plate broker. To Gene, trading dinner plates combined art with commerce, a unity as clear to him as the practice of law was murky.

Gene's offices were in 10 East 49th Street, off Fifth Avenue. The address was convenient for his exit at Fortress East. It was near Doris, who worked in Rockefeller Center. His offices could have seemed small if they ever held more than himself, his secretary, and two thin clients. They comprised his own two-window office and a five-by-six anteroom where the secretary sat near a duct so she wouldn't suffocate. Doris had decorated both rooms with artifacts from (allegedly) the Bangwibangwi and the Gunduwalambala. There were two wuramus; a hunting scene painted on bark showing birds and kangaroos and supposedly done by a Marakula dua man; and a sacred didjeridoo, each represented as having come from the heart of Arnhem Land. Doris had bought the collection from her employer for forty-five dollars. Her employer had taken the collection in settlement for a bad debt of one hundred dollars across the board on a horse named Fred Foaley. Gene was sure the artifacts had been made in Akron, Ohio, where he knew of the existence of a firm of industrial designers who had once been retained by the State Department to create retroactive designs for the "ancient" folk culture of South Korea because no such souvenirs existed for the GIs to buy to bring home to prove they had been there.

To complement the aboriginal artifacts, Doris had furnished Gene's private office in the style of a Vermont country lawyer at the turn of the century. It had a large roll-top desk with sixty pigeonholes, two rocking chairs for clients, and a swivel chair for Gene. Down to the multicolored hooked rugs the effect was one of demonstrated, simple honesty.

However, Gene's secretary, Alice Trudy Kehoe, was no primitive. She had masses of intricately worked red-gold hair, a face of melting, compelling purity, and a pair of legs to complete that crazing figure which could not have been exceeded in appeal by the sculpture of Pygmalion. In spite of this, the relationship between the lawyer and his secretary was as correctly formal (sexually, that is) as that between Calvin Coolidge and his Chief Justice, William Howard Taft, in the early fall of 1923.

It was Gene's habit to enter his office, greet Miss Kehoe (who always seemed to be there), make a small joke while hanging up his hat and umbrella, then take the four steps into his private office to stow his lunch in the middle, left-side drawer of his desk. He always carried an umbrella to the office because his gloom was so overwhelming that no matter how much the sun was shining, to Gene it always seemed ready to rain.

To get through the day, he would plunge into the complicated business of following the dinner-plate market. Totting up his imaginary holdings in plates painted by Salvador Dali, Norman Rockwell, Bing & Grondahl, and Dwight D. Eisenhower, Gene estimated he could have made just under sixty thousand dollars in the six and a half months of the year so far—if he had had the money to trade dinner-plate issues.

He kept up with kiln and firing gossip, the plans of the big private mints, the chatter about which painters were swinging toward or away from which potteries (it was said the English were raiding). He had to work it all out on paper because he was so poor, but he refused to project

69

even imaginary action with mutual plate funds, or plate hedges, or pools with over-the-counter potteries. During four years of keeping his own records of his own imaginary trading, he had earned (on paper), with a fantasy investment of five thousand dollars, the total clear-capital amount of three hundred and twelve thousand dollars.

He had made himself a master of plate cycles. He had worked a potter's wheel at the Y. He had apprenticed at ovens on weekends. He had tried polishing. He had dusted and sold crockery both at Macy's basement and at Plummer's. He knew inventories, style changes, and everything about packing, crating, shipping, and export. With absolutely nothing else to do to get him through the days for eight years, he had lived speculative dinner plates. *He knew plates.*

On the fateful morning when he was expecting a new client, if it were a client, Gene sat at his desk and unpacked the lunch in his brief case: a single Hero sandwich made only with raw green peppers. He was already feeling desperately hungry and it was only twenty minutes to ten. He sat motionless trying to think of the best way to get the most out of his client. He summoned dignity within simplicity. He imprinted upon himself an expression of interested wisdom. He practiced balancing the fingertips of one hand upon the fingertips of the other.

Miss Kehoe put her head in at the doorway. "I've begun the count-down!" she said gaily. "Four minutes, twenty seconds to blast-off!" Gene appreciated that kind of effort.

He began a game of solitaire with a deck of forty-nine playing cards. Someone (the cleaning woman?) had stolen three cards, making it impossible for him to win out.

Palmer Mahan was announced at the stroke of ten o'clock. With a supreme effort of will, Gene did as he had been taught at law school. He kept the client waiting for twelve minutes before asking Miss Kehoe to send him in.

In the reception room, Miss Kehoe and Mr. Mahan were as cordial as two boxers at a weigh-in. After a silence, Mr. Mahan blurted, "But what is he *doing* in there?"

"He plays cards. He keeps a record of hourly outside temperatures and he plots his imaginary investments. It's pathetic really."

"Then why is he keeping me waiting? I am a client. He has no clients. This could be his big chance."

"It is a ritual all lawyers must perform. He *must* pretend to be busy for twelve minutes."

"Why?"

"After all, Palmer," Miss Kehoe said with asperity, "he doesn't know he died one and two one-hundredths seconds ago. Like every other lung fish in another place, he is the result of his in-puts. Whatever he does, or believes, it is the result of how we programmed him for this assignment."

"Of course." Mahan flushed at being corrected. "Sorry. But, just generally, why do lawyers keep clients waiting?"

"Because lawyers are programmed to believe that if a client thinks they are occupied, the client will understand better when the lawyer charges him more money."

"More than who?"

"More than any lawyer who could think that an appointment is a verbal contract, or even good manners."

Mahan shook his head with the hopelessness of an Eskimo staring at his first cricket match. "It's no use, Alice," he said, "I'm never going to get the hang of these lung fish money rituals. They're going to have to replace me in this job."

"Don't be silly, Palmer. You haven't even met a lung fish yet. Give the whole thing a chance."

"Have you met one?"

"I *am* his secretary. He *did* have to pass me to get into his office."

"What are they like?"

"He seemed very nice. He was clean. He wasn't at all obsessed with sex the way we were warned."

"I must say you are looking very well."

"Really? I had never tried hair before. Do you like it?"

"Which is the hair?"

71

"Here." Alice touched both sides of her head.

"Oh, yes. Very nice."

The buzzer sounded.

"Mr. Quebaro will see you now," Alice said. She unwedged herself from behind the tiny desk and opened the PRIVATE office door. As Palmer Mahan entered, Gene rose.

Gene had been expecting an older, perhaps a pleasanter-looking man. What he saw was tall and quite thin, dressed in bottle green with very high slashes at either side of a hacking jacket cut in the English mode with a pinched waist and a flaring skirt. There were small, blood-shot black and glittering eyes; the mean-cold eyes of a top surgeon who would much prefer to work without anesthetics. His skin was sallow, his mouth prissy. Mahan's voice was flat, his manner unpromising rather than unfriendly; unappetizing rather than repulsive—in short, the model businessman. Haurus had designed Mahan's mien with a sure sense of double con. Single con would have been to plant a happy, enthusiastic fellow before the needy lawyer, but Haurus was too subtle for that. He chose to present Mahan in a human form that was congruent with his real one, but then, after the impression had been struck to unsettle Quebaro, he added Mahan's wondrously sunny, even irresistible smile and his moulinage of words which were purest, supplicating silk. It was the great con of olden times long gone before, in the days before the President of the United States had undersold it, back in the happy times when it was forever said that Attila the Hun or Hermann Goering was the most charming man some poor, doomed bastard had ever met.

With innate courtesy, since he had only four cigarettes remaining for the entire day and evening, Gene offered his guest an Argol and struck a match for him.

"Thank you."

"Not at all. May I help you, Mr. Mahan?"

"I don't know."

"Perhaps you might begin by telling me about the problem that brought you here."

"In which branch of the law do you specialize?"

"Mine is a general practice."

"Is your time freely available?"

"This morning?"

"In the immediate future."

"I shouldn't think so. It would mean re-mak-
ing a rather busy schedule."

"Perhaps I could make that worth your
while."

"How did you happen to seek *my* counsel, Mr.
Mahan?"

"The usual inquiries."

"The *u*sual?"

"Yes."

"Well! That is most flattering."

"For seventy dollars I was able to buy from
the Treasury Department a copy of the computer reels from
the IRS which establish you as fourth lowest in income-tax
payments among all the lawyers in Manhattan. To me, this
establishes you as either a high-powered tax counsel or as a
weak earner. Which is it?"

"To each his own," Gene snarled.

"The Consumers' Credit League rates you at
their J level, the lowest possible rating, which was attained
not so much by the amounts you owe as by the different sorts
and numbers of accounts you have failed to pay—such as the
account of your stepfather-in-law."

Gene bounded to his feet. "My stepfather-in-
law?" The size of the question mark showed the paralysis of
his credulity. His eyes and mouth made perfect circles giving
the impression that, should he lean forward, his *machismo*, a
delicate mechanism, would drop out and shatter on the
floor. "Dr. Norman Lesion?"

Mahan nodded.

"How—— Why this is out*rage*ous! That was
a personal loan! How dare he report me to the Credit
League?"

"He didn't report you for the loan, Counsel-
lor. He reported you for non-payment of a three-thousand-

four-hundred-and-eight-dollar bill you ran up over a period of three years at his delicatessen."

Gene had never forgotten the first time Doris had taken him to her stepfather's delicatessen. He had never been able to afford to go there. It was a gastronomic legend among your true American gourmets, he told her. Doris had gotten them a table with an effortless phone call four days in advance.

"How does he get this effect with the pickles?" Gene had asked his bride. The dinner was a wedding present from Dr. and Mrs. Lesion, in lieu of cash or flatware.

"The doctor doesn't do it himself, silly."

"Why not?"

"Because he's a healer. It just happened that a grateful patient left him this delicatessen in her will."

"But how do they get this effect with the pickles?"

"The doctor marinates in champagne plus truffles then slices on the bias."

"Wow!"

"Everything is gourmet here, Gene. And you won't get a lot of allergies breaking out on your skin, either, because the doctor puts lecithin into every dish."

"This is a gourmet *pal*ace."

"The doctor won a Medoc *pot* for seventy-four for moving more Chateau Lafitte than any other American delicatessen."

"Also, let me say this is the all-time most in pastrami I have ever eaten."

"That is your Charolais beef," Doris said. "It is saffron-flavored, then the doctor has them rub in a few pounds of lark paté before marinating in the honey-wine combination."

"Dry method or wet?"

"First dry, then wet. The cattle itself have also been naturally flavored by feeding with two strictly Mediterranean fish. Then the little ortolans and rice birds the doctor feeds the cattle cancel out any fishy flavor."

"Then why feed them fish?"

"It adds to the price, of course. Then a goat

is roasted inside the beef. The whole method makes an un-
forgettable pastrami but it costs, naturally."

"You get what you pay for," Gene said chew-
ing ecstatically. "Eleven ninety-five isn't a lot for a sandwich
like this. Have a beer."

He should never have opened a charge account.

Gene was trembling with rage. Mahan flashed
the first of his wonderful smiles. *"Please* forgive me, Mr.
Quebaro," he said. "I have offended you where no offense
was meant. Is it possible that you conceive that you are one
of very few in this hard-pressed city who are in financial
straits? The very state of your credit shows that you are an
honest man. *That* is why I have come to retain your counsel
if I can."

"A retainer?"

"Would you accept ten thousand dollars a
year? With all fees to be set by you, of course."

Gene sat down. Mr. Mahan took out a choco-
late-brown wallet so sensually soft that it seemed to have
been made out of dyed ghee. He put the wallet in Gene's
hand. Gene did not lift the wallet to examine its contents.
Instead, he asked numbly, "Fees for what services, Mr. Mahan?"

"Think rather of the money you owe, Mr.
Quebaro. Think of the mortgage on your apartment, which
must be paid this week. Think of your furniture, such as it
is, strewn out upon Third Avenue while your neighbors
snort their contempt."

"But I must know the sort of legal work you
will require before I can accept a retainer," Gene said
weakly.

Mahan's entire body deprecated his re-
sponse. "I want very little for my money, actually," he said.
"First I want you to keep this little valise for me." He lifted
a small aluminum case from the floor beside him. "And
other equally simple things for which all your expenses will
also be paid."

"You want me to *keep* other things?"

"Do other things."

"What other things?"

"Well—for example—there is a package I would like you to bring me from Peru."

"Peru?"

"Yes. You know, where the cocaine comes from."

Eight

On her way to work on the 49th Street cross-town bus, Doris became conscious of a man studying her with a more concentrated interest than any man had ever shown her before. It happened that Doris was not only a gulpingly beautiful Greek-American girl, but that she was also able to dress herself very well because a garment manufacture client of her employer, Mr. Violente, had bet his entire company and, when he lost, Mr. Violente had divided the dress stock of the man's $399.95 line (wholesale) among Mrs. Violente, her sister, Mr. Violente's secretary, and Doris. In the actual sharing, since Mr. Violente's sister-in-law was so freakishly fat, and because Mrs. Violente preferred to wear men's clothing, only two of them could share, and Mr. Violente's secretary was sixty-four and would not have looked good in the Courrèges copies which made up the man's stock. Doris was wearing something which gave girls with legs and figures like hers the power to turn parts of men to stone.

What bothered Doris about the man who was staring at her so lewdly across the bus was that, only a few minutes before, he had been staring up at her from the back seat of a long, chauffeur-driven limousine. At a red light he had left the limousine to board the bus apparently to be able to regard her even more ravenously. He was a well-built man of about thirty-five. He wore a really good, glossy, black moustache. In fact, in every way he was a disturbingly attractive man.

She left the bus at the Rockefeller Center stop. She went to the sixty-fourth-floor offices of Mr. Violente's Mesilla Trading Company, said good morning to each fellow-worker she met, then locked herself in her office to begin the day's visualization of American track results. Suddenly a panic gripped her. She had just seen a vision as clear as the nose of a winner breaking across a finish line. She grabbed the direct line to Mr. Violente's office, which was twenty-three feet away.

"Mr. Violente! It's Doris. I have just had a very bad vision. I have just seen the future and it isn't going to work."

"The tracks aren't even open yet. What happened?" There was panic in his voice.

"We are going to be raided."

"Raided? Wha'?" He began to laugh a great big hearty laugh. "Raided? Me? Don't be crazy, honey. The U.S. Army wouldn't even have the nerve to raid me." At that moment, the New York City police crashed down his door and took him under arrest.

The raid happened at twenty minutes after ten on the morning Gene was expecting his client, so she could get no news from him. Nineteen uniformed policemen and seven detectives herded one hundred and twelve Violente employees into the elevators while a TV camera crew, four press photographers, and three reporters yelled questions at them. Doris's employer, Mort Violente, was speechless with outrage as he was led out, shielding his face from the cameras with a wastebasket dropped over his head. He could only shout obscenities. The reverberations of the sounds inside the metal tub made the curses awesome to the viewers of all prime-time news shows that evening, giving them the instant knowledge that he was guilty of whatever he was being arrested for. For over thirty years his position as the nation's first bookmaker had been inviolate. He was the head of a Mafia Family in metropolitan New York. If he were hindered from continuing, as was threatened today, the bulk of American gambling on such industries as professional football, racing, baseball, hockey, and impeachment could grind to a halt. Stop Mort Violente and take all the pleasure, maybe the only pleasure, out of elections.

Mysteriously, during the raid Doris was

treated with elaborate courtesy. She was sequestered from
all the others and protected from the press. She was not
escorted from the offices until all other Violente employees
had been dragged off. She was driven to the Municipal
Courts building in a limousine with a uniformed police chauffeur. At the midtown courthouse, obviously a new venue,
lawyers and bail bondsmen were everywhere. Word was
passed to her that Mr. Violente wanted her to attend a policy
meeting at The Restaurant at eleven thirty. Then came the
surprise. Sitting as muncipal court judge in charge of the
Violente proceedings was the man who had ogled her on the
crosstown bus that morning! She stared up at him in a daze
of both fright and pleasure while he set Mr. Violente's bail
at $250,000. Then as all the Violente employees awaited
their fate, he called a recess and strode off to his chambers
while Mr. Violente was led off to the paddy wagon to be
taken to the Tombs. A policeman asked Doris to follow him.
He led her along a circuitous route to the Judge's chambers,
but passed her into them alone. The Judge locked the doors,
seated her on a sofa, then sat beside her, their thighs touching in a disturbing way. He smelt of some refreshing and
crazing scent she had never smelled before. He said, with a
scandalously moving voice, "I am so sorry to have caused
you this trouble, Mrs. Quebaro. May I introduce myself? I
am Judge Joe V. Zeuss and I was wondering if you would be
free for lunch today."

"*Lunch?*"

"To begin, yes."

"I can't, Your Honor. My employer has called
a policy meeting for eleven thirty."

"Not to worry, you beautiful woman. There
will be no meeting. He is in the Tombs now. Therefore you
can come to lunch with me."

"This is a very, *very* serious matter for Mr.
Violente, Your Honor."

"Shall we meet at the Thessaly Restaurant at
Twenty-eighth and Eighth at one thirty?"

"Yes, Your Honor."

o

Outside the courthouse a Violente Family car was waiting to take her to Sal's Smorg on West 56th Street for the eleven-thirty meeting. Mr. Violente had chosen to pay the $250,000 bail.

Mr. Violente, agitated almost beyond recognition, was waiting for her, alone, in a private room.

"How come you knew about the raid?" he asked harshly. "And how come you didden tell me yesterday?"

"It came to me the minute I locked the door in my office. Like the horses come. It just came. Anyway, you wouldn't believe me. If it *had* come to me yesterday, you would have laughed at me in the same way."

"Yeah. Okay."

"Mr. Violente! You didn't think I—"

"Doris, tell me something. Why the judge called you inside?"

"He wanted to ask me to lunch."

"Lonch? *Lonch?* What you tole him?"

"I told him most certainly not. I told him that I was a married woman and that you had called a policy meeting."

"What he said?"

"He said if I didn't go to lunch he would double your bail and keep you in the Tombs until I had lunch with him."

"What you tole him?"

"I accepted, so that you could be free."

He stared at her, nodding. "I'm ashameda myself for thinkin' what I was thinkin'. You are a great kid, Doris. And you got yourself a twenty-dollar-a-week raise the way you handled this." He peeled off a hundred-dollar bill from a head of kohlrabi he carried in his canvas-reinforced pocket and pressed it into her hand. "A little bonus. You go out an' get your hair done or something while I take care of this certain son of a bitch of a nothing nowhere muncipal court judge." He gave her his hand to kiss. Then he said, "But no lunch with this animal, you hear?"

Doris heard but she didn't hear. She felt sad and loyal as she left Sal's Smorg. Wasn't Mr. Violente's No

Lunch policy all for the best? Why fool around? She could only end up getting herself in a great big mess because that judge had something for her. She got *tremendous* vibes out of him; absolutely the most colossal, heroic, gigantic vibes she had ever felt except for the morning she had been all alone in the Lincoln Memorial in Washington with Mr. Lincoln. Stay with Gene, she ordered herself. Love Gene. Gene should be the only man for her, she insisted, unaware that the subjunctive was the alibi tense of the language, unaware that she had become such an instantaneously responsive instrument from constant, endless hour-upon-hour sex (since they couldn't afford any other entertainment in their lives), honed down so fine she could, if necessary, respond, wet and throbbing, to even tertiary male stimuli like a collar button. Judge Zeuss was, to her, primarily, primely, and primetidally exhilarating in the most dizzyingly carnal way. She felt torn. As she struggled with herself, she wasn't quite sure which man she was struggling to join or get away from. What has gotten into you, she demanded hotly of herself. *Not Judge Zeuss, that's for sure,* was the instant self-answer.

She had not quite made it to the corner of Broadway and 56th Street with this colloquy when three police cars came screaming around the Eighth Avenue corner on inside wheels and geeked to a stop in front of Sal's Smorg.

Many large policemen hosed out of the cars and into the restaurant. She stood transfixed. In her clairvoyance (and elsewhere) she knew that somehow the Judge had ordered this second raid because he had somehow found out about Mr. Violente forbidding her to go to lunch. It seemed supernatural. She *felt* that. But she also felt the Judge was going to be a supernatural experience all-around. She watched Mr. Violente manhandled out of the building by the police, shoved across the pavement, then flung into the second police car. To Doris it was as if this were all being staged as an aphrodisiac for her. The police convoy started away toward Broadway where she was standing on the corner. As it passed her, Mr. Violente leaned out of the car window and yelled, "So take him to lunch, fah God's sake!" Then with sirens wide open the cars sped across town.

She was under orders. She had to save her

employer. She was going to have to have lunch with Judge Zeuss and felt greatly relieved that the decision had been made.

She ran to a telephone booth to try, some-how, to lessen the pressures she felt. She called Gene's office. "Is he still with the client, Alice?" she asked. It was high noon.

"No, Mrs. Quebaro. I'll put you through."

Gene came on.

"Gene?" Doris was determined to try to keep talking until she could stop feeling what she was feeling. "Did you score? I mean, did you close with the client? What happened?"

"Doris? Violente's lawyer just called. They want you at Sal's Smorg at four o'clock."

"Honey, listen to me. I got a twenty-dollar raise this morning and a hundred-dollar cash bonus. So let me take you to lunch, Gene. Please, let me take you to lunch." She held her breath. She had to say that or she would never be able to face herself again. He couldn't turn her down. He could not possibly turn her down—but if he did —well—then it would all be his fault. She forced herself to think of that green pepper sandwich Gene ate at twelve ten every day, all alone, and she wanted to weep. And she was very hungry herself. The trouble was, she was just a little bit hungrier for lunch with Judge Zeuss.

"Okay," Gene said listlessly. "Pick me up here."

"What about the new client?"

"I blew it." He hung up.

Doris counted to twenty slowly, then she called Judge Zeuss at the Muncipal Court.

"Your Honor? This is Doris Quebaro. I won-dered if we could change our luncheon date from one thirty to a quarter to two?"

o

It was twelve fifty-five when Doris got to Gene's office. She listened with horror as Gene told her about Palmer Mahan's evil proposition.

"He has no right to fool around with cocaine packs," she said indignantly. "That is the Mastrogianni Family's privilege for which they paid plenty. Why, if I were just to mention this to Mr. Violente, that man Mahan would be behind a Brooklyn billboard full of nine-gram units by this time tomorrow."

"Just the same," Gene said, "I blew it. How could I fall back on a lot of crappy principles! Money was involved here."

"I am proud of you that you threw him out," Doris said. "You have been under such pressure about money, my God." She grabbed him to kiss him, but he had remembered something that had sent him all rigid.

"Not now," he said with new steel in his voice. "There is something I want to talk to you about right now."

Doris felt a chill go over her. How could he possibly know what she had been thinking about Judge Zeuss? He didn't have The Gift. "What? What is it?" she said, too loudly.

"Mahan told me that your stepfather reported me to the Consumers' Credit League for non-payment of the sandwiches."

"The *Doc*tor?"

"For less than three hundred sandwiches he had the nerve to report it as a debt—at retail prices."

Doris dropped her head in family shame. Dropping her head made her see the small aluminum case on the floor beside the desk. "What's that?" she asked.

Gene followed her gaze. He stared down at the case, then slowly pushed Doris to one side. "Jesus *Chr*ist!" he yelped. He dropped to one knee in front of it.

"What is it?"

"It's Mahan's. He offered me a year's pay just to hold it for him."

"Why?"

"I don't know. I told him no."

She knelt beside Gene. "There's a key in it," she said in a whisper. "Open it."

"No."

"Gene! Open the case!"

"It's illegal to open it."

"It was illegal for him to leave it here after you refused it. There could be a bomb in there. It is your duty as an officer of the court to find out what could be in there that could possibly be worth a year's pay."

Gene put the case on its side and turned the key. He opened the top. The case was filled to the brim with tightly packaged, neatly stacked, primly labeled five-hundred-dollar bank notes; twenty packages of one-hundred-dollar bank notes: a dazzling visual echo chamber of the faces of Benjamin Franklin and William McKinley. Instantly, Gene banged the lid shut, locked the case quickly, and stared bleakly into his wife's paling face.

Doris gulped. "That man must be a crook. Even Mr. Violente doesn't walk around with money like that."

"We mustn't say that, dear," Gene said shakily. "We don't know it is true."

"But he doesn't. Mr. Violente never carries more than twenty thousand dollars."

"I meant we mustn't say Mahan is a crook. After all, your stepfather probably has a trunk filled with cash like that."

"That's different. He's a dermatologist."

"I have to *think!*" Gene gripped his forehead with both tense hands and paced in short circles, then he lifted the case to the top of his desk and slammed the roll top shut over it. He picked up the telephone. "Miss Kehoe, did Mr. Mahan leave us an address or telephone? Good. Oh, fine. Will you call the number?" He put the phone down.

"What time was he here?" Doris asked.

"About two hours ago."

"He'd have to be awfully absentminded to forget this kind of money for two whole hours."

"Yeah."

"And why did he leave the key in it?"

"Yeah."

The phone buzzed. Gene picked up. "Yes?"

he said anxiously into it. He punched a phone button. "Hello? Who am I speaking to? Miss Stein? I'd like to speak to Mr. Mahan, please."

"Mr. Mahan isn't here, Mr. Quebaro. May I help you?"

"Mr. Mahan was at my office this morning. He left an aluminum case here."

"We know that, Mr. Quebaro."

"Do you also happen to know what is in the case?"

"Oh, yes. Please hold on to the case and I'll tell Mr. Mahan you called when he gets back from Peru."

"That won't suit me at all, Miss Stein. I flatly refused to hold this case for Mr. Mahan and, more emphatically, I refuse to keep it now. Therefore, as inconvenient as it will be for me, if you'll give me your office address, I'll bring it to you."

"That would be contrary to my instructions, Mr. Quebaro. So sorry. Bye-bye."

"Miss Stein!"

"Yes?"

"Miss Stein, I have been put in an intolerable position and I flatly, irrevocably refuse to hold this case and I am telling you that in the presence of witnesses. I am absolving myself of all responsibility for it and this conversation has been recorded on tape as evidence should the matter ever reach the courts."

"Pfui," Miss Stein said cuttingly. "We know you do not own a recording device and that you could not afford to rent one. No cheap threats, please. What kind of twits do you think we are? I have the receipt you signed when you agreed to keep that case. It is right here on the desk in front of me."

"Re*ceipt?*"

Miss Stein hung up on him. Gene wheeled on Doris with as blank a look as has ever been recorded on a cartoon strip. "They are going to flash a forged receipt," he said. "Why—this son of a bitch is trying to frame me!"

Doris reached for the phone. "You just let me

call Mr. Violente's caporegima and report this cocaine business," she said firmly. "Then we'll see who Mr. Smartypants thinks he is going to frame."

"Not yet!"

"Why not?"

"Baby, I have to figure this out. Why would a total stranger want to frame me with that much cash? I'm so poor I don't have an enemy in the world. There has to be a reason for this conspiracy."

Doris stood there swaying like a tree in a hurricane. She knew why. She knew who, what, why, when, and where. She felt herself filling with the three-dimensional presence of Judge Zeuss. She wanted to weep at how impotent Gene had become but that wasn't all she wanted to do. The telephone buzzed. Gene picked up.

"Yes?"

"The Fortress East office is on One, Mr. Quebaro," Miss Kehoe said.

Gene hit the One button. "Hello?"

"Mr. Quebaro?" a preposterously southern voice said. "This is Laura Bergquist? Your friendly building manager at Fortress East? Where safety is more than a word?"

"Oh, yes, Miss Bergquist."

"I am calling from our Mortgage Division? About your mortgage?" Crumpled, Gene listened to their doom. As Doris watched his panic form, it seemed to her that all the character had run out of his face since she had looked at him directly above her this morning. Her eyes fell to his crotch involuntarily, to see if his balls had fallen off. Gene hung up.

"Either we pay the twenty-three hundred bucks by five o'clock Friday or Miss Bergquist is very sorry but she will have to throw us out on the street."

"I could get the money from Mr. Violente?"

"Not at thirty per cent a week and have them wave my own arm in my face."

Doris rolled back the desk top. She opened the case. They stared down at the money.

"It's a terrible thing to tempt people," Doris

said abstractedly, seeing Judge Zeuss stripped to the buff in place of McKinley's face on every five-hundred-dollar bill. "Gene, I don't feel like having the victory lunch anymore. Okay?"

"Sure."

"I'll see you at the bowling tournament tonight. Okay?"

"Sure."

She turned to him mechanically. She kissed him in a sisterly fashion on the cheek. She left the office worrying about what she might be going to do.

Gene buzzed for Miss Kehoe. She sat across from him, arranging her spectacularly beautiful legs. Gene said, "Miss Kehoe, what would be your reading of Palmer Mahan?"

"Dreadful."

"In what way?"

"Evil."

"Do you intuit anything criminal?"

"Something much worse."

"But appearances aren't everything, are they? I never met a skier I really liked yet surely all skiers are not unlikeable, are they?"

"Every skier I ever met was."

Gene took a different tack. "Suppose I were to tell you that, because of Mr. Mahan, I might be able to pay all your back salary. Wouldn't that change your mind about him?" Gene could feel the heat of the money in the aluminum case. He knew that if he could win approval for Palmer Mahan from this young woman, then he would be able to become much more realistic about the whole thing. He had to get money but he could not accept this money without approval from somebody. The approval had become the currency he could spend because the currency had been, all the time, other people's approval. He waited intently for Miss Kehoe's answer.

"Let me ask you this, Mr. Quebaro. Could money change your opinion of Mr. Mahan?"

"Not so far."

"So far?"

"He offered me ten thousand dollars as an annual retainer for legal services."

"What legal services?"

"That was the catch." By withholding approval Miss Kehoe had released him in a different direction. He saw the absurdity of a member of the bar becoming a messenger for Mahan for a few crumbs of money. How could he have thought, even for a moment, that he needed money that badly.

Miss Kehoe crossed her legs. He began to wonder how a girl without any salary could afford such sheer, gun-metal panty hose—if indeed that was what she was wearing. Could she be accepting lewd employment on the side? Impossible! He had never looked upon such bonity. He grasped himself tightly around the middle with both arms to keep from tearing her clothing off, and rocked back and forth in his chair.

"Stomach ache, Mr. Quebaro?"

"No, no. Just trouble. Mahan left behind a case filled with money. I don't know what to do with it."

"I could have the bank send for it."

"If the bank had any clue that I had this kind of money at hand, they would tie it up. I am badly in debt to three banks, Miss Kehoe. No, Mahan will have to take this money back."

"But—where is he?"

"All I need is an address. If we can get the telephone company to give the address for that telephone number, I'll take the money there and just dump it." He paused significantly to let a different idea form itself. "Or I could invest it in plates for Mr. Mahan."

"Oh, no, Mr. Quebaro, I don't think—"

"My God! That's it, of course. Furthermore, I would be required to return to Mahan only the precise amount of money which is in that case." His life's dream could be realized. He could go into the plate market!

"I should think there would be all kinds of interpretations on that interpretation," Miss Kehoe said severely.

"I am the lawyer here, if you don't mind. We are going to count and re-count that money; then I am going to invest all of it in signed, limited editions of dinner plates and when Mahan gets back from Peru and demands his money, I will sell those plates and keep the difference."

"Oh, no, Mr. Quebaro!"

"It will be entirely ethical. I have been given no instructions about money which I refused to agree to hold in the first place."

"But—keeping the difference!"

"The difference, Miss Kehoe, is my fee as an unwilling custodian—yet that fee will not have cost the client one thin dime."

They each counted the money separately. There was exactly one million dollars in the case. The New York Plate Exchange would be open for two more hours. Gene thumbed frantically through the telephone book to find the number of Kullers & Company on East 57th Street. He dialed the number and asked to speak to John Kullers himself. His frantic manner softened and became reverent. John Kullers was his hero in the world of speculative dinner plates. He made an appointment at the Kullers brokerage in twenty minutes' time, advising that he would arrive with one million dollars in cash. He identified himself authoritatively. He took a deep breath and said, into the telephone, "While I am en route to your offices, please prepare to buy, in my name, for cash, two hundred and eight Edward Marshall Boehms from the Smiling Collie limited edition of thirty thousand plates at nine hundred and sixty dollars a plate. Yes, sir. Then eleven editions—1931 through 1939—of Bing and Grondahl Christmas plates, then anything, in any quantity you can get, of James Richard Blake's portrait plate series on that little Irish family. I want thirty-seven N.C. Wyeths, three hundred of the Chaim Gross Passover plates, and all the kiln-fresh Norman Rockwells you can put your hands on." He ordered Wedgewood, Rosenthal, Franklin Mint, Spode, Royal Copenhagen and Belleek. He wanted three dozen of the priceless plates Winston Churchill had painted for the Hallmark Ramadan greeting card series.

While he issued his buy orders, Miss Kehoe got Palmer Mahan's street address from Victoria Saxe-Coburg.

By the time Gene, feeling like a giant, reached the Kullers brokerage, there was an open line working to the plate exchange traders. The old man led Gene into his private office where, framed on the wall, was the plate Luke had eaten from at the Last Supper, a priceless example of the ceramist's art with the reliquarial stains of the original lasagna still on it.

Together, they counted the money. "Good," Mr. Kullers said. "Where do we send the plates?"

"Send, sir? The plates?"

"I have my Back Room Operation to think of, Mr. Quebaro."

It had not occurred to Gene in all the years of his imaginary speculations that he would be required actually to receive the plates: the round, hard, physical plates, which had considerable weight. Investors in U.S. Steel didn't expect to have to take delivery of part of the electric arc furnaces when they bought stock shares. Not in any way attempting to guess how many plates he had bought that afternoon, he gave Mr. Kullers his home address and asked him to send the plates there.

o

Gene left the brokerage office on a high wave of elation. At the rate Americans were at present collecting dinner plates, his investment would appreciate at the rate of one-half of one per cent: five thousand dollars a day. He had instructed John Kullers to sell three specified plates the following afternoon, yielding $270 in profits. With that money he would pay off the interest on his mortgage while guaranteeing to make the full payment due in thirty days' time together with a bonus addition of 50 per cent additional interest.

He had decided to sit tight and let Palmer Mahan find him, knowing that the more ways the inevitable meeting with Mahan could be postponed, the longer the plate investment could accumulate aggregates of one-half of one per cent. He would stay away from Mahan's office.

Then, suddenly, his true jeopardy hit him with cruel force. He stopped walking. Mahan's secretary had said she was holding a receipt he had signed. Even though that was criminal forgery, if Mahan could prove he had accepted the money and the retainer, then Mahan would be entitled to every cent of profit from the ever-rising market. He had to get that receipt or lose five thousand dollars a day —five days a week.

Nine

The Thessaly Restaurant, at one forty-five on a sleepy, near-summer afternoon, was marvelously glamorous to Doris. It had lazy-turning apple-green ceiling fans. There were sweet bouquets of flowers standing in old-fashioned crystal vases beside cruets and condiment bottles on each table. Waiters glided in black Eton jackets over floor-length white tablecloth skirts. Muffled voices burbled strephonades. Heavenly smells seemed to be shaped by the Greek alphabet, urgently tempting another of Doris's working appetites. Because of the stained-glass roof in the main room, the restaurant encased a light-violet shadowiness, mysterious and serene. She began to feel the Greek woman syndrome, which was mainly a tragic feeling of pain and loss for never having slept with Pericles. She was all Greek today. She had been raised speaking Greek. She was feeling in Greek now.

A majordomo appeared. Doris asked for Judge Zeuss. The man bowed so low she feared he would clap his head on the tile floor. He beckoned her to follow him through the anagram of Greek cooking smells. They passed across the main restaurant to a staircase at the back covered with a Turkey-red carpet, softer than steam. They ascended one floor to stand before an enormous mahogany double door. The headwaiter opened it.

"Good afternoon, my *dear* Mrs. Quebaro," Judge Zeuss said. "You are more beautiful than this morning and it is your fate and my ecstasy that you shall look ever and ever more and more beautiful."

The rapid thlocking action began at her clitoris as he motioned her to the center of the private dining room which was furnished as a Caliphate harem with thick rugs, cushions, dim light, and the sound of soft, clear, distant Greek music: a man singing "The Canary Song," which told the story of a youth who was awakened each morning by the song of a canary near his window. He sings to the canary, asking her not to tease and lure him with her song but to come into his room and become a part of his life. The lyric was in Greek. The rhythm of the music, in 7/8 time, its scales different from those of Western music, made it exotically appealing to her.

"How do you know how to speak Greek?" Doris asked breathlessly, breathily, throwing back her shoulders to increase her breadth. "I thought Zeuss was a German name."

He chortled with pleasure. "No, no. Think again on your heritage. Zeus is an old Greek name. Oh, yes. One of the oldest." He reached up and helped her to descend to a cushion beside him. He gave her a glass of cold wine. "Warm the wine with the lips and give it ardor," he said huskily (a quality which had come from thousands of years of eating olives), "just as I must use its careful chill to cool mine."

She felt very light-headed, very much alive, and *very* ready. Gene seemed to have backed away into the shadows of memory. Soon he would disappear for just a little while. Not that anything would *happen* if he disappeared. But —if anything did happen—it would be Gene's fault for always being so broke that they had to fill in all of their time together with sex, then more sex. She was always on the verge of orgasm. The Judge's voice had such *maleness* that she was afraid it might set her off at any moment. That made her resent Gene. It wasn't exactly that she didn't want to be set off; she hadn't yet quite made up her mind. She was merely trying to get used to feeling things pour out upon her from this man after not so much as being aware of other men in the three years she had been married to Gene. She had to talk about something else!

"Judge Zeuss?"

"Yes, my little dove?"

"Why did the police arrest Mr. Violente?"

"The police aren't responsible."

"Then—who?"

"You. You are responsible."

Doris gasped.

"I saw you and I adored you. Instantly. On sight. I had to know you." He kissed the palms of both of her hands, which shivered Doris in a very old-fashioned way. No one had done that to her since high school. He was staring burningly into her left eye. "I ordered the raid. I had Violente arrested, then re-arrested. Those were not police. They were my men wearing rented uniforms. I wanted to have you in my power for one tremendous moment so that I could tell myself my life had not been in vain."

"Judge *Zeuss!*" she moaned. She had an insistent desire to undress him. "But I am married."

He pressed a REMOTE button on the eight-track equipment. The voice of the Greek singer was switched to "The Girl from Egion," which told a story in the form of the lament of a lover who sings to his sweetheart about his unhappiness and his eternal love for her, although she is to marry another man because of a promise made by her family. It was alluring and very sad against a background of clarinet, lute, bass, and bouzoukis. "There was a Neriades in the ancient Greek religion," Judge Zeuss said softly. "Thetis Neriades, a Thessalian sea-goddess, one of the fifty Neriades girls. She was chosen to be the wife of Zeus, but Zeus was a fool. An all-potent oracle told him not to do it and it almost broke his heart. You are the image of Thetis. You are the single reincarnation of all the unforgettably beautiful Neriades sisters."

Her minikin resolve to struggle against him melted away. Something had to be done or she knew she would be panting and pantless among the rugs and cushions. Then—oh, *shit!*—there was a knock on the door. Judge Zeuss glared as if he wanted to fling a thunderbolt through it. The majordomo opened the door and entered the room.

"Is it that Your Honor is ready to be served?" he asked. Without waiting for an answer two waiters began to roll wagons of food into the room.

Grinding her teeth, Doris leaned back against

the cushions, bitterly saved from herself; faithful to Gene. Judge Zeuss stabbed so viciously at the control button on the eight-track that he snapped the top off a fingernail. The solo song switched into the song-story of Sapphire, a girl whose father became very rich and who wanted his daughter to have everything her heart desired. She wanted to become a dancer in the King's harem. This was beyond the reach of her father's wealth because Sapphire's face had been exposed and she was forbidden to wear the veil of the harem.

The waiters began to serve the food. There came a procession of: pastourma, peinirli, kaccavia, htapodi, krassato, katsokaki, psito, kolokithokeftethes, and floyeres. "The food is ambrosia here," Judge Zeuss pronounced.

Doris forced herself to smile.

In seventy-two minutes, within three minutes after he had swallowed the last morsel, Judge Zeuss was fast asleep on the cushions. In a green rage, Doris stamped out of the room.

Ten

The Mahan offices were in the gigantic Fortress Midtown which had been built as one ninety-seven-storey block on a space that had previously been called Central Park, from 59th to 110th Street, from Fifth Avenue to Central Park West. The words of Anne Knauerhase Fortress, which had made the building possible, were in every schoolbook: "Cities are for people, not for trees."

The Mahan office was on the Fifth Avenue side, near the 72nd Street set-back entrance. The security office got Miss Stein's approval for Gene to be allowed to go up, then punched out the coordinates on the computer to provide him with a small map. Gene found the door of 67J48BE1 with ease. He rang the doorbell. He found himself facing a hypnotically beautiful woman. She had the most smolderingly, questingly, sexually obsessed eyes he had ever seen. For a flash he thought of them as "evil" but he rejected that notion instantly because that would have been tantamount to believing that active sex was evil. And active sex was Gene's only rewarding hobby.

Phyllis Stein was seeing her first lung fish up close. She had only observed a few of them on the street below from her sixty-seventh-storey window. She was utterly unprepared for the effect a close view would have upon her. Separated from her normal work in Hell for this assignment, Phyllis had been determined to do an outstanding job. Being a librarian she had access to all the books about lung fish but, through an accident, she had, unfortunately, read only the work of American novelists instead of a more general mix. This had resulted in a cultural overload. She had been convinced that lung fish were obsessed with sex while, in truth, it had no more importance in the combined total human interest than tennis or lynching compared with the energy and interest the lung fish gave to their true obsession: money.

Through the illusions of novelists rather than the hypocrisy of lung fish (their manner of handling their preoccupation with money), Phyllis Stein had separated money out as a *problem,* rather than seeing it, as they did, as their one chance to attain ecstasy or despair. (Sex, really, was their *problem,* since they were fast reaching the point where they preferred to watch it: on movie screens, on Scrabble boards, in "dirty" books, by exhibition, with the help of their Polaroids, on PORN-CATV, at lunch clubs, on matchbook covers and TV cassettes, and there were some who got a slight *frisson* out of watching themselves at various sexual work positions in mirrors and shiny belt buckles. It was a collison course with disaster, in the main, for soon the question would be: who could be persuaded to do it while they watched it?)

Money was the purpose. Miss Stein had misread the signs along with the lung fish experts themselves. She had looked at John Kenneth Galbraith and had seen Dr. Kinsey. Because of this prodigious reading preparation she felt continually raunchy in her new lung fish form, without understanding what she was supposed to do about it.

Looking at his six-foot, four-inch frame, dropping her eyes to his trousers while he involuntarily adjusted his clothing, she achieved a phenomenon even for fallen angels. She lusted for him.

"Oh, *honey!*" she mumbled, pulling him into the entrance hall and slamming the door behind him. She began to devour his mouth while, instinctively, she burrowed like a mole within the front of his trousers with her unzipping hand, scooping out the contents like the prize in a box of Crackerjacks, working with all her lost soul until Gene did what any American boy would have done. He laid her like a carpet on the carpet just inside the front door, and a very thorough job he did.

As a field agent who herself would require surveillance, Miss Stein had no idea whatsoever that she was being covered by J($\Uparrow$)CES cameras and that her every action was being flashed in glorious color on the giant NixonVision screen at Liederkranz Hall.

Watching, the J($\Uparrow$)CES convention was crumpled with shock, some seeming utterly puzzled, most totally unbelieving.

"This is out*rage*ous!" sputtered Azza$\downarrow$, a.k.a. Shem-yaza, a fairly typical reaction from him since he had once been suspended between heaven and earth for 11,600 years (according to rabbinic tradition) as punishment for having carnal knowledge of a mortal woman. It was also Azza who had wised up Solomon, making him the smartest politician on earth at that time.

"What are they doing when they bump each other on the floor like that?" N'Zuriel Yhwh yelled above the hubble-bubble. "Will somebody please tell me what they are doing?"

"They are making sex," Pharzuph$\downarrow$, angel of lust, genius of fornication, said blandly.

"Is there money in that?"

'It depends.'

"This is a different subject entirely," Azza cried out. "And I'll tell you something else. She wasn't sent there to study that subject, so how come she learned to do it so good, I'd like to know."

The entire assembly turned appalled eyes upon Haurus, Chief of Mission. Haurus said instantly that he would have to consult the actual data sheets before he could express an opinion. He said that Miss Saxe-Coburg was directly in charge of individual tactics in the field. It was immediately demanded that Miss Saxe-Coburg be sent for. She appeared instantly. By the time she appeared, Phyllis Stein, up on the giant NixonVision screen, was doing something entirely different. She was seated on the end of a sofa, weeping her way bitterly through post-coital triste, about some event they all seemed to have missed. The male lung fish wasn't even in sight.

Miss Saxe-Coburg said she was sorry to see Miss Stein weeping but that she didn't see anything so terrible about it.

"Never mind the crying," Raziel said. "She was also making sex with a lung fish a minute ago. Gack!"

"That you have to expect," Miss Saxe-Coburg said coolly. "Sometimes you have to use flies to catch a honey. However, if this is a court-martial I must have time to prepare a defense."

"The court-martial comes later," Raziel said. "Right now we want to know how this disgraceful business happened."

"Raziel. First of all, I am surprised at you, a sophisticated angel," Miss Saxe-Coburg said, calmly poised. "Second, I am disturbed and shocked by you. This convention approved of stealing, lying, even murder for this field study, so why not anything else a lung fish happens to want to do? She was sent out there as a woman, wasn't she? So she has rights. That is a brave, brave angel we are looking at up there on that screen. Could any of you do what she had the courage to do? Could you make sex with a *lung* fish? Go ahead and judge her—but before you judge her, you'd better remember she was a woman when she did it and, as a woman, she has as much right to make sex as any man, maybe more."

"How can it be more or less?" N'Zuriel Yhwh asked in a baffled voice. "It takes two to tango."

Azza stood on his chair and yelled. "I *demand* that we vote to bring this angel back now. She must be tried. This is dis*gus*ting!"

o

Gene walked dazedly away from Fortress Midtown. He could not believe that it was possible for anyone to forge his signature with such compelling accuracy. He also could not believe that Miss Stein could have found it possible to weep so inexhaustibly. He had explained after three acrobatic copulations that he had to leave so he could watch his wife in the bowling finals at Fortress East. Didn't they bowl at Fortress Midtown? Miss Stein had insisted that he stay there with her. He even remembered, as wild as it seemed in retrospect, that she had said he must never leave her. What kind of talk was that? He had *told* her he was married after the second bang.

He stopped at a phone booth on his way home to tell Doris that she could put the spaghetti on and the margarine to melting.

"Doris?"

Doris was feeling guilt about what had almost happened at lunch with Judge Zeuss. She really didn't want to talk to Gene.

"Mother's here," she warned.

"You won't believe it and neither did I, but that momser this morning actually did have a forged receipt."

"Mother! Don't eat that! It's wax!"

"I went to his office where he had this secretary and got the receipt back."

"How?"

"Well—that's how it worked out."

"Did she ask you for the aluminum case?"

"No. As a matter of fact."

"Then where is the money?"

"I invested it in dinner plates."

"For Christ's *sake*, Gene!"

"Now we'll be able to pay off the interest on the mortgage."

"Pay off the mortgage? Oh, Gene!"

"I didn't say that. I said, pay off the interest on the mortgage."

"Will we also be able to pay the doctor back?"

"Are you crazy?"

"Hold on, dear." Doris spoke across the telephone into the room. "Yes, Mother. Gene has a wonderful new client. Yes, yes—we'll be able to pay back the doctor. Isn't that marvelous? Isn't Gene brilliant?"

"Have you lost your mind, Doris?" Gene said heatedly into the telephone. "What about the *entire* goddam mortgage? What about the three personal loan companies who are baying for twenty-eight hundred and ninety dollars? And the banks? And the two credit card companies who are trying to have me arrested for a lousy two thousand six hundred and ten dollars? If we were crazy enough to pay back your stepfather, a rich dermatologist, as if there were any other kind, I'd have to re-borrow thirty-eight hundred dollars at the point of a gun. I can't even pay my secretary, Miss Kehoe, or the Anne Knauerhase Fortress supermarket. Baby, the office rent is coming up. How can I make a living if I don't have an office?"

"Now you've made Mother cry."

"How could she hear me all the way across the room?"

"Because she is interested enough in us to want to hold her head next to the phone, that's how. Never mind, Mother. Home for dinner, darling?"

"Where could I go? Mr. X closed his soup kitchen."

"Mother! My God! Don't eat that!" Doris hung up.

o

That night, Doris won the Fortress East Silver Bowling Shoe Award as the best woman bowler in her elevator bank. The Silver Shoe Award had a long four-year tradition. Each year the retiring champion donated her left bowling shoe to the Sports Committee who had it silvered. The champion preceding Doris had worn size 11 1/2 DDDD so, in a sense, Doris's cup ranneth over. It was the largest Silver Shoe ever awarded. It brought tears to Gene's eyes.

They went to Elaine Shubagger's shower in a security group with the Feinschmeckers because it wasn't exactly intelligent for two people to walk alone in the building corridors, then they tipped two building policemen to walk them home and ride the elevators with them to their own flat. Doris tipped them with nine hundred Plaid Stamps which she had saved for just such an emergency, asking them not to worry that this would cut into their Christmas gifts.

Gene closed the main door to the flat, bolted it, locked it in the three positions, then pulled down the

101

welder-proof door between themselves and the outer door and locked it into the floor. It was wonderful to be home safe and sound again after their first night out in four months. They were just too tuckered out for much sex. After only one coupling they went right to sleep.

Eleven

Carlotta had to do a lot of testing and tinkering in her workshop to get the results she wanted. She had thought it all through. Then she set it all down in careful designs, which she intended to give to Dad Quebaro to hold for her so she could patent them once she got Gene back. She established a parallel tri-series of reversals on the structure of radio galaxies: interferometry, pencil-beam antennas, and a method of lunar occultation all worked out in opposite forms so she could get her effects. She hammered, soldered, and jogged metal and electronics components to approximate a reversal in directional force of the synchrotron process, polarizing her emissions to make sure that the magnetic field was in no way tangled and experimenting with a range of sizes as a reliable astronomic radio source, from double sources contained within an optical galaxy to components having separations of a hundred kiloparsecs or more on either side of her galaxy finders. She made a series of models which became, each time out, more effectively integrated. She never left the house, frequently forgot to eat or sleep. She completed the final mode of her astrono-electronic prayer wheel whose power exceeded the range of both pulsar and quasar beams on a Box^{22} ratio.

Carlotta merely built upward from the quarks she was able to construct. Neutrons and protons are made up of these sub-atomic quark particles which have charges of 1 2/3 more than that of an electron. She designed her emission signal to pulse every 1.33730113 seconds, wishing she could achieve a tighter accuracy. The signals would reach their destinations at fluctuating periods, which would vary from destination to destination, between 1/30 of a second and 8 1/17 seconds, the actual strength of the pulses varying in a completely irregular way. The biggest single problem she had to work out was building her own, home-achieved, on-line, communicating computers to realize the limitation of the size of the emitting region to that which was no greater than the distance light travels in the time over which an object varies. Essentially, what Carlotta was determined to achieve was a mechanism that would closely resemble the properties of the nuclei of the Seyfert galaxies, or certainly the type of explosion which takes place in those galaxies.

The old-fashioned Lamaist prayer wheel had been a mechanical contrivance which, when spun in the hand, had the effect of multiplying the production of prayers written on twelve strips of paper, each with forty-one lines of formula repeated sixty times, sending 3,542,000 prayers heavenward with every turning, repeating, as the text of each prayer, "Om mani padmane hoomn," meaning "The Jewel of the Lotus, amen." By night, these wheels would be turned by the wind to repeat the invocation in written form tens of thousands of times an hour on many wheels.

However, Carlotta's electronic prayer wheels left nothing to chance. By her calculation it was entirely probable that deities had not bothered to learn to read. Each of Carlotta's finished models, duplicated from her perfected design, transmitted her prayer by electrono-astronomic means on an extraordinarily narrow band. Some, such as the device she designed for reaching Northern Irish deities, were much narrower than others.

Carlotta's invocation was simple and direct: it was three D7 bleeps followed by the spoken words SEND QUEBARO HOME AMEN followed by three G Major bleeps.

She arranged her advanced prayer wheels along the periphery of the deep conversation pit of the Quebaro house. Connections from each ran to a central switch so that all wheels could be turned OFF or ON simultaneously. The wheels were individually adjusted and aimed precisely at the central divine headquarters (as placed in the cosmology) of the Zoroastrians, Amish, Buddhists (an all-sects band), Catholics (Roman, Russian, Greek and Irish),

Jews, Moslems; Greek and Scandinavian mythological deities; Hindus (Shatism and Vishnuism exclusively, as it happened, because Carlotta had not heard of the Shivaists who, after all, have not been aggressive with missionary work); the Taoists, Druid top management, the Manicheans, and the Mithra crowd, as well as Shinto executives and Sikh deities. She lumped the 436 Protestant faiths together in one high-frequency band because although their dogmas were oppositional cosmetically they were one solid mass of male sky gods, just as the four branches of the Catholics represented one Earth Mother.

Carlotta felt no awe about intending these intrusions. They—one of them anyway—had interfered with her existence by removing Gene. She wanted Gene back. She had always been maniacal about her policy of dealing only with the top and that most certainly went in the case of godheads. The astrono-electronic prayer wheels were the only way she could determine to reach the absolutely first-string theoarchs. With deliberate care she covered the Mayans; Aztecs; Sunis; Priscillians (*that* Gnostic gang, she thought); the Melchites, those trendies of the anti-Menophysite doctrine; and the Chiliast theolatries. Each prayer wheel was oiled with chrism and was able to repeat SEND QUEBARO HOME AMEN in each of the 149 languages, out of the 3782 extant, spoken by more than 1,000,000 people. These multi-coded messages had been recorded on tapes phonetically, by Carlotta herself, after having been translated by polyglots at Oxford University, where Carlotta's first cousin, Ferdy Fairfax, was an executive bill collector for the Merchant Tailors of Greater London. The prayer wheels operated on 110 volts AC with competent anti-feedback devices. They were transmitters only. Carlotta reasoned that if the deities who were responsible for kidnapping Gene could not figure out a way to send back replies in order to open negotiations with her, then they could not have had the power to snatch Gene in the first place.

She decided to build the prayer wheels with an altazimuth mounting so that they could move on a vertical and horizontal axis in order to compensate for the rotation of the earth, but it just wasn't satisfactory. Things like latitude and longitude came into it. Geography wasn't her field. So she built later models with an equatorial mounting so the motion of only one axis was required. It was *so* much less complicated that way. But it didn't work. So, for the final model, she went back to the altazimuth by building in a computer servo-mechanism which directed the prayer wheels in a complex double motion. After that it was only a matter of projecting her particular radio waves, getting tight force-focuses on particular regions of the firmament, different for each prayer wheel, then just broadcasting her simple point-to-point prayer against a standard Hertzspring-Russell Diagram. She estimated that her call was reaching out about 9000 million light years.

She knew she would get through. She tried to figure out why they had taken Gene away from her and she became convinced that a plan was underway for a gigantic conglomerate in which all the religions had decided to combine in one giant, economy-size. Of course they must have seen that they would need Gene to sell it. Theirs was good thinking as far as it went, she conceded. But what they obviously did not know was that they would only be getting half of Gene's value without her. Gene needed her to merchandise his efforts, and to do the book-keeping and the chartmaking. Gene was a closer, but he was a lousy setter-upper. She was a setter-upper and if the religious crowd didn't get the message, they were going to piddle along with a very low-volume yield.

Therefore, she had to get through. She didn't eat much. She slept fitfully in the conversation pit because in the event of equipment breakdown that was equidistant from all the prayer wheels. She did not try to fathom how she had stumbled on the designs. It was as though no one had ever really had the interest or the need to reach a major or minor deity before and had just stopped abruptly with the time-waste of prayer. The egotistical anguish of forty-two millennia had pretended to be desperate about reaching gods with petitions for this or that but they had all failed for the reason that they could not have cared enough. It wasn't that Carlotta's own need had happened to parallel her existence in such a universally massive technology or that her hobby happened to be home electronics. If Carlotta had lived in the fourth century and had found herself in the same agonizingly unacceptable predicament, she would have rigged something different (teleportive herbs?) but just as effective because Carlotta loved Eugene Quebaro to the square root of the furthest reaches of feeling by the human spirit, or what had been endured emotionally in the libretti of operas; in the plays of Shakespeare.

Consistent with the measure of her love for Gene, Carlotta also believed in the appreciating value of their joint estate. By cutting corners she was able to bring in the entire battery of 149 electronic prayer wheels for just under $216.

Carlotta knew she was getting through—in spite of moments of delirium here and there—because whenever she turned on commercial radio for use as a possible response system, she would hear, almost at once, contrasting awesome voices doing readings from Sarah Flower Adams, St. Thomas Aquinas, Horace Bushnell, W.P. Lemon, and Charles Mackintosh with such encouraging quotations as Blaise Pascal's: "What reason have atheists for saying we cannot rise again? What is more difficult, to be born, or to rise again? That what has never been, should be, or that which has been, should be again? Is it more difficult to come into being—or to return to it?" Notwithstanding such powerful logic there was—as yet—no direct response.

She continued her vigil. She refused to see Dad Quebaro on his daily, then twice-daily visits. She began to cough a great deal at about the fourth month because she often forgot to dress beyond a filmy nightgown and she never checked to see whether the furnace was still operating. She overlooked eating more often than not. She lost a great deal of weight, which so upset the delivery boy who brought the food Dad Quebaro kept sending that he reported her condition to her father-in-law, who agonized over interfering where she had made clear he was not welcome but who then broke a window and climbed into the house.

He wept when he saw her. He sat in his overcoat, an old man with his face in his hands, and sobbed over what she had become. She seemed transparent. He thought of an X-ray projected on a white sheet. They sat in the kitchen. She was feverish and, he thought, more than slightly delirious. She kept asking what the hell was the matter with *him.* Instead of talking to her he went to the cellar and got the furnace going. Then he made them a pot of tea.

"Carlotta, I think you have to be committed."

"That's okay. You're allowed to think that."

"Jesus, you look terrible."

Carlotta shrugged. "There's nobody to look at me."

"Listen—for old time's sake—will you smile for me?"

She smiled.

"Jesus, Carlotta, you have a beautiful smile. There are two things I'll always remember about you. From the first night I saw you at that carnival. Your earnestness. And your beautiful smile." He wept again. Then he poured more tea. "Don't think I don't understand. I think it's right to grieve. There isn't grief enough in the world for what we've lost. Grief is the ultimate way of respecting the loss of important things. But follow me on this. We weren't given just the one emotion, were we? And the others get rusty if we don't use them. We have to get to the end of the grief and start up with—say—an appetite for steak and potatoes. Then there comes an end to that and we need to sleep or hate or just smile—or any of the things you don't do anymore."

"Dad, I—well, I can't explain it. I am not grieving. I am negotiating. This is a very, very big deal and I have to concentrate more than I ever concentrated before."

"What's the deal?"

"I'm getting Gene back."

He stared at her blankly. Tears poured down his face. He turned away from her in the chair.

"Dad? If it will make you happier, I'll get dressed and make us a good dinner, just like the old days. We can talk about anything you want to talk about. You can fill me in on politics—or football. Then, after a while, you have to understand that I'll have to get back to my work. Okay?"

"Okay. But you may be dying from whatever you're doing."

"Dad, they took Gene for reasons of their own. I understand that and you don't. But I don't want you being sad. You have my guarantee that I will not die. Not until they work out a way that I can take the money Gene and I made together, the whole thing, down to the last cent, with me."

"It definitely says TILT across your forehead, sweetheart," Dad Quebaro told her.

o

Carlotta *was* getting through to cosmic management in almost every instance. The prayer merely confused or bored deities such as Buddha, the Great Druid, St. Clare, the Patron Saint of Television, and Salmon P. Chase, God of the Republicans. Neither Ra nor Mohamet would take the call, so bugged were they about what Golda Meir had said in the Knesset the day before. BUT both Zophiel↓ (openly identified as "God's spy") and Hermes (messenger of the gods) monitored Carlotta's prayer at their respective message centers and, since it was the first human prayer that had ever gotten through, they tended to take it seriously, if only for the novelty value.

Zophiel had handled all counter-intelligence for Satan™ during "the troubles." In fact, it was because of his really rotten information before Satan™'s second attack that God® was able to push The Adversary™ and his legions over into the abyss. Zophiel has been identified by more than one expert as "the herald of Hell." In one book, Zophiel is a fallen, but not evil, angel. In anybody's book he was a thoroughly incompetent spy but obsessed with counter-intelligence information of any kind. Zophiel was the *only one* in the Upper or Lower Departments of the Firmament to maintain a "listening post." Not that very much came in. Throughout the aeons the only extra-angelic bleep he had picked up was Eddie Fisher singing "My Mother's Eyes" and the noises from some sort of gala which was being held on the far side of one of those "black holes" in the universe which did so much for Sunday supplements. The only part of the "message" (if it was a message) that had come through clearly in that case was a woman's voice saying "Move over," expressed in liquid mathematical symbols.

In the case of Carlotta's prayer, Zophiel was making his usual bachelor breakfast, earphones clamped over his head, when, to his e*nor*mous pleasure, he heard the three D7 bleeps followed by SEND QUEBARO HOME AMEN in Amharic, Hebrew, Sumerian, Assyrian, and Chaldean, followed by the G Major bleeps. Then he had the utterly clued-in pleasure of hearing it wrapped up in modern English, with a pronounced Surrey accent.

Zophiel was simply ecstatic. He spent the entire morning on the trace-back. By a quarter to twelve he had the name and address: Mrs. Carlotta Quebaro, 2535 Long Ridge Road, Stamford, Connecticut 06903, plus a voice print.

He sensed it was a big breakthrough. He had debriefed his share of western clergymen in the anteroom compound. He had a notion of their jargon. He vaguely remembered some of them referring to the use of something called "prayer" so he went to the dictionary which Raziel had ordered be compiled and looked the word up. The definition for "prayer" was: *A solemn and humble request to God* (aha!), *a supplication, petition, or thanksgiving, usually expressed in words.*

Zophiel classified SEND QUEBARO HOME AMEN as a sort of cablese petition. It was certainly no supplication or thanksgiving. He dressed carefully, as always, and went to find Raziel.

o

Hermes a.k.a. Mercury a.k.a. Casmillus a.k.a. Cyllenius a.k.a. Argeiophontes a.k.a. Anubis a.k.a. Thoth— son of Zeus and Maia; inventor of the lyre; roast-beef enthusiast; patron of thieves and travelers; deity of gain (honest or dishonest); deity of sleep and dreams; messenger of the Gods and conductor of mortal souls to the realm of

Hades—sat on the toilet seat of his father's bathroom while Zeus was shaving and explained the message he had picked up that morning which was, even then, pouring endlessly into the monitors at Hermes's message center.

"The message was in Greek?" Zeus asked. "It said SEND QUEBARO HOME AMEN? That's all?"

"In Greek and English. Pretty mangled Greek. But ancient Greek."

"Hm."

"What does it mean, Pop?"

"What kind of English?"

"A woman. Kind of a Surrey, England, accent. Maybe near Wonersh."

"Hm."

"What does it mean, Pop?"

"What is her name and address?"

"Carlotta Quebaro. She lives in Stamford, Connecticut, a slave dormitory. If people think they can just start up with asking favors from you, Pop, you've got some pretty busy days ahead."

"She must be a remarkable woman to think up a thing like that."

"Like what, Pop?"

"The man she wants back is Quebaro, the dummy that religious sect put out in the field for tests on money."

"How can she get him back? He's married to the Neriades kid."

"Only for their field test. This one in Stamford is the real wife. Aiee! I can certainly thank my lucky stars that my wife isn't that smart."

"What should I do, Pop?"

"Herm, you're a sophisticated fellow. You have always been like my ronaldreagan, the buddy the good guy could always talk to. I am not ashamed to say that I have very big eyes for the Neriades kid."

"Well—ugly she isn't."

"Also, I have reason to believe, she has very big eyes for me."

"It figures."

111

"So, if Quebaro's *real* wife comes on the scene with the kind of an eye for a target she seems to have —a woman able to figure out a way to actually pester the *gods* with her problems—then Quebaro is suddenly going to have his hands very full, if you see what I mean."

"And you'll make a run around her end to score. Right?"

"Right. But, and this is a big but, it shouldn't look as if it came from me. Everything will march much better if the other side thinks it's their idea."

"How?"

"Easy. Their field test just isn't working out. Quebaro doesn't know the first thing about money or how to get it. With him all alone out there—after all, the Neriades kid is a fixed race, a clairvoyant bookmaker, what can they learn from that?—they are never going to find out. Build them a Gross Earnings File on Quebaro from The Other Place. It figures that, with a wife like this, the man must have been knocking down six figures because she had to be doing his thinking for him."

"How come?"

"Male lung fish can't think, Herm. They're a bunch of dreamers. The women think and convince the men that the men are thinking; in exchange the men go to work while the women shop for appliances. It was always that way. The men in the caves used to throw spears, miss, then get home late without any food for the family—all cold and wet. The women had planted some rutabagas behind the cave and that was how they survived."

"When do you want me to go in with this?"

"Watch them at Liederkranz Hall. At the first sign that they have finally realized that Quebaro isn't working out, start spreading the word about Mrs. Quebaro. They'll do the rest."

Twelve

Somewhere a bell was ringing. Gene tightened his grip on Doris's crotch. They rolled toward each other in sleep, banging their heads together. They awoke, stared without focus, registered that the ringing sound was coming from the front door and turned, as one, to look at the digital clock on Doris's side of the bed.

Doris sprang up, jammed her pink feet into mules, put on a robe, and swaddled to the front door. It was daytime. She worked as fast as she could with the padlock on the roller door, then on the three main door locks, exclaiming loudly, "One moment. Just a sec. Be right with you." The metal roller door made its crashing noise going up. Then Gene could hear the snap of the bolt and the clunks of the three locks. Doris's voice said, "Who is it?" There was a muffled colloquy, then Doris sang out, "Dear! It's men with crates of dinner plates they say are for you."

"Oh, yes. Let them in, please, dear." He rolled out of bed, grabbed at clothing, and ran into the bathroom.

Two thousand four hundred and seventy commemorative dinner plates were encased in heavy wood carriers, one hundred plates to a box, on average: twenty-five crates. These were trundled into the small apartment on trolleys. They were set down to line the entrance hall from floor to ceiling, then were stacked up along two of the walls of the living room. Doris watched with dismay, not uttering more than a muffled "My God!" or a bleated, "But, Jesus, fellas——" When the crates had been safely stored, she pretended she was only a woman and did not know about things such as needing to tip delivery men. Gene cowered in the

113

bathroom wearing one sock. Doris got the men out some-how. Gene emerged.

"Gene, you've never seen so many crates."

The news made him grin broadly. It was the first time he had smiled in the morning in almost two years and her heart went out to him. "Honey," he said expansively, "you have one million dollars right in your apartment."

"How could you do such a thing?"

"Baby! These plates are appreciating at the rate of one-half of one per cent a day. Five thousand dollars a day. How does that grab you?"

Doris thought of Judge Zeuss. "But suppose the dinner-plate market goes down for some reason?" she asked piteously.

"Never. Impossible. Plates are the surrogate currency of this country."

"But just suppose. Suppose that happened?"

"I cannot suppose because it just cannot happen."

"Sup*pose,* I said."

"Doris, please! Why are women so negative? Why—these plates have already paid the interest due on the mortgage."

"But we can hardly move around here! What's the use of living here? We'll have to entertain in the john."

"Doris, fahcrissake. Mahan could be arrested for what he's doing and get life. Do you have any *idea* of how much that would bring us at twenty-five thousand a week?"

"If the plate market stays up. *If.* If you sell the plates at the top. *If.* It isn't as though plates pay dividends, like stock. You have to sell the plates to make a profit and if we drop just *one* of those plates, Gene, we've had it."

"You are kidding around with the American economy."

"And if the plate market goes down just five per cent, you'll owe that man fifty thousand dollars."

The doorbell rang. Gene ran into the bathroom like a mountain child. Distraught, Doris flung the door open as if the city, and probably the building, were not filled with cocaine-packed rapists. She faced a burly man in overalls. He said, "I got ninety crates of plates for Eugene Quebaro."

"Ninety crates!" Doris shrilled.

Gene came streaking out of the bathroom, but fully dressed. He eased Doris into it. "You get dressed, darling," he said. "I'll handle this." Doris backed away, her knuckles at her mouth like a heroine in a horror movie. She locked the bathroom door.

It took well over forty minutes to install the second delivery of crates in what remained of free space in the apartment. It was necessary to put all of the furniture except the double bed and one chair out into the public corridor so that the valuable plates could be stored inside. This caused one of those freak accidents on which the odds against happening could have been a thousand to one, as Gene explained to Doris much later. The family across the hall, that of a rich oil company bookkeeper who was being transferred to the Middle East, were being packed and moved. The team of moving men who were on *that* job mistook the Quebaro furniture, which was temporarily in the corridor, as part of the oil fellow's shipment and moved it out. This caused a lot of honest confusion four months later when the shipment was unpacked at Khabrat ar Radifah.

"That's a helluva big load for your floors," the foreman said to Gene.

"It's okay. It's evenly distributed." Gene said.

"Yeah, but I'd hate to be the people downstairs."

In the end, Gene had to say flatly that he did not believe in tipping, that tipping was degrading to the tipper and tippee. The delivery men did not agree but, at last, they left, doing no more than kicking the crates and making a lot of unnecessarily obscene references to Gene. When Doris came out of the bathroom fully dressed, she would have cried at what she saw were it not for her fresh make-up. The crates seemed to be packed into almost every available square foot of the apartment, from floor to ceiling, blocking out all light, smelling of excelsior, and allowing only one very narrow aisle in which the Quebaros could stand sideways, except for a tiny area around the bed and the bathroom door. Doris began to whimper.

"Never mind, sweetheart," Gene said. "What do we care? One-half of one per cent a day. So what's a little inconvenience?"

Doris jigged in a tantrum. There was a light creaking sound from the floors. "You are such an *idiot!*" she shrilled. "What are we going to *do?* This is supposed to be where we *live.* And—oh, *Jee*-zuzz—I invited mother and the doctor for dinner tonight."

"How come? The doctor hates spaghetti."

"I spent my twenty-dollar bonus," she wailed. "I bought a steak." She beat rapidly on his chest with both fists. "And I can't reach them to stop them. Mother is going to be getting the sun on the Staten Island ferry all day and the doctor is at the county skin games." She looked around at the bulging, threatening crates, then she ran out of the apartment, telling herself what a failure Gene had been. He was marvelous with sex and always helped with the washing up, but he was a failure. She tried to imagine a humiliation such as these crates happening to Judge Zeuss. If he could afford to buy a million dollars' worth of dinner plates he would be a grafter, of course, but the crates of plates would be stored in a warehouse and she would have had the home she had worked so hard for.

Gene made his way with difficulty through the piled crates back to the bathroom. As he shaved, he was able to tell himself that things were looking really good. Uncle Raimundo's eight or nine hundred thousand dollars was going to look like a lapel's worth of dandruff. He would be able to lease the penthouse at Fortress Midtown. His turn at the top had come. Then he heard Doris's voice inside his head: *"Suppose the market slumps, Gene?"* But he had no choice. He knew that. He had to stay in the plate market until plate prices had risen enough for him to pay off the mortgage.

o

The court-martial was held in a private room at Liederkranz Hall. Phyllis Stein admitted her guilt but pleaded for clemency, "for reasons of temporary insanity induced by an alien culture." She was still in deep culture shock. Even the lung fish themselves had a word for it, Victoria Saxe-Coburg, hot with indignation, told the court.

"I de*mand* justice for this exploited tool of the bosses," she cried out. "She was sent out to do Hell's bidding. She carried with her a fountain of willingness to win for them. Exiled among the lung fish, was she at any time expected to accomplish her tasks by using the methods of angels or does it seem more likely that she would win Hell's goals by using upon the lung fish the devious and carnal ways of the lung fish? She is your instrument! This is not a rutting, lascivious Azza whom you try. You commanded her to find ways to persuade the lung fish to give up their deepest secrets. Yet you would bring her down for serving you too blindly and too well. Shame to you, I say. Shame! Shame!"

The President of the Court, Raziel, spoke. "Nonetheless," he said, "she seemed to be having a very good time while she endured the pain and sorrow of making sex. Also, there was nothing in her orders that said she had to do it with him the very second she laid eyes on him. Show me the orders which told her to do that and I'll dissolve the court."

"*Murder* was in her general orders," the counsel crowed. "Barratry and arson were in her general orders."

"She is an agent of Satan™, not a psychiatric social worker," Raziel insisted. "The point here is: she seems to have decided to have fun on a very serious job. Is that angelic? Money is a serious business or we wouldn't be wasting all this time. Let her be serious."

"She repents, Raziel," Miss Saxe-Coburg said. "IF she happened to do the wrong thing—which she most certainly did not—then she repents."

Miss Stein sat in the dock downcast, wearing black, high-fashion wings, her pointed tail extending out demurely under her elegant red robe. That she appeared to be genuinely contrite could have been because, immediately before the trial, Haurus had broken a sturdy youths' Flexible

Flyer sled over her head, knocking her through a steel-meshed window, crashing her down into a courtyard six storeys below.

The court ruled that Miss Phyllis Stein would have to remain out-of-play for the rest of the present sequence. Until allowed to return, she was to be suspended between heaven and earth.

"She could get hit by one of those seventy-two hundred satellites they have flying around up there so they can see the same prizefight all over the world," Miss Saxe-Coburg said bitterly, pointing accusingly at Raziel. "I know your type. Let the women do all the work and you'll take the credit and sit around drinking beer and farting. *You*, Raziel, formerly an ineffable angel of angels, have become the lung fish, not my helpless, persecuted client."

○

Athena reached her father by Aircall at the Cross-Rhodes Barbershop and Hellenic Philately Center, Eighth Avenue and 21st Street, where he was having his moustache marcelled and his fingernails given a high, flesh-pink polish.

"Poppa?" Athena said into the phone.

"Yes, darling girl."

"They have had to discipline Phyllis Stein."

"Why?"

"Instead of carrying out her assignment, she made sex with Gene Quebaro."

"So?"

"They are against that between angels and people. It's a hanging offense."

"Hanging?"

"They hang them between heaven and earth."

"That's a real suspended sentence."

"But this time, because Stein got herself a good lawyer who hit them with women's lib, the only punishment is that they are benching her."

"Listen, Athena—did Quebaro make good sex with Stein?"

"Stein thinks it was fantastic."

"Is Quebaro that good?"

"What does Stein know? It's her first. Still—from what I could see—which was plenty—Quebaro is very, very good."

"How good is that?"

"His wife must be a happy woman."

Zeus snorted. "By their standards."

"Poppa, the point is—what do we do now?"

"We send in Aphrodite."

"But can she follow instructions?"

"She can follow these instructions. Find her and send her right over here."

"If I send her all alone she'll never get there. She'll grab some guy."

"Send Apollo with her. You keep watching the NixonVision. Tell them to take a cab. I'll be waiting out front." Zeus went back to the barber's chair.

When the cab rolled up, Zeus waved at Apollo to stay in it as he helped his younger daughter out. Aphrodite was a radiantly beautiful girl with the charoptic expression of a new, young whore the morning after her first Saturday night in a car trailer flat joint parked outside an army camp.

"Hello, Poppa," she said happily.

She took her father's arm and they walked slowly along Eighth Avenue, turning at the corner into 21st Street toward Ninth. Zeus spoke slowly and carefully so he could be sure she understood him.

"Would you like to help Poppa with his work, baby?"

"Oh, yes, Poppa."

He was thinking so hard about the effects of his plan to import the original Mrs. Quebaro that he had to talk slowly himself so that he could be sure to intermesh all the strands of the plan.

"Good. That is very nice, baby."

"I mean—it depends," Aphrodite said hesitantly. "Like if it's not too hard or—you know . . ."

"I know. But it's all right. There is this very

119

handsome, sexy young fellow and I would like you to spend all the time you can with him."

"That's all?"

"It's not so easy. They are going to try to put cameras on you. And even if you might like that, I don't want it. As soon as I give him to you, you'll have to move fast and get him away while I draw the cameras off you."

"But I love that kind of problem."

"It would help Poppa if you could keep him busy for a couple of days. Like a couple of days and nights or so."

"Poppa, I'd *love* to help you."

Zeus was very pleased.

o

When the decision of the court-martial was flashed, Haurus called Palmer Mahan to a booth at the back of McCrory's on Third Avenue. They drank Southern Comfort with a Guinness chaser perhaps because they were just a little bit homesick and wanted to feel like Hell.

"Your little friend certainly goofed off," Haurus said. He had resumed his favorite form as a leopard and the sort of expression he put into those words could be said to be chilling—coming from a talking leopard.

"She isn't my little friend," Mahan said. "You picked her. Remember?"

"Don't dwell on it."

"Well, I mean—"

"Enough!" Haurus snarled.

"So we pull the plug."

"How?"

"Whatever goes up comes down. We let him have a few hours of fool's paradise, then we dump about sixty thousand great-greater-greatest dinner plates into that Plate Exchange at low-lower-lowest prices and we drive that market straight into a slump. Then I get back from Peru, show him a copy of the receipt, and demand my money."

"Stein gave *him* the receipt. Instead of a dozen neckties. He tore it up."

"So what? You'll make another receipt. Our

job breaks into two halves. We've got to throw their country into a panic by ruining the plate market so we can see how they all react in the crunch."

"That's the high-level," the leopard agreed, "but on the working level, we'll have Quebaro where we want him. He'll owe more money than he'll ever see in his life. He'll never be able to pay it off unless he does whatever we say or right into jail with him for the rest of his life. We'll see real field research then: on the mass and the individual level."

"It could work," Mahan said, as if it wasn't his own idea.

"It *has* to work," his boss said, as if it were his. "Go and do it."

"I'll need a lot of very good plates, Haurus. I mean Hudson River Valley primitives on bone china. Also Warhols. Also about five hundred in a limited edition showing the covers of the Sears, Roebuck catalogue of 1889."

"Why 1889?" Haurus asked.

"They had a big special on buggy whips, what else? And ask your boys to please shuck out about seventeen hundred and fifty plates with the Hurd portrait of Lyndon Johnson and about twenty thousand of Winston Churchill's Japanese Mother's Day cards. Always—all the James Richard Blakes with the little Irish family you can get, please. I can begin to dump at cut-rate tomorrow morning and the bottom will fall out of the market."

"You'll have to do a little better than that."

"How do you mean?"

"You'll have to buy up Quebaro's mortgage, take over his notes at the banks and loan companies and buy up his debts to the credit card companies. Then—pay off the stepfather-in-law so we can own that sandwich debt; then we'll be in an all-around squeeze position to see just how far he'll be willing to go to get money."

"You mean—?"

"I mean murder, child molesting, skyjacking, White House politics, orphanage arson, oil company lawyer —we'll find him some lulus."

"Okay. And how about this? We tell Violente

that Quebaro's wife was the real cause of his two falls—so far, two—and he'll fire the wife, maybe even have her hit. With that money stopped they will really be stretched out on the stones. They'll *really* have to do anything for money."

"Palmer?"

"Yes, boss?"

"You know why you'll never get anywhere?"

Mahan went pale.

"You always have to have the last word. You always have to top everybody. That's why you'll never get anywhere."

o

Af, Chief of Mission, was so somberly preoccupied as he faced Kehoe and Case in the Lexington Avenue ice cream parlor that he had fallen into the tick of making alternate snouts and compressed lip grins over and over again while he thought through his campaign.

"How is yours?" Justin asked Alice quietly about her banana split, unwilling to disturb his chief.

"I think the strawberry flavor may be artificial," Alice answered in a whisper, "and this whipped cream may come right out of an aerosol can."

Af's piggy eyes became intent upon them in a Churchillian look of gloom/doom. "We are fortunate," he said, "that our superiors have, for the past nine aeons, maintained efficient industrial espionage among the fallen opposition. Due to this foresight, it has been passed down to me from the leaders of the Michael Brigade that our programs are in jeopardy from The Adversary™'s team. Our plumbers have been monitoring a bug in a certain Third Avenue saloon and I can tell you that these lung fish of ours are being set up for a demmed bad fall. I speak of eternal damnation, among other things, which would be just cause for our grief even if we did not know, were not responsible for, the souls in question. It goes without comment that, if this happened, it would be sheerest tragedy for souls which have been placed directly in our charge. Do you follow." Af had even achieved the Churchillian ring of extremely faulty bridgework.

"Yes, sir," the two angels chimed.

"Then let me put it still more clearly. If Haurus and his thugs succeed in this, I will be fired off the Michael Brigade and put to janitorial work somewhere, if you catch the distinction. I am not one to threaten. But—if that can happen to me, by George, you can undertake to threaten yourselves with what will happen to you."

Kehoe stopped eating. Case pushed his banana split away from himself.

"Let us respond, then, to the intolerable pressure," Af said piously. "Let us show—*as we have been ordered to show* that goodness is not just a smiling metaphor but a positive force for positive action, as Dr. Peale has taught The Great Architect®. Hm? How, you ask? We are forbidden to supply our lung fish with money directly, which must mean that, in a far shrewder gaze than my own, money is considered evil in itself—a conclusion to which we, personally, must not subscribe until we have proof positive. No one—and I will repeat that—*no* one knows what money is or can cause, given its own will."

"I would say," Alice murmured, mushing her whipped cream into her artificially flavored strawberry sauce, "that if we give them money we could at least be in a position to see what they do with it. The way they have been programmed, one feels we will never know even that."

"And we never will find out with this man Quebaro!" Justin said passionately. "Money seems to shun him."

"Do not natter," Af said. "Stare at now. The problem is now."

"I think we should send him clients," Alice said. "That could not possibly be interpreted as giving him money. He would have to earn his fees or he wouldn't be paid."

"Hm." Af said. "Gurm. Um. Yes. That is, I see. I shall refer that to Higher Authority."

"Just you keep referring and waiting for an answer," Alice said, tears forming in her perfect eyes, "while the hounds of Hell run off with another soul to damnation."

"I shall do my best, Alice," Af said. He bit off

123

the end of an enormous cigar, then lighted it with such care one would have thought he enjoyed cigars, which he did not; he smoked them because someone had said they made him look even more like Churchill whom he had of course met, personally, in the anteroom outside the happiest place. To even things out, he blew cigar smoke directly into their faces across their ruined banana splits. "Now hear this," he said. "Hell and Haurus propose to dump rare plates into the market at cheap prices. They will drive the market down to penury, then foreclose on our friend Quebaro. They also propose to buy up all his debts and have his wife discharged from her job so that the two of them have no income or resources—or dwelling for that matter. Then they are going to apply the crunch."

"Oh, Af!" Alice wailed. "What are we going to do?"

"We are going to postpone Plan A and move into Emergency Procedure. I will not refer and wait. I shall take the responsibility."

"How brave!" Alice sang.

"Last night I took the initiative by appearing in a dream of the Pope's while he slept at Castel Gandolfo. I appeared in my basic, unimproved form which, as you know, is five hundred parasangs high—all chains of fire. Really terrified the blighter. In his dream, I commanded him to release dinner plate rights to the Michelangelo ceiling in the Sistine Chapel and I think I may have persuaded him to throw in some other extremely valuable designs as well. I'll appear to Chairman Brezhnev tonight and sew up the best of the Hermitage in Leningrad. If necessary, I am going to request that The Almighty® recycle every layabout painter now using our facilities from Fra Filippo Lippi to the Span-iards. We are going to acquire plates which will sweep that plate exchange ahead of us, with paints baked in the original pigments."

"And that isn't all we should do," Alice said grimly.

"What else *can* we do?"

"We should let Mr. Quebaro save the market himself, personally, by representing his client, Mr. Justin

124

Case, who will own all these great plates."

"Capital!" Af cried. "Justin hires him or re-
tains him—whatever it is lawyers prefer to call it when they
sell themselves—and that will fill Quebaro with self-confi-
dence and cause him to go onward to do great things with
money."

"Justin will have to arrange to misplace all
those bank records and credit card files and mortgages concerning Mr. Quebaro's obligations," Alice said. "Not
forever, of course. Only until he turns his great victory in the
plate market."

"And Zeus must see that Mr. Violente is held
incommunicado in the Tombs, to protect Mrs. Quebaro."

"That leaves only the delicatessen debt to Dr.
Lesion," Af said. "The doctor is a highly respected dermatologist who would be inclined to regret it very much if
any ignoble information concerning him got into the hands
of some crusading dermatology trade paper editor, so it is
going to have to be Alice's job to fuck him, then Justin will
blackmail him, pretending to be her husband and—"

"*Fuck* him?" Alice said with horror. "*Me?*"
She was totally horrified. "It is simply impossible to think
that heavenly angels could or would solve anything with
blackmail and sex. *Grab him, Justin!*"

They pinned Af to the corner of the ice cream
parlor booth. But it was not Af. It was Haurus disguised to
appear as Af. He had gambled on having both of the Up[t]
Team members court-martialed and banished in disgrace so
that he and Mahan would have a clear field. But he had lost
and at the same time revealed the plans of Hell to bring
about Quebaro's downfall. Because he was of such high
rank, a great duke of Hell, he could not be brought to trial,
but he had been stopped. He confessed that Af lay bound
hand and foot in the storeroom of the ice cream parlor. His
total confession was made on the full NixonVision screen at
Liederkranz Hall.

"Hell certainly fielded a team of nudknickers
this time," Raziel said loudly in the convention hall.

At the ice cream parlor Alice looked mistily at
Justin and said, "He gave us some *wonderful* ideas. We could

never have thought of them all by ourselves. Let's get out there, darn it, and do something about it." They left the ice cream parlor and, in their excitement, hung up the store for the bill for the banana splits.

No one remembered about Af being tied up until three fifty-eight the following morning. The Upper Chair had to have a team of plumbers break into the shop and free him, later justifying the action to the convention on the grounds of "security."

Thirteen

Dr. Lesion had developed a knack for persuading elderly lady patients to leave him their worldly goods in their wills. He had inherited considerable cash in this way, also 68 percent of a hockey team playing out of Indian Head, Saskatchewan, two liquor stores in Harlem, and the flourishing delicatessen in midtown Manhattan. Dr. Lesion, like all healers, was extremely keen about money. He watched his own very carefully. His medical duties were light. When General Ina Amin Dada expelled the wealthy East Indians from Uganda, Dr. Lesion had applied to sponsor four of the most capable physicians in that exodus. He had trained them well under the cover of his own license to practice and while they worked off their seven-year contracts with seven-year options with him at thirty-five dollars a week, he made sure they were sustained as men of science, not bogged down by the sight of fees or the paper work that goes with them.

He spent at least four evenings a week with elderly lady patients, trying out his hypnosis theories, leaving his own wife at home in the bathtub with a box of cannabis fudge. It was these sweet old ladies who made him an extremely busy man. Considering his repugnance for both his stepdaughter's husband and spaghetti in margarine, it was a kind action for him to appear at the Quebaro flat that evening.

It was hysterically dismaying to Mrs. Lesion that there was only room to stand sideways between the rows of bulky crates stacked in the Quebaro apartment. But she was even more upset because she could not see how they were going to eat. The doctor was gripped by the unexpected scene. The fact that the crates had crowded out almost everything the Quebaros had ever owned gave the crates a monetary value, riveting the doctor's attention upon them. Gene arrived home as the doctor was making Doris almost frantic with his stream of questions.

"Gene!" she burst out as she saw him crowd into the inner alley of the crates. "Oh, my God, Gene, everything is gone. Where is the furniture? Where are our priceless aboriginal artifacts? We've lost everything but the bed and the chair, Gene. Do you understand what I am saying to you? How could you do this? How could you possibly do this?"

"The furniture?" Gene said blankly.

"What are all these crates, Gene, old man?" Dr. Lesion asked genially. "What is the big secret here?"

"How are we going to eat in this place?" Mrs. Lesion said stridently. "I didn't come all the way out here tonight to stand around a warehouse."

Gene quopped with rage when he realized it was the doctor standing there in front of him. "How *dare* you report me to the Credit League for a few rotten sandwiches?" he trembled.

"It was over three thousand four hundred dollars' worth of sandwiches," the doctor replied blandly. "I was forced to report it to show a legitimate loss on my tax return."

"Gene! What happened to my furniture?"

"I don't understand it, hon. The men who brought the crates didn't take it, I know that."

"What are we going to *do?*"

"Tell me, Gene," the doctor asked confidentially. "What is in these crates that could be important enough to crowd out your furniture?"

"Crappy dinner plates," Doris wailed. "That's what's in those crates."

"But what good are plates," Mrs. Lesion asked philosophically, "if you don't have a place to eat off them?"

"Or food to put on them," Doris sobbed. She saw Gene naked. A flop. A failure. A half-man who didn't give a damn about the nice things his wife had spent a marriage putting together to make a home. He was a man who let his wife live on borrowed sandwiches and yuk-making spaghetti while he waited out an inheritance like a spineless parasite. She knew one thing: Judge Zeuss wouldn't throw his home away for a stack of crappy plates.

"But where in heaven's name did you get the money to go into the plate market?" Dr. Lesion was saying. "Why—this amount of plates must represent a very large investment."

They were standing in a four-file in the long alley leading away from the front door. Gene was nearest the outside corridor next to Dr. Lesion. Then Mrs. Lesion lumped out the area. Doris was at the end of the line. The entrance door was open so they could have some light coming in from the public corridor. "It happens to be a million dollars' worth of plates!" Doris sobbed.

"Baby, baby." Gene cried out across the Lesions. "What's happened here? Why are you crying?"

"A million *dollars*?" Dr. Lesion repeated incredulously.

Gene wheeled on him. "Yaaaas! A million dollars which a valued client handed to me and asked me to invest as I saw fit—wherever I thought best."

"Why am I *crying*?" Doris wailed.

"You put all that money in plates, Gene?" the doctor asked.

"Where else can you earn one-half of one per cent a day cumulatively—three hundred days a year—one hundred and thirty per cent on your money every year?"

"One-half of one per cent a *day*?"

"I certainly don't see how we are going to eat here," Mrs. Lesion said, "but Doris is a good little manager. What time is dinner, dear?"

"I tried to explain the whole thing to you three months ago," Gene snarled at the doctor.

"I'm getting out of here," Doris screamed, psuhing past her mother and the two men. "This just isn't my little home anymore." Wrenching past them, she squeezed through to the public corridor and sprinted down the hall. Gene started after her but Dr. Lesion's heavy hand held him tightly.

"Gene! Wait!" he said urgently. "What do I buy? How do I do it? What kind of plates?" He clung to Gene's arm with an iron grip until he was fully briefed and had the address of Kullers & Company. It was well over seven minutes before Gene could break away into the labyrinthine corridors of Fortress East to try to find Doris.

As she ran, Doris worked hard to sustain the reckless hysteria of her mood because it fully expiated any guilt she might feel if Judge Zeuss happened to be waiting at her front door with his limousine and she happened to get into it and go off with him to do what had been on her mind to do since she had met him. Her imagination palpitated like a baby rabbit stuffed with live mice. Her eyelids shook with REM. She was concentrating on what must happen in the great beyond, in his actual bedroom, which was a fantasy out of reach of even her imagining since the restaurant in which he merely ate was a duplicate of the pleasure rooms of the Abbasid caliphate.

Just before her relatives had arrived that evening, Doris happened to have patted on a dipperful of the insidious Turkish perfume, *Opium,* which cost ninety-two dollars an ounce, but which Mr. Violente gave to key girls at the office at Christmas because he got it from a friendly fence and because, by giving it to everybody else, he was provided with excuse acceptable to his wife for giving it to her sister as well. It was a perfume that could turn Gene into an animal.

It also just happened that she was dressed in her best green, heavy-velvet dress which, if Gene accidentally happened to brush against it as it hung in the closet, gave him an instant erection. The dress had a very low neckline—so low, in fact, that when she wore it she imagined everyone could see the back of Gene's head. As she ran through the corridors of Fortress East she knew she hadn't prepared all these things merely to welcome her mother and the doctor to dinner.

She had only one thing in mind as she fled. She had to make it out of the building entrance on Third

Avenue before Gene could catch up with her. Somehow, every time, Judge Zeuss seemed to know what she was going to do before she did it. Now that she was doing it, she felt certain Judge Zeuss would be waiting for her out there.

o

As top security agent for Angelic Operations Executive, Justin Case had had a busy day. As soon as the banks and personal loan companies opened for business, he had slipped into their file rooms and had misplaced all records of loans made to Gene Quebaro. Then he had cleared up the difficulties at the credit card companies that had been hounding Gene. In the mortgage department at the Anne Knauerhase Fortress central office, he not only removed all records of the mortgage held on the Quebaro flat but all evidence that the Quebaros even lived at Fortress East, or that their apartment existed, hoping to save them the worry of the monthly payment of rent. The only remaining financial problem was the outstanding debt to Dr. Lesion.

The work had taken him all day. He had, only now, tracked down Judge Zeuss to persuade him to prevent Mort Violente from firing Mrs. Quebaro.

The long, shiny black limousine caparisoned with the flanking flags of the Municipal Court was waiting on Third Avenue at the 49th Street exit from Fortress East. Case materialized beside the car and spoke earnestly to Judge Zeuss through the open window.

"Judge Zeuss?"

"*Aaaaa*akkk!"

"Oh. Sorry if I startled you. It's just that the bail for Mrs. Quebaro's employer must be rescinded again."

"Who are you?"

Justin took out his gold buzzer and pushed it under Zeuss's face and said, "Hell is trying to ruin Quebaro financially by getting his wife fired so they won't have any money source."

"Ah."

"Can you do it?"

"Yes. Violente will be rearrested tonight. I will go from here directly to Police Headquarters."

She came rushing out of Fortress East. As soon as she saw the long limousine she slowed to a casual stroll. She gasped as she saw the tall, beautiful young man wearing a marvelously cut sand-colored suit chatting into the car. He was so gorgeous. She had dreamed of men as captivating as this but she had never really seen one. He was an absolute angel. She moved forward into a destiny of sensations. She walked slowly past the car with the absent-minded air of a woman retracing her way to pick up a sable coat left behind at a laundromat.

If one were studying Doris, it might seem as if she were a susceptible woman. That assumption would have been unfortunate. The fact was, since her death and the beginning of the field tests, Doris had been under sexual pressure of more than 9200^2 pascals, yet she was not being pressured by any mortal man. No human female, no matter how self-righteous or simply faithful, could have withstood the sexual pressures of the principal god of the ancient Greek pantheon. She was being wooed by a divinity who had had more experience in and out of beds, over the millennia, than any other single manifestation. Further, she was greatly chagrined by her husband's failure as hunter-provider. She was as powerless as a love-starved maiden lady who had been fed cantharides, in chocolate creams, by a great film star of the thirties.

However, it was not Doris after all who had come rushing out of Fortress East. It was Aphrodite. Judge Zeuss's plan to decimate, even eliminate, the heavenly team was now underway. He knew Phyllis Stein had been eliminated. He knew Haurus was in trouble. The more of the whole opposition that could be taken out of play, the better would be his chances of having the original Mrs. Quebaro brought in to take up Doris's husband's attentions and leave Doris alone and available for Zeus. Justin Case must go. If possible, they all must go. Except Doris Quebaro.

Justin had never seen Mrs. Quebaro. He made the natural mistake of assuming that Aphrodite was Mrs. Quebaro, as she had come out of Mrs. Quebaro's building and because Judge Zeuss had leaned out of the car window and called out, "Mrs. Quebaro! What a pleasant surprise! What an unexpected pleasure! May I introduce Mr. Justin Case?"

Justin had not only never set eyes on such a magnificently beautiful woman, he had never even set eyes on a woman at all at such an intimate distance. He liked it. But, instantly, he became aware of the certainty of the existence of sin, which is, to an extent, he found himself telling himself, what women must be for. He became dizzy at the thought of the consequences. All at once he saw it as his duty to, if possible, keep Mrs. Quebaro from falling into sin herself with this corrupt lecher, Judge Zeuss. He decided, even as he looked upon her, that, if necessary, he would seduce this woman himself to keep her from sinning.

Aphrodite filled one of Mademoiselle Chanel's "little black dresses" in a manner more glorious than its creator had ever aspired to. The dress was of the vintage 1971 so it must have worked relentlessly for Aphrodite on many different occasions, but it was trendless over her rolling hips, her magnificent shoulders and that bust—reproductions of which were, even at that moment, being gaped at in several hundred museums of the world. It was an evening suit of black crepe printed with gray, orange, and black patterns that mingled with beaded embroidery, but Aphrodite's professionalism, symbolized by a female standing under a lamppost, swinging a handbag, was diametrically opposite to Mademoiselle Chanel's, who had said, "What is tough is never to be careless for one moment."

Somewhere at the back of Justin's sensibility he seemed to realize that this impossibly sensual beauty could not be mortal. But he knew she was not an angel because of the thrilling development of her chest. As a heavenly representative, he was incapable of thinking that a father could ever use a daughter in the ways Zeus often used Aphrodite. But Justin threw away what he sensed and inhaled her like cocaine.

"I am on my way downtown to police headquarters, Mrs. Quebaro," Judge Zeuss said. "May I drop you anywhere?"

"No, thank you," Aphrodite answered demurely.

133

"May I drop you, Case?"

"No, Judge. Not at all. No. Quite all right. Thank you, but no. Thank you very much."

Judge Zeuss bade them good evening. As the enormous limousine moved up Third Avenue and then bore left as if to go across town, the Judge ordered the re-arrest of Mort Violente on the car's radio-telephone. Justin flagged a cab and decanted Aphrodite into it. "Where to?" he panted, because the insurance company pamphlets he had read had convinced him that lung fish were obssessed with sex.

"I thought some nice, cosy hotel," Aphrodite said huskily.

By the time Judge Zeuss's limousine had made it around the block and had re-parked in front of the Quebaro building exit, Hermes had telephoned his father to report that Aphrodite had gotten her target away without any surveillance interference, which meant that the giant NixonVision screen had not informed the Liederkranz convention of Case's possible defection. Luckily, the immortals were as strapped by lung fish technology as the lung fish were by the immortals' morality.

Doris came plunging out of the building. She spotted the limousine, pretending she had not.

"Mrs. Quebaro!" Judge Zeuss called out. "What an unexpected pleasure! I was hoping with all my heart—and more—that we would meet this evening." He opened the limousine door. Doris entered the luxurious car. "Where are we going?" she asked tremblingly.

"I thought we might enjoy the Thessaly Restaurant," Judge Zeuss said, kissing the palms of her hands.

Fourteen

The system that projected motion pictures in forty-one colors on the big screen at Liederkranz Hall was an entirely mortal, reasonably simple system if the electronics were bypassed. The Director, an angel of the Cherubim discipline who had once directed "What's My Line"—a network television sub-extravaganza—worked in a booth at Liederkranz Hall with multiple cameras that stayed with all possible components of the field study to photograph a complete video tape record, which was also shown on dozens of monitor screens. The most currently significant were edited instantly by the Director and routed through to be projected within the convention hall on the giant NixonVision screen. There was nothing "supernatural" about it. It was an ordinary White House surveillance device that worked well. The J($\Uparrow$)CES had merely borrowed it for use around the clock in their own special pursuit of law and order.

By mistake, editing on the monitor screen with many camera choices, the Director, St. Clare, Patron Saint of Television, had held on Judge Zeuss's car as it had pulled away, ignoring their own operative, Case, and the newcomer. The only two mistakes St. Clare had made during the entire extremely intricate and difficult simultaneous filming operation concerned Aphrodite. St. Clare had decided the walk around the block by Judge Zeuss and his daughter was just some family stuff of no interest to the field study, and she had decided that Judge Zeuss, as a principal actor, should have the single camera that was covering the scene. But St. Clare had a ruggedly tough job and the Joint ($\Uparrow$)Committee had given her a margin for error. Nevertheless, the shocking fact remained: the Up† team had suddenly lost one of its two operatives. No one had the faintest idea of what had happened to Justin Case. He had vanished just when Eugene Quebaro needed him more than ever before in his life.

o

Gene broke free from Dr. Lesion's grip on the fifty-second floor of Fortress East. He sprinted down the corridor on the trail of his wife, who had a seven-minute start on him. He had only to hare along behind her crazing spoor of perfume, which drew him through all the correct corridors (where it had already seeped under doors, turning normal family men feral).

When he came out on Third Avenue, there was no sign of Doris. He felt frustrated and guilty. He was dismayed. He resented that Doris made him feel such weak emotions because, since she had the only money between them, he couldn't even take up the faultless excuse of finding a comfortable bar with four juke boxes playing "Star Dust" and get drunk. He couldn't even gain weight as a kind of revenge because he couldn't buy food, and he was damned if he would go back upstairs and eat spaghetti standing up with the Lesions, even if they could find the stove. He had twenty-eight cents. He could either buy half a hot dog and have three cents left over or he could call Phyllis Stein, his new friend, and see if he could get a meal out of her. It would cost crucial money to call her, but he would have to take a chance.

While Gene looked for a telephone booth, Victoria Saxe-Coburg noticed that Justin Case was missing. She telephoned Alice immediately at the Quebaro office, where Alice spent twenty-four hours of the day. She had no place else to go and mortal time meant nothing to her.

"Is Justin with you, dear?" Miss Saxe-Coburg asked.

"No. He's out misplacing the bank loans."

"The cameras have lost him."

"But that's awful!"

"You people really need him, don't you?"

"*Need* him? He's the whole key!"

"Let me rerun the film. I have a hunch. Alice, dear, in the meantime, Quebaro is very down. His wife left him. He has only twenty-eight cents and he's very hungry."

"Why—that's terrible."

"Why don't you buy him a good dinner? No rule against that. Sweet talk him a little bit. Get him sleepy enough to go home and go to bed."

"That is my duty. Where is he?"

"He's about to step out of a telephone booth in Dag Engelson Plaza. He's been calling Phyllis Stein and he's going to lose his quarter."

"I'm on my way."

o

Gene listened to the Stein number ring twenty-eight times without answer. He hung up. His quarter didn't fall. He shook the phone and hit it but the quarter still didn't fall. He now had three cents. He stepped out of the booth and almost into the arms of Alice Trudy Kehoe.

"Miss Kehoe!"

"Why, hello there, Mr. Quebaro."

"I couldn't believe it was you. In fact, I've never seen you outside the office."

"I just got stood up. My Aunt Helen, who sent me a gift certificate for three dinners at Chock Full O'Nuts was going to help me use it tonight—the last night it's effective—but she sprained her ankle." Five lies in one sentence.

"That's too bad."

"It's a darn shame. Are you free, Mr. Quebaro? Can you join me?"

o

After dinner they strolled north along Madison Avenue. "It seems so early just to call it a night," Alice said.

"I have some funny cigarettes," Gene said. "We can sit on the wall in front of the Seagram Building and watch the traffic lights change color in the smog along Park

Avenue." They walked, holding hands, each facing a different direction, Gene walking backwards, so they couldn't be
surprised by attackers. They sat on the low wall and lit up.
Gene said he was thinking of getting a night job in some
restaurant.

"But—your uncle's estate."

"Only at night, I mean. I'd continue to prac-
tice law in the daytime. It would bring in *some* money. I could
pay you something on what I owe you."

"Please don't go thinking about *that.* I have
a small income from Australian nickel stocks."

"Everything seems like such a drop in the
ocean since somebody told me I'll owe Palmer Mahan fifty
thousand dollars if the plate market goes down by five per
cent."

"Then you must sell those plates."

"No. I can't. I owe you a responsible debt. I
have a mortgage, the banks, the credit card companies and
—oh, a lot of other things. And now, due to some horrible
accident, we'll probably have to buy all new furniture."

"But if the plate market fell only one-half of
one per cent, you would owe that man five thousand dollars,
which is much more to the point. He's capable of having you
arrested, Mr. Quebaro. You could be disbarred. You would
have to sacrifice all the years you've poured into the law to
inherit from your Uncle Raimundo. I tell you, Mr. Quebaro,
I could just weep."

"I have always wanted to tell you that I think
you are a very beautiful girl."

She looked up at him tremulously. Oh, *God!*
—he thought. I have never *seen* any thing this beautiful up
close. How had she stayed a legal stenographer? She should
be married to the heir to the British throne and be starring
in four forms of world entertainment. He couldn't *stand* it.
He reached out and pulled her to him. He kissed her wet,
mushy mouth so fiercely that they appeared to have fused
together.

It was a famous first for Alice.

As he let go of her, she grabbed him, pulled
him down to her mouth, and did it all over again. "Is this

138

sex?" she babbled. "Is this it? Oh, it's so wonderful! Are we doing it?"

"Baby," he mumbled, running his hands over her body, "we are about to make history. Where do you live?"

Alice lived nowhere on earth. Time flashed by so instantaneously in this slot that she just sat at her desk. "Why?" she asked helplessly.

"Because we are going to explode the sex rumor and turn it into a living myth, a legendary thing. We have to go to your place to do it because my place—"

Alice ran through the codes Victoria Saxe-Coburg had put into her head for every single conceivable emergency. She immediately retrieved the code for this one. "I'll have to call. I'll have to see if my roommate is in or out."

He kissed her again until she was afraid she was going to have to tear his clothes off right in front of the Seagram Building. "Call," he said hoarsely. "We'll run to that Waldbaum's on Lexington. Then I'll find a cab or commandeer a car. Go!"

They leapt off the wall, ran to the corner, and headed east along the pavement. Alice slammed into a telephone booth and called Vickie Saxe-Coburg. "Vickie! I've got him so he'll tell me absolutely anything!" She hated to lie for the second time in her life as a lung fish but she didn't know what else to do. It sounded too frivolous to tell Vickie she was going to bed with Eugene Quebaro and that she was almost out of her mind about it.

"Sure," Miss Saxe-Coburg said. "And you need a place to make him talk—right?"

"Yes!"

"Take him upstairs in the building you are in now. Apartment 12F. The key is in the door. Be sure to make the bed nice before you leave."

"Thanks, Vickie."

"And, Alice?"

"Yes?"

"Just make sure you cross-examine him about money, or you'll get into the same kind of trouble as Phyllis Stein."

o

Gene had never heard such sexual sounds. It was as if feeding time in the lion house had been crossed with the Vienna Opera company and the complete performances of Artur Rubenstein. He thought Doris had mastered the entire aeolian encyclopaedia but this was a totally new and cosmic recording. Further, he knew he had never experienced such transmuscular power and fitness. He had never known that a woman had so many orifices of such fantastic tensile mobility. He had never realized that a woman could have such a multiple capacity for orgasm, and so frequently. He had never known any woman who was capable of transforming him into a creature possessing supernatural sexual powers. It was well on into dawn before they paused. For three years this fantast of sexual feeling had been an arm's length away from him and he had not as much as reached out. But if he reached once more he was afraid he would perhaps lose the top of his head and all his toes and, even more likely, never be able to stop again and he had other obligations to face. He lay limply on the bed. She panted on his thighs.

"I don't know how I could have thought that first kiss on the wall in front of that building was *doing* it," she mumbled with a bleared voice, sobbing into his crotch. "We have nothing in Heaven. *Nothing, nothing, nothing.*"

They lay silently, he thinking of Uncle Raimundo's executors, she thinking of eternity.

"Mr. Quebaro?"

"Yas."

"Am I better than Palmer Mahan's secretary?"

"What about her?"

"Oh, Gene. Everybody knows."

"They do?"

"Am I better?"

"Alice," he said with awe, "those are questions which mere technicians ask. You are a great *poet* of sex. You are a great *innovator,* a vise, a force, a simple mysticism.

You are loving and beloved and com*plete*ly adorable. You must have known the inventor of all of it."

"As a matter of fact, I——" she started to say but she thought the better of it.

"But what did you mean—everybody knows about me and Miss Stein?"

"Well," she fumbled. "Executive secretaries do talk. They do pool information, you know."

"Do you *know* her?"

"Well, no. Not actually. I think I may have read about it in our trade paper."

"They print facts like that in a *trade* paper?"

"Well, you, see a really *good,* that is a top-class secretary has to *know* her employer inside out, if you know what I mean." Hurriedly she changed the subject. She remembered she was supposed to be getting information. "Do you think it will help a great deal to inherit your uncle's nine hundred thousand dollars? Will it make much of a difference?"

"Jesus. It sure will."

"How?"

"I'll take it into the plate market and triple it."

"Then what will you do with the two million seven hundred thousand dollars?"

"I haven't thought about it, really. My wife hasn't seen a movie for a long time. She needs stockings."

"Are you scared, Mr. Quebaro?"

"Good heavens, Alice. What is there to be scared about?"

There was a longish pause. He spoke again in the dawn's early light. "Yes. I'm scared. I can't remember when I wasn't scared. I've been scared since I was a little boy and knew I'd have to find food and clothes and a roof for other people someday, just like my father had to do. Somehow, it all works out. Everyone is able to do it, but that doesn't mean it doesn't scare you till you can hardly get out of bed some mornings."

"It was a frivolous question, Mr. Quebaro. I

haven't even figured out what money is and you're scared there isn't enough to go around. I mean, you have real problems."

"Yeah. And I have another one. I think my wife left me." He was propped up on a pillow discovering how much he was getting to like looking at the top of her head.

"Oh, you poor man."

"Maybe she didn't."

"Of course she didn't. You are a wonderful, wonderful man."

"I can't make money," he said dreamily, "so how can she respect me? Money is the only measuring stick left to us. And the actual, factual fact is that if a woman can't respect a man, she can't love him. The other fact is, unless I can figure out how to make money while it is practically snowing money on everybody else, she's bound to walk out on me. I can't blame her. It's a matter of respect."

"Mr. Quebaro, why is money important? When did that happen?"

"Well, what the hell, Alice," he said. "There has to be something to maintain the male mystique and keep the scales balanced. As long as everybody wants money and the men have only one job in life, which is anything related to bringing it in—then everything else we do is all tied up with money. There are so many more people now. People need the money to keep up with what the advertising tells them they need. Jesus, how do I know? Anybody who can't make any money—then how can anybody have any respect for them? I mean—that's how we're taught, isn't it?"

o

In the back row at Liederkranz Hall, after having watched many hours of NixonVison on a split screen that showed them what Doris and Gene were doing separately and simultaneously, Tipperah[†] whispered to Kavod. "So what do we find out? Nothing." Tipperah was a wife of Moses, but because of all the hard work she put into making the Old Testament a best seller, she had been made a Virtue in the Women's Division. Kavod was an all-around utility

angel who could do a great Irish tenor imitation except that
once he got started, it was hard to stop him but that, after
all, is only part of doing an Irish tenor imitation.

o

Gene left Alice collapsed on the bed at 6:59
A.M. and walked home. He was at home in bed with Doris—
who he found waiting for him—within fifteen minutes.

Spaced out beyond self-recognition, Alice
slowly pulled herself together. It took her twenty-three minutes to dress. With the mechanical movements of a sleep-
walker she "made the bed nice," then left the vault of her
virginity to walk downtown to 49th Street, planning to sit at
her desk to dream about sex until the business day began
again. There wasn't a cab in sight, nor did she think of
looking for one. She was mugged and beaten by three bull-
dykes at 51st Street between Lexington and Park. She was
found by a Sanitation Truck crew and taken to the Midtown
Hospital. Watching all of it at Mission Control, Miss Saxe-
Coburg knew the team of the Heavenly Host was in ghastly
trouble. Case had disappeared. Kehoe was permanently out
of action. Of all the starters only Palmer Mahan was still on
his feet.

Fifteen

Judge Zeuss's gleaming black Mercedes 600 had rolled downtown on Ninth Avenue, its chauffeur turning east on 28th Street in order to pull up in front of the Thessaly Restaurant. The Judge had been murmuring archly to Doris, sometimes alluringly, sometimes seductively, after he found, at last, that he was actually able to talk after the first maniacal sexuality that had come over him because of her perfume. As the car turned onto Eighth Avenue, he happened to look across at the front of the Thessaly. He made a terrible choking sound. Without hesitation, he pushed Doris forward in her seat and jerked her abruptly to the floor of the car, holding her there firmly with his foot.

"Judge Zeuss!" she cried out, face down upon the thick pile carpet. "What happened?" She was in an extremely undignified position, but she didn't think of that. She was convinced that soldiers of the Violente family were waiting with drawn guns outside the car.

"Stay down!" he barked. "Don't move!"

"But what is it? What is happening?"

"My wife," he said in a terrorized voice. "My wife is standing right there in front of the restaurant."

"Your *wife?*" Suddenly Doris overtook the grotesqueness of her sprawl.

The Judge yelled into the communicator at the driver. "Straight ahead. Fast. Move it. Left at Thirty-first Street. Take me to the French Hospital on Thirtieth Street and I'll get myself admitted retroactively. Then get to the nearest phone booth and call Athena—*but don't go near that restaurant.*"

"What about me?" Doris shrieked from the floor of the car.

"Oh! Ah, yes!" He took up the communicator again. "And after you call Athena, drop this young lady off wherever she wants to go."

The big car turned into 31st Street, heading west. The Judge was biting his lip, thinking frantically. He seemed to have forgotten that Doris was sprawled at his feet, under his foot.

Doris made it to her hands and knees in a series of necessary but unforgivably graceless movements from the floor of the lurching car. She pulled down the jump seat directly in front of Judge Zeuss, drew back her handbag to maximum arc, then crashed it forward into the Judge's face, knocking him unconscious into the corner of the tonneau.

The limousine stopped for a red light at Ninth Avenue. Doris got out, slamming the door. Thinking twice about the chauffeur who had been witness to her disgrace, she changed her mind, tottering with fury. She went back and opened the door, leaving it open so he would have to get out of the car to close it. She picked up a tall wire waste basket, provided by the city, filled with discrete but indiscreet debris, and flung the whole thing with all her strength into the rear of the car, at the Judge, the wire of the basket lacerating his face and causing ichor to flow. She hailed a cab and rode away.

Judge Zeuss was admitted to the French Hospital with a broken nose and facial contusions. Athena brought his wife, Hera, to the hospital. Hera keened sharply all through Zeus's story of the mugging he had suffered in broad daylight at the hands of four giant Puerto Ricans on the streets of one of the biggest cities in the world. Hera sat beside his bed all night in uxorial vigil, Athena having slipped her father three seconals whispering, "Thrice happy and more, those whom the marriage bond unbroken holds."

Hera was so exhausted from sitting up all night that, by ten o'clock the next morning, before Zeus was willing to open his eyes, Athena had to find a room for her, in the hospital, to get some sleep.

o

Doris tiptoed through the Quebaro apartment into the heinously crate-crowded bedroom. Gene wasn't there. A cruel mixture of anxiety and guilt burned into her as she sat on the edge of the bed. Where had the poor man gone? He was penniless, hungry, friendless, and it was terribly unsafe for him to be roaming around the city. She undressed, took four aspirins, and stayed awake as long as she could, worrying.

o

Mort Violente was out of the Tombs for the second time that day. He was about to enjoy the primary, secondary, and tertiary sexual characteristics of his almost completely deaf and dumb sister-in-law (a woman of 318 pounds who stood, whenever he gave her a chance to stand, at five feet, one inch) in his custom-made, foam rubber-lined, superwide bathtub designed for two consenting adults. In the past twenty-one hours he had neither eaten any of the food he lived for nor had he made love to the only woman in the world who really reciprocated the way he felt about sex in the bathtub (and he knew this was no con because the water made her feel about a hundred and fifty pounds lighter).

His wife was in West New York, playing *bocce*. A large pot of *ragu** which, in all the world, only his sister-in-

*1 8-pound turkey cut into cubes	1/3 cup raisins
2 onions, roughly chopped	1 tortilla
1 stalk celery	1/4 teaspoon ground cloves
salt to taste	1/4 teaspoon cinnamon
2 chipotle chilis	4 peppercorns
6 mulato chilis	3 cloves garlic, chopped
1 teaspoon seeds reserved from chilis	1 quart turkey stock
	1 ounce unsweetened chocolate
4 pasilla chilis	3 medium tomatoes, peeled
4 tablespoons lard	
3 tablespoons sesame seeds	
1/3 cup almonds	
1/3 cup peanuts	

law knew how to make,—and which made him helpless with respect when he ate it, covering pasta with it to the point that he now found it difficult to eat pasta in any other way—was bubbling on the stove ready to enrich a mountain of tortellini under a half pound of freshly grated Parmesan from the right side of the river. His sister-in-law might not talk much or hear so good, but she was one sensational cook. And what she was like when the two of them got into that bathtub was something that could not even be spoken about.

It is possible that Marat had not been served as badly in his tub as Violente was to be served in his because Violente was sexually readier than Marat had ever been (perhaps than he would ever be again considering his age and the difficulties in obtaining mulato chilis). His sister-in-law's mute hand signals on his bare back were developing into wild punches, so ready was *she,* when Judge Zeuss's cops broke down the bathroom door.

The humiliation of Violente's arrest (the word was out across the Five Families within hours), naked and wet, to be thrown on his head into solitary in the Tombs for the third time on the same day on a charge as unbelievable as bookmaking was in direct relation to his loss of face as one of the most influential criminals in Fun City. A direct comparison: if the police had broken into the bathroom of a figure (if such eminence were possible) who was the combined head of First National City Bank, Chase Manhattan, Exxon, and the Combined Chiefs of Staff, had pulled *him* off the pleasures of his sister-in-law who respected him deeply in or out of the bathtub, and arrested him on a charge of vagrancy. The palpable injustice, the lack of respect shown, required that Violente now would have to have an even greater number of people killed when he was released to establish, beyond any doubt, the amount of respect which had to be paid to him in order for his position and his business to survive.

Sixteen

Raziel had given careful consideration to the message Carlotta had gotten through with her astrono-electronic prayer wheel after Zophiel brought it to him but, at first, his interest in it was entirely abstract, related to his interest in science, indeed in all things pertaining to lung fish.

"Well!" he said to Zophiel when he heard the news. "And they say there is nothing new under the sun."

"It's such a neu*rotic* thing," Zophiel said. "Why should they address pleas of any *kind* to us? Do you think this is going to start some sick trend?"

"No. Actually, you see, I *think* they have been trying like this for some time."

"Not a chance of it. If there had been any other sort of message of any kind from them it would have had to come through me. I *know* none of them has tried to get through."

"No. You are mistaken, Zoph. They tried. It's some kind of power play or perhaps even a put-on by their religious leaders. Talk to Samuel[†] or Pacelli[†] or Billy Sunday[†]. What the lung fish have been doing—insofar as I am able to reconstruct it—is called *praying*, which means kneeling and asking for something—anything. In this case, the woman wants her dead husband back. But their religious leaders encourage them to ask for anything, anything at all."

"Ask *who?*"

"The Great Architect®. The Boy. The Boy's Mother. It depends upon their sect, you see. It's all perfectly harmless. I mean, until this woman, no one's ever gotten through."

148

"But there are *billions* of them! Suppose they all start this praying? How am I going to get any work done?"

"Just keep it away from the All-Knowing®. No sense bothering Him with this boobery because you are quite right. They could all start up."

"Are you going to give the husband back?"

"Of course not. How can I give the husband back? Just because she got the first prayer through, it doesn't mean we all have to jump, does it?"

Nothing more was said about it (at the time). Zophiel turned his receiver off, the message was so monotonous. It was not until both field staffs were entirely eliminated, not until Raziel began to see that, despite a really tremendous expenditure of time and attention, they had so far learned absolutely nothing, that he gave Athena a ring.

He played it cool. He pretended he was calling about Irish Sweepstake tickets, a form of money. "Did any of your people ever win this?" he asked.

"I never even heard of it," Athena said.

"You know, we have run up quite a background chart on Quebaro. One gets interested to know what his batting average was with money before he came here. That sort of thing."

"Oh, his wife—the wife in the other place—is the key to that," Athena said blandly, winking across the telephone at her father.

"You think so?"

"We know it. We've charted her very carefully."

"Very interesting."

"It is, actually."

"Is that so? Well. I'd love to see the file sometime."

"We've been catching a lot of flak from that wife demanding her husband back."

"As a matter of actual fact, so have we."

"My brother Herm is an authority on the wife," Athena lied with pleasure.

"Well. You know I really would like to see

149

that file sometime. I'd really be much obliged."

"I'll be happy to send it over."

o

Raziel and Dagon went over the file minutely. "How could this be?" Raziel asked Dagon rhetorically. "The man was a six-figure man over there, but over here he can't get arrested."

"The wife. Read about the wife."

"What about the wife?"

"The one he had over there but he doesn't have over here is that wife. She's the first one ever to get through to bother us with appeals, so she's got to be some smart cookie. You watched Quebaro. You certainly know he isn't any smart cookie, so it stands to reason that he only knows how to get money when that wife tells him what to do."

"You could be right," Raziel said.

"How could I be wrong?"

"Maybe if we could get the woman over here she could pep up the whole field study."

"Send her the husband's ear *oder* his necktie or something and she'll come. Also, he happens to need a secretary *beim* his office now that the one from Thrones got banged up."

"We can't do it direct."

"Why not?"

"Somebody is sure to complain. Either the Upper or the Lower angels. They are so orthodox."

"So have the Greeks send somebody."

"That's good. That's what we'll do."

PART TWO

One

Hermes rang Carlotta's front doorbell at 2535 Long Ridge Road, Stamford, Connecticut 06903, and waited. He was wearing a well-tailored covert cloth suit with a single vent in the back. He had on a tweed fedora. His black shoes were brightly polished. He was a most pleasant-looking, if slightly campy young man. Carlotta answered the door wearing a sweater and skirt, short socks, and brogans. She looked haggard.

"What?" she said across the taut door chain.

"My name is Hermes, ma'am? The Greek Pantheon?"

"Yes?" Carlotta said tentatively.

"Your messages? They have been coming through? We thought you might like to talk about it?"

Carlotta closed the door, loosed the chain, opened the door and pulled Hermes in.

"The Greeks have Gene?" she asked tensely.

"Well, yes and no," Hermes said.

"Come on! Give me the scam!" Carlotta snarled.

"We are sort of in on the operation, but your husband's main sponsors are the Upper and Lower echelons of the Judeo-Christian hierarchies."

"Then why didn't they come?"

"Internal politics."

"But you can handle the problem?"

"I represent them."

"Please," Carlotta said. "Come into the living room. Suddenly, roses had bloomed in her cheeks. They sat down near a window in facing chairs above the conversation pit.

"How *is* Gene?"

"Well—he's dead."

She made an impatient gesture. "I know that, but how *is* he?"

"Fine, Mrs. Quebaro. Just fine."

"Why did they take him?"

"They didn't take him. He got killed at precisely the right moment when they were setting up a field study on money."

"Gene doesn't know anything about money."

"So they found out. But they want to know about money. They can't figure it out. They think it's the cause of all amorality and so forth but they don't know how, so they're making a study."

"They're studying *Gene*?"

"Gene and his wife."

"*Me?*"

"You're not his wife over there. He has a different wife. She doesn't know anything about money either. She's a Greek girl, which is maybe how we came into it." Hermes had no idea of how they had gotten into it except that Doris was beautiful and he knew his father.

"I don't buy any other wife. But let it go," Carlotta said. "The hard fact is that you can't find out anything about money studying Gene. Gene is a salesman, period. I'm the one in the family who knows about money. We were some team, believe me."

"Yes. Well. We wondered if you'd like to work with him over there?"

"Why should I?"

"Why should you? I thought that was what you were knocking yourself out for."

"I want him back here."

"He can't come back here. It simply can't be done. But you can go over there. We can arrange that."

"You can arrange it because you need me there."

"Well—"

"I only have your word that Gene can't be sent back here."

"Oh, no. No, no, no! That is absolutely a universal fact. I mean, dear woman, he is *dead*. Dead, dead, *dead*."

"Okay. Let's work out a deal."

"What *is* this? Do you want your husband or don't you want him? Anyway, I don't have the authority to make a deal."

"Then bring in the people who can."

"It's getting very *butch* out, isn't it? All this hairy big-executive shit. I'll be back." Hermes disappeared.

Carlotta felt so much better that she made herself a large pot of tea. She was pouring it when the doorbell rang. She opened the door on the chain. It was Hermes with a smartly dressed woman and two sweet-faced, elderly men. "This is the negotiating committee," Hermes said. Carlotta took everyone into the dining room. They sat around the table. Carlotta poured tea, acknowledging the introductions of Athena, Raziel and Dagon.

"Mrs. Quebaro?" Raziel said flatly. "What is there to bargain about?"

"Well—for example—if I don't like it over there, can I come back here?"

"Over there is a replica of over here. Nobody could tell the difference except us. What else?"

"There is another point, very important. I have just been paid a million dollars in insurance money plus two hundred fifty thousand dollars in damages from the City of New York. Also, when I liquidate on investments and total up our cash and property values, jewelry, stock shares, cars, wheat futures, et cetera, I will have maybe another six hundred thousand and I am definitely not leaving that here—if I go."

"But there is no way we can transfer that. No way exists," Raziel said firmly.

"Then you'll have to get along somehow without me. Forget it. Forget the whole thing."

"Terrific health we can guarantee you. And youth, for instance. If you would like to look twenty-two when you are—say—ninety-one, that we can do. We can make sure you are popular. After all, a person likes to be liked. But transferring wealth from here to Over There, impossible." He shrugged. "It can't be done."

"Then I am not going. I also suggest that you two gentlemen, as august as you are, are not top management. By that I mean you are not the Highest, Final Authority."

"Of course not," Dagon said. "Who would want a job like that?"

"Mrs. Quebaro, be reasonable. Be smart. Be fair to yourself. Even if you do get through to The Ancient of Days®, it won't change a decision like this. He is a great executive. That's why He is where He is. He'll back us up," Raziel said.

"Besides," Dagon interjected, "He can't think in one person-two person terms. He has too many people on His mind—trapping them in forest fires, arranging earthquakes, famines, hurricanes, and floods. It is entirely His Multiple Personality Capability which got Him the job in the first place. Raziel and I are on a very high policy level, believe me."

"Gene and I worked too hard to get our money together, and since it is now my total responsibility or—let me rephrase that—totally my responsibility—I am not leaving that money behind. I *am* sorry, but that is final."

"Maybe my father could arrange it through a Greek bank," Athena said.

"Swiss banks only," Carlotta said. "Although I think you should know that this house does not need to be transferred. It could be that we *can* get back and we'll need a place and we like this house."

"The house is already there, lady," Dagon said. "Don't ask me to explain, but there is ten of everything."

"Let us handle it," Athena said. We can set up a credit with parallel banks Over There, and your people don't understand how all that works yet, Raziel."

"Are there taxes over there?" Carlotta asked.

"Are you kidding?" Dagon said, misunderstanding. "There are taxes on every corner and they'll take you anywhere absolutely free, no tipping."

"What do you want me to do if I do go?" Carlotta asked.

"It works like this. You'll be Gene Quebaro's legal stenographer. He's a lawyer Over There. You'll be programmed to know all about his law practice, and you'll be programmed with a certain amount of limited information about the people you'll have to work with in the field tests—base, functional information like that," Raziel told her. "So you won't have any trouble working with him, on the one hand, and working indirectly for us with him on the other."

"What about his wife?"

"She is the wife. That's done. That's the way it is. But as the secretary you'll have a fair shot at him and —who knows?"

"I am going to hate that part of it."

"Mrs. Quebaro, you won't know. I can't tell you why or what happens, but when you go Over There, something happens in the head. You forget over here and everything that happened over here. We have to have it that way or the people would always be yelling to be somewhere else."

"You will be Over There, and all you'll know is you work for Quebaro; you'll help us to help him, and you'll have a different name because we certainly can't call you Mrs. Quebaro," Dagon said.

"Why doesn't he have a secretary now? If he's a lawyer, what happened to his secretary?"

"She was mugged," Raziel said.

"Listen, it happens," Dagon said.

"This is a very chancy thing, Mr. Raziel, Mr. Dagon. I am being asked to take an awful lot on faith here."

"Faith? That's the name of the game, Mrs. Quebaro. Please," Raziel said. "Hear me out. I am Raziel with a nickname, which is 'The Secret of God.' In the cabala I am the personification of Cochma, which means "divine wisdom." I am second of the holy ten sefiroth. In rabbinic lore I am the author of The Book of the Angel Raziel—

"Sefer Raziel" they call it—wherein all celestial and earthly knowledge is set down. I helped Adam. I helped Enoch. I helped Noah and Solomon. I am one of the nine archangels of the Briatic world, which is the second of the four worlds of creation. I am chief of the order of erilim. Lady, listen to me. Do you think an angel like me would stoop to flim-flamming a woman like you?"

"I suppose not."

"All right. Athena is the daughter of Zeus. She is a member of the Olympian assembly. She is known to be—absolutely known to be—a direct emanation of her father's noblest self. She is allowed to hurl a thunderbolt. She has the power of prophecy. She is Zeus's deputy in maintaining law, order, and justice. She is THE patroness of art and learning. She presides over all useful inventions and discoveries. She is the irrefutable guardian of all women. Do you think a goddess like Athena would flim-flam you?"

"No," Carlotta said. "If you both counter-sign the transfer of my funds and give me your personal guarantees that I can take my money with me, then I'll take the job."

"That's agreeable," Raziel said. "But, I warn you, Mrs. Quebaro. You are going to be programmed so that it will be impossible for you to give any money away to Eugene Quebaro. He is a controlled experiment."

"When do we leave?"

"Five days? A week?"

"A week then. Do I go through the rigama-role of conventional death?"

"That is routine."

"Then—oh, well. Never mind. Can your bankers be here this evening to get the financial arrangements settled?"

"Athena and I happen to be bankers. We'll settle everything right now. What name will you use Over There?"

Carlotta pondered that one. She walked to the window and looked out for a while; then she turned and said, "Charlotte Pimbernel, I think. It was my mother's maiden name. Yes. That will suit nicely."

o

On the morning of the sixth day, Carlotta left the house for the first time since Gene had gone. She went to Dad Quebaro's showroom-garage in downtown Stamford. There seemed to be Volkswagens everywhere, as though he bred them. Dad was talking benignly to a man named Meltzer. He took Carlotta into his office and closed the door.

"Well!" he beamed joyously. "You're looking normal and beautiful again."

"Thank you, Dad"

"So it's finally all over."

"Yes. All over."

"And you're going to rejoin the world."

"Dad, I just came in to say good-bye and to thank you for all you've always meant to me."

"Where are you going?"

"I contacted the authorities who have Gene, Dad. I made my deal."

"Now don't start that again, Carlotta."

"Well, I did."

"Carlotta, please——"

"They came to see me five days ago and they need my help to help Gene help them. We worked out all the details. I've liquidated everything and I am going to be able to take it all with me. Isn't that nice? Is there anything you'd like to have?"

"Well, if you don't want them I'd like to have the *Century Cyclopedia of Names* and your copy of Keifetz's *The Sensation*."

"Fine."

"But—where are you going?"

"They call it the Other Place. There is ten of everything, Dad. I don't understand it either."

"Carlotta," he said desperately. "Now, you listen——"

"Don't be frightened."

"Carlotta, *please*——"

"Remember that second Christmas when

Gene brought you the red wooly bathrobe and everyone was in such a good mood for three whole days? Remember the way we sang? Real three-part harmony? I wish we'd had a tape recorder then. I wish we could play it all back now."

"I remember," Dad said wistfully. "I can hear the music."

"When I'm gone, please think about those days, not this past year. And will you remember the summer you taught me how to cook? Will you remember that, Dad?"

He ran his huge, veined hand across his eyes. "You mean it. You mean every word you're saying."

"Gene and I belong together, Dad."

He lowered his head into his arms on the desk. Carlotta got up. She leaned across the desk, bent over, and kissed him on the top of his head.

Two

Two minutes after Gene arrived at the office the next morning, hung up his hat and umbrella and made his usual small joke for Miss Pimbernel, his new secretary, Kullers & Company telephoned. After he hung up, Charlotte went into his office. Gene was lying on his back on the floor, staring absently at the ceiling.

"Anything wrong?" Charlotte asked.

"Not really," he answered dreamily.

"But it isn't like you to lie on the floor."

"I suppose not."

Charlotte went back to her desk and called Mr. Kullers. "How is the plate market this morning?" she asked.

"It opened four per cent off yesterday and it's getting worse."

Charlotte hung up. A four-per-cent loss meant Mr. Quebaro owed that Palmer Mahan forty thousand dollars. Programmed, she responded. In moments of trouble she knew she had a friend to call.

"Vickie?" She asked Saxe-Coburg. "Charlotte. They have started dumping plates." Charlotte was *thoroughly* programmed. "The market opened at four per cent off."

"I know."

"When will Justin be here, luv? Gene is lying on the floor of his office in a daze."

"We are working on it."

The bare outlines of vital statistics on Miss Pimbernel, Miss Kehoe's replacement, were that she was a very beautiful, blond English girl of seemingly great intellec-

161

tual strength and follow-through with no small amount of physical stamina. She had told her employer that she was independently wealthy and would not mind at all if she were paid annually or by any other arrangement he would propose. She explained earnestly that she was far too young to bear the thought of retiring and had always gotten *keen* pleasure out of legal stenography, so on the chance to work for Mr. Quebaro arising, when her dearest friend Alice Trudy Kehoe had been hospitalized, she had jumped at it. She was enormously decisive and filled with productive, new, profitable ideas that would have been enormously helpful if Mr. Quebaro had had any law practice to support them.

She thought Mr. Quebaro was a pleasant, anxious, thoughtful, and frightened man. There wasn't enough work. There wasn't any work actually. But Charlotte felt it very much her duty to protect Alice's job for her, for when she got out of the hospital some day. When Miss Pimbernel finished her day at the Quebaro law offices, she commuted to Stamford where she had a house on Long Ridge Road.

So much for the bare vital statistics on Miss Pimbernel. Her emotional response to Mr. Quebaro was something far, far, far less routine and dull than that. She had been waiting in the anteroom to the offices on the morning she had been hired, waiting for Mr. Quebaro to come in so that she could apply for the job. The office door had been unlocked because Gene had lost the keys two years before and had not been able to afford to replace them. When he had arrived, carrying his umbrella, she had leaped to her feet to greet him; had stared into his eyes, face and spirit—as he towered, as a wooden Indian towers, so far above her. Her entire permanent-yearning system, that built-in psychological miracle of aspiration which gets people out of bed in the morning, often to get into yet other beds, was activated. She felt devastated by pity/lust for him, the unbeatable, irreversible combination for the most lasting female adhesiveness to the body and soul of the male. She felt exalted just to be near him. She felt transformed into an analogue of Puss In Boots running out ahead of the Marquis de Carrabas to win kingdoms for him and to find him happiness. She was transformed, by a flicker of his eyes, by a stretch of taut skin at the corner of his mouth, by an habitual crinkling of his black eyes peering through his feral Filipino face on the body of a Viking. It would not be enough to state that Miss Pimbernel had fallen in love with Mr. Quebaro because such descriptions have become the meaningless shorthand of popular songs and graffiti. She *loved* him in every lasting, fulfilling, multi-dimensional sense of that lost and exalting word. She loved him so deeply that, in the instantaneous human-female sense, she was determined to save him.

"Nothing can really delay Justin, can it, Vickie?" Miss Pimbernel asked anxiously into the telephone. "Mr. Quebaro is in desperate trouble."

"Give me a little more time."

"Vickie—a *panic* is building in dinner plates. At noon there will be only three trading hours left. It could be too late. I mean, all you have to do is read '*Springvloed: Beschouwing over industriele ont wikkeling en prijsbeweging*' or '*Des crises commerciales et leurs retours periodiques en France, en Angleterre et Etats-Unis*' and you can chart your own graph of Kondratieff, Juglar, Matson, Kitchin, and Van Gelderen cycles of plate price fluctuations since nineteen hundred. I am telling you now that unless Justin appears here as The Big New Client who will give Gene the means to act fast, one hundred and seventy plate exchanges in the world will be in for acute panic."

○

N'Zuriel Yhwh pushed the FREEZE button on the arm of his chair at Liederkranz Hall. Charlotte Pimbernel's picture went silent and still on the big NixonVision screen. It is not known whether, when he did this, all the noises and motions of life on the planet went into suspension but it is likely, because of the time-phase factors involved. In strike-prone countries such as England, for instance, FREEZE seems to happen much more often than it happens actually. In any event, this kind of angelic FREEZE action also accounts for why otherwise perfectly normal people cannot remember where they have just put their eyeglasses down in their own houses.

"I want to talk with this Charlotte Pimbernel," N'Zuriel Yhwh told the convention. "She is the first one who sounds as if she has anything resembling a clue to this money business." He spoke to the screen, pushing the HOLD button. "Charlotte, why should there be a panic in dinner plates? What happened? Dinner plates are the whole backbone of your economy."

"It goes in a vicious cycle, sir," Charlotte said into the hidden camera. "You see, there is a cumulative expansion of productive activity which is fed and propelled by a continuous expansion of credit."

"Use shorter words if you can, dear." N'Zuriel Yhwh said. "Try to make everything very clear for us here in the Hall."

"Well, sir—the basic trouble builds this way: the banks merchandise their money and lure businessmen into borrowing it by lowering the cost of hiring money."

"How do you like that?" Dagon said, aside to Raziel. "They rent money just like we could rent a harp."

"I hope the rented money works better than our rented harps," Raziel replied.

"Please!" N'Zuriel Yhwh thundered. "A certain young lady is talking! Please proceed, young lady."

"Well—the businessman increases his inventories because it is now easy and inexpensive to do it. This brings bigger orders to the people who produce the goods the businessman needs."

"I follow you," N'Zuriel Yhwh said, making notes as he stared at Charlotte on the screen, "very clear."

"All this increased production and selling causes more consumer spending as the money from the firms who produced the goods circulates out to labor and small producers. This causes the businessman's stock to be depleted, which produces still more orders and more consumer spending until the banks decide to make money still cheaper—until everything together causes an inflation, which means that there is now a *lot* of money from all that unrestricted activity around, money which by now is pretty worthless."

164

"The people must hate that," Dagon said to the screen.

"They hate being wiped out, yes."

"I can see it!" Raziel said with excitement. "When the money is worthless it ruins all confidence in business, industry, and government and, at about the fourth time around of all that fiddling, things begin to collapse into panic, which causes complete economic collapse."

"Can't they fix that?" N'Zuriel Yhwh asked anxiously.

"Can they fix people?" Charlotte asked from high on the NixonVision screen.

"I mean—why doesn't your government do something?"

"But—I just don't understand."

"I am asking why the governments don't step in and stop all this in time?"

"But, sir—" Charlotte answered with some confusion. "When has any government been of any help with anything, except in making war? Government is just a living for people who can't make a living anywhere else. Manifestly, they don't *understand* what they are doing and they are always being replaced. Thank God."

"You mean—like a Home for the Mentally Infirm?"

"Exactly! They are in further over their heads than anyone else because the *only* thing they understand is getting re-elected. Everything politicians do to *help,* as you call it, only postpones the fatal collapse that is the normal part of the business cycle except that, if the government doesn't help, it may only be a small collapse."

"Then what can anybody do?"

"The important thing is to stop credit expansion in time."

"Then do it! We'll make them do it!"

"In all history governments have only acted to stop collapse after it was too late to stop it, because when credit expansion stops, the boom stops. If the boom stops the people might not re-elect the politicians who should have stopped it and the banks can't rent their money at such marvelous profits."

"And that's where we are right now?"

"Yes, sir. The plate market is on the verge of super-crisis. The dinner-plate economy is peaking out, which caused the government to suspend the gold convertibility of dinner plates. A vicious downward spiral is the only outlook possible. There is a dire need to get Mr. Case to this office instantly, posing as a client. Believe me, sir, there is only a relatively short span of time when this vague feeling of public insecurity appears and, as that feeling grows, so will the panic-based expectation of collapse grow until— well, sir—it is simply *essential* that Mr. Case be sent here at once."

"So find Case!" N'Zuriel Yhwh shouted at the entire convention. *"What is his Chief of Mission doing? Where is the resident here?"*

Victoria Saxe-Coburg appeared instantly. "Resident reporting, sir. We greatly fear Case has been kidnapped."

"Kidnapped? Who would kidnap him?"

"Unknown, sir."

"I want him found—now!" N'Zuriel Yhwh had agitated himself exceedingly but, on the other hand, he was enjoying it. He fell back into his chair, pushed the ACTION button, and turned to Raziel. "All this talk. All these panics, disasters, crashes," he whispered in a baffled voice. "Where does money come into it? I don't get it."

○

With the pushing of the ACTION button, Charlotte went on speaking into the telephone to Miss Saxe-Coburg. "I have to go in there and get Mr. Quebaro ready for what he has to do."

"All right," Vickie said grimly. "Count on Justin for eleven o'clock."

Three seconds after Charlotte hung up, the phone rang again. It was a bitter, bitter Dr. Lesion.

"This is Dr. Norman Lesion," he said. "Put Quebaro on the telephone."

"One moment, Dr. Lesion." She buzzed Gene who took a while to get to the phone because he had to will himself to pick himself up off the floor. Charlotte listened in on the call, intently.

"What is it?" Gene said listlessly into the telephone.

"What is it? You dare to greet me with a what-is-it? I am on my back in the Beth Joyce Hospital because of what you did to me."

"Don't come snuffling around me for a get-well card."

"Last night you worked on me to buy into the dinner-plate market. One-half of one per cent a day you promised. Like your Australian nickel mine stock, like your bottomless belly for sandwiches. What did you make out of this deal? On your urging, I went into the plate market this morning and it immediately took a high dive out of the window, landing on me whose whole life savings are involved. I am lying here in a hospital with the closest thing to a stroke that the human condition can survive without paralysis and I can only say thank God Dr. Youngstein had not already left for the Yacht Club when Mrs. Lesion reached him."

"If what you want from me is sympathy, that is impossible," Gene said.

"What I want from you is immediate repayment of the three thousand four hundred dollars you owe for the sandwiches."

"Also impossible."

"Either you pay it before the close of the business day or I will get a court order confiscating every single crate of dinner plates in your apartment."

"You would grab a million dollars' worth of dinner plates to settle a thirty-five-hundred-dollar debt?"

"By the time that market closes today I'll be lucky if those plates are worth fifty cents." Dr. Lesion slammed the phone down. Gene slid out of his chair and lay down on his back on the floor directly next to his desk.

Three

While she was settling her stepmother in bed in a private room at the French Hospital, Athena was desperate to talk to her father alone. But, when she got back to his room, she found that since Zeus had written GREEK in the religion spaces on the thirty-one forms he had been required to fill in before admission, the Archmandrite's office had been informed as a matter of course, the information routed to the local parish, and a young Greek Orthodox priest had been dispatched to comfort Zeus.

"I don't know what you are talking about," her father was saying as she came into the room. "What does Moscow or Constantinople got to do with Greek Orthodox? We believe in the living pantheon at Parnassus. And that's it."

"Parnassus?" the young curate asked blankly.

Athena guided the priest out into the hall, asked him to accept ten dollars for the poor and to realize that her father was recovering from shock. When she got back Zeus was up, looking for his trousers and his aegis. "I've got to get out of here before Hera comes back," he said nervously. "How did she find me? Who told her?"

"The Heavenly Host."

"Well—how about that?"

"Poppa, I am talking about the whole Commission. Officially."

"But why? Give me one reason why they would do such a horrible thing?"

"Poppa, that angel, Justin Case, your friend, has disappeared. They know he is with Aphrodite but they can't find him. They are panicking. I warned you not to interfere in this thing, Poppa."

"They can't find one of their own people in New York but they can find my wife in Greece."

"The angel won't answer any calls they are sending out and they are sending out like crazy."

"He probably can't hear Aphrodite in the same bed with him. She probably has his whole head enveloped."

"They need him badly, Poppa. Telling Hera where you were was just a warning to convince you to send him in."

"A *warning?*"

"They didn't tell her anything yet. They only said you needed her, but they didn't say anything about you-know-who."

"They didn't tell?" His whole face lighted up. "Well! That was very friendly. What time is it?"

"Ten seventeen."

"I'll handle Case. You spread the word that we're changing headquarters to Popina Matsoukis on East 18th Street off First Avenue. And—I don't need to say it—don't tell Hera. Send Herakles over to the Thessaly to bring all the cushions, the hi-fi, the water pipes, and the halvah. Tell Mastrogeonocholis there I am sorry but—" Zeus shrugged "I'll send him a little something by Praxiteles."

o

The telephone on Gene's desk buzzed. Miss Pimbernel announced Mr. Palmer Mahan in the outer office. As Gene whirled in his chair to face the door, Mahan was already in, sneering. He swaggered to the rocking chair across from Gene and settled himself in.

"I have come for my aluminum case, if you please, Mr. Quebaro," he said, in the English manner.

"You have, have you, you one-balled, two-faced supercilious son of a bitch?" Gene answered, in the American style.

"Yaaaasss." Mahan drew the word out like a long, reedy oboe note.

"You left the key in it."

"Yaaasss."

"Therefore I opened the case."

"You shouldn't have, you know."

"As an officer of the court, I was duty-bound to ascertain whether the case held anything illegal, dangerous, or contraband."

"And what did you find, pray?"

"One million dollars."

"Give me the case, please."

"I don't have an office safe. We have wooden doors, no burglar alarms. I had refused to hold the case for you. You trapped me with the case and its contents and I had to protect it."

"Then fetch it from wherever you put it, please."

"You'll have to wait."

"*Wait?*" Mahan had transformed the oboe into a cavalry bugle.

"It could take a few days."

"Out of the question." Mahan was stalling, drawing time out and tying it into intricate daisy chains, and every minute that adorned those chains gave his people who were trading for him on the floor of the plate exchange more opportunity to drive the market down, down, and down. Time was all he needed, so he pretended graciousness. "But I am no monster," he lied. "Either you return the case and its contents within twenty-four hours or you will be arrested, charged, and disbarred."

"You'll have to be a damned sight less monstrous than that," Gene said, faint with apprehension. "The plate exchange is a highly regulated business with red tape and new rules accumulating every year. To protect your money, I invested it in the plate market."

"You—invested—*my*—money—in—*crock*ery?"

"Yes, and my broker, like every other, has a compliance department whose sole function is to supervise and supplement the regulations of the Plate Exchange Commission, the exchange itself, and the NADPB—the National Association of Dinner Plate Brokers. If I were to sell out at this instant and be able to send in all the plates I hold in good delivery form, you couldn't have the money in less than five days."

"Five days?" Mahan said creamily. "I see. Yas."

"I'm sorry, Mahan, but that's the way it works. Those are the rules which any court of law will uphold."

Mahan rose. "Very well. Five days, my friend." He giggled madly. "Try it on for any longer and you'll be disbarred." He whinnied with pleasure; then he turned and sauntered out of the office.

Gene buzzed for Miss Pimbernel. When she came in he said, "Why should that son of a bitch be so cooperative?" he asked rhetorically. "And why should he be so goddam delighted that he has to wait five days to get his money back?"

"He framed you once before, didn't he?" Miss Pimbernel asked. "An absolute stranger came in here, left a million dollars, then pulled the phony receipt dodge on you, didn't he?"

"What do you mean? What? What are you saying?"

"Obviously he has an even bigger double-cross up his sleeve."

"Why? *Why? WHY?*"

"Mr. Quebaro, does it make the slightest difference right now *why* he is doing it, if he is actually doing it?"

"Doing *what*, Miss Pimbernel?"

"Using the five days you gave him on a silver platter to force the plate market prices to plummet lower than they have ever fallen before until you will owe him the greater part of that million dollars and be *utterly* in his power."

Gene's legs gave way. He crumpled to the floor. He lay on his back, staring vacantly at the ceiling.

171

Four

Justin and Aphrodite, a lattice of flesh, were locked like a double granny knot and twisted into a bowline on a bed in a sun-filled hotel room that towered over Brooklyn Heights as it faced the 900,000 glittering glass teeth of the buildings of lower Manhattan. No mortals could ever have achieved the inextricable position of sexual dynamics into which they had worked themselves. But that is just as well. Had any two mortals been capable of so doing they would have perished from the resultant ecstasy. Aphrodite, the most experienced copulatrice in the short pre-history before the present coupling series, was dazed, amazed, and tearfully grateful to have found such a friend as Justin. He, altogether new at this sort of thing, had proved to be a quick and ready learner. They had been at it without halt for fifteen and one-quarter hours. Aphrodite, who had begun to keep score after her forty-seventh full orgasm, had achieved 1,203 more. With ineffable pleasure and an only inconsequential number of blackouts, Justin had been clocked for 196 ejaculations. The ultimate position into which they had worked themselves could have called for a total rewriting (even massive burning) of all sex manuals from *The Perfumed Garden of Shaykh Nefzawi* to Dr. Reuben's *Everything You Always Wanted to Know About Sex but Were Afraid to Ask.*

If he could have learned how to achieve that position, any Boy Scout could have ruled the world. It is just as well, therefore, that the only eyes to witness this degree of co-convolution were those of Hermes, himself a god. Hermes had been sent by Zeus. After knocking at the door to show his sister minimum courtesy, he picked the lock and entered the room. Working with enormous patience and a watchmaker's concentration, he succeeded in untying the two in thirty-eight minutes. He knelt beside Justin's ear as soon as he could find it. "Now hear this," he said. Justin tried to lift his head as Hermes filled him in. It fell back, but his eyes stayed open. Gradually, they began to focus. At last, they registered alarm. When Hermes finished the run-down on the Plate Market panic, he explained to Justin that, unless Miss Saxe-Coburg could establish kidnapping, the angel would be tried for desertion by Liederkranz Hall.

"De*ser*tion? I am here on orders!"

"Don't try to talk! Get dressed and run." He helped Justin to his feet. He half-carried him to the bathroom and held him under a cold shower. Somehow, he got Justin dressed.

"Baby, baby, *baby!*" Aphrodite moaned pitiably from the furrowed bed. "Where are you? Mama needs you. Climb back on Mama, baby." Justin tottered to the bedside and knelt at her head.

"I have to go," he said. "I will never forget you."

*"Go? For*get?*"*

Hermes pulled at Justin's arm. "Come on, kid," he said.

Aphrodite grabbed at Justin. "Where are you going? You *can't* go. Are you crazy? We are in *love,* lover!"

"Wait for me, Doris," he pleaded. "Wait for me."

*"Dor*is? I'm not Doris."

"You're not Doris?" His bewilderment was abject.

"How can you call me Doris after what we've meant to each other?"

Horror filled Justin's eyes. "You are not Mrs. Eugene Quebaro?"

"Are you deliberately trying to break my *heart?*"

Justin fled the room.

o

When Justin burst into the Quebaro outer office, Miss Pimbernel handed him a note which he read quickly. It said: NIXONVISION CAMERAS LOST YOU ALL NIGHT SAXE-COBURG COVERING YOU. Case ate the note, nodding and saying, "Taag mif vin to Qilborgo." He swallowed the paper.

"He's on the phone with his plate broker."

Gene was listening with fright as John Kullers explained market conditions. "They are dumping very great plates cheaply on the San Antonio, East Orange, Pasadena, and St. Petersburg exchanges. No one can find out who is behind it. Panic is building. It could be worse than Black Friday, which led to Dish Nights in the movie houses from coast to coast in the thirties."

"What can be done to stop it?"

"The only thing that can stop it is if someone could go onto the floor of the exchange and offer even greater plates at higher but moderate prices which would begin a supply and demand cycle to get magnificent plates which had never been seen on the market ever before. But that is out of the question, because such plates simply do not exist."

"How much is the market down?"

"Twenty-seven per cent and falling. Your own investment is off two hundred and seventy thousand dollars. The Narodny Bank of Russia and the full Big Six of the Japanese Zaibatsu have combined with the Arab world and have gone Bear."

Gene hung up. He could not stand any more. Miss Pimbernel came in. "Will you see a Mr. Case?" she asked.

"No thanks, Charlotte," he said. "I am thinking of killing myself."

She pulled him off the floor by his necktie and shoved him into his desk chair. "We will have no more talk like that, Mr. Quebaro," she said. "You will straighten up—*now*. This man may be an important client." She hauled off and whacked him across the left cheek with the fullest force of her open palm. Gene took a deep breath, then exhaled. "Send him in, please," he said.

Case, a strangely pale and emptily transparent-looking young man, entered. They shook hands. Gene seated him. "I have been sent to you by Judge Zeuss of the municipal court. He is a friend of your wife's, I believe. He recommends you as *THE* authority on Dinner Plate law."

"He *does?*"

"I will be brief and to the point because our nation faces disaster. The life savings and holdings of millions of people face total wipe-out unless plate prices are forced up again and that market is stabilized."

"It can't be done," Gene said hopelessly.

"It can be done. The patriotic syndicate which I head has stockpiled hundreds of thousands of the most spectacularly valuable dinnerware ever seen. All from hidden private collections. We have plates by Michelangelo —I speak of *signed* plates—by Joseph Mallord William Turner, Rembrandt, James Richard Blake, and Van Dyck. We have the contents of the Vatican and the Hermitage museums on signed, hand-baked plates in fantastically limited editions. We have original birthday card designs that Winston Churchill did for the Buddha's Birthday Card line of the Ah Fong Trading Company of Singapore and we are asking you to take charge of trading these plates on the floor of the New York exchange, to make those plate prices find their true value again across the entire market and to restore America and the world to an even keel."

"In what quantities do these plates exist?" Gene asked, on fire with excitement.

"Perhaps three hundred thousand plates. The pool represents two hundred million dollars' worth of plates."

"I would have to see some of them."

"Of course. But after that, man, you've got to act." One by one, Justin took plates out of the large black box he had been carrying. Each plate was more magnificent than the one before.

"I have never *seen* such plates!" Gene's voice was shaking. "I never knew such plates could exist!"

Justin handed him the warehouse invoices.

"Every plate we own is now in your hands, sir. For the greater good of our country. But my group must remain anonymous. If there is any credit to be given, you must take it. If there is to be blame, it must be yours."

"I accept that challenge," Gene said simply.

Five

Zeus refused to ride across town with Athena. "I have to think. This is a terrible time for me. I am in love."

Athena did not smile or chide her father for acting the youth because she had seen that simple declaration lead to dozens of wars and tens of thousands of deaths. She knew it would be best if Zeus wore out his brooding by walking and worrying. But, when he finally reached the Popina Matsoukis all the way across town, he had worked himself up into a rage at the Angels for informing on him to Hera, imperiling the great love of his life with Doris. He stalked into the Popina, ignoring all greetings. He summoned Athena to his private rooms.

"I have made up my mind," he said with steel in his voice. Athena shut the door hurriedly.

"Think nice, Poppa," she said. "It's better."

"I am not going to hold still for this kind of treatment from a bunch of Sumerian cultists and holdovers from Mohenjo-Daro."

"Poppa, please! We are on camera."

"Not in here we aren't. I had Matsoukis line these walls with Dacron and olive paste in a cork chip mix. Their goddam NixonVision doesn't work in here."

"But you aren't supposed to have anything to *do* with this! You initialed the treaty! You can be sent by it to Olympus. We all agreed. You can only get into trouble."

He snorted like a stallion. "I am Zeus!" he thundered. "I *make* trouble!" He lifted his aegis over his head and shook it and the resultant electrical storms and flash floods caused four million dollars' worth of property damage from Dover, New Jersey, to Far Rockaway. "Which one of them is the most obnoxious?"

"The one called Palmer Mahan, I think."

"Which faction is he?"

"Hell, I think."

Zeus had gone very red in the face. "Seventeen thousand two hundred women have been proud to bear my children," he said, "and now those angle-shooters have to snitch to the only woman I ever married." His pitch soared. "They must pay! They must be taught a lesson they will never forget! I command that Aphrodite's little boy, Eros, will now shoot one of his arrows into Palmer Mahan's heart to produce an irresistible passion for Eris, the ugliest female I can think of in all the corridors of time—Eris, my own goddess of strife and discord! What a wife she will make for him! I command that Eris will refuse all ardent pleas by and from that rotten minion of Hell unless he marries her in one of the lung fish churches. Let them record *that* with their NixonVision cameras." He stamped to the house phone to issue his terrible orders. Then he commanded that his Mobile Luncheon Facility be made ready.

○

Eris, an unrelievedly sickening-looking creature, was dressed in rose corduroy rompers, with yellow suede Space Shoes and positioned in front of the 72nd Street exit to Fifth Avenue of Fortress Midtown so that Palmer Mahan could not, no matter how he tried, avoid looking at her when he left the building to direct the dumping operations at the plate exchange that morning. Each day was a new operation to the traders he used on the floor of the Plate Exchange. They depended on him to deliver the invoices of the plates he wished sold that day. Today was the second day of Mahan's planned market debacle.

As he came through the building exit, the wave of rupturing nausea that flooded him as he looked at Eris suddenly changed to an unredeemable emanation of heart-filling, ineradicably sentimental love for her as four candy arrows of Eros (three for good measure by Zeus's command so that they could have a total effect upon Mahan's evil heart) pierced his thorax and entered his ventricles. The arrows, made of re-stressed cotton candy, had been marinated in a mixture of the juices of the red Nigerian serendipity berry (Dioscoreophyllum cumminsii), Sicilian marzipan of the Taormina region, and a chemical solution of 1-n-propoxy-2-amino-4-nitrobenzene, making them the sweetest beyond intolerable sweetness. Mahan never had a chance. He fell instantaneously, irretrievably, hopelessly, utterly and forever in love with Eris. His mind emptied of everything but her. She allowed him one little kiss *(gaaaaacckkk)* to seal his doom, then crossed her legs with a snap, crackle and pop. He promised her the world and bottles of Arpège but she held out for a simple gold wedding band. After he had begged, wept, and pleaded, they were married that morning in the fashionable Anglican church at 71st Street and Madison Avenue. The bride wore white cheesecloth, black Space Shoes and carried one dozen calla lilies. She looked disgusting. She had a bad drool tik. The groom glowed with the *sacré feu* of love and need which seemed to burn through the lenses of the NixonVision cameras.

The brute force of the shock waves that hit the convention at Liederkranz Hall could not be measured. The Upper House merely recoiled in horror at a fallen angel of Mahan's caste choosing to marry a pagan monster in a religious ceremony under the sanctified roof of an overwhelmingly fashionable church. But the shock wave that rocked the spacelessness as far out as Alpha Cygni (Deneb) was the reaction of The Adversary™ himself. His rage over the contemptuous defilement of his *amour propre* had him ready to make a cinder out of the sun that warmed the planet that held the church that had disgraced him by consenting to marry his servant. Indeed, The Adversary™ found himself simply incapable of believing what had happened. He insisted upon replay after replay, then screamed louder than the echo of an honest man's death when fullest understanding came unto him. He plucked Palmer Mahan out of that church at 71st and Madison and flung him outward further across the firmament than has ever been measured.

o

Phyllis Stein↓ was still serving her suspended sentence in outer space. Alice Trudy Kehoe↑ was still in the Midtown Hospital. Justin Case↑ was suffering house arrest on Callisto, in lieu of punishment. Haurus↓ was *haurus de combat*. Af↑ was totally baffled. The only field agent he and Miss Saxe-Coburg↓↑ had left to run was Charlotte Pimbernel, a semi-mortal lung fish-retread who was now required to represent both Heaven and Hell in the projected field study. The bear raid on the plate exchange was totally defeated, now that Eugene Quebaro had mounted his massive bull operation (with no chance of continuing opposition). Without being in the slightest way aware of it, Zeus had saved the international plate market and had made Eugene Quebaro into an American money hero.

Six

Warmed to the cockles of his heart by the wondrous gratification of his revenge, Zeus rode serenely uptown in his Mobile Luncheon Facility, munching on Armenian tzitayough derevaoatat, delicious stuffed grape leaves, and sipping a red Turkish Feltu '59. He dismissed everything from his mind except how to win Doris back.

Although there were more than thirty-six exits from Rockefeller Center, it so happened that when Doris chose one of these at random as she left the building for lunch that day, Judge Zeuss was waiting on the pavement with an adhesive plaster across the bridge of his nose.

"Don't you dare come near me!" she cried the instant she saw him approaching her.

"I am a judge," he said abjectly. "I am a man. I demand the right to an explanation."

"Anyone who thinks he can explain what you did to me is criminally insane," she said hotly.

"If you do not accept my explanation—for any reason—I will go away and you will never see me again."

Doris wavered. He took her hands. He fondled the inside of her wrists with the fleshy pads of his long fingers. "I can renew your faith in us," he crooned. "I can show you, in a few tragic sentences, an injustice which almost cost us everything."

"All right. Then tell me."

"Not here."

"I am not going to that Eighth Avenue restaurant."

"No, no. In my Mobile Luncheon Facility." He waved to the formidable landyacht, more enormous than

181

the largest house-moving van, itself drawn by a large truck. He led her across the pavement. He pressed an invisible button. A door slid open. Retractable steps untracted. She stepped daintily upward and entered the Facility, Zeus directly behind her, staring at her bottom with rolling eyes. As she crossed the threshold she was in a dining room with a round, highly polished rosewood table which held a sparkling service for two. Wine was chilling in a silver bucket. Many vegetables exposed their garish sexual organs called flowers, scenting the air deliciously. Hung on the walls of the Facility were Van Gogh's "The Olive Pickers" and Douanier Rousseau's "Tropic Zone," which the Metropolitan Museum had been persuaded to sell. From somewhere above came Scott Joplin's alluring rag "The Easy Winners," its joyous beat matching the increasing thlocking of Doris's clitoris.

As the Facility moved up the Avenue of the Americas, she and Zeus were standing in a domed, oval room whose baroque effect was altogether dazzling; whose ceiling was supported by four pillars of Apuanian marble. Painted across the dome was the figure and the course of the classical huntsman as he set out for the chase. All of it, including the mirrored walls, was set off by superb rococo woodwork and elegant frescoes.

"My God!" Doris exclaimed.

Zeus bowed his reflexive acknowledgment.

"This must have cost a fortune!" Doris said.

Zeus shrugged. "One must lunch," he said simply. "And one does get crumpled in restaurants."

"You use this only for lunch?"

"It is pleasant to drive around the edges of Manhattan Island—as we shall do today—sipping good wine and nibbling—on delicious food. Please. Come this way. As a native-born American you must see this room." He guided her to a doorway. She stared in at the perfect bedroom, which had a full-length four-poster double bed with a great chest studded with brass nails at its foot. "This is a replica of the Mother's Room at Stratford Hall where Robert E. Lee was born," he said. "I am a Civil War buff."

Doris moaned.

182

"And I thought I should have a bedroom aboard in case anyone got sleepy after the wine."

Doris yawned widely. Then, all at once, she remembered how this man had affronted her. "We seem to have overlooked your explanation," she said coldly.

"My darling girl." His eyes held enormous pain. "My wife is a homicidal maniac whom we have had to keep institutionalized for many years. Somehow, she escaped from her wet pack yesterday, and when I saw her out there, standing in front of that restaurant with madness in her eyes, I was swept by only one consideration—to protect you."

"Judge Zeuss!"

"You are the only thing which has any meaning to me. You are the only birdsong of wonderment in my sad, suffering life. I flung you to the floor of that car to prevent your assassination even though it might have meant my own."

"Darling!" Doris outcried rapturously. "Life must have been a living hell for you."

"Rather, say it has been a living hell for her. Out of loyalty, a precious quality, I have to stand by."

With a sob of joy, Doris stepped toward him and held up her trembling mouth. He downzipped the front of his trousers and took her in his arms, his right hand moving like a SAM missile under her dress, just as a U.S. Mail truck driven by a temporary named James Nolan, who was, unfortunately, not sober, smashed into the side of the Facility as it was crossing 57th Street at Tenth Avenue.

By the time Doris and Judge Zeuss were able to drag themselves out through the badly damaged vehicle, neither was any more interested in sex than a calendar is interested in a light-year.

Seven

Harvey Zendt, a religious affairs analyst for the soybean industry, worked at home. He was sifting through a dietary peculiarity of Jacob Amman's when he leaned backward, away from his IBM MC-82 electronic typewriter, seeking new creative thrust. He was staring at the ceiling of his flat in Fortress East. Without pause, he screamed for his wife Rita and ran toward her out of the room.

"What is it? My God, Harvey, what is it?"

"Take a look at the ceiling. In my room." He grabbed her as she started in. "No! The hell with it. Come on. We'll just get the hell out of here."

"Let me see it!" She ran into his workroom. He heard her outcry.

"It's bulging," he said.

She came running back. "Bulging? It's drooping. Harvey! Quick! Call Boatie Bergquist in the Building Office. I'll get your manuscript and the canary."

Harvey lunged at the phone. He dialed three digits with fumbling fingers. "Gimme the manager," he barked into the phone. "Miss Bergquist? This is Zendt in 51BZ4G5. Yeah. Now don't get talking because I am going to say it once then we are going to run the hell out of here. The ceiling right over my head is bulging downward. Yeah. Yeah. Right above in 52BZ4G5. I'll leave the door open." He grabbed the canary cage as his wife went racing past and they left, flat-out.

Laura "Boatie" Bergquist, building unit manager and three times winner of the Anne Knauerhase Fortress Award for General Excellence, took less than five

184

minutes to get to the Zendt apartment. She took one long, considering look at the ceiling, which was now bulging like a fanny in a hammock, then bolted for the telephone on the BZ line of elevators. She called her office, her voice harsh and rapid. "Put ever' gol-durned soul you know on our phones an' call ever'body in the BZ line," she said. "An' check their names off as you call 'em so's you don't miss a one. When you call all them folks you start off to callin' ever family on either side of the BZ line, you hear? An' you better send up some wheelchairs for old Mr. O'Connell an' people like that. Now you tell all them folks that this section of the buildin' is in danger of immediate collapse and I'll call you back at this number in ten minutes. So keep this one line clear after you notify Miss Fortress."

She hung up. She pressed the elevator button for floor fifty-two. When the door opened, she leaped out with master keys in her hand. She opened the door to the Quebaro flat, took one look inside, turned, and fled into the elevator, punching the button for the main floor and telephoning Police Emergency as she did. She asked for disaster footing, which meant every ambulance available in the region and all fire-fighting equipment and His Honor, the Mayor. As she rushed out of the elevator on the main floor she brushed past Dr. Norman Lesion and a New York County Sheriff, who entered the car and pushed the fifty-second-floor button.

"Hey! No! Wait!" Miss Bergquist yelled as the doors were closing. She sprinted across the lobby to her office. On the way she stopped a Pinkerton special and ordered him to keep anyone, no matter who, even Anne Knauerhase Fortress herself, from entering any elevator in the BZ line. She raced into her office yelling, "Who the hell lives in 52BZ4G5?" Her secretary spun a large circular file. "Nobody lives there. It isn't even on our records."

"Sumbitch!" Miss Bergquist shouted. "Some smart-ass found it was empty and figured he'd use it as a free storehouse. Are those goddam tenants responding? Are they gettin' out?"

"They're moving like red-ass birds," a fat lady answered from one of the nine telephones in use.

"You tell Miss Anne Knauerhase Fortress?"

"She said not to bother her again until the building started to go."

There was the chaotic sound of police cars, emergency trucks, ambulances, and fire engines arriving at the 49th Street entrance. Boatie Bergquist ran to meet them. She stopped a burly police captain wearing a shiny black rubber coat and a steel helmet as he ran into the lobby followed by two cops and a fire lieutenant, all of them geared out with ropes, poles, and axes. The lobby was almost filled with tenants who were disgorging from the seven-car elevator bank, everyone talking at once with excitement and fear. Everyone was carrying a precious possession; some of them extremely embarrassing.

"Get them out of here!" the police captain bellowed. "Clear out this goddam lobby." Up ahead of him Miss Bergquist gestured frantically, then ran. All police and the fire lieutenant followed her. Somehow they all packed into the BZ line service elevator and, out of the masses of rubber coats, MACE cans, and gray sweaters, Boatie's hand snaked out to press the button for the fifty-second floor. She explained on the way up. They were all brave men. They clomped out of the car at the fifty-second floor, behind Miss Bergquist. They collided with Dr. Lesion, who was fiddling with keys at the lock on the door of 52BZ4G5.

"This is the *place*, fercrissake!" Miss Bergquist yelled at the cops.

"Show them the Writ," Dr. Lesion said to the Sheriff calmly. The police captain slammed them both out of the way to allow Boatie to open the door with her master key. She swung the door open gingerly, holding the others back from putting their weight over the threshold. The crates seemed to be a painting of boxes which were being pulled downward into a deep whirlpool.

"Holy Jesus! What's that?" the fire lieutenant said.

"Those are my extremely valuable plates," Dr. Lesion said. "My personal property."

"Arrest this son of a bitch," the Captain ordered. "Come on. On the double. Get the hell out of here."

They sprinted along the corridor to the service lift, dragging Dr. Lesion behind them.

The official party spilled out into the street floor lobby, which was now even more densely crowded with adults and children in every stage of dress. The police captain snatched an electric bull horn from the hands of an Emergency cop and brayed through it, ordering everyone out onto the streets as far west as Lexington Avenue. "This part of this building is going to collapse," he said, "and when it goes it's going to take a lot of the adjacent architecture with it." The people got out of the building quietly enough. Outside, a gauntlet of police and firemen passed them across and far up into 49th Street.

Thirty-eight minutes later, at 3:18 P.M., the floor under Apartment 52BZ4G5 gave way and just over two tons of crates crashed eight feet three inches to the floor below. One million dollars' worth of rare and extraordinary dinner plates, described later in reports by Federal, State, and Municipal investigators as "crockery" or "resembling crockery," plunged downward, as if descending steps, at a gradually accelerated pace, floor by floor, taking with them as they descended: pianos, washing machines, bidets, hair dryers, billiard tables, rowing machines, television sets, dolls' houses, electronic sex devices, light and heavy furniture, large steel safes, illimitable clothing, countless books and phonograph records, bottles of all known sizes of wine, whiskey, seconal, cantharides and methadrine, jewels, canned goods, carpets, money, dildoes, cellos, bales of marijuana, air conditioners, stoves, shotguns, movie projectors, photo albums, cosmetic jars, beer cans, and refrigerators; through floor after floor, until, at seven floors below the Quebaro apartment, the combined, terrible weight stress began to widen the base of the building collapse to begin bringing down apartments in the AZ and CZ lines on either side of it so that, when all parts of the fifty-two storeys crashed into the basement level, the Quebaro apartment was the least altered, the debris from the fallen building units choked Third Avenue to the level of nine storeys and 48th, 49th and 50th Streets, almost to Lexington Avenue, were choked with it, filling lovely Dag Engelson Plaza with rubble the way lava had smothered Pompeii. A total of six and a half linear blocks of Fortress East itself was in a ruin which could have been duplicated only by a hydrogen bombing. Ninety-one thousand people were homeless in a city known throughout the world to have no available housing. All their clothing and furniture and most of their worldly possessions were gone but, miraculously, not one tenant, not one pass-erby, not one neighboring resident, not one policeman or fireman was hurt—thanks to the intelligence and courage of Laura "Boatie" Bergquist. The Mayor ordered that new, all-steel garbage scows be washed down and refurbished and two circus tents pitched on each of them. These were an-chored in a long file in the East River, approximately oppo-site the vanished AZ through CZ lines of Fortress East so that none of the people had to suffer the social shock of being required to live on the West Side. Boatie Bergquist, nicknamed "The Gallant Superintendent" by the world press, was subsequently awarded a Congressional Medal of Honor and was kissed with inordinate passion by a Metho-dist bishop for the lives she had saved by her unselfishly courageous actions. Insurance company estimates put prop-erty losses at "over seventy-one million dollars" but there were the outcomes of sixteen thousand tenant family civil suits still to be faced.

o

N'Zuriel Yhwh pushed the FREEZE button on the arm of his chair at Liederkranz Hall exhaustedly. Wit-nessing so many details of motivation and happenstance of the Fortress East disaster had taken a lot out of the Joint(⅄) Commission. The action on the giant NixonVision screen was frozen at the scene of the disaster. The lights went up in the hall.

"Now, please," N'Zuriel Yhwh said, mopping his forehead with a linen handkerchief, "we will review this. This, I mean all this we have just seen and suffered, must be significant. A man buys a few thousand dinner plates be-cause altogether he doesn't have any confidence in the money of his country and besides his greed has developed massively at the first scent of profit. The dinner plates weigh so much, and are so unwieldy, that they crash through the floor, ruin five entire buildings, make tens of thousands of people move from luxury to garbage scows and cause a loss, so far, of about seventy million dollars. I know that part is right so don't interrupt me. We had nothing to do with it. The bear raid on the market had nothing to do with it. When Palmer Mahan left the million dollars in this nudnick's office, neither he nor anyone else had any idea that the dufflehead was going to quick use the whole thing, every last cent, to buy crockery. The fact is: have we chosen the right man here for our field study tests? An even worse question: would it have made any difference which man we chose for the tests? This man, Eugene Quebaro, seems to me to be just a tiny bit more than useless to us. Money has got to have another side except the Quebaro side. Can I have some kind of a tentative report on this?"

Raziel summoned Miss Saxe-Coburg to reply to N'Zuriel Yhwh. "We all realize," she began, "that it *seems* as though Mr. Quebaro is a failure as a field study subject, but the selection, by Raziel, of Mr. Quebaro's former wife and long-time supervisor as a *combined* field study team just all rolled up into one, that is, representing both our Upper↑ and Lower↓ teams, is going to have a marked effect on real revelations about the meaning of money throughout the rest of this project."

"What can she do that is so special?" N'Zuriel Yhwh asked.

"Well, she has a power over him that no one else in all time has ever had over anyone. She loves him more than anyone has been loved since the lung fish walked out of the oceans—and before that. Our own Aura Tests show that she is hopelessly, helplessly, willfully, and determinedly more in love with this man, with whom she had been combined on Level One to create the greatest Salesman-Merchandiser force ever known to the insurance industry, than has ever before seemed possible, within emotional indices, for the human species. Allow them to work together, throw them together on this single field study problem, and—in time, because the male human is far dimmer about these things—you will awaken the latent reciprocal emotions

189

which are now dormant in Quebaro as she runs him through his paces into which she had previously trained him. She simply cannot be stopped. She will deliver the goods far more efficiently and securely than any emissary of Heaven or of Hell. In fact, she is already both of these and more. That is what the love of women like this is all about."

"I like it and I don't like it," N'Zuriel Yhwh said.

"Personally, I like it," Dagon interrupted.

"What is it that you don't like about it, sir?" Miss Saxe-Coburg asked N'Zuriel Yhwh.

"What about Quebaro's wife?"

"That is a problem, isn't it, sir?"

"Are you telling me that we, the Heavenly Host, are going to break up a marriage between two young people?"

"If the marriage is broken up, sir," Miss Saxe-Coburg said, "and I see no reason it should be, then we should bring ourselves to see the breakup as part of the money study *in extensis* as it were, as if the marriage were a casualty in their own war for money and, in that sense, one more fact unit in our research. I would say, essentially, that such stresses are a part of our studies here, aren't they, sir? And we *are* here on a *money* study, sir, aren't we? We have not assembled this enormously prestigious deliberative body to gossip or even to judge the private affairs of two young people, have we, sir?"

"All right, arreddy," N'Zuriel Yhwh said irritably. "But we expect razzults, you understand? I'm busy. Give us what we got to see and we'll keep funding your program." He pressed the ACTION button and the picture on the giant NixonVision screen became animate again.

Eight

At his arraignment before the Grand Jury, the
dazed, deeply shocked Dr. Lesion admitted that the contents
of the crates which had caused the Fortress East disaster
were his property. He was tried within two days of the disaster and sentenced to thirty years at hard labor with no time
off for good behavior; a severe sentence for a man of his age
with a wife and six East Indian dermatologists to support. To
prevent his being torn limb from limb by the angry mob, he
was spirited away to an unknown prison at the dead of night.
His family lost track of him.

Doris rallied round her mother. She had been
transformed by guilt over what she had almost done with
Judge Zeuss into an attentive and wonderfully considerate
daughter. Besides, her mother had a lovely flat at Fortress
Midtown and Doris had no place to go because she had not
been able to bring herself to speak to Gene to find out how
he was managing to live, since he had caused the doctor's
terrible conviction.

Mr. Violente was still in the Tombs. Doris
had explained to his Caporegima, now standing in as operating head of the family, about the doctor and her mother, and
she had secured an indefinite leave of absence, at least until
Mr. Violente could be sprung.

Doris moved in with her mother. They ate
two meals a day at the doctor's delicatessen. She could have
had all the free dermatology she wanted also, her mother
said, because the doctor was away, if she needed any, which
she did not. Mrs. Lesion was badly confused, mostly from
overeating because she did not have the doctor there as a
brake to keep the check down. As far as she was concerned,

her husband had just disappeared, then she had gotten a flash of him on the six o'clock news, when he had disappeared again. "How did he get on television, dear?" she asked Doris pitiably. "I didn't even know he knew Walter Cronkite. Where has he gone? He never does this. If he was ever on television before, he never told me, and that isn't like the doctor, dear."

During this first week or so, while Gene was striding toward greatness by his salvation of the American plate (as we know it), Mr. Kullers, his broker, had arranged to have him put up at the Hotel Piedmont on East 56th Street. During the doctor's lightning trial Gene and Doris had spoken on the telephone, trying to piece the whole story together. Gene said, please, she was not to worry, to leave everything in his hands, which was why people were so glad to have a lawyer in the family.

However, the Fortress East disaster had become such a national matter that the President had taken an interest in it and had ordered an invisible seal to cover the entire Lesion trial. Gene was, therefore, unable to get any information concerning whether Dr. Lesion had, in fact, actually been sentenced, where he had been imprisoned or, if he had not been sentenced, where he had disappeared to.

Naturally, since there were still some sixty-nine blocks of Fortress East still standing, as healthy as ever, Gene was able to keep calling the main management office for information but he was turned away as some kind of crank when he tried to identify himself as the head of the family which had been occupying Apartment 52BZ4G5. He was forced by circumstance to brush the whole thing aside anyway. Truly he had had hardly a moment to think since Justin Case appeared at his office with the bottomless supply of good dinner plates. Beginning at just after three thirty peeyem of the day Case had retained him, when all invoices, inventories, and descriptions of the Case Syndicate plate stocks had been wholly organized, Gene had gone forward into action. Eugene Quebaro, an unknown New York lawyer, had waded into public panic and emerged with the national salvation in his pocket, as one of the American Titans. It was a four-day battle against no opposition and he won. During

192

the nights, high in his aerie at the Hotel Piedmont, while the ordinaries slept and dreamed their tiny dreams, Quebaro was hardly ever off television: live and replays. His secretary, Charlotte Pimbernel, had moved into the hotel, although discreetly not on the same floor, to be on instant call. She and Gene had settled in to work sixteen-hour days. She was his assistant, his soul, his secretary, his courage, his buffer, and his brain. More than once he interrupted the awful significance of his work to stare at her oddly and say, "You have a good—uh—mind, Miss Pimbernel." He felt safe with her, a condition great men frequently find hard to attain, he explained. He felt as if he had known her.

He asked her, once, about her background. She said, "Oh, just a general beegee, Mr. Quebaro. I was a steeplejack for awhile. I spent some time as an agent in British counter-intelligence. I ran a rather good Mexican restaurant in London called The Mexican Stove. I played billiards professionally, and I was a bartender at the Hamburg Opera House."

"A good background."

"I was just trying things out to find out what I was meant to be."

"Did you find out?"

"Please go to bed, Mr. Quebaro. You are so tired. You have given *so* much and tomorrow will be another terrible day for you."

"It's no use, Miss Pimbernel. I can't sleep. An innocent man is in prison because of me."

"Won't you leave it in my hands?" She pleaded with him with her beautiful eyes, with her soft hands which only touched his elbows lightly, willing a current of safety and love to pour into him.

"What can you do?" It was not said scornfully, but hopelessly.

She drew herself to attention out of respect for the long line of Republican Presidents. "You have saved your country and have helped to make it great," she said simply. "And I happen to believe that our President, who has already shown, in spades, that gratitude is his longest suit, will be proud and happy to pardon—at your request—this simple dermatologist who has suffered enough." She eased him into a chair, then stood behind him gently massaging the back of his neck. He leaned into the sensuality of her hands and was released from tension.

When she had brushed his teeth and tucked him in, Charlotte telephoned Miss Saxe-Coburg and poured out her problem. Miss Saxe-Coburg said of course she would help, that Af would appear in a dream of Gene's and order him to call the White House as soon as the Dow peaked over a thousand for the Plate Market.

"Then Af will appear in the President's dream and order him to welcome the call and cooperate with it fully."

"Oh, thank you!" Charlotte breathed.

"Not at all. We did it for Mr. Nixon so you can be sure it works."

"So *that* is how Mr. Nixon arranged the pardon!" Charlotte cried as though an electric light bulb had just gone off in a balloon over her head. "No *wonder* the President appeared so baffled and confused!"

"I also think," Miss Saxe-Coburg continued, "that it will be perfectly safe to have the President order the prosecution of Palmer Mahan to pay for the Midtown East crime. Palmer is now two hundred thousand light years beyond Quasar 2C 05–34, thirteen million light years away from Earth, and he still has sixteen to twenty thousand light years to go—if one believes the oscillation theory of cosmology—because Lucifer™ has a magnificent pitching arm."

o

On the telephone with Gene the next day the habitually grateful President agreed instantly that Dr. Lesion must be freed from jail in the Aleutians where he had been placed in solitary under a "temporary" Defense Department name, and to turn the Federal forces of prosecution upon Palmer Mahan.

When, dazed, he hung up the telephone, Gene in his turn was so grateful that he wanted to kiss Miss Pimbernel "all over."

"All over?" she cried in a shocked tone.

"All over this wonderful service you have performed for my family," he said.

She turned him off. In her professional voice she reminded him calmly about *his* services, about the matter of fees and disbursements.

"Justin Case owes you a bundle, and by my way of figuring you should have a small fortune coming to you from the Association of American Plate Brokers. You saved their lives."

"Case owes me a fee, yes. But it would be unethical to ask any broker for a kickback."

"I'll get the bills out tonight."

"Thank you, Charlotte. The Case bill should be for five thousand dollars."

"*Five* thousand."

"That's right."

ŏ

Dr. Lesion was flown back from The Stockade on Attu Island blindfolded and lightly sedated so that he could not know where he had been. On landing, while the network TV crews waited outside the plane, he refused to read the grateful speech (prepared for him by Charlotte). He said he was going to spend every cent he had, if necessary, to put Eugene Quebaro behind bars. The MP Brigadier assigned to his security told him they'd fly him back north and throw him back into the goddam stockade unless he read the grateful speech. So Dr. Lesion agreed to cooperate. He had to be reunited with his waiting wife off-camera because she had hiccups from too much chopped chicken liver. On camera, with his beautiful stepdaughter, Mrs. Eugene Quebaro, he expressed his everlasting gratitude to the President for fighting his cause "when every man's hand was turned against me" but stoutly denied any guilt. The glow went out of his voice after that as he thanked "our country's savior, Eugene Quebaro, the man who saved the dollar and saved me."

o

At last Doris was free to go home to her mate. Forlornly, at six o'clock that evening she was let into the penthouse suite at the Hotel Piedmont listening to an assistant manager explain with pride that Mr. Quebaro was in Curva, Arizona, opening the largest supermarket in the free bloc.

Doris felt bleak and alone. This wasn't her home. In succession she: longed for her lost Australian artifacts; wondered what could have happened to Mr. Violente; resented Gene's adulation and national celebrity; then thought about Judge Zeuss. But she simply could not stand to think about him so she turned the radio up loud and wandered aimlessly all through the expensive luxury feeling as though she had been locked in the furniture department of some downtown store and struggling within her mind to try to imagine how Gene had become such a national hero that he was invited across a continent to open a supermarket.

He hadn't even bothered to leave a note for her, she thought self-pityingly. Her mother was depressing, but this was worse. She drifted to the thatched bar and made herself a Cointreau and Dr. Pepper, then lighted a joint from a box printed with greetings from the hotel management. She stared off into nothing at all.

Then the telephone rang.

Nine

Dear Miss Fortress:

As one American who must have had a great deal at stake during the perilous plate crisis, you will be appalled to learn, I know, that Eugene Quebaro, the man who saved the dollar, is now homeless due to the catastrophe at Fortress East. As the nearest acceptable (safe) residential neighborhood outside your housing developments is in Vermont, a long commute, he is in dire trouble. If he is needed in the crises to come, perhaps you, and America, will be in grave trouble as a consequence. I know you will want to help Mr. Quebaro find adequate housing. I am told of a sudden vacancy in flat 67J4BF1 at Fortress Midtown, formerly occupied by a Mr. Palmer Mahan who has fled the country. This six room unit would be most suitable for Mr. and Mrs. Quebaro's needs in that it is furnished. The FE disaster left him wholly without furniture.

Sincerely, Charlotte Pimbernel

o

Then Charlotte wrote to John Kullers suggesting that the APBA, and his own brokerage, reward Eugene Quebaro for the measure in which he had served and saved, causing a tremendous volume of buying and selling and literally saving the American plate as a sound investment for all tomorrows. She suggested an award to Mr. Quebaro that would be equal to fifty per cent of gross national plate brokerage commissions for the week during which Mr. Quebaro traded on the floor of the exchange.

197

o

TO: Justin Case
FROM: Eugene Quebaro

For Legal Services Rendered . . . $50,000.00
o

That was when N'Zuriel Yhwh punched the FREEZE button.

The lights came up in Liederkranz Hall. "What *is* this?" he asked loudly. "Didn't I distinctly hear Quebaro tell her to charge us five thousand dollars just a little while ago?"

"Well," Dagon said, "she didn't charge expenses."

"Just when I was really beginning to think this girl knew her stuff," N'Zuriel Yhwh said. "And she was the first one out of the whole bunch, and that includes our own people."

"Well, let me say this," Raziel put in. "Although I didn't think it was exactly the right time to talk about it, I am going to say that if it weren't for this former wife from the former life, our whole field study could have gone up the flue."

"Why?" N'Zuriel Yhwh demanded.

"Because this man Quebaro, on whom we wasted all this time—even if he did the best he could—well, the guy is simply not a self-starter."

"Raziel," N'Zuriel Yhwh said with some scorn, "let's not walk around the bush when a straight line between two points is what I was talking about. We have here a woman who has added forty-five thousand to a bill we happen to be stuck with." He pressed the HOLD button for Charlotte's screen. "Young, lady," the Executive Angel said, "tell me something. Your boss told you to bill Mr. Case for five thousand dollars. Correct?"

"Yes, sir."

"So—did your hand slip or something when you were typing out the bill? You wrote down *fifty* thousand."

"Mr. Quebaro doesn't know the first thing about fee structuring," Charlotte said. "He has hardly ever had a client worth more than a hundred dollars."

"But fifty thousand!"

"It should have been half a million. If you analyze the volume of trading he generated for the Case plates, just plain arithmetic would tell you that the fee should be at least five hundred thousand dollars. But if he were paid that, he wouldn't accept it because he is a twit about money."

"We won't pay!" N'Zuriel Yhwh shouted at the screen. "You can just forget it."

"You'll pay the fifty thousand," Charlotte said, "or you'll end up paying more."

"We made Quebaro a big hero with his people. For what we did for him—never mind that—that's not why we won't pay. We won't pay because he belongs to us. We brought him back to life so he owes us a couple of favors. Did you ever think where he'd be if we weren't trying to figure out money?"

"I refuse to argue. I shall inform the press that Mr. Case has turned his back on the man who saved America. And Mr. Quebaro will bring a suit for treble damages—that's three times fifty thousand dollars. There isn't a court, there isn't a jury who won't order you to pay—right up to the Supreme Court where Mr. Quebaro will take the case if necessary."

N'Zuriel Yhwh banged his fist down on the FREEZE button. "What kind of a lung fish is this?" he said rhetorically. "This is ruthlessness at its very worst."

"I certainly agree," Raziel said. "But since this fee involves the man who was her beloved husband in a former life—I tell you, with all respect, that you'd better pay her if we're going to get out of this safely and continue the field study."

"I hate it when they haggle," N'Zuriel Yhwh said.

"I must warn you. I am telling you. This woman is capable of seeking an injunction to stop all people from going to churches and synagogues until we pay."

"Enough!" N'Zuriel Yhwh gargled and prestidigitated fifty thousand dollars. He handed it to a cherub to pass along. "First, the man dies. Then the woman dies. We had nothing to do with that, but that was good for what we needed because we could re-program them with the kind of a background we thought they ought to have to struggle through money problems. We were completely scientific. So what happens? They threaten us with a law suit after we give them their big chance." He pushed all ACTION buttons. The screen went back into movement and sound.

Raziel stood up slowly. Gravely he stared into faces all around the room. "I think I am ready," he said, "to tell you what is on my mind."

Suddenly everyone in the hall seemed to be mumbling the word rhubarb aloud because they sensed something important coming up. Raziel was lashed by a sea of mumbles. Shards and splinters of unseemly crowd sounds lay in jagged forms around the speaker's feet until the noises became soft sand, then withdrew into every larynx except Raziel's.

"Do we want to arrive at a new and workable code of morals for these lung fish?" he cried demagogically.

"*Yas!*" It was a massive collective affirmation.

"To accomplish this are we willing to discard one old moral which they didn't pay much attention to anyway?"

There was no explosion of sound. The angels sat silent. Dagon said, "It all depends."

"Why can't we ever have a straight discussion?" Raziel pleaded. "Every time we are getting somewhere, some amateur stands up and says, 'It all depends.' This is nineteen seventy-five. You are very sophisticated creatures with real information sources. Give me a yes or a no."

A voice far in the back yelled, "Would you accept a maybe?"

Dagon stood up. "As everybody knows, I am a Down↓ member. We stand for anything that is evil. But nothing is evil unless it can be changed from good—and vice versa. Therefore, we got to have rules. So, we call the rules

morals. But whatever they are—all they are is a choice between good and evil. So if we go around saying that six of
the old kind aren't worth one of the new kind, then what is
the basis of temptation, if you follow me. Let me put it this
way: a moral is a moral."

Raziel shrugged. "Everybody is critical all of
a sudden, but nobody knows what I am trying to say."

"All right," Dagon said, "say it. It couldn't
hurt."

Raziel addressed the assemblage, "Will the
leader of the Arab bloc please stand up?"

Monker↓ got to his feet. Monker was one of
the two blue-eyed black angels in Arab demonology. His
work was the examination of recently deceased souls to
judge whether they were worthy of a place in Paradise.

"Monker," Raziel said. "you are an Arab. Do
you think it is the most important thing in the world that a
man ends up with the wife he started out with?"

"It all depends," Monker said.

"We are playing that game again! How many
wives do male lung fish have where you operate?"

"Up to four. Legally."

"Suppose, out of four legal wives, he decides
to stay with just one—would that be immoral?"

"Why—no. Absolutely not."

Raziel sighed. "Thank you, Monker. Can it be
that we are actually getting somewhere? I put the question
to you on a practical basis. I am saying to you—are we going
to spend the whole summer in this place or are we going to
hammer out a new moral code for lung fish on a practical
basis? What I am offering you here is a solution."

"What is he offering us?" N'Zuriel Yhwh said.
"Did I miss something?"

Raziel held up his hands to quiet the ensuing
uproar. "I am offering a solid proposition," he said impres-
sively. "The former wife from the former life knows her
onions. Believe me, she is the cat's pajamas. I am saying, in
slang terms, that she is a very exceptional little woman. In
every way, if I were a lung fish, God Fabbid, she would be
my type. For that same reason she also has a benign influ-

ence on the subject of the field study. But she is limited. She can't deliver the goods because of a big restriction."

"What restriction?" N'Zuriel Yhwh asked loftily.

"The new wife of the new life," Raziel said and sat down.

"Wait!"

"Finish!"

"Explain!"

Raziel got to his feet again. "I am saying that we have to arrange everything so that the new wife in the new life goes away so that the subject can be one-hundred-per cent guided by the former wife from the former life."

"How," Dagon asked.

"We start by appointing a Ways and Means Committee to investigate the best way. I recommend that the committee be constituted by Af, a Chief of Mission and a member of the Michael Brigade. And Haurus, who, although he happens to be under house arrest, should be brought back because he is a Chief of Mission also and, as we all know, gives always very true answers on matters of dogma. Then, to keep those two opposite delegates on the tracks, I propose, as a neutral member from the Permanent Undersecretariat, Miss Victoria Saxe-Coburg."

The motion was carried.

Ten

Doris picked up the phone in the Hotel Piedmont suite. "Hello?"

"This is Judge Zeuss. I am downstairs. May I come up?"

"No! Absolutely not!"

"Why not?"

"This is my husband's headquarters!"

"Your husband is in Arizona with his gorgeous secretary. I am here. I need you. I must see you. I am going crazy with what is happening to us."

"Not on the phone."

"Not anywhere!"

"I'll be right down." She hung up.

Judge Zeuss was waiting at the curb in a hideously long Lamborghini whose eighteen-cylinder engine was chuckling flatulently at the idea that it could only deliver six miles to the gallon. The top was down. Judge Zeuss dominated the street with the mauve and yellow car as he sat behind his burnished moustache, his teeth flashing blindingly, his shirt open to the belt buckle. He waved gaily as Doris emerged. She approached the car tentatively, as if she might be expected to buy a ticket to look at it.

"I cannot see you again," she said bitterly to the Judge. "I simply cannot. What never ever happened is now all over."

"You can say such a thing?"

Her face was knotted with sacrifice, but she still looked hauntingly lovely. "This is good-bye, my dear." When Metro was at its height, Greer Garson could not have read that line any better.

"Get in the car."

"No."

"Get in the car! We have to talk."

"No!"

"We will drive once around Manhattan; then I promise to deliver you back to this door. We can never be strangers again after what we have almost meant to each other. We have to talk this thing through. We have to understand it." He opened the door. "Get in."

Doris got in, refusing to ease the martyrdom on her face. The Lamborghini was standing still, then it was driving up Park Avenue.

"Jesus!" Doris screamed. "Not so fast!"

They did not speak again until the car reached the West Side Highway. As he went up the ramp, heading north, Judge Zeuss pressed a button and the top went up instantly, fastening itself in Italian, enclosing them in Photo-Dym glass. Doris pretended not to notice this. The Judge dropped his free hand upon her upper thigh. She pretended not to notice that either.

"Now, let us talk about the nonsense." he said masterfully.

"The fact is," Doris said, "well, the fact is—" she had to lift his hand off her thigh to be able to think. "My husband and I have been miserably unhappy since the day I met you. We were radiantly happy for years and years; then you arrived and we have been miserable and my husband doesn't even know you exist. Since the day I met you, my employer has spent most of his time in jail. My stepfather was committed to a military prison in the Aleutians. Because my mother needed me, I was separated from my husband at the moment of his national greatness. His was a truly annealing experience which we never shared because of you—and now I sense he is gone from me."

"What has that got to do with me? Any of it?" He put his hand back on her upper thigh. "Are you saying I caused all that? How can you do this to us, Doris?"

Perhaps because she was rattled, her hand fell on his upper thigh; high. He grasped it and pressed it into himself. "Be fair, Doris. Be fair!" he groaned, his trousers tenting. "I can't stand it! I can't *stand* it!" He slammed on the super-powerful quadruple braking system (which could have stopped a mortar shell in its flight), sliding his hand directly upward under her skirt while the other arm pulled her to him eagerly, and caused the most extensive freight-train collision in the traffic history of the West Side Highway, his car holding like a rock mountain while the seventy-one cars directly following crashed and telescoped into each other in a long row of steel that crumpled into itself for almost a quarter mile down the elevated roadway behind them, bringing dozens of shouting, gesticulating motorists out of their ruined cars to sprint forward toward the Lamborghini at the head of the line. Judge Zeuss gallantly drew the angry mob away from Doris by getting out of the car in fullest view so that he could be identified as the driver who had caused the catastrophe; then he ran for the railing, vaulted it, and began to shinny down the pillar, pulling the crowd behind him.

Eleven

Gene hung up his hat and put his rolled umbrella carefully in the stand in Miss Pimbernel's office. Little did he know that the Ways & Means Committee were, even then, meeting to discuss extraordinary changes in his future. He made his little joke, then asked about Miss Kehoe's progress at the Midtown Hospital, as he always did.

"She goes into traction today," Miss Pimbernel beamed. "They have her out of the tank for seven out of every twelve hours now. And it looks as though the kidney machines will be off by the ninth."

"That's just wonderful," Gene said, entering his office. Miss Pimbernel followed him in with a trayful of mail and telegrams.

"That isn't all the wonderful news," she said. "John Kullers called to say that the APBA *insists* on sharing their commissions with you for the glorious fight you made for them."

"Well! Wasn't that nice?"

"Yes. And that means an extra two million seven hundred thousand dollars."

"Two mill——what was that?"

"Yes. And Mr. Case laughed merrily when I told him you were going to charge him five thousand dollars. He not only insisted on paying fifty thousand dollars but he sent the money by messenger and here it is." She extended the cash, in greenbacks, on a wooden tray.

Gene stared at the money, opened the middle drawer on the left side of his desk, took out a green pepper hero sandwich, broke it into three parts, and dropped it into the wastebasket. "Call my wife and invite her to lunch, please," he said dazedly. "Anywhere very expensive. Anything else in the mail this morning?"

"There are a few hundred telegrams of congratulation from the great and near-great," Miss Pimbernel said, "and I am proud to say that quite a few companies have invited you to sit on their boards."

"I'll consider all legitimate offers providing that I may serve in my capacity as a lawyer."

"You've put in a lot of years as a lawyer. But I know one thing. You have the makings of a great salesman. You have the looks that bring security. You have the height that gives authority. You are near-sighted, which makes you seem intense. And you have the essential con."

"I have the makings of a great lawyer," he said with no little offense. "The events of the past week proved that."

"Proved what?" Charlotte answered scornfully. "It proved you were a great salesman, a walking, talking inspirational television commercial. You sold this country back on dinner plates as their backup currency. What did being a lawyer have to do with it?"

"What is so distinguished about being another salesman?"

"What's so distinguished about being another lawyer? Where's the challenge? There are six hundred thousand-odd lawyers in New York. We have over *five million* salesmen. You'll really be competing. That's big-time."

"Tell me something," he snarled. "Does your woman's intuition tell you what I should be selling?"

"Anything. What's the difference? Whatever people need. There's a fortune in it. We are a service economy. We don't make many things anymore, we just apply the grease. But that's good. That makes stress. So the people need comfort and peace of mind. That's *it!* You should sell insurance."

"Insurance? *Insurance?*"

"A great opportunity."

"Well, that's not the way I see it," he rasped, his voice rising. "I'm going to finish my ten-year sentence as a lawyer and take Uncle Raimundo's by-then million bucks and my wife and maybe a nice little chicken ranch in the Tuamotu Archipelago with a TV cassette supply of two or three hundred great old movies, a giant deep freeze filled with choice shell steaks, four thousand cases of Czech and Mexican beer, and let the other fellow knock himself out."

"Is that all having a million dollars means to you?" Charlotte said with disgust.

"That's all having a million dollars means to anybody. *Any*-body."

o

At Liederkranz Hall, N'Zuriel Yhwh looked at Dagon, startled. Dagon shrugged.

o

"What about the children of the world?" Charlotte said stridently. "What about people who have to have help or go under? What about music and paintings and books—the kind we should build our lives around? How about the three seasons that never get to the South Pacific? And outdoor plumbing? How come *people* don't mean anything to you and how come you don't care about pro football?"

"Come *on*. I'm tired out. It's been a tough week. Let's cool it, okay?"

"Whatever you say. But whatever it is you are thinking, I've got to keep you from doing it. That's what I'm here for. I know it. I feel it. You are a man, and if you are left to yourself you are just going to fritter your life away, propped up in the sunshine at the middle of a pile of used beer cans. But that isn't the way it's supposed to be."

"Are you telling me to turn my back on Uncle Raimundo's money?" he shouted.

"Gene—listen. You now have two million, seven hundred and fifty thousand dollars. I can get you sixteen per cent on that with no risk. That's a nice three hundred and eighty thousand a year, a steady seventy-six hundred a week. And for the rest of your life. That's a lot of money. Money is what made America great. Money is love.

The one thing left is—you don't *need* your Uncle Raimundo's estate."

"I have suffered like a bald Siberian dog for Uncle Raimundo's money!"

"I'm not asking you to throw his million away! A million dollars was real money when he was alive. But now we have inflation, Gene. In your Uncle Raimundo's time your seventy-six hundred a week would have been worth exactly a hundred and sixty-eight eighty-five a week. I worked it out on my little Hewlett-Packard."

"But you just said I didn't need the estate."

"You don't need it to survive. Not the way you did before." The telephone rang. Charlotte ran to take it in the outer office. When she came back, she was wreathed in smiles. "That was Anne Knauerhase Fortress herself," she said. "She heard you were homeless. She is so grateful for what you did for dinner-plate investors, of whom she is one, that she wants you to have, rent free, a furnished six-room apartment at Fortress Midtown."

"Rent free?"

"Gene, listen to me! Now you have everything you need. Now you can tell the Surrogate in charge of Uncle Raimundo's estate that you are going to specialize in the practice of insurance law. We'll make a deep study of insurance law, but most of all you'll be using your marvelous new contacts to sell insurance—every kind of insurance—industrial, life, annuities, golf ball, everything—and I am going to be right behind you, backing you up, on every move you make."

Twelve

Af, Haurus and Victoria Saxe-Coburg, the Ways & Means Committee, hammered out the euphemisms by which the Joint (⇵) Commission would be able to abandon one old moral morally before it had been determined what its replacement would be. Af and Haurus were *very* old friends. Af held no grudge because Haurus had had to face the tactical necessity of tying him up in the closet of that ice-cream parlor. They were real old pros. However, they did oppose each other classically and realized that they faced no easy task.

They were seated in their shirtsleeves, looking rumpled after a six-hour session. Miss Saxe-Coburg, despite the sizzling summer's day, looked crisp, cool and indifferent. She was wearing a flat napkin on top of her head, to keep the air conditioning out, she said, and it looked fetching.

"Af, please," Haurus said. "There is no use keeping up the argument that the lung fish would give a damn whether we shuffled a few morals around and happened to lose one. They are not morals-oriented."

Af had taken his square Churchillian billycock bowler off sometime before, revealing that he wore a scarlet zucchetto underneath it.

"But we are not losing one moral, Harry," Af said. "We are deliberately setting up a condition involving only two people out of billions and saying that it would be perfectly all right if the husband broke his marriage vows in order to desert the wife in order to go off with his secretary for the very mingy reason, to me, of accommodating our own R and D facility."

"Af, I like you, but sometimes you are a hairsplitter. I could even say that sometimes you can't see the chicken for the chickenshit."

"Watch it, Harry. There is a lady here."

"If that's a lady, then so am I," Haurus said. "That's an angel who is temporarily standing in as a female lung fish."

"There is still no call for that kind of language, Harry," Vickie said. "Is that how it is all the time in Hell? With everyone yelling shit every time he feels like it?"

"Never mind about Hell. Let's scatter the scatology and theorize on the theology, if you don't mind. Af, you will agree we are talking about two people—Doris and Gene Quebaro—who, no matter how you measure anything, are living in something they call time, so they'll be dead soon, right?"

"All right. Right."

"The rest of the present population in the country they live in is about two hundred and ten million—right?"

"Okay, Harry. Right."

"At the rate they breed, there is no counting how many lung fish yet unborn will be affected by the new moral code when the Joint (⚕) Commission finally sets it down for them—right?"

"Yes, but—"

"No buts, Af."

"I have to say a but, Harry. There is a prime necessity here. Eugene Quebaro is not only married to Doris Quebaro in this other place but, if you will study the screen footage, and if you will re-run that footage on him from the day we convened, you will find that he is deeply in love with his wife. That is *pert*inent, Harry."

"He was programmed that way."

"Good. You said it. And you are stuck with it. He was programmed that way and he is deeply in love with her."

"So what?"

"I know you don't understand love, Harry. Love is hardly Hell's bag."

211

Haurus blinked.

"But let me re-phrase," Af continued. "Marriage is a contract. Marriage is a legal community necessity for the protection of any resulting children. Do you understand that, Harry?"

"Perfectly clear."

"By enforcing this decision we are supporting three morals, not one. Hell is no *depart*ment of a Heavenly holy system. Hell is an entirely separate operation. We are separate outfits and we compete for souls into eternity. But here we are with good and evil, which is *who* we are, and the three morals this decision supports is, one: the contract of marriage; two: the moral right of children to be protected by their sponsors in a society before they enter that society; and three: the overwhelming personal *choice* involved. Quebaro loves his wife deeply; therefore he would have chosen to marry her because he is young, would have been single, and that's how it works. So—and mark me well, Harry —we would not only be violating these first three morals if we agree to allow this Quebaro marriage to be broken, we are betraying this male lung fish by denying him the essence of his soul: his emotional capacity to make and abide by an emotional contract. He *loves,* Harry! That is what love is, the soul's involvement in natural law,"

"He screwed Phyllis Stein."

Af shrugged. "A biochemical explosion meaning less than nothing."

"How about the night with Alice Trudy Kehoe?"

"Don't deliberately provoke me."

"Then," Haurus said with a straight face, "you are nailing this whole thing down on a single moral base. You are saying that, because this one man loves and was married to this one woman, we may not discard one moral for our purpose of redesigning the moral security of hundreds of millions—born and unborn?"

"That is correct, Harry."

Haurus licked his awful lips. "Af," he said, "you better get your options straight. Why did the Uppers† show their contempt for the love felt by his former wife from a former place by bringing her to work again at his side, totally tempting her to lose herself to him all over again while showing her that his new wife from this place stood in the way of her ever possessing him?"

"I was waiting for that," Vickie said.

"Then you should have said something," Af told her hotly.

"Not me. I'm neutral. But this is the first and probably the last time I'll ever hear Hell using Heaven's arguments while Heaven is caught with its pants down."

"Quebaro was killed. He died," Af said indignantly. "We had nothing to do with it!"

"Is Raziel from Hell?" Haurus asked mildly.

"*Raziel?*"

"You are jolly well right he isn't," Haurus said.

"What are you driving at?"

"Raziel negotiated the cross-over of the female lung fish—now known as Ms. Pimbernel—while she was *still alive* in The Other Place. He brought her here setting horrifying precedents. When he had her here, he *used* her. He not only *used* her, he made her work at the side of the man for whom she has feeling so far beyond your so-called soul's involvement in natural law that she became the first lung fish *in all time* to get a prayer through, to get him back. So I say to you that hers was and is the *prior* right of contract, based on your own arguments, the *prior* right which *towers* over what you try to insist are the rights of this—this concubine—the present wife of the present place."

Af took off the zucchetto and wiped his sweating face with it. "That's a good point, Harry," he said.

"Then you are willing to make a deal?"

"Not yet."

"Why not?"

"I am convinced that the man, and his former wife from the former life, can become adjusted and get a fair shake if we make this deal. Basically, that is what a well-made moral provides. But, until I am reassured that the present wife of the present life will be able to adjust to the change equally, *no* deal can be made."

"Af, are you keeping something from me?"

"How?"

"What do you do with your time here? You must be into something."

"Harry!"

"Well, you haven't been watching the giant NixonVision screen, that's for sure. You don't seem to know what everybody knows—that Doris Quebaro is out of her mind about a certain municipal court judge."

This was a true charge. Af *hated* movies and television. He spent most of his time in Mexican food-supply outlets, wholesale and retail, depending on Miss Saxe-Coburg to fill him in.

"She is?" Af gasped. "The wife is cheating on the husband? The wife?"

"She tries. So far, no luck. But the terrible intent is there."

Af looked at Vickie. She nodded solemnly. She said, "There is only one problem left. The woman's needs are provided for, but what about poor Quebaro himself? He happens to be in love with the present wife from the present life."

Af and Harry stared at each other. Af spoke first. "A thing like that can't be forced, Harry."

Haurus turned to Miss Saxe-Coburg. "What do we do now?"

She took a deep breath. "I understand the Greeks have a process that looks like a cherub. They call it Eros. When Eros shoots an arrow at someone who is looking at a member of the opposite sex, the one who is hit falls irrevocably in love."

"All right," Haurus said with relief. "That means it can all be worked out. The main thing is that we have found the Ways and Means for the Joint (⚕) Commission to proceed."

Thirteen

The negotiations to gain the cooperation of Zeus on the matter of Eros and his arrows were so delicate that N'Zuriel Yhwh decided that he should become a part of the Contact Delegation. Raziel encouraged this to cut down on second guessing. However high N'Zuriel Yhwh's rank among the angels, it did not approach Zeus's ranking as Chief of State of his religion. Even Lucifer™ with his position as head of the Lower House↓ could not match Zeus's rank. As it was, the Greeks were fielding a team of three full-fledged major deities. Each one outranked the angels. But at least two of the angels were keen negotiators. Athena and Hermes were just as keen, but Zeus had decided to include Aphrodite in the package. And the angels had N'Zuriel Yhwh.

To set the meeting, word was passed from Raziel to Hermes to Zeus: a joint council meeting was requested by the angels.

"But what *for,* Herm?" Zeus asked petulantly. He had been brooding about Doris. He felt poorly. He was on the top floor of the Popina Matsoukis on East 18th Street having his beard ironed into sausage curls by a clever little hairdresser from Lacedaemonia. Her place was the one with the pink store-front, not right *in* Sparta, but in the high-rent suburb called Lelex which was named after the brother of Agenor, the uncle of the Theban founder, Cadmus. She had a terrific body odor, which was like fresh hot-cross buns crossed with Viennese coffee fumes. While he brooded, she curled and he overate little things from the big trays which Matsoukis kept sending in.

"It's a funny thing," Hermes said, "But they

215

don't seem to have caught on that you are also Judge Zeuss of the Municipal Court. I can't understand it.''

"You can't understand it? I'm the master of disguise throughout history. I mean—for like fifteen thousand years I've been known as The Man with Ten Thousand Faces.''

Hermes rolled his eyes. "The only difference is, you wear a business suit and you don't wear a beard.''

"That's the whole *trick!* Less is more. Well! This news is very, very gratifying.''

"Raziel thinks everything might move faster if we could break up the Quebaro marriage so that Quebaro could remarry the former wife from the former life.''

Zeus's feeling of doom/gloom was expelled. "They are going for it hook, line and sinker. My own plan and now they want a little help on it. You see how a real brain works, son? But you share the credit. You fed it to them. I am very proud of you.''

"Thanks, Pop,'' Hermes said. "Can I have the car tonight?''

"What?''

"That's what the children say here whenever the father is pleased.''

"When do the angels want to meet?''

"Tonight.''

"Where?''

"Uptown. At the Cloisters.''

"What's that?''

"An indoor-outdoor museum on the Hudson.''

"How many angels?''

"Three. One is their top brass.''

"Who?''

"N'Zuriel Yhwh. He is one of the highest ranking princes in their Merkabah. His official work, listed in their directory, is Angel of Hailstorms.''

"Big deal.''

"He *could* be a little dim when you come right down to it.''

"Athena can handle them. But this time I

want you on the team instead of Apollo because you have been working with them very well."

"Thanks, Pop. Can I have the car tonight?"

"And I want Aphrodite to be the third member."

"Aw, Pop!"

"Listen, don't knock it. You never know. One of them could be very susceptible. We'll have Athena to close with them, you to keep them amused, and Aphrodite to keep their minds off business."

"Okay, Pop. Then can *Athena* have the car tonight?"

o

As it happened, the angels were sitting on the lower deck of the Number 4 bus to Fort Tryon park while the Greeks were on the upper deck. They met at the end of the line with many exclamations about it being a small world. The time was a quarter to ten. The park was closed and the Cloisters were closed, so they all materialized inside the walls in a pleasant, covered nook. Athena recognized her father the instant she materialized. He was standing on a seven-foot pedestal, about fifteen feet tall, closely resembling a statue of Zeus with a very curly beard. No one else but Raziel glanced at the statue, and if he had been less preoccupied with the issue at hand, he might have wondered what a statue of Zeus was doing in a musuem of medieval art.

"It's nice to see you again," Athena said. "May I introduce my sister Aphrodite?" Aphrodite shimmered her left tit at Raziel, then at Dagon, finally at N'Zuriel Yhwh. She struck a stone wall with the first two. Definite shudders and susceptibility vibrations came from N'Zuriel Yhwh.

They all sat down. Somehow, Aphrodite sat squarely on N'Zuriel Yhwh's hand and squealed with delight. The tips of his wings grew very red.

"We asked for this meeting to demonstrate the harmony we feel with your Godhead and your pantheon," Raziel began. The statue smiled benignly. "We have completed our Time and Motion studies of the Quebaros and we wanted to share these with you, as well as the tentative conclusions we have reached and the recommendations we are prepared to make."

"How interesting," Athena said.

"Jolly good show," Hermes added.

"The case studies show," Raziel continued, "even at these early stages, that Quebaro doesn't know what money is, has rarely seen much of it in his life and that his wife, Doris, is no help either."

"You have beautiful—and very lively—hands," Aphrodite whispered to N'Zuriel Yhwh.

"However," Raziel went on, "the former wife from the former life, who has been here for just one of their days or so, has already made him almost three million dollars—and she figured out how to get every dollar herself. So it seems apparent—to us anyhow—that if Quebaro could be switched away from the present wife of the present life and instantly mated with this former wife, we would be greatly enhancing both the forward movement as well as the depth of our field studies. Do you agree?"

Athena looked at the statue. The statue nodded. Athena spoke, "Yes. That may be an excellent plan. But will the Quebaros cooperate? Will the former wife want to?"

"We say yes. Yes, she will. Given your cooperation."

"Our cooperation?"

"I think of the candy arrows of little Eros."

Athena nodded vaguely in the direction of Aphrodite, whose hand was now resting lightly on N'Zuriel Yhwh's thigh. "Eros is my sister's little boy," she said.

"Are his arrows as effective as ever?" Dagon asked blandly.

"Unfailingly," Athena answered.

"May I ask for a recess?" Raziel said. "I have a cramp in my leg." They all stood up. Aphrodite turned N'Zuriel Yhwh away from the group. They strolled off, chatting. Hermes got talking with Dagon about a marvelous piece of fish he had gotten one time in Lebanon, the first time he had ever had fish with green peppers. Raziel and

Athena wandered away from the open atrium. Zeus stood motionless on the pedestal.

Raziel said to Athena, "Don't think I didn't notice your father standing up there. It took me a minute to realize it was he. But I do feel that there are one or two things we might discuss beyond his hearing."

"My father is a very inquisitive sort of god," Athena said, blushing with embarassment.

"That is a rewarding quality in a deity," Raziel answered. "Ours is so busy that He can't enjoy little qualities like that. Not that He doesn't have them. Frequently, His eye is on the sparrow. Often. But tell me—since your father's authorization is necessary before little Eros can loose his arrows—how do you think he will respond?"

"I can't see how he could have any objection. But he would feel strongly about one thing. All three people involved must be helped by Eros to make the adjustment."

"You mean—?"

"Quebaro, his wife Doris, and his former wife."

"To whom can we expose the wife Doris?"

"We have reason to believe that she is very much interested in a Judge Zeuss of the Municipal Court."

"Is he single?"

"Why?"

"The exposure must result in marriage. That is an all-important condition with us."

"Let me investigate that," Athena said.

o

"I found this wonderful little hotel in Brooklyn Heights," Aphrodite was saying. "What a view! Lower Manhattan is so close you imagine you could touch it—if one were to take the time to look out of the window."

"I could touch it," N'Zuriel Yhwh said.

"Do you ever get to Brooklyn Heights?"

"Well, not as a general rule. But I sure would like to see your little hotel because you never know when you are going to need a great little hotel like that."

"How about when this meeting breaks up?" Aphrodite said breathily. "I could show it to you then." She ran her soft tongue all around her soft, pink lips.

"You mean—you and me?—"

"Oh, honey!" Aphrodite moaned.

o

"They took the fish and dipped it in a butter-oil mixture, you follow? Then they sprinkled it lightly with flour and threw it in a pan with two large tomatoes, peeled and sliced, and a large sweet onion ditto. Then in there with all the rest was a half of a small green pepper, seeded and chopped, a quarter cup of coarsely chopped black olives, the tip of a bay leaf and a little salt and pepper. That's *all.* You never had anything like it."

"They grow a very nice olive in Lebanon," Dagon said.

"You're telling me?"

"I was the national god of the Phoenicians, then later the Philistines."

"Oh, well. Then you should know."

"Yes. As a matter of fact, a real coincidence, I am commonly represented with half the body of a fish."

"Well, this recipe was for red snapper."

o

Zeus listened to all three conversations simultaneously on three channels. What he heard made him proud of his kids. Aphrodite had tied up the biggest boob in knots. Hermes had nailed one of the very smart ones right to the stage. Athena just happened to have worked out the deal of Zeus's dreams, with the angel's eager help, and without giving anything away. He felt light-headed with the euphoria of being in love. He hummed: "Just Doris and meeee/ An' baby makes threeeee/ We're happeee in my bloooooheavunn." Doris was his, at last. And she couldn't get hurt. She was twenty-four of *their* years old and if she stayed very, *very* healthy she might live to eighty. What was eighty years of fidelity? Nothing. Also, he would need to go away on trips. He would marry her to keep the bargain with the angels, then he would invest fifty-six little human years then—*gavoom*—he would be free and clear. Who could beat a deal like that?

He was going to give Eros a new bow and arrow set.

He transmitted his will from his brow to Athena's brow in a very tight band. "Take the deal," he instructed. "I happen to like it very much."

o

N'Zuriel Yhwh never got to the Brooklyn Heights hotel that night. Raziel and Dagon bundled him right out of Fort Tryon park and straight back to Liederkranz Hall. He couldn't think quickly enough to get away from them. Zeus took Aphrodite back to Popina Matsoukis with him. He sent for his grandson, little Eros, set up an archery butt in the big room on the top floor, and said they were going to stay right there until the boy scored six bull's eyes out of six.

The fact was, despite success in the Palmer Mahan case, Zeus didn't trust the boy's shooting and was afraid it might have gotten rusty since they had come to the city and he wanted to take no chances in a matter so close to his own heart. His mother was greatly embarrassed. "What is going to happen to fucking if you shoot like that?" she asked reproachfully.

"You must think about what you're doing, boy," Zeus said. "The bow was probably the first mechanical device in which energy could be accumulated slowly and released suddenly under control and direction. Let the bow express that little thought, Errie."

They worked hard. Within the hour the boy had it all back again. His mother beamed at him with real pride. "Grandpa wants you to double-dip the arrows in the passion solution this time. This is a very important case."

All the subjective meaning of that sentence hit home with Zeus. He broke out into a rich baritone song, "Just Doris and meeeeee/ And babeee makes threee/ We're happy in my bloooo heaven."

Fourteen

Doris was fulfilled to have such an apartment at Fortress Midtown; not only richly furnished and with a new addition of a magnificent set of dinnerware (on which Diamond Jim Brady had actually dined—or was it Jack "Legs" Diamond?) from John Kullers, but also Gene had been sweet enough to move all of his own Bangwibangwi and Gunduwalambala artifacts to the apartment, out of his own office where they had brought him such good luck. They *made* the reception hall. The kitchen was one of Doris's dreams come true, not pulled out of a wall but out of the pages of a magazine. The dining room was so genuinely Regency that its sideboard had a right-hand compartment for port and a left-side compartment for the silver chamber pot which the gentlemen would use in turn while they pretended to be drinking port before they joined the ladies. Doris was made so euphoric by the firm, gigantic beds and the lapis lazuli bidet that, impulsively, she called Judge Zeuss at his chambers and asked for a pardon for Mr. Violente.

"Certainly, my dear. Anything. Ask me anything but tell me when I am going to see you."

"No, my dear," she said in her gentle Greer Garson voice. "That was then. This is now. We are all over and done. And in our hearts we know it is the best thing that we never see each other again."

Then she called Sal Lavocca at the restaurant and reported that she had arranged to have Mr. Violente freed and asked, for her part, only that his friends be there to greet him when he came out. She knew gangsters were notoriously sentimental people, but the kind of joy Mr.

Lavocca conveyed seemed to miss the point. "Now we can really give it to them," he said.

o

As Mort Violente emerged from the Tombs his consigliere, Amadeo Kranz, and two of his caporegimas, Sal Lavocca and Herbert "Little Pasquale" Ganglia were waiting for him. Joyously they pelted him with confetti and paper streamers and The Boss took it all with undisguised good nature. This merry scene was soon jarred when a young policemen wearing a rookie armband came pushing in among their horseplay, grabbing their throwing arms and forcing them down. "What are you guys *do*ing?" he asked belligerently. "This is a disgrace. Doesn't pollution and waste mean anything to you?"

"I don't get it," Amadeo Kranz said.

"You are throwing paper everywhere. You are littering and wasting," the young cop answered. He took his black summons book out of his back pocket. "All right, Mr. Litterbug," he said to Kranz, "what's your name?"

"Kid, are you crazy?" Kranz said.

"Crazy?"

"You know who this is?"

"The summons is not for him. It's for you. What's your name?"

Violente looked hard at Kranz and nodded. Kranz took out his wallet. He extracted a new one-hundred-dollar bill and tucked it into the young cop's shirt pocket. "All right," he said, "now get the hell outta here."

The cop drew a chain of nippers from a loop at the back of his trousers and threw it around Kranz's wrist. "Under arrest," he said. He turned to Herbert "Little Pasquale" Ganglia and said, "Now—what's *your* name?"

Ganglia looked at The Boss helplessly.

"Tell him your name!" Violente snarled.

Ganglia answered all the cop's questions respectfully. He pocketed the summons silently.

"Kid," Sal Lavocca asked civilly. "How olda you?"

"He's maybe eighteen," Kranz sneered.

"I am twenty-one years of age," the policeman said.

"Is this your fayst day onna street fomm The Academy?" Sal inquired, in a kindly way.

"Yes. It happens to be my first day. There has to be a first day."

"Kid, do you know what is gunna hoppen to you? You are gunna be transferred—on your very fayst day —to duty on a deep-sea garbage scow which it is about twelve miles *off* Staten Island. You unnastan'?"

"You have threatened an officer," the cop said. "No summons for you. You are under arrest. All right, you two," he said to Kranz and Lavocca. "Against that wall, hands on the wall, feet twenty-three millimeters apart." Kranz and Sal did as they were told. The cop frisked them and found two .38 caliber Hoodlum Specials and, on Kranz, six decks of heroin he was taking to a sick friend. Paying no more attention to Mr. Violente or to Herbert "Little Pasquale" Ganglia, he marched the two men ahead of him, into the Tombs.

"And we wanted it to be such a happy occasion," Ganglia said.

"Some coming-out party," Mr. Violente answered bitterly. "Get in the car."

Ganglia drove the large car uptown. Mr. Violente sat in the front seat beside the wheel. "Amadeo is dead as a consigliere," he said. "He has no paper for the gun. And carrying junk won't help. I'll do the best I can for him." His spirit seemed broken.

"You'll square it, boss."

"The way things have been going, I'll be lucky if I can square your summons for littering."

"I never heard of luck like we've been getting it."

"Who is the best mechanic we got?"

"Me. Even if I say so myself."

"All right. You know what I found out inside?"

"What?"

"You know where they took us, the first time they raided us, they said it was the Municipal Court?"

"Where?"

"The Inishfail Ballrooms on Third Avenue. They hold dances there. He turned it into a courtroom. It cost him plenty. He fooled my own lawyer, supposed to be the smartest inna business."

"But—"

"Don't think. This is what you do. Drop everything else. Let Sam Tubasi stand in for you. Find this Joe V. Zeuss. I want him quick, and when you find out where he is, bring him in and I'll blow his fucking brains out. You unnastan'?"

"Sure. Where do I look for him?"

"How do I know?" Violente flared. "Put fifty soldiers onna street. Find him!"

o

Herbert "Little Pasquale" Ganglia was in and out of nearly every bail bondsman's office in the city. Nobody had ever heard of a Judge Joe V. Zeuss. Of the people who had been arraigned at the fake municipal court, some said Zeuss had a beard, others said he wore only a moustache, with 12 per cent represented by "Don't Know." It was impossible to put an Identikit picture together. Then Little Pasquale figured out that if Zeuss were a phony judge and they were all fake cops, how come Mr. Violente had been dropped into the worst solitary cell in the Tombs three times in a row? He talked that over with Mr. Violente, who put his best lawyer on it. The lawyer's report stated flatly that there was no record whatsoever that Mr. Violente had ever been admitted to the Tombs. Not only no record—all prison personnel from the Warden down denied hotly that Don Mort had ever been confined there.

"This momser really has muscle," Mr. Violente said ominously. "This kind of a hustler is no good for *any*body. You gotta find him, Herbert. I am goin' outta my mind."

It took eight days to remember the link between Judge Zeuss and the Violente organization's chief statistician, Doris Quebaro. Mr. Violente called her into his office.

"I wanted to thank you, Doris, for getting me out," he said.

"Nothing has made me happier, Mr. Violente," she said.

"How you done it?"

"You remember that judge—Judge Zeuss—the one who wanted me to go to lunch with him—the one who ordered the raid?"

Mr. Violente nodded. He was watching her carefully. He saw that she was blushing deeply and he misinterpreted it. In his increasingly paranoiac way he decided she must have been plotting against him with Judge Zeuss. But he did not accuse her. "Where he took you to lunch, Doris?" he asked.

"Well—it was upstairs in a private dining room at a Greek restaurant on Eighth Avenue called the Thessaly."

"Did they know him there?"

"Like he owned the place. How come you are interested in Judge Zeuss, Mr. Violente?"

"Well, I wouldn't want him to think I was sore at him. I wanted to send him a case of cigars. I mean—a judge is a judge. Did you ever have to get in touch wit' him directly, yourself?"

"I have called him on occasion," she said carefully.

"Where did you call him, Doris?"

"At the Municipal Court."

"What's the number?"

"I just look up Municipal Court in the telephone book."

"There is no Judge Zeuss at the Municipal Court!" Violente shouted at her. Doris was startled. Her employer got a grip on himself and tried to be more temperate. "I mean—I keep tryna get him there but no dice."

"Then someone called the wrong number."

"I dialed it myself, Doris," Mr. Violente said through gritted teeth.

"Then look up the number in the book and I'll dial it. We'll dial it together." Mr. Violente reached for the book. He found the number. He wrote the number in large markings on a slip of paper. He walked around his desk to stand beside Doris, placing the slip of paper beside the telephone. He watched her read the number and dial it letter by letter, number by number.

"May I speak to Judge Joe V. Zeuss, please?" Mr. Violente put his head next to the receiver and listened to Judge Zeuss report that he was fine indeed. He heard the Judge ask when he would see her. He recognized the olives-ravaged voice. Doris queried Mr. Violente silently as to whether he wanted to speak to Judge Zeuss. Mr. Violente shook his head.

"Actually," Doris said into the phone, "I dialed your number by accident. I must be thinking of you unconsciously," she said gaily and hung up.

When Doris left his office, Violente called his contact at the telephone company and told him to put a tracer on the line, numbered as it was in the telephone book, which led into the Municipal Court switchboard but which had been trans-switched because the man telephoned was unknown at the Municipal Court in any capacity. The telephone company vice-president said he would run it down.

Mr. Violente called Sal's Smorg and told them to have Little Pasquale to cover the Thessaly Restaurant and to trace Zeuss through the owner and the waiters.

The paths of the telephone company vice-president and Herbert "Little Pasquale" Ganglia crossed with hairline precision at the Popina Matsoukis. Mr. Violente was able to confirm that Judge Zeuss was in residence on the top floor.

Little Pasquale planted himself to set down Judge Zeuss's daily routine, his habitual movements around the city, so that the organization could know where the Judge was likely to be at any given time as well as who he knew, what places he habituated, and what he did. Judge Zeuss was being set up for a highly professional hit.

Fifteen

The new apartment made Doris so euphoric she felt she had to celebrate. She called Gene and asked him if he could take her to lunch. He agreed with delight. She said she would go right downtown and pick him up at the office but he said he could get a cab quicker and easier than she so he would dash uptown, pick her up, and take her to lunch at Twenty-One. "Be at the Fifth Avenue entrance in fourteen minutes," he said.

Judge Zeuss's wiretap on Doris's telephone kept him informed of these developments. Eleven minutes later, the Zeuss limousine arrived at the 72nd Street entrance to the Quebaro apartment building on Fifth Avenue and Zeus lined up the hit. He showed Eros where Doris would emerge and how he, Zeus, would appear in Doris's direct, inescapable view, in Eros's line of fire. She would be looking directly at Zeus when she was shot through the heart with Eros's candy arrows.

"Just make sure she can see me before you fire," Zeus told the lad, "because I think she wears contact lenses—something has to be giving her that dopey look—and if you fire too soon she might not be fixed on me."

"Okay, Gangrad," the child said.

Eros took up his position among the plants at the main exit so that he would be behind Doris when she emerged. She came through the door in three minutes' time and started across the widely recessed pavement to the curb. As Zeus opened the door of his limousine, perhaps too hastily, Gene's taxi stopped directly behind the Zeuss car. As Zeus came out, his foot slipped on the stainless steel door riser and, instead of going up into Doris's line of vision, he went down and backward, stretched out on the wide floor of the limousine. Gene, meanwhile, bounded out of the cab yelling Doris's name, impelling her instant attention at the moment Eros loosed a rapid two-arrow volley. One of these caught Doris squarely in the heart as she stared at Gene. She had started to run toward him so that the second arrow sped harmlessly past where she had been but went cleanly into Zeus's chest as he came out of the limousine, staring at Doris.

Husband and wife stared at each other in the bright, clear sunshine in front of their wonderful, new home and were possessed by redoubled ecstasy. It was a case of love at 14,328th sight.

Agape, bereft, crushed, and confused, Zeus stood beside his giant Mercedes and watched Doris ignore him as she got into the taxi with her husband. He watched them kiss passionately upon the rear seat. The cab moved off. Zeus turned to his tiny grandson, doing a slow, slow burn.

"What happened here, you little twit?" he said, trembling with he knew not what.

"You goofed, Gangrad," the child said. "You fell down as I shot. I hit her with nummer eins but she twisted around and hared away so I missed her with nummer zwei."

"But why do I feel so terrible?"

"Because nummer zwei kept going and it hit you."

"*ME?* No!" He tottered. "Eros! Is there an antidote?"

"No *known* antidote, Gangrad. Maybe, if you asked Momma—"

"What am I gung do?" Zeus cried out pitiably. "I have this feeling I can't live without her. How long do the effects of the arrows last?"

"In the way of counting in this place, about seventy-nine, eighty years."

"You mean she'll be a hundred and four when she gets over him?"

The boy shrugged.

Zeus began to weep. The boy led him to the car.

o

The news of Zeus's goof-up threw Raziel into a towering rage. "He is the most fat-headed, balloon-brained idiot ever to hold high office and that even includes American politics," Raziel spluttered at Dagon. "We would have done better planning the whole tactic with your aunt's elderly parakeet. Now what are we supposed to do? Hang around this miserable town for eighty years until the Quebaros return to their senses?"

"Well—eighty years. That's not so bad," Dagon said. "We could see all the shows. We might even get out to Sheepshead Bay for some crab."

"Listen, already—*please!* Do you know how long eighty years is to lung fish?"

"No. How long?"

"I'll tell you how long. The insurance companies kill all the males at 67.4 years and all the females at 71.3. Quebaro is thirty-two. He'll probably be dead within forty-five years, that's how long it is. But it's not only him! It's the other two hundred and ten million American people, let alone the rest of the world who are out there breeding geometrically and operating their lives with an absolutely useless, outmoded moral code."

Dagon brooded on the Convention's half-admitted understanding of the problem: The lung fish-into-people had invented their gods because they weren't at all effective in controlling themselves and they fervently hoped that this invention—gods with rules and rituals called religion—would take over the task of controlling them to lead better lives. They had expected of their invention, at the very least, that it would become an effective conscience beyond their own too-accommodating consciences. However and alas, nothing could be invented which could save the lung fish from their own natures, *but their gods had not understood that yet.* People were people. They persisted in behaving like people, i.e. they "sinned" by their own private and personal definitions. The child molester thought the usurer was sin-

230

ning. The usurer thought the topless waitress was going to Hell. The more the lung fish "sinned," the more the gods intervened because, as an invention of convenience, that was what they had been programmed to do. But no matter where the lung fish were, no matter if alive or "dead"—they remained people—unchecked and uncheckable. It was frustrating to be omnipotent.

"I see what you mean," Dagon said finally. "That's serious."

"I can't bring myself to say that we'll just have to make the best of it."

"You just said it."

"Said what?"

"You said—we'll just have to make the best of it."

"What are you, some kind of a quitter? There has to be a solution to this. What we are doing is terribly, terribly important work. We are outlining *useful* sins. But where is the solution? What are we going to do?"

Dagon shrugged. "We could maybe talk it over with the former wife from the former life. I'll never forget how she got that prayer through."

Raziel rubbed his chin. "Maybe you got something there."

"Let's play back all the film we got on her and see if anything whistles Dixie."

They rented a Movieola and ran through every foot of the NixonVision material on Charlotte Pimbernel when she had been Carlotta Quebaro. They spent four totally bleary-making days staring at the clock-sized screen. At last it was over.

"Did you see it?" Raziel said.

"See what? I can't remember a thing. Not a single frame."

"You have to admit that you never saw a woman love any man as completely as that Carlotta Quebaro loved her husband."

"Fantastic. But what does she see in him?"

"She is Mrs. Love-That-Man-Like-Nobody-Else. Is that how you see it?"

231

"Absolutely."

"What chance do you think a sweet, dumb girl like Doris Quebaro is going to have against that—and I don't care if they shoot her up with fifty of their candy arrows!"

o

Zeus lowered Eros down to the window ledge of the Quebaro law office on a coil of nylon rope. Zeus was on the ledge of the offices directly overhead, invisible to human eyes, as was Eros. They had to work invisibly; otherwise the people working in the office directly beside Zeus, and the woman who was looking out of the window from the Scribner Building, would have called the police.

Eros found firm footing on the window ledge, unpacked his bow and arrows from the tiny violin case, and looked into the room. Miss Pimbernel was facing Mr. Quebaro directly as he dictated to her. Eros waited until the woman was looking directly into Quebaro's eyes; then he loosed three, rapid-fire, triple-dipped arrows at point-blank range. The arrows pierced Miss Pimbernel's heart in quick succession. Eros waited tensely for her to moan and melt and fling herself across the desk at Quebaro because this had been the strongest dose he had given anyone since he had made his own personal arrangements to get Psyche.

But nothing happened. Repeat: nothing happened. He loosed two more arrows. He saw them hit and sink in but they had no effect. Zeus was jerking on the rope. He began to pull Eros up, hand over hand. When Eros was on the upper ledge, Zeus said, "Don't you think five arrows are kind of a lot? We want her to fall in love, not turn into a mad dog."

"Gangrad?"

"What?"

"I *had* to shoot five arrows."

"Why?"

"The arrows didn't work."

"You missed her? At that range?"

"The arrows hit. Three. Center target. Nothing happened." Eros had a high, soft voice and a babyish lisp, probably against the day when talking Valentine's Day greeting cards would come in, but he was a serious kid.

"Nothing *hap*pened?"

"So I sent in nummer fier und fumpf. Macht nichts."

"What is it with you and this pidgin German all the time?" Zeus barked. "You are a Greek boy. Speak Greek or I'll give you such a klaps you won't be able to hear. What macht nichts?"

"She was looking straight at him, Gangrad."

Zeus fell back weakly against the building wall, pale. "Do you think I've lost my powers?" he asked pitiably.

"We're invisible, aren't we?"

"Yes."

"Then you have your powers."

"Go get the arrows back. They are used arrows. I'll put a special spell on them and you'll shoot them at that lady who is looking out the window in that building over there. Five arrows." He lowered Eros to the Quebaro ledge. Eros passed through the window and pulled all five arrows out of Charlotte. He tugged on the rope and Zeus pulled him up.

Taking the arrows, Zeus said, "Cover your ears." The boy clamped his hands tightly at the sides of his head. Zeus turned away and whispered something in Mycenaean at the arrows and turned them upside-down, mysteriously. "Okay," Zeus said, "the arrows have the refill. Do your thing."

They looked across the courtyard from the back of the 49th Street building to the back of the Fifth Avenue building. At last, the door behind the young woman opened. An elderly mailman who had surely lied about his age when he had entered the Postal Service and who was almost certainly nine years over the retirement age came shuffling into the room as the young woman turned to look at him and Eros loosed the rapid-fire with the triple dip and Zeus's own whammy on them. The gods watched the arrows penetrate the balloon of her left breast as she turned to look at the ruin of the mailman. They could, of course, hear no sound as she covered the distance between herself and the mailman in four bounds. She ripped the front of his trousers off with the inspired strength that had come over her and bore him down upon the floor, out of sight.

"Well, one thing we know, Gangrad," Eros said. "You certainly haven't lost your powers."

"There is something fishy about that Charlotte Pimbernel."

"Fishy?" Eros said. "There has to be something absolutely *zahlungsschwierig* as far as I'm concerned."

"You mean—you think she's *gleichgeschlect-lich?*"

"Gangrad, the five arrows she got were triple-dipped!"

"I am going to look into this personally," Zeus sobbed, "if I can only stop weeping about my lost Doris." The boy helped him off the ledge, through the busy rooms, and out of the offices.

PART THREE

One

Through two entire sessions at Liederkranz Hall, after the conference at the Cloisters with the Greeks, N'Zuriel Yhwh had sat blandly, centered on his own aplomb.

Then a truth detonated inside his head. Like the flash that follows the explosion of a ninety-megaton H-bomb whose shock waves have the power to circle the world four times at an average speed of 31.2 hours and 11 minutes per circuit, N'Zuriel Yhwh suddenly realized that every movement, every word, every second in which he had made a fool of himself with Aphrodite had been projected on that giant NixonVision screen at which he was now staring, absent-mindedly munching popcorn. *This entire assembly —Upper and Lower Houses—every one of whom he absolutely outranked—had watched him and had listened to him make an assignation with that Greek woman in a Brooklyn hotel!* The length of each fraction of fractions of moments he had talked with her in the total view of the most prestigious angels in the Firmament, stretched out in his mind longer than the 244-foot daisy chain which had been completed by the Coronation Secondary School, Pembroke Dock, Wales, on May 12, 1971, and cast a shadow over his *amour propre,* which was so huge as to make Charles de Gaulle's have seemed like Father Damian's, chilling his self-esteem as though it had been touched by the forefinger of Clarence Birdseye. He wanted to shrivel up into the size of a mouse and scurry out of Liederkranz Hall. He got up abruptly, looking at no one, and strode to the MEN'S ROOM on that floor and locked himself in a stall, trying to get time to think. *"How could you have done such a thing, N'Zuriel?"* he kept asking himself.

If he were ever to pull himself out of the

depths into which his herculean ego had cast him, he would have to invent something so magnificent that it would capture the imagination of the entire convention. He had to find a way to recreate his stately, ever-error-free image which he knew had always glowed within the minds of his peers when they thought of him. He had to come up with a scheme that would beggar the efforts of Raziel, Dagon, and anyone else who had some remote idea that they were among the front-runners of the convention. In one fell swoop he had to motivate Quebaro into providing solutions so that he, N'Zuriel Yhwh, could be seen as the angel who had cracked the case, who had come down from the Mount, as it were, with the answers by which the convention could reframe morals and rewrite sins for the lung fish. But—*what?* He closed his eyes. After a day and a half on that toilet seat it came to him. Raziel kept trying to tell them about wage drifts, arbitrage, expense accounts, conglomerates, macro-economics, cemetery care investment funds, loss leaders, buffer stocks, payola, the karat scale, and the Kennedy round. But nobody at the convention—perhaps least of all N'Zuriel Yhwh—could understand any of it. What was the epicenter of all money? At last he had the answer—banks! All right. So he would appear in a dream to the lung fish President and command him to appoint Eugene Quebaro as National Banks Czar. Working at the center of it all, Quebaro would then be *living* the story of money and demonstrating everything as he went along. They wouldn't have to depend on whether the man knew what he was doing or not. He would just be the man on the spot, the lung fish at the right place at the right time. N'Zuriel Yhwh had solved everything! And would, as always, be the envy of heavenly princes for his dignity, authority, and circumspection.

He hurried from the loo at the back of the great hall and looked down at the delegates, pages, security men, stenographers, firmamental journalists, cherubs, harpists, cabalistic enumerators, hayyoth, seraphim—and the four evil angels Puziel, Guziel, Psdiel, and Prsiel who were guarding the exits in case anyone thought they could slip out unnoticed and take in a movie. N'Zuriel Yhwh could smell the aromatic plants placed all around the hall. He listened with growing reassurance to the sacred music arranged for dulcimer, lyre, and cymbals. "It's that old gang of mine," he said sentimentally.

Raziel was addressing the convention, trying to explain assets, stripping, uptick, leverage, big board, tax havens, Marx & Galbraith, buffer stocks, slumps, monopolies, and capital formation. He was exhorting them about stock splits, gross domestic cash flows, rigging the market, business cycles, forward purchase, mortgages, pyramiding, and the Euro-bond market. He urged them to try to understand, while N'Zuriel Yhwh worried that it was already past the President's bedtime, such elusive concepts as near-cash, Dow-Jones, pump priming, ergonomics, credit unions, price-earnings ratios, proxies, cost benefit analysis, the consumer price index, and the Common Market.

N'Zuriel Yhwh could not stand Raziel taking all the attention for such a lot of flap-doodle when only he, N'Zuriel Yhwh, knew what must be done. "I AM GOING TO TELL YOU HOW TO FIND OUT ALL THAT!" he yelled from the back of the hall as he advanced rapidly down the aisle with his hands held high, to interrupt the business of the convention.

After he had given his long speech about what banks were, explaining his plan to have Eugene Quebaro appointed as National Banks Czar, the Joint (⚕) Commission voted its unanimous acceptance of the N'Zuriel Yhwh Plan. When he had accepted the congratulations of the various caucus leaders in the Liederkranz cloakroom, N'Zuriel Yhwh left for Washington and entered the President's dream. He issued his instructions. Until he got well out of the dream, N'Zuriel Yhwh was oppressed by the smell of toasted breakfast muffins. It was very confusing inside the President's head.

Two

Charlotte lay on her stomach in her room at the Hotel Piedmont continuing in her mind the debate with Gene, for she knew he could be THE super insurance salesman. She knew it. She filled her mind with his small, brown, ferally beautiful face which could open into a dazzling smile whiter than any collie's, giving, always giving to the world through his soft, sweet, brown salesman's eyes under the marvelous shining black helmet of his hair. He was the handsomest, dearest, kindest man ever born—towering over ordinary men with his enormous bones, his thrillingly broad shoulders and waistlessness, yet with hands so gentle, so dexterous! He could probably cook. He could probably sing. She closed her eyes and found herself bathed in a puzzling vision of herself and Gene and an older man who must be his father on a porch in the summertime singing the medley of "Du Gamla, Du Fria," Sweden's national anthem, "Bayang Magiliw, Perlasng Silanganan," the Philippine national anthem and "Battle Hymn of the Republic." The blend of all of it came out of Gene like a love song for a *ménage à trois.* And what a dancer he must be! But everything he did edified her: She imagined that as his wife she would be the perpetual envy of other women; even blind women who couldn't see him could still smell him and imagine what it must be like to be Charlotte Quebaro—imagine but fall short by about one million miles.

Something had happened to what must be his man's sure knack of dressing himself more smartly than any other man but she put that down to the indifference and ignorance of his clottish Greek-American wife who probably hung her laundry on the chandeliers and chewed bubblegum. If Gene were the first target, that woman was the first obstacle. Gene's obviously unrestricted genius for selling life insurance was the second target. Gene's useless law practice was the second obstacle.

She called down for some consommé and toast at 6:11 P.M. and, as an afterthought, asked them to send up an evening paper. She sharpened some pencils and laid out two fresh writing pads on the stainless steel and glass table. She would spend the time until Monday morning planning her campaign to sweep the Greek-American bint from the seas so that she could settle down to fulfilling Gene's purpose, which was her purpose. She had to get Eugene Quebaro established in the insurance business.

The doorbell rang. It was the waiter with the consommé. She sat down to sip soup and read the newspaper. Tumbling out at her in bold two-column headlines came detestable news:

PRESIDENT NAMES QUEBARO AS U.S. BANKING CZAR TODAY

Damn those manipulating field study teams, she raged. Oh, damn, damn, damn! She read the story intently. *Gene had already accepted without consulting her! Bank*ing czar? All the files had shown he had known *some*thing about trading dinner plates, but he wouldn't even know where to start with banking. Oh, damn, damn, *damn!* This meant she would have to devote every night next week to a crash course at the public library cramming on Federal and State banking systems, which meant she would have to put off getting rid of that blotchy Greek-American woman until the week after next.

The telephone rang. It was Gene. How thrilling it was to hear that voice and know that he was hers!

"Have you seen the papers, Charlotte?"

"Yes. What a nice surprise."

"I told the President I couldn't start until a week from Monday. And it isn't going to create any problems with Uncle Raimundo's estate."

"That's nice."

"But I certainly wouldn't want to be the all-powerful Federal Bank Czar if I didn't have you there to keep little details running smoothly."

"How very kind, Gene. In that case I think I should take the next week off just to brush up on banking procedures. I mean, you'll be busy with the press and Mrs. Quebaro and probably one of us ought to take a refresher course."

"Damned good notion, Charlotte. You do that. What would you say if we met for lunch a week from today—at the Plaza—and you could sort of brief me on what banking tips you had been able to pick up?"

Heaven help him, she thought. A kosher corned beef resting on a delicatessen steam table was sharper than Gene about almost everything. "Jolly good," Charlotte said. "The Oak Room at one o'clock. I'll book the table."

o

N'Zuriel Yhwh could not wait to get the N'Zuriel Yhwh Plan underway to reestablish his self-esteem and to return him to a place of highest regard among his peers by showing that his Banking Czar solution had been *the* solution to the entire J($⫟$)CES convention study. So he juggled time a little bit. But he made a mistake. He only advanced Gene Quebaro and Charlotte Pimbernel by one week to get them into their jobs all the more quickly. But he forgot to advance the rest of the people living on the Tenth Level to stay even with Quebaro and his assistant. This mistake altered things a great deal.

o

Instantaneously after they hung up from making the luncheon appointment for the following week, Charlotte and Gene sat thigh-by-thigh on a banquette at the Hotel Plaza. Gene was saying with astonishment, "But—you are absolutely beautiful!"

This flustered Charlotte. "Why, thank you! But I look just as I have always looked."

"It's your glasses," he gasped. "You aren't wearing the glasses you wear at the office!" He knew suddenly that the plots of all the old Betty Grable-Bette Davis movies on television were based on *truth.*

Charlotte dimpled and hit him with a numbing, toothy smile. "Beauty is in the eye of the begrudger," she said.

They had a wonderful time at lunch. Charlotte was so happy it was contagious. For once, they talked about everything but money. "I had a little trouble getting away today," Gene said. "My in-laws were going to stop by at our place—they haven't seen the new place yet—and somehow my wife had forgotten to tell me. Well! Are you all briefed out on banking?"

"Oh, yes."

"Is it difficult?"

"Not a bit."

"Well, we'll just move slowly on it."

"Gene, I wonder if you could help me this afternoon?"

"Anything at all."

"I've decided to sell my house in Stamford, and I need your legal, stable, male opinion."

They drove to Stamford in a rented car, Gene at the wheel.

"Do you make this drive often?" Charlotte, asked as they headed out on Long Ridge Road. "You certainly seem to know the way."

"Well, *yeah.* How about that? I mean I've never even driven to *Stam*ford before. Are you saying we're also on the right road?"

"That's the house just up there."

"Well—how did that happen?"

"Stop right here."

He stopped the car. "But——"

"It's nothing supernatural. I mean you read about things like this all the time. It must be coincidence," Charlotte said.

They went into the house. She walked him right past the living room with the deep conversation pit and all the electronic prayer wheels. They stood in the large square entrance hall. "How do you like it?" Carlotta asked.

"God*dam*, Charlotte. I have the eeriest feeling."

She turned to face him in her thin summer dress, standing very close to him. "What is the feeling like?" she said in a low, husky voice; not a trick voice, but a voice choked and strained with hunger for him. She blinked her eyes slowly and ran her pink tongue over her lips lasciviously.

"I have the eerie feeling that I have lived in this house. And—I mean, what the hell—how could I drive straight to it unless I had driven here before?"

A weird sense of recognition ascended through Charlotte's body. Impulsively, testing herself and Gene, she asked, "Listen, can you show me where the dining room is?"

Abruptly, he led her along a short hall to a room which had been well out of his sight. And it did look much more like a dining room than, say, a gymnasium. "This is where we ate."

"We?"

"It looked like this because we liked to pretend we were eating in a restaurant while, at the same time, we were actually saving money because my wife was extremely sensible, you see—"

"Your—who?—dearest."

Gene was getting more dazed. The impact of those little tables was jolting.

"Just the two of you?" Carlotta whispered.

"Yes," he said, disturbed. "And we had Muzak. My wife built it. She made the wine we drank." He stared through the walls of the past. "It was really wonderful wine. You might not think that vintage turnip wine could be wonderful, but it was. Full-bodied, soft—enormous mouth —and so good for you. I would lift my glass to her from across the room at a distant table. She would smile at me through the mists of the Muzak. I would cross the room and we would dine together. How we would dine! Swedish-Filipino cuisine. No use trying to tell you about *that*, but I can taste it now." He ran his hand over his eyes. "But I don't seem to be able to pronounce it anymore."

244

"Are you all right?" Carlotta asked from the edge of hope. "Woofie?"

The room seemed to tilt on him. He reached out to grip her arm as he went backward two short steps. She looked up at him longingly.

"*She* called me Woofie," he said brokenly. "Only Carlotta ever called me that—thank God." They stared at each other, silent for a long moment. He blinked as if he were staring into a minor sun. "Charlotte—are you Carlotta?"

"Yes, Woofie, dear."

"What happened? Where did we go?"

"Do you think you could lead us to the bedroom?" Carlotta said, panting heavily.

"We can figure everything out later, much later," Gene said, picking her up and carrying her along a different hall to another room.

Ω

As the convention watched the Quebaros flailing about on the bed on the giant NixonVision screen, N'Zuriel Yhwh dabbed at his eyes with a handkerchief and said, "That was ex*tre*mely touching." He punched the FREEZE button. "It was so much like one of those wonderful old Warner Brothers movies on television where Kay Francis and George Brent—oh, boy!"

"Did you see the one with Kay Francis and William Powell, they were on a ship?" Dagon said. "I bawled like a baby."

"I am only worried how she is going to get us out of this after they are finished on the bed?" Raziel said.

"She'll find a way," N'Zuriel Yhwh told him. "This is one terrific kid."

"She knows the whole story," Raziel said. It all came back to her the minute she saw him in that house. By now she has figured it all out."

"If she ever tells him the truth, we are going to have some big brainwash on our hands," Dagon added.

"Why should she tell him the truth?" N'Zuriel Yhwh demanded. "She probably saw the same Kay

Francis movie. She'll explain everything."

"In my humble opinion," Dagon said, "this is better than the movie. Even the production is better. Look at that lighting! Pauline Kael couldn't have lighted it better."

"Let them finish and wash up," Raziel said. "Let's let them start talking." He pushed the ACTION button.

While he was tying his necktie, Gene asked her point-blank what had happened to him and when and how. She decided that the true explanation could only unbalance him so she said, "Woofie? Do you remember a Kay Francis-George Brent movie? Called *They Packed Twenty-four Hours into a Lifetime?* Like he was a great insurance salesman who was hit on the head and the blow gave him total amnesia?"

o

"See," N'Zuriel Yhwh said. "What did I tell you?"

"This is the smartest little lung fish that ever happened," Dagon said.

"Remember you said that," Raziel told him. "Real talent isn't just lying around the streets."

o

Gene said, "Yes. I remember the movie. George Brent got terrible amnesia and he walked out into a new life. He forgot his entire past. He married another woman. An innocent woman." Gene shuddered. The bouncing ball of awful memory began to careen around inside his head. He felt almost unmanned as he remembered. His legs turned to water. He felt straight downward into a chair. "My God!" he gasped. "What am I going to do? I am married to Doris!"

"Those things happen, dearest," Carlotta said. "Remember George Brent."

"But—I'm a *big*amist! I loved you yet I married her because—and maybe this is a terrible thing to say —I love her, too. What am I going to do?"

"You are going to stick with the plot of the

movie like everybody else," Carlotta said patiently. "This is your life, Eugene Quebaro. Run it through. Kay Francis came to work as George Brent's secretary. But the audience knew she was his wife from the other life. She wore glasses so George Brent wouldn't recognize her but then he got another hit on the head and it all came back to him."

What had come back to Gene with cruel force was a vision of Doris's sweet face, which had never lost its smile of belief in all the bad years they had struggled through. He was frightened. He felt helpless. The only life-line was the thread from the plot of a forty-three-year-old movie. The lifeline snapped. He was carried out to the raging sea again.

"We can't stay with the plot of the movie, Carlotta."

"Why not?"

"Because George Brent's second wife was killed rescuing a kitten in a flood."

"I remember," Carlotta said softly.

"So this *isn't* an old movie. This is a real problem. I owe Doris a great debt. She loves me and she stood by me. This has to be faced and I don't know how to face it."

o

"Now she has to spill the beans," N'Zuriel Yhwh said. "I was wrong."

"No." Raziel was emphatic.

"I agree with him, Raz," Dagon said. "After all, she's only a lung fish. She has no place else to go. She has to tell him now that there were no years he and Doris had together, that the whole thing is just an illusion of programmed inputs."

"No, she won't," Raziel said.

"Who can it hurt? A little brainwash and everybody is home free."

"Don't underestimate her," Raziel said. "She is a very special woman."

o

"This is out of your hands, Gene," Carlotta told him. "There is no way for you to face it or ever to solve it."

"Out of my hands?"

"This has to be between Doris and me."

"How?" He was wary.

"You are as innocent of wrong intent as she is. But she has to know in her heart that you are rightfully mine."

"Doris may not see it that way. But, even if she agrees, what is she going to do?"

"She'll just slip away. Your marriage has no legal meaning. It just never was. A ticket to a far place, I think."

"Well, you don't know Doris."

Carlotta put a soft finger to his lips. "No fretting," she said tenderly. "Women know. She will understand. You are mine."

o

The tensed convention broke into instant, relieved applause.

Three

Although N'Zuriel Yhwh had been able to arrange for Charlotte and Gene to "jump" a week directly into their vital meeting for lunch at the Oak Room, that did not mean that the week had not happened.

In many ways Gene and Charlotte had missed eventful times. The American banking industry, led by a direfully outraged banker named Bennett Johns in San Antonio, Texas, had expressed horror at the President's announcement of a Federal banking czar who would "have unlimited powers to close, audit, merge, rearrange, regulate and control all banks in the United States of America." Johns had convened a powerful banking committee of his own and they had immediately suspended all banking operations in the country and had called in all paper, loans, mortgages, and other financial obligations that they were holding on any part of the American overcommunications industry: the press, television, radio, and comic books. They cried out that the President was seeking to rip the heart out of America.

The overcommunications industry immediately got the point and began a high, median, and low-level attack upon the President's concept of a watchdog-ruler for banks and all of its possible considerations including Eugene Quebaro. The man who had become one of the nation's mightiest heroes in four days was now diminished, shrunken like a hobby human head of a picturesque South American Indian. Eugene Quebaro, the man who saved the dollar, was transformed overnight into an agrarian Maoist plotter whose lust to bring Communism was laced with armor plates of Hitlerian fascism, whose engorgement of power over a weakened and hypnotized President had swollen him out of human proportions into revolting, monstrous shape. During the week that was to be forever missing to Gene and Carlotta, he was torn to shreds as the overcommunications industry fought, day and night, to convince all banks and bankers, great and small, that they were in a holy war against a fiend. While the dollar Quebaro had restored slumped alarmingly, Eugene Quebaro, to the utter glee of the press, had disappeared. It is possible that, had Quebaro been able to show his face anywhere in the United States during the week he had missed before recopulating in Connecticut, he would have been mobbed, perhaps lynched.

The President's first announcement of the Quebaro appointment appeared in the "light" papers on Saturday morning so that the news could germinate into sturdy think pieces in the "heavy" Monday and Tuesday papers and in the weightless news magazines. The really terrible screams from the bankers were not registered until the six o'clock news on Saturday night. By Sunday morning the mortgaged overcommunicators had been whipped into line and had begun to promise disaster. Monday morning carried the President's denial of ever having made such an appointment, implying that a sinister force was impersonating the President.

On Tuesday, the White House revealed the contents of tapes which proved that the President had not considered the banking dictatorship nor had he offered any fictional post of "banking czar" to Eugene Quebaro, but had, instead, offered him the embassy in India. But, for whatever reason, no one would believe these tapes. Then, miraculously and compassionately, everything was totally forgotten on Thursday when Raquel Welch sat on a beehive with shocking results and the country went into half-mourning. The Welch disaster so dwarfed the banks' rebellion that, by Friday, in clusters of states, the banks began to reopen for business. The President went on to make new mistakes. Then came the blessed, healing hiatus of the weekend which began on the Saturday when Carlotta and Gene met for lunch at the Oak Room and drove out to the house on Long Ridge Road.

o

N'Zuriel Yhwh watched the havoc his time-tampering had caused, seeing his dream of making Quebaro a banking czar slip away as the American establishment spent itself in rage, but he was utterly unable to move quickly enough because one week to his own sense of timelessness went by faster than an eyeblink to a human. As the Quebaros got into the rented car outside their house on Long Ridge Road, he adjusted the time difference, making everything equal again, except that the Quebaros did not know they had gained one week in one day; they did not know a week had passed away forevermore. They had no conception of the trouble they were in.

Carlotta drove back to New York. Gene was too immobilized with thoughts of Doris to be able to concentrate on anything. When they got into the city, he decided he couldn't face Doris. He decided to spend the weekend at his office, pleading the pressures of the new banking czar job, giving himself time to think.

o

Doris had been frantic with worry about Gene's disappearance. She had appealed to the International Mafia through Mr. Violente. She had sought the counsel of Judge Zeuss, driving him almost out of his trousers with the heat of the opportunity inherent in her husband's absence, but thirty to fifty press, radio and TV members, the six FBI men, eleven special (undercover) agents of the Bankers' Protective Association, the Russell Harty Show from London, and two attorneys from the Senate Banking Committee were covering the front and service entrances to the Quebaro apartment building against the probability that, if Quebaro surfaced, he would probably get in touch with his wife. Doris's telephone at Fortress Midtown held six different wiretaps. Her appeal to Mr. Violente brought headlines that linked Eugene Quebaro to the Mafia. On telephoned advice from Judge Zeuss, she made two appearances a day in the street-floor lobby of Fortress Midtown to report to the nation's press that she had heard nothing from her husband and "feared foul play."

Zeus wouldn't chance running the gauntlet of the press. Of course, he could have simply materialized in Doris's apartment but he couldn't figure out how he would explain that to her. He was even ready to risk it, just for the chance to get at Doris in her loneliness, but Athena convinced him that the NixonVision cameras would pick him up and reveal what he had in mind with Doris. That offended Zeus's sense of personal daintiness. His terrible lust was abated only when Doris told him (over the telephone) that her mother and Dr. Lesion had moved into the apartment to keep her company, which, fortunately, violated his opportunity.

o

The rented car carrying Eugene Quebaro came along 49th Street from Madison Avenue at five ten Saturday afternoon to drop him at his office.

"Hey! There must have been a fire in my building," he said as the car came nearer the horde of newsmen in vigil outside.

"It's probably just a Heroin Sale," Carlotta said at the moment Stone of the *Times* spotted Gene.

"Holy *shit!*" he screamed with professional ecstasy. "Here he is!" Eighteen hands reached into the car and dragged Gene out through the open window while Carlotta shrieked at them to let him go and pulled at Gene's middle from the other side. They got him out almost before the car could be stopped.

Carlotta got the car door open somehow, left the car in the middle of 49th Street, and fought her way through the press of bodies until she saw that the only way to get to Gene would be to swim across the tops of their heads and shoulders, so she ripped her way back to the car, climbed to its roof, and dove flatly toward the entrance to the building. She got a grip on the nose of a policeman and squeezed hard as she screamed, "What are you *doing*? What are you doing to Mr. Quebaro? We demand police protection! This man is a ranking federal official." The cop whose nose she was squeezing responded wildly to the pain by clubbing three men and a girl on his right side, scattering teeth but clearing a small space in front of Gene, into which Carlotta dropped. She stood between him and the mad dog mob of overcommunicators, making a fence on either side of him with her arms outstretched behind her.

"*STAAAHHHHPPPPPP!*" she yelled in a mighty voice.

The CBS-TV cameraman bellowed, "Cheat this way, lady. To your *right,* baby, to your *right.*"

There were cries of "Who's the broad?" and "Get that goddam woman out of there!" while the police worked their way in front of all news cameras except the *Daily News* as though protecting Carlotta and her chief. One tall man with a moustache wrenched his way to the front line and, for the moment, was the horde's spokesman. "Howdy, ma'am," he said. "I'm Mort Stone of the *Times?* Who are you-all, ma'am?"

Carlotta put her hand on Stone's chest and held him off. "I am Charlotte Pimbernel, Eugene Quebaro's executive assistant in the Federal Banking Administration, and I demand an explanation for this outrageous conduct. I will state right now that Mr. Quebaro will make no statement whatsoever until this pavement has been cleared by the police and Mr. Quebaro and I have been given safe conduct into this building and his offices."

Very few of Carlotta's words were heard after she said that Quebaro still considered himself to be the banking czar. But Stone turned to the rest of the press, winking heavily, and pleaded for them to give the little lady a chance to talk. They got quiet.

"First of all," Charlotta said, "let's understand one thing. As Federal banking czar, Mr. Quebaro is only an instrument of the people. Now, I'll give you this little fillip so you can go away with something to write about. On behalf of the American people, it is his intention to socialize the American banking system and to socialize the system of money as we know it."

"*Lynch the son of a bitch!*" the policeman nearest Gene screamed, lunging. Carlotta threw a necklock on him, sunk her fingers deeply into his upper hip pressure point and threw him high in the air over her shoulder into the dense crowd. She dragged and pushed Gene ahead of herself into the building. She slammed and jammed the main door, raced Gene into the elevator, and dragged the door shut, sending the car to the eighth floor and Gene's office. She rammed Gene into the office and closed the door. Then, with a magnificent British sense of understatement she wheeled on Gene and said, "Something went wrong."

As a man who thought he was a member of the administration team, Gene said, "It must be the goddam Washington *Post.*"

A siege began. On and off through most of Saturday night, the nation kept watch on its television screens. Every hour on the hour, the screens showed the same shots of Carlotta declaiming in the street, throwing the cop away, bolting with Gene into the building, while even-voiced commentators explained that there were no new developments. The Sunday papers carried banners which shouted

COMMUNIST BANK CZAR
OFFERS FREE MOOLAH

having decided to ignore the fact that, some days before, the President had denied that the office of a banking czar had ever existed.

Four

The news ticker at Popina Matsoukis brought the word to Zeus that inasmuch as the heat was now directly on Doris's husband, the heat was now entirely off Doris. Zeus threw himself into materializing directly outside the Quebaro door on the sixty-seventh floor of Fortress Midtown. He rang the doorbell, concentrating with all of his terrible force on willing Doris not to turn on radio or television to learn that her husband had returned from wherever he had been. The door opened.

"*OH!*" Doris cried out. "It's *you!*" Her right hand covered her left breast in classical style, in a body language Zeus had learned to read well over the millennia.

"Is your mother here?" he said, breathing shallowly.

"No. She and the doctor are getting some sun on the Staten Island ferry."

"I had to see you," Zeus said. "I can't stand it. I can't work, I can't eat. I can hardly breathe. You have filled my life. I adore you. I want you."

"Please come in," Doris said. "I am very worried. I need advice badly."

Zeus shut the door and locked it behind himself. "Your husband has deserted you," he said. "He has run off with his secretary."

"Im-possible!"

"He loves her, the fool. I love you. You are mine. You will always be mine."

"Judge Zeuss, *please,*" Doris said weakly as he advanced on her, his eyes gleaming dully. "I want my husband back."

Judge Zeuss took her in his arms. She writhed steadily, perhaps to escape, but she just didn't seem to be strong enough. Beyond her will, as if moving by its own decision, her hand worked its way into the fractional space between their bodies, shocked her deeply by tugging at the zipper of his trousers.

"No, *no!*" she moaned whenever she could get her mouth free, but her mouth was hardly ever free. Her legs gave way. She sank to the floor, unable to cope with her real desire, which was to order Judge Zeuss to leave her house immediately.

"Aaaaaaa!" she argued. They thrashed about the floor in a storm of high legs and flashes of skin.

"Oooooooooh! Eeeeeeee!" she protested. "Oh! Sweetheart! My God! You're en*or*mous!"

"That's just the starter," he gasped.

"Ooooooh, *Judge!* My God, *Judge!*"

In position at last, Judge Zeuss began to work with the immeasurable skill of thousands of years of regular, steady practice toward perfection. Doris wanted only one more thing to make it perfect. "Sweetheart—darling—please—please reach up right beside you and switch it on. I've got to have music with this—this *magic.* We must have all this inside walls of wonderful music." Reflexively, as he worked away, Zeus's hand ascended blindly and turned on the radio switch, his eyes rolling wildly in his head, and the meaty voice of a news commentator boomed into the room.

"After fighting their way through the twenty-three-man-deep density of television cameras, press and police, Eugene Quebaro and his beautiful executive assistant—as she calls herself—found refuge in his law offices at ten East Forty-ninth Street where now they are both barricaded and where they are prepared to spend the night together, if necessary."

One half of the violent movement on the floor seemed to have stopped; the lower half. After a few short moments the top stopped its movements. "What's the matter?" Zeus asked tragically.

"Get off me, please, Judge Zeuss," Doris said. "What?"

"Please get *up!* Judge *Zeuss!* Get off me this *instant!*" She changed the level of the plateau under his limpening body and rolled him over to her left. There was a THLOCK sound, like a very large champagne cork popping. Doris got to her feet, straightened herself out with a few quick movements, and dashed out of the room. "Doris——" he yelled after her. "How can you do this after all we've been through? What happened? Doris, tell me what *hap-pened* here?"

The news commentator's sunset gun voice got through to him:

"Quebaro, bewildered, arrived on the scene so unexpectedly that the press corps who had been standing vigil in front of that building for five days may have over-reacted, observers say, but the police soon had——"

Zeus snapped the set off. He took three steps away from it, as if he were going to follow Doris down the corridor to her bedroom; then he reversed himself, went back to the radio, ripped it out of the wall and ran with it to the kitchen where he executed it by flinging it down the incinerator shaft. Then he jammed his hat on his head, zipped up his trousers with a brutal wrench, caught one of his testicles in the steel zipper, screamed, unzipped, adjusted, rezipped, then, almost fainting with the fear of the effects of the sudden self-mutilation, opened the main door, stepped limping out into the hall, then slammed the door shut with a tremendous bang, the sound resounding through the building.

Doris had cleared her mind of everything but the fact that Gene and that woman had reappeared together after a week's absence and that he had not even bothered to come home to put up a false front to cover up his disappearance with lies. She wanted to remember only two things: that she was wronged and heartbroken. Her wonderful, wonderful marriage was in ruins. Her husband had deserted her in a way that proved she had never meant anything to him. Now he was holed up with his mistress in his rotten little two-by-four office. She was sure of only one thing. She wasn't going to let them get away with it.

She put on her make-up twice. She felt a few knives of regret for the way she had treated Judge Zeuss. It might have seemed tactless but this was reality. The Judge was something else. She changed into the one dress she and Gene had both always been crazy about. She drenched herself in the perfume he loved the most, then she rushed out of the apartment and fled to the street where, without the slightest delay, she was able to flag down an empty cab, which happened to be driven by Zeus in his red wig and red moustache. She gave the address of Gene's building and the cab headed downtown.

Five

Hermes, who had been watching the giant NixonVision screen at Liederkranz Hall, raced up the broad steps through the expensive cigar smoke of the convention to a telephone booth in a public corridor. He telephoned Athena. "Sis? Herm. Well, it just hit the fan. Anything can happen now."

"What happened?"

"I'm at the Liederkranz. Pop just showed up on the giant screen here. He was at the Quebaros'. He scored Mrs. Quebaro—except not entirely—on the floor of the entrance hall. Then, through an accident that is too sad to even try to explain, Mrs. Quebaro found out where her husband was—at his office, downtown—and she is now riding there in a cab driven by Pop in disguise."

"One of *his* disguises!"

"The red wig and the shredded moustache."

"O, Herm!"

"Well, they're pretty dumb up here. The main thing is: has Aphrodite been able to come up with an antidote for Eros's arrow in Pop's heart?"

"Not yet."

"What should I do?" Hermes asked.

"Just wait. We've got to give Aphrodite a chance. Go back to the Hall and watch."

As Hermes returned to the convention, N'Zuriel Yhwh had the floor and the complete attention of the convention.

". . . and I am very gratified to accept your congratulations on how nicely the national bank czar thing worked out. I am glad I thought of it. I feel we have learned

259

a good deal about the lung fish because of it. Please permit me, in advance of expert technical analysis, to project what I feel are only some of the meanings of our field study. We did find out that money is the most collective thing they share but—the very fact of the desirability of money to them prevents any possible collectivization. Their credit system, by which the very fact of money is achieved, insists on pretending that money is individual, not collective, with them. We also found out that, although money is the single material thing desperately needed by all lung fish, the banks and the lung fish who guard the banks, the government and the lung fish who manipulate the government do not want all the lung fish to have money. In fact, they will do anything in their power to subvert any efforts of any lung fish to get an equal share of this substance which is vital to all lung fish. Now here's the *most* peculiar point: all the guardians of money, from the President down to that outraged policeman who was so shocked that anyone could wish to socialize money, all responded violently in opposition to the very idea of socializing money, though they would be depriving themselves—as well as all others—of an insured fair share. Surely, this is a very important discovery. Surely, this must be one of the key points at which their morals went askew two, maybe three hundred years ago. They value money. They all agree that everybody must have it. They secretly admit that it belongs to all, yet all—each and all—rich, middle, or bottom—refuse to share and would instantly accuse anyone who suggested that they did share of being a dangerous radical. I mean, take a look. You will see that they maintain a collective refusal to admit to the collectivity of money. Take a look and you'll see that my idea about making Quebaro banking czar is the big key to their whole faltering moral code."

"You could also give them a little help with their manners," an angel yelled from far in the back.

"Don't get into manners here, please!" N'Zuriel Yhwh barked. "That is the subject of a whole different convention all by itself." He made a little bow to the Hall. "I thank you for thanking me," he said and sat down to what the cosmological trade papers later referred to as "heavy mitting."

Raziel took the floor. "As always," he said as the applause was allowed to die down, "it's no surprise to any one of us here that N'Zuriel Yhwh did it again. He pondered this banking solution and he has offered us the only analysis which can be drawn from it. However, let us pay our attention to the invaluable contributions made by that outstanding lung fish, Carlotta Quebaro. Not since Ezekiel—indeed not since Enoch—has a lung fish provided us with so many opportunities for quality research and development. Therefore, I respectfully request that a vote of confidence be entered into the record as our token of gratitude to this swell fish." He sat down to a storm of enthusiastic applause.

The convention settled down with total absorption, shuffling their Bingo cards absentmindedly, to watch the events on the giant NixonVision screen make new moral history.

Six

Herbert "Little Pasquale" Ganglia followed Doris riding in the cab driven by Zeus. Thriftily, he was on a Moped. He watched the cab leave Doris in front of 10 East 49th, a building with a big crowd in front of it, then he stayed with the cab as it moved past the crowd. He watched Judge Zeuss take off the wig and moustache and get out. Little Pasquale came around the back of the cab and jammed his Hoodlum Special into the judge's back at kidney level.

"Back inna cab, creep," he snarled.

"Why?"

"Because say no and I blow you apart."

"You are wasting your time."

"Move it! You want that little broad dropped inna river?"

"Who?"

"The Quebaro broad! The one you are workin' wit' to take over the Violente family, yah crazy bastid. Inna cab!"

Zeus did as he was told because the man had appealed to his curiosity. Why would anyone want to harm Doris?

Little Pasquale gave him an address on West 82nd Street. Zeus reached over to start the taxi-meter.

"Don't throw that clock, yah fink! You're not gettin' a dime outta me."

"We can be stopped by a hack inspector. I am warning you."

"Aaaaa. Go ahead and throw it."

Doris fought her way through the mob. "Let me past, damn you!" she yelled. "I am Mrs. Eugene

Quebaro and I demand to be allowed to see my husband."
The police cooperated by flinging her against the building
wall so the press photographers and the television boys
could work up a little feature. After a dozen or so humiliating
questions and a couple of friendly feels, they let her through
the main door and up to Gene's office.

o

For the seventeen minutes they had been inside, Carlotta and Gene had made only a token attempt to
find out what might have gone wrong with the banking czar
appointment. Gene stared listlessly into the courtyard while
Carlotta called her friend Vickie Saxe-Coburg and got the
whole story. Carlotta explained it to Gene. "Oh, the hell with
it," Gene said. "What good is the job, even if it were still
there, if I don't have Doris. It's—it's just all too much for me,
Carlotta."

"But you'll get used to it," she said. "And
she'll understand it the minute I explain everything to her."

Doris burst into the room trembling with an-
ger. "I heard you!" she squeaked, then she wept so robustly
that she was unable to speak. Gene darted across the room
to soothe her.

"It's very complicated, honey," he said.

Doris threw her head back and wailed.

"Oh, for Christ's *sake!*" Carlotta snarled.

"Doris—Doris, listen to me," Gene pleaded.
"You remember that 1931 Kay Francis-George Brent movie
we saw before we had to sell the television set? Where
George Brent gets hit on the head and goes away somewhere
and marries another woman even though he is still very
much married to Kay Francis?"

Doris nodded into her handkerchief as she
wept.

"Well, you have the Glenda Farrell part."

Doris stared at him incredulously. Her head
turned slowly to stare at Carlotta while she spoke to Gene.
"And she has the Kay Francis role?"

"I'm not George Brent, honey," Carlotta
snarled.

263

Doris squealed with rage. She ran to the wall, ripped away a heavily framed steel engraving of Warren G. Harding and ran at Carlotta in full attack. The three bodies converged at a single point, as if choreographed, and formed an idyll, six hands high over three heads, two hands intending to smash and crash, four intending to prevent; a unity as graceful as a fountain piece by Bernini, when the door opened noisily. Without changing position, the three heads turned to see Miss Phyllis Stein filling the doorway, more pregnant than Elzire Dionne had once been. Miss Stein had spent eternity as a fallen angel, but nine seconds after she had met Eugene Quebaro she had become a fallen woman—and it showed. She seemed to be carrying Gene's baby (or babies) high and low, on the sides and fore and aft. She was apparently about to give birth to an adult Kodiak bear.

"Who is *she?*" Doris shrilled.

Miss Stein ignored the two women. She stared longingly at Gene. "It's no use, Gene," she said simply. "I can't hack it alone. You'll have to marry me."

The fountain group scattered. Frozen with disbelief, Doris still held the picture over her head.

"Marry you?" Gene said, "I'm not sure I remember you."

"Mr. Quebaro is married to *us,*" Carlotta said icily.

"I remember now," Gene blurted. "We met about five days ago when I went to get that forged receipt back from Palmer Mahan. Five days, lady. How could I possibly get you into a condition like that?"

"I've been gestating like *crazy,*" Miss Stein said.

With a scream, Doris crashed the picture down on Gene's head. He sank slowly to the floor, his eyes crossing. Doris renewed her sobbing. Carlotta put an arm around her shoulders and patted her soothingly. Miss Stein waddled to Gene's side, assaying how to get closer to him at his level. She plumped herself down on the carpet and lifted his head into her super-circumferential lap.

o

N'Zuriel Yhwh pushed the FREEZE button. "How did that fallen angel get in there? What is all that padding she's wearing everywhere? Who is her Chief of Mission here?"

Haurus materialized, facing the convention hall. Raziel glared at him. "As President of Miss Stein's court-martial I was dismayed to see her appear at the subject's private office to demand that he marry her. Why has she been recalled?"

"We were helpless to continue, Your Beatitude. Her sentence was up for good behavior. I had to have field staff. Palmer Mahan is gone irretrievably. I applied for permission to return Miss Stein to work and we devised this little pregnancy ruse to mitigate the problem which was certain to arise between Quebaro's two wives."

"Mitigate?" Raziel cried. "You made double trouble, you fiend out of Hell."

Haurus sniffed indignantly. "Of course I am a fiend out of Hell," he said. "How could you ever have thought otherwise?"

o

As Gene returned to consciousness and sat up dazedly, looking around himself warily like a horse just fallen at a steeplechase jump, they could all hear the outer door open. There were odd, dragging sounds. The inner office door opened bringing Alice Trudy Kehoe into the room on one crutch, her neck in a high, rigid cast, her head bandaged and her right arm raised in clinical traction in the startling appearance of a perpetual Fascist salute. It was her heavily plastered right leg which had been making the scuffling sound.

"Oh, Gene," she exulted, oblivious of everyone in the room except him, "the hospital has released me. We can be together." She made little mews of ecstasy. "I haven't been able to think of anything but that wonderful night. That pulled me through. Oh, Gene," she moaned. "I want more. I have to have more. I have to have more and more and more and more. Oh, hello, Mrs. Quebaro."

"Have you lost your mind, Miss Kehoe?" Doris said.

"Yes," Alice breathed. "Yes, yes, yes. I lay on that bed, in pain, always stuffed with tubes, rigged with ropes and pulleys, reamed with catheters and gravity feeds, and I told myself it was all worth it, all of it, because we just don't have anything *like* what you people have where I come from. I *knew* you would give him up, Mrs. Quebaro. I knew you would see that mine is the greater need."

o

N'Zuriel Yhwh punched the FREEZE button and yelled, "Chief of Miiissssshhunn!"

Af materialized.

"Did you send that player in?" the Executive Angel asked.

"No, sir. And I am deeply shocked, sir. I am shocked and troubled and grossly offended that one of our people should allow herself to become thus degraded."

"But why is she doing it?"

"I hate to say."

"Say it!"

"I am forced into the belief that she is some kind of nymphomaniac, sir."

N'Zuriel Yhwh jammed down on the ACTION button.

Simultaneously, at Liederkranz Hall, sixty-three angels pushed their FREEZE buttons. Raziel leaped to his feet. "I command that those two angels be removed from that place at once! he thundered.

Outcries rang out.

"Clarify!"

"Specify!"

"Who should remove them?"

"Gavreel!" Raziel yelled. "Now!" Gavreel was the name for Gabriel used by the Ethiopian Hebrew Rabbinical College. At the moment the command was made,

Gavreel removed Stein and Kehoe from the Quebaro office.

Doris stared at the two empty places which two considerable young women had just been filling, began to weep again, and ran out of Gene's office.

Seven

Mort Violente sat in the barely furnished room facing Judge Zeuss, who was tied to a chair. Herbert "Little Pasquale" Ganglia sat close by, leaning forward intently. A simple soldier of the Violente Family, Dimples Tancredi, lounged on an orange crate at the far side of the room. Mr. Violente was grim, sweating lightly in his passion.

"You raided my office and ran me in, right?" he asked the Judge.

"Yes."

"Then you let me out on a phony bail because you ain't a judge, right?"

"Yes."

"Then you had me picked up again. Then again. I am tryna be fair witchew. Right now you happen to be on trial for your life and, between us, you are losing. You made me look like I was some poolroom hustler to every Family in this country—and God knows what they are sayin' about it in Sicily."

"Yes."

"Why you done it?"

"You wouldn't believe me."

"Try me."

"You felt a little bad when my men came in and dragged you out of that bathtub?"

"I felt bad."

"Then, maybe you'll understand. Listen—I did it because I had to meet a woman who works for you, Doris Quebaro."

"That's how you meet women? What happened the last time you picked up a broad—World War II?"

Zeus shrugged. "I had to know her. That's all. I tried to figure out a grandstand play. So I organized the raid and so on—to impress her."

"All the same *morning?*"

"I am a strong organizer. I swear to you, she was more beautiful than I think I ever saw a woman. She was like a girl I knew a long, long time ago. Kind—you know? Sweet, very sweet. When she smiled it turned on all the lights."

"You act like a Sicilian. Ain't Zeuss a Hungarian name?"

"Zeus is Suez spelled backwards," Little Pasquale said.

"Yes," Zeus acknowledged, "it's just a little boustrophedonic. But," he said to Mr. Violente, "to answer your question: it is a Greek name. The Greeks colonized Sicily, after all. But I want you to know that I am truly sorry, on your account, about the way things happened to happen."

"You better believe you are sorry because I am gunna blow a cave into your head."

"Don't be silly. Can't be done."

"You think that's silly? I am a man sixty-six years old. I got maybe two pints wortha passionate conduct left in me an' I am wit' the one woman in the world who turns on music for me whenever she moves, standing or on her back. I can never get it back how I felt before your fake cops busted in. Maybe I never will. And you say it's silly?"

"You are the biggest bookmaker in the history of mankind, Mr. Violente. I know. That means you are a sporting man."

"I got eleven sportin' computers on lease, maybe four hundred sportin' addin' machines, and don't forget my sixteen very sportin' collectors which it is two of them you can see here, now."

"But you do accept wagers. This is what I am going to offer you. I will bet you two million dollars on any horse running at any track you choose, today."

"What horse?"

"That's the sporting part of the bet. You pick the horse and I will bet on it."

"What kinda bet is that?"

"It is a two-million-dollar bet."

"What happens after?"

"What always happens in these things. If I lose, I pay you. If I win, you pay me. And you forget about killing me. But you pick the horse."

"How do I know you got two hundred dollars, never mind two million?"

"Untie me," Judge Zeuss said with simple authority.

"Untie him," Mr. Violente said to Little Pasquale.

"Take the rope off," Little Pasquale said to Dimples Tancredi.

Tancredi untied the Judge, who reached very, very slowly into his breast pocket and took out a thick, black wallet. He placed it on his knees and opened it. He took out a sheaf of mint-fresh ten-thousand-dollar bills. There were twenty of these. He counted them aloud, slowly, then handed them to Mr. Violente. "That is a ten-per cent deposit," the Judge said. "And perhaps you will accept my check for the remaining one million eight?"

There was the sort of silence that is easy to recognize, for it is the silence that the sight of twenty ten-thousand-dollar bills always brings. The Judge said, "If you will bring me a phone while you and your men look up the telephone number of my banker, Jack Crouch, at Manufacturer's Hanover, we can telephone for a confirmation of the availability of the money."

"Get the phone!" Mr. Violente barked at Tancredi, eliminating the middle man.

Mr. Crouch confirmed the availability of the money.

Something occurred to Mr. Violente. "Listen," he said. "Did you figure out this crazy bet so nobody can say you paid me ransom to get out of here?"

"No, no," the Judge said irritably. "You are a bookmaker. I am making a bet. If the horse wins you are going to pay me off at track odds. Is that clear?"

Violente grinned evilly. "Suppose I lose? As if I could lose such a bet. If I lose I'll pay off but you'll be right back where you started with a big hole in your head."

"No. Look here. Suppose the horse you choose is in the morning line at eight to one."

"Okay."

"Therefore, you would write a check to me, at the moment the bet is made, for sixteen million dollars and we send this check to my son, Hermes. I enclose a note which says Herm is to hold the check for three hours—to allow time for the race to be run and the winning horse confirmed to him—then he is to deposit your check to my account—if my horse wins. Follow?"

"You think we can't take the check away from some kid?"

"*Mis*ter Violente—I am merely setting down the rules of the bet."

"Okay. Good rules." Mr. Violente couldn't stop grinning. "Now we pick your horse—okay?"

"Indeed, yes."

"Make your bet."

Judge Zeuss wrote out a check for $1,800,-000. On the obverse side he wrote, "In full payment of a wager of two million dollars made with Mort Violente on the horse_____ running at _____race track on the 27th day of June, 1975: To *Win.*" He showed the check to Mr. Violente who nodded eagerly, grinning. Mr. Violente made a long distance call to Boston.

"Hello, Beniamino?" he said into the phone. "You know who. Look, put the computers on a little problem and call me back. Yeah, Tessie is fine. Here is the problem—ready? What is the absolutely very worst, nothing beetle that is running in the entire United States today—this afternoon. The *worst.* Call me. At Dimples'." He hung up.

They waited seventeen minutes. The Judge amused them with card tricks. Beniamino called back. The name of the horse the computers had selected was Al's Lady-boo. It was running in the fourth at Narragansett. The odds were 87–1.

"You're sure?" Mr. Violente said anxiously into the phone. "A real dog?"

"This horse is not only slow," Beniamino said. "His running style is two steps forward, one step backward. This horse is not only very, *very* slow but this horse is a rotten-*lazy* horse who hates the business he's in and who runs even slower until they finally fire him."

Mr. Violente then agreed on a minor technicality because it was so much in his favor. The bet would be paid off based on the odds in the morning line, 87–1, not on track odds. Judge Zeuss noted the horse's name, the track, and the true date on the back of the check. Mr. Violente initialed it.

Mr. Violente made out his check, grinning wildly, in the amount of $174,000,000. Both Herbert "Little Pasquale" Ganglia and Dimples Tancredi then accompanied Judge Zeuss to a post office where he posted the check, with a note, to Hermes while Ganglia made a note of Hermes's address.

During the short time the mailing party were away, Mr. Violente made another call to Beniamino in Boston.

"Hey," he bellowed into the phone. "lissena me. I want you to shoot dope inta that horse, Al's Ladyboo, in the fourth at Narragansett."

"Dope? That horse?"

"Yeah. Then I want you to wedge two of those little iron chestnuts under his back shoes so he could go a little lame in the race."

"Mort, whatta you doing? This here is totally unnecessary!"

"You do it, you hear?"

"Okay. All right. I'll do it."

When Judge Zeuss and the boys returned, Mr. Violente had arranged for a direct wire from his office which fed into an amplifier-caller. To pass the time while they waited for the fourth race at Narragansett, Mr. Violente had Herbert Ganglia sing the aria by Magnifico in *La Cenerentola* as Giuseppe de Begnis might have sung it. Both Mr. Violente and Tancredi accompanied him on mandolins. Then Judge Zeuss sang, *a capello,* from *Orfeo Idomeneo* in the style of Giorgio Kokolois, causing all three Sicilians to batter their hands with applause, weeping openly. "This is like one of the great afternoons of my life," Mr. Violente sniffled.

At that moment, the call for the fourth at Narragansett began.

"It's the fourth at Narragansett coming up with thirteen dollars and some change added,"

the harsh, hoarse voice of the caller said loudly and clearly.

"The starters are at the gate in a field of seven horses—Captain Barrett at the rail, Shady Parrot number two and fighting his rider. Moving out past Shady Parrot, it's In A Garret, Zany Ferret, Sadie Jarrett, Lady Carrot and Al's Ladyboo."

Mr. Violente, unable to stop grinning, passed around a box of three-dollar cigars. Judge Zeuss listened intently, concentrating hard.

"There are no scratches. The form today at the fourth at Narragansett at post time is—THEY'RE OFF!!!"

"Two million bucks at eighty-seven to one," young Tancredi babbled hysterically. "I mean, even if the race *is* fixed—Holy *shit!*"

"Don't worry! Don't worry!" Mr. Violente chattered at double speed.

"And now it's Lady Carrot breaking strong across the field and straight to the rail with Shady Parrot and Captain Barrett close. At five lengths back—length to length—it's In A Garret, Sadie Jarrett, Zany Ferret and Al's Ladyboo. From here it looks like Al's Ladyboo could have developed a lame back foot. Shady Parrot is moving up.

At the turn it's Lady Carrot, Shady Parrot, Captain Barrett, In a Garret, Zany Ferret, Sadie Jarrett and—seven lengths back—Al's Ladyboo.

Mr. Violente was giggling girlishly. Happy tears were pouring down his cheeks. "You got a bet down on a water buffalo," he guffawed, wetting his pants, pointing at the Judge.

The Judge held a finger to his lips, nodding toward the speaker system.

"Al's Ladyboo is moving up. Yes, I said Al's Ladyboo, running at the tote board odds of one hundred and thirty-six to one, is moving like an express train past Sadie Jarrett, Zany Ferrett, and In A Garret. I have never seen speed poured on like Al's Ladyboo is paying it out today. It's Al's Ladyboo overtaking the leaders! Al's Ladyboo! A horse which has not finished better than last in one hundred and thirty-two starts!"

Mr. Violente was shaking his head in small, eccentric circles as though gently trying to dislodge a concept which persisted in trying to plague him. He began to pull on Herbert Ganglia's necktie heavily, in frantic jerks. "What? What did he say? Did I hear him or I didn't hear him?"

"You heard him," said Judge Zeuss benignly.

"It's Al's Ladyboo! Yas, yas! It's Al's Ladyboo going past Shady Parrot. He is neck and neck with the leader, Lady Carrot. He's in the lead. He's pulling away! Al's Ladyboo is four lengths in the lead and widening the gap. Folks, it's got to be a track record for the distance, he's across the finish line. The winner is Al's Ladyboo eleven lengths ahead of the nearest horse in the race. Yas, it's Al's Ladyboo ladies and gemmin, commemorating the Sport of Kings by winning at one hundred and thirty-six to one!"

"You saved quite a bit of money there, not having to pay those track odds," Judge Zeuss said pleasantly.

Mr. Violente's limp body hit the floor. Dimples Tancredi, a young but intelligent young man, put on his

hat and ran out of the apartment immediately. "Little Pasquale" knelt beside his boss and patted his cheek, talking
rapidly in a western Sicilian dialect. Judge Zeuss, puffing
smoke, said, "A very good cigar, this," and leaned over to
turn off the excited babble of racing the reportage as the
word came through that Al's Ladyboo had just set a world's
record for the distance.

Mr. Violente missed that statistical thrill. He
was getting mouth-to-mouth resucitation from "Little Pasquale" and his complexion was slowly changing from deep
black to light purple. Judge Zeuss got up, walked close to
where the two friends gave-and-took saying, "Let me help."
He gave Mr. Violente a violent kick in the rump. Mr. Violente's eyes opened, rolling. "Is—it—true?" he said.

"It's true, boss."

"Too bad," Judge Zeuss said, "that little
race cost you one hundred and seventy-four million dollars."

The bookmaker wept. "My entire life's savings. Gone. I'm broke. He cleaned me out."

Judge Zeuss said, "You are a real sportsman,
sir."

"Hit him, Herbert!" Mr. Violente yelled.
"Kill the son of a bitch!"

Herbert sprang to his feet, pulling a revolver
from his waistband. Judge Zeuss closed with him. The two
men grappled. There was a short, intense struggle for the
possession of the weapon. The gun fired. There was a
scream. Ganglia fell back, staring downward with horror. He
had shot Mr. Violente in the foot. Ganglia then did the
humane thing. He rushed to the hallway, grabbed his hat,
and ran like hell out of the apartment.

"Get a priest, fahcrissake," Violente moaned.
"Get me a priest."

Judge Zeuss knelt by his side. "Your men ran
out on you, Mr. Violente. If I leave, you'll be all alone and
you may bleed to death."

"No!"

"Give me your sister-in-law's number. I'll get
her here. She'll take care of you."

"She's deef an' dumb, fahcrissake! Get a *doc*tor!"

"That will only make trouble with the police."

"Are you kiddin'? Get me a doctor—a bone man or a foot man, but a real great. Please—please, Judge."

Judge Zeuss went through the classified directory. "Nothing under doctors," he mused. "Ah—here!—see Physicians and Surgeons." He leafed through the pages leisurely. "Well!" he said, "twenty-one pages of them, all in small print, and not one of them will make a house call."

"Look up my wife's sciatica man. His name is Youngstein—Max E. Give me the phone when you get him. O, my God, the pain. That was every dime I had in the world."

Judge Zeuss dialed the Youngstein number and gave the phone to Mr. Violente. There was a very short conversation. Mr. Violente hung up.

"He's on his way?" Judge Zeuss asked.

"He won't do nothing!" Mr. Violente bleated. "So much for the Hippocratic Oath. He says the way I give my wife sciatica, I should bleed to death. Bocce and wrestling and touch football give my wife sciatica!" He began to weep. The day had been too much for him. "I'll get that fink. I'll give him a case of sciatica like he never had."

Ganglia burst into the room followed by a tall WASP carrying a medical satchel. "It's okay boss," Ganglia said. "I tore him right off the City Desk of *Clinical Trends in Urology*. My uncle works there. You're gonna be all right."

The doctor removed Mr. Violente's shoe and sock. "Small toe gone," he said.

"Will I be a helpless cripple?"

"You'll be all right," the doctor said. "But this is a gunshot wound and I am required by law to report it."

"Of course," Ganglia said.

"The law is the law," Mr. Violente added.

Eight

Frustration, humiliation, rage, guilt, shame, disappointment, shock, fear, helplessness, hopelessness, confusion, horror, disbelief, outrage, jealousy, aggression, disillusionment, excitement, envy, haplessness, and hostility sent Doris flying out of Gene's office, snatching the last remaining Australian aboriginal artifact from the wall, a sacred bullroarer engraved with concentric circles, loops, and zigzags. She went through the mob of the press and cameras in the crowded corridor, whirling the bullroarer over her head to generate its frightening sound. The crowd parted hastily, letting her through. She took the elevator to the top floor, jammed the door to stay open and immobilize the car, ran up the stairs to the roof and crossed over the roofs of two buildings before she went down to street level through 424 Madison Avenue, well around the corner and out of sight of the dense mob of overcommunicators waiting in front of 10 East 49th.

Doris had never really had a chance in This Other Place. Gene had been allowed to develop exactly as he had always been, but Doris had awakened, faced the day gaily, then had gone across town to her work to face a police raid, then the titanic attentions of Zeus. No being had ever trod the soil of the earth who had had more experience with women of every kind than Zeus. Doris, from her first steps into an utterly, totally new life, had been swept off her feet like a wood chip in a flood. Her faculties, from the other life never had a moment to surface. She was the victim of a circumstance over which she had no control. She had become Zeus's bauble—and he, hers.

Zeus had signaled Hermes to be waiting for

her with a taxi when she emerged. She thought it was a miracle (which it most certainly was) that an empty cab should be standing there on Madison Avenue. She leaped aboard saying, "Just head downtown. I'll tell you where when I think of it." As the cab turned into 49th Street moving toward Gene's building, she crouched on its floor out of sight. Hermes dematerialized the cab, then materialized it again in front of the Popina Matsoukis.

"Okay, lady," he said.

"Okay, what?" Doris said, raising her head. "My God. What happened? Where are we?"

"East 18th Street. This is maybe the second-best Greek restaurant in North America."

"But—how did we get here?"

"You said downtown. You look Greek. So I figured this is where you wanted to go."

"But I just got in the cab at Forty-ninth and Madison."

"Maybe you fell asleep. Anyway, there is a dollar ninety-five on the clock."

Confused, Doris got out of the cab and paid. As she turned away, she found herself face-to-face with Judge Zeuss. "Mrs. Quebaro!" he said ecstatically. "How wonderful! What good fortune! How sweet and marvelous to meet you here directly in front of the Popina Matsoukis. You must come in and have a cup of Turkish coffee."

o

"What are you going to do with our lives?" Carlotta asked.

"I'm not sure," Gene said. "You know how much I love you, Carlotta. But I need a yardstick to measure this thing."

"There isn't any."

"You saw her. You heard her. She can't handle this. She'll go to pieces."

"AAAAaaaahhh!"

"Carlotta, listen—it's a case of advance and be recognized. I have a deep, deep commitment to Doris and I can't turn my back on that, I can't throw it away." '

"You're going to stay with Doris."

"I love Doris, too, Carlotta."

"Are you going to stay with Doris?"

"Please—bear with me—Doris does have rights that you don't have. Admit that."

"Drop dead."

"I mean—this is *her* marriage. We are discussing this on *her* time, in a way. I am only trying to be fair, Carlotta."

"Well, you can fucking well stop trying to be fair." She reached up with both hands and pulled him to herself. She kissed him fiercely. "I won't accept this kind of talk, Gene, you hear?"

"You have to accept. Most of all, I have to accept it. Do you think I *want* to accept it? I *have* to."

"Tell me something—did you ever see your marriage license?"

"Why not?"

"Did you? Do you even remember getting married to her? The actual wedding ceremony? Just answer yes or no, Gene."

"No." He stared at her, greatly puzzled. "But I could have been hit on the back of the head, like George Brent."

"Oh, sure."

"What are you driving at?"

"You aren't back with her yet, are you, friend?"

"What do you mean?"

"I read her just a little bit differently than you do. I'll wait, Gene. I'll just wait." Her eyes flooded with tears. She kissed him again. She straightened his tie, then turned away and left the office. He felt absolutely helpless and lost. He walked to the window. There he saw what helpless really was. Across the air-space, in the Scribner Building, a naked, deepchested woman was sexually assaulting a pitiably elderly postman, trouserless and without drawers under his Confederate gray uniform coat.

279

Nine

Dazed, Doris allowed Judge Zeuss to lead her into the Popina Matsoukis. She was still trying to believe that it could be possible that Gene could have been married to another woman all this time. If he meant it, if it were true, then she was alone in the world—an enormously healthy unmarried woman who had been living in sin with a sex-crazy bigamist.

Judge Zeuss took her into a glorious room which, he said, was a reproduction of the inner, hidden, secret harem room of the twelve favorites of the Caliph Bocca (seventh century). He poured her a glass of coffee and urged her to try some dear little honey cakes which had the oddest aftertaste of hasheesh. She nibbled and supped.

"You need a rest, my darling," Judge Zeuss crooned. "You have had a very, very difficult few days, my dear."

"You will never know how difficult," Doris said with a choked voice.

"I am insane with love for you. I need you, little doe."

"You need a little dough?"

"No, no! Aaaah, how I adore you!"

"It is very nice of you to say that," Doris replied, trying to balance her status as a (probably) married woman with the effects of the strange little honey cake. The cakes *must* be drugged! How oriental! In motive, that is, she thought. "May I have another little cake?" she asked. He passed the plate with such eagerness that all the sticky little things slid off the plate, into her lap. They had a marvelous time while Judge Zeuss plucked each cake off the velvet dress which covered her thighs. It wasn't hasty work, the way the Judge did it, nibbling after each tiny crumb. When he had finished and she had eaten another little cake, he said hoarsely, "I have this little place off the Salonika road just inside the Macedonian state line, on top of Mount Olympus," he said. "It has a gorgeous view. Really, you'll see what they mean when they talk about Olympian detachment."

"*I'll* see what they mean?"

"I want you to rest there. I want you to spend just as much time there as ever you want, Doris dumpling. You need this rest, and I know positively that your employer will release you for a little holiday for as long as you wish to stay in Greece."

"Greece!" She sighed like a chimney filled with winter wind. "How I have dreamed of seeing Greece one day."

"And, don't forget. Mount Olympus is the best section. Totally restricted. No Turks. No Cypriots. Tennis, golf, centaurs. The food is ambrosia and you can take my word for that. And—the deep, sweet peace of the double bed." As he caressed her inner thigh, she took another little bite on the cake, stared into his eyes and asked, "Will you be there?"

"You bet your sweet ass——" He caught himself. "Yes, my dear. I will be there."

"Oh, Joe! May I call you Joe?"

He nodded, hardly hearing her, thinking of the confidence he had in Athena to keep Hera doped to the gills in the French Hospital for twenty or thirty years while he got it off with this wonder woman. "Can you leave tonight?" he asked. "Olympic Airways has an eleven o'clock flight."

She looked at him levelly. Her eyes were straightforward although there was the slightest hint of a goldfish swimming around in the eye to the right. "I have very, *very* deep feelings for you, Joe," she said huskily, now very, *very* high. "But until I am sure that there is no shred of evidence that my husband needs me, I cannot allow myself to run away from him."

Judge Zeuss's hand, high at her legs, was

working like a dachshund at a badger's den. The little honey cakes and the Judge's fingers, the scents and softnesses of the room, the very sense of fantasy which the entire day had brought upon her, made her loath to rush out to find Gene to inquire of his need. Instead, she moaned, "Oh! My *God*, Joe! Aaaaaahhhhh! *Joe!* Oh, Joe, you *are* enormous!"

○

Doris tottered out of the Popina and into a taxi driven by a man who must surely be wearing a red wig, she thought vaguely. She fell back upon the seat and closed her eyes in utterly ecstatic exhaustion. Then, all at once, what she had just done came over her like a sótnya of Cossacks. She had been unfaithful to Gene! The sharp stab was gone almost as soon as it arrived, however, when she realized that she must be falsely married to an already-married man, a fact which made Gene unfaithful to his wife—that washed-out boxing glove of a busted British cooze—for almost five years.

The truth engulfed her. She had run away from him before Gene had made his choice. The contest had not been resolved! Running madly, barefoot through her mind went the chorus of "Is You Is or Is You Ain't My Baby?" When Gene had made that choice, it would be time enough for her to decide about Joe. She tried to refuse to think about Joe but she found it impossible not to feel him within her—and not entirely in the regions of her heart of hearts, either.

Ten

Before Judge Zeuss had left Mort Violente in the apartment on West 82nd Street, a key conversation had taken place.

"I don't know how you done it," Mr. Violente said, "but I know you framed me on that bet."

"How could I frame you? You picked the horse. You picked the track."

"I donno how, but it is like dealing seconds or making the Cortlandt shot with dice or something. I can't figure it out, but you framed me, pal, and I am now beginning to worry very bad about whether my boys are gunna be able to head off that check you mailed to your son." He covered his eyes with one tightly gripping hand. "What hurts is that forty years inna business an' I take a two-million-dollar bet at eighty-seven to one. That is what hurts," he said with a choking voice.

"Would you like to get the check back?"

"Get it back?"

"I mean it."

"How do I get it back?"

"I require specialist services and I believe in paying well."

"He asks me if I want the check back." Mr. Violente seemed to be approaching hysteria. "You hear me, Herbert? You heard what he wants to know?"

"But what does he want for it, boss? He could want things which it would even be terrible to you."

"Whatever it is," Mr. Violente said, eyes glassy, "I want that check back." He wheeled on Judge Zeuss, in place, his foot propped up and grossly bandaged.

"So what do you want from me to give the check back, mister?"

"Your bathtub? Your sister-in-law?"

Violente turned green. "Okay. Take them," he said. "I knew it. I knew you wanted Tessie all the time." Tears welled up in his eyes.

"No," Judge Zeuss said. "I was only testing. You keep Tessie. There is a man named Quebaro—Eugene Quebaro—husband of your employee Doris Quebaro——"

"And you want him hit. What else?"

"No." Judge Zeuss leaned forward and squeezed Mr. Violente's wounded foot where the small toe had once been. Mr. Violente's scream was terrible to hear. "One thing," Judge Zeuss said, "you must guarantee—or no check—that nothing harmful or violent or even the slightest bit discomfirting can be allowed to happen to Eugene Quebaro. If I agree to hire you for one hundred seventy-four million dollars, you will see that he is treated with enormous courtesy and care."

"So whatta you want, fahcrissakes, arreddy?"

"I want you to abduct him."

"Abduct?" Mr. Violente looked from the Judge to Herbert "Little Pasquale" Ganglia.

"Snatch, boss," Ganglia said.

"Kidnap," the Judge explained.

"Oh."

"When you have him, I want you to take him to a very small, very comfortable island which I own in the Tuamotu Archipelago. I will provide the longitude and latitude. I have it stocked with beautiful, unliberated Polynesian women and a lifetime supply of chilled, canned Czech and Mexican beer. There is a small chicken ranch which he can run. There is an enormous freezer big enough to drive a truck into, filled with prime T-bone and sirloin steaks. The coral lagoon has no sharks. He will have a large, pleasantly cool house with TV cassettes of 800 movies made before 1965, a copy of *The New York Times Book of Home Repairs* and a flush toilet."

"Jeez," Little Pasquale said. "Sounds great."

"That's all you want from me?" the astounded Violente said. "Then you give the check back?"

"Not quite. I want you to persuade him to write a little farewell note," Judge Zeuss said. "The text is in here." He handed Mr. Violente an envelope.

"When you want him to leave?"

"As soon as you can arrange for an extremely comfortable charter ship to take him non-stop around Cape Horn to the South Pacific."

"No problem. He goes on my yacht the *Little Sister*. You want us to take him right now?"

"The sooner the better," Judge Zeuss said.

o

When Herbert "Little Pasquale" Ganglia arrived with two men and a driver in front of 10 East 49th Street at seven o'clock that evening, they passed Carlotta on her way out. All members of the press and television had been pulled off the Quebaro story and were following up the dozens of leads on that week's new Washington scandal, which had just broken.

Unhindered, the three Violente soldiers left the large pick-up truck parked in front of the building. They jammed into Gene's inner room and moved in on the astonished man with drawn guns.

"What the hell is this?" Gene said, staring at the Magnum pistol in the right hand of Marvin "Bummy" Banjolini.

"Shaddup!" Herbert Ganglia replied.

Eleven

"Hello-oo!" Doris sang out in a gay, two-toned greeting at the threshold of their apartment at Fortress Midtown. "Anyone home?"

There was no answer. She went from room to room calling Gene's name. It was twenty minutes to eight. At first she was glad he wasn't there because she wouldn't have to lie about where she had been. She shucked off her street clothes and got into something yearningly domestic. She decided to make his favorite dinner as a reminder of the good, old days: spaghetti with margarine sauce, then, to add a contrasting richness, two knockwursts and a bottle of Pontet-Canet '66. She took the knockwurst out of the freezer, lined up the spaghetti box, filled a six-quart pot with water, reamed the margarine out of its tub, and opened the wine, but that was as far as she could go until she actually heard his key in the lock.

She was a little hungry, so she spread some carrot butter on a piece of raisin bread, sprinkled a teaspoon of lecithin on top of it, and poured out a glass of the wine to keep up her gala spirits. She settled down at the round kitchen table under the adorable captain's light with the good little Greek grammar/phrase book she had picked up that morning. The next time she looked at the clock, there wasn't much wine left and it was twenty minutes to ten.

Before the dismay the realization brought, she had built up the solid conviction that the time had never been righter for a trip to Greece because it could help her so much with her language studies. Greece! The very conception excited her. My God, she thought, Joe Zeuss is simply e*nor*mous!

Then she looked at the wall clock. In mid-flight of fancy she realized she was now free to go to Greece or anywhere else because Gene hadn't come home, which meant he had chosen his other wife as inevitably as George Brent had had to do. She had never felt so rejected. She didn't know how to act because rejection was such a totally new experience. She tried on a full inventory of emotions. She thought of their happy years together. She wept softly into a dish towel. Then the image of the *extent* of Phyllis Stein's pregnancy loomed large in her mind and she turned bitter at Gene's deceit, but the betrayal feeling had much admiration in it because she couldn't understand how a man who had been as broke as Gene Quebaro had been for the past five years could find and seduce such a cultivated, well-dressed woman as Stein. But worse, oh, *Jesus*, much worse was Gene screwing his secretary whose *salary* he didn't even bother to pay. Stein, after all, was a stranger. He could have banged her in a subway phone booth, but Alice had been welcomed into Doris's family as a friend and equal, then she had jumped right under Gene just the same. What a fool she had been! Three women that she knew about, so Heaven knows how many more. Yet, like a tigress, she had fought off the most compulsively sexy man in the history of New York civil service; a full-fledged judge, a millionaire, she had fought him off because she had loved her husband and could not bear to be unfair to him.

She felt like throwing all the furniture out into the street. She felt like taking a razor blade and turning both of Gene's suits hanging in the closet into bags of ribbons. She felt like heating up the spaghetti water and throwing his goddam personal scrapbook into it for a good boil.

But—*supposing he hadn't chosen that British bint?* Supposing he had stepped out into the night city and—*swish* went a razor. Suppose he had just been walking along in front of some perfectly innocent, well-lighted place like Bloomingdale's and some crazy junkie with a big Izzro had grabbed him and knifed him? She was no masochist. Why was she just sitting around here and torturing herself? She rushed to the kitchen wall phone and dialed the number at Gene's office. No answer. She looked up the Piedmont Hotel. She dialed and asked for Miss Charlotte Pimbernel.

"Pimbernel?" she said abruptly. "This is Mrs. Quebaro. Put my husband on the phone, please."

Carlotta did not get confused and blurt out that Gene was not there. If this one was calling to talk to her husband, that meant her husband was not with her; a big edge for Carlotta. "You wouldn't want me to drag him along to the phone, luv," Carlotta said. "He's sleeping."

Doris slammed the phone down.

She had lost him. It was all over. She looked at the wall clock. It was twenty minutes to eleven. She looked up the number of the Popina Matsoukis and started to dial. Then she hung up. Supposing Gene had gone weakly to Pimbernel's hotel to talk everything out and he had fallen asleep there after the terrible events of the day. That was natural. He had to be exhausted. Suppose he suddenly woke up at, say, one o'clock in the morning, realized how very much he had wronged Doris, got dressed and raced home. Then suppose, because she had been lonely and hurt, she had happened to call a friend (such as Judge Zeuss) to keep her company while she sat in vigil, and her husband found her friend and his giant member in bed with her? Her every basic motive would be misunderstood. Then Gene would *really* have been given reason to go back to his other wife unless that whole George Brent story was a lot of bullshit.

She emptied the last of the bottle of Pontet-Canet into a glass, put one of the knockwursts into a saucepan of water, and lit a fire under it. No sense in being heartbroken *and* hungry, she told herself. She had to do a lot of thinking before she called Judge Zeuss.

Twelve

The *Little Sister* rounded Sandy Hook and headed out to sea. Gene was playing gin rummy for a quarter of a cent a point with Herbert "Little Pasquale" Ganglia in the luxurious main cabin. Marvin "Bummy" Banjolini lounged in a nearby chair, his jacket off, his Magnum in its holster, picking his teeth with a pipe cleaner.

"You're not kidding me, now, Herbert," Gene said eagerly. "In the Tuamotu Archipelago? You don't know what that can mean to me. I was in an awful bind. I had a terrible decision to make and I couldn't have made it."

"It happens to be true. I'll take you up to the captain tumorra."

"And my own chicken ranch?"

"Plymouth Reds. Rhode Island Rocks."

"God, you even make it sound like I own two baseball teams. Six points."

"Fantastic," Herbert said. "Two points." Herbert marked the score and shuffled.

"Czech *and* Mexican beer? Pilsener Urquell?"

Herbert nodded as he dealt the cards.

"Tres Equis? Bohemia and Carta Blanca?"

"Yeah. And like five dozen beautiful native guapas all equipped wit' ukuleles and a natural need to fuck."

"Why don't you guys stick around when we get there?" Gene asked.

"Listen—I am sorely tempted," Herbert said. "My old lady can be a real pain in the ass."

"I always wanted to raise Belgian hares," Marvin said. "I could send away. There is real money in that."

"I don't suppose I'll ever know who did this for me," Gene said wistfully, picking up his cards and sipping at a can of cool Bohemia. "But if I ever know, I'll never forget him."

"Well, we'll see," Herbert said. "In the meantime, what's the name of the game?"

"Gin," Gene said.

"That's it, sucker," Herbert said, laying down his perfect hand.

PLATE CRISIS HERO SUICIDE
EX-BANK CZAR BREAKS
UNDER STRAIN

New York, June 28—Eugene Quebaro, The Man Who Saved the Dollar, hero of the international plate market crash which he, single-handedly, averted, the man nominated as Federal Banking Commissioner, an inoperative post, disappeared last night for the second time in twenty-four hours, leaving a suicide note in his office.

The note was found at 8:53 today by the lawyer's secretary, his former Executive Assistant at the projected, White House-denied, FBA, Charlotte Pimbernel, with whom Quebaro had disappeared for one week while he was being sought by the nation's press.

Interviewed this morning, Miss Pimbernel said, "I do not believe Mr. Quebaro has killed himself. It is my conviction that Mr. Quebaro was kidnapped, quite possibly by the CIA as an accommodation to the White House, and that he was required to write and sign the false suicide note which was dictated to him by persons unknown."

For reasons as yet unrevealed by the police, investigations were said to have been undertaken immediately in the Scribner Building which overlooks the Quebaro law offices. (See box for facsimile of suicide note.)

QUEBARO SUICIDE NOTE CALLED AUTHENTIC

To whom it may concern: I have been hounded and pressured beyond human resistance because I sought to serve my country. There is no other way out except to kill myself. On completion of this letter, in which I leave my entire estate to my nephew, Raimundo Quebaro, 7 San Antonio, Magallanes Village, Makati, Rizal, Philippine Islands, on the condition that he practice law for a period of twenty years, I shall fly out to sea in a light hired airplane carrying five gallons of gasoline and keep flying until the engine fails.

God help us all,

(Signed) Eugene Quebaro

PRESIDENT WILL OFFER EVIDENCE PROVING QUEBARO SOLD CARRIERS TO THE CHINESE

Washington, June 29—White House aide Frederick "Fritzie" Schmuck, Presidential Chief of Staff, stated at a White House press conference today that Eugene Quebaro, missing lawyer believed to be a suicide, was "palpably guilty" of the secret sale of three United States aircraft carriers to Red China.

"The President is appalled that such a man could as much as conceive of selling such large naval units to a foreign power for personal gain regardless of their probable obsolescence."

Thirteen

Doris Quebaro was shocked, in a deeply satisfied sort of way, when Carlotta Quebaro refused to attend the memorial services for Gene that Judge Zeuss had so kindly arranged at the Garment Center Greek Orthodox Church, which was quite near the Popina Matsoukis on West 18th Street. Doris was poignantly lovely in exquisite black widow's weeds with a sheer black peekaboo veil and memorably filled black stockings. She had scented her little black handkerchiefs with Opium, a favorite perfume of the deceased. She seemed serenely composed because Judge Zeuss had assured her that there would be no difficulty in breaking the wrenching bequest to Raimundo Quebaro which might have left her penniless.

Judge Zeuss supported her in every way. He accompanied her to the services, which were conducted in Macedonian—which was not quite Doris's ken, she being more a student of Modern Greek—but she knew the sentiment was there and appreciated it. After the service a eulogy was spoken by Dr. Norman Lesion, made directly to the press in the first two rows.

The heartbroken widow and Judge Zeuss drove away immediately at the end of the services, to elude Doris's mother. "You were a brave, wonderful girl," Judge Zeuss said as they rode uptown in the Mercedes 600, sipping Metaxas brandy and nibbling on little honey cakes.

"Doris, darling?"

"Yes, Joe, dearest?"

"When I ask you what I am going to ask you, please try to feel your answer from all the secret and wonderful places of your heart."

"Ask me anything, Joe."

"Will you marry me?"

"Joe!"

"What does your heart tell you?"

"Of course I'll marry you. But—that is—just as soon as a respectful amount of time has passed after—what Gene did."

"For reasons beyond our control, it must be today, right now. The special flight goes to Athens tonight. When we board that plane, we'll be going home to my mom, Doris. And I know you wouldn't want me to bring a girl home to meet Mom if we weren't married."

"What girl?"

"You, silly." That had been a lot of blather about Zeus's mother. He hadn't seen his mother, a *very* old lady, for over nine hundred years because she always embarrassed him by asking him to sing "Danny Boy." Zeus had to marry Doris because the Judeo-Christian oligarchs had delivered Doris unto him, by contract, and, by contract, he had to marry her.

"But Gene is hardly cold," Doris said.

"Oh, he's cold. A plane crashes into the mid-Atlantic and believe me, that's cold. Please, Doris—do it for my Mom?"

Shyly, Doris accepted.

The limousine went directly to the Municipal Building. Athena was maid of honor. Hermes was best man. The ceremony was shown in every detail on the giant Nixon-Vision screen. A contract had been honored.

Going uptown to Fortress Midtown, Zeus said to his bride, "We'll be in Greece before you can say Jack Pappanopoulos. Pack your little bag. I'll pick you up in exactly six hours—at half past nine tonight—and we will fly to that wine-dark sea, that sceptered isle—that England."

"Greece, dear."

"Of course! I mean Greece."

o

Raziel materialized in the public corridor outside the Quebaro office and knocked on the door. "Yoo hoo,

Mrs. Quebaro," he said loudly. "It's me, Raziel."

Carlotta opened the door. She greeted him warmly and drew him into Gene's room. She seated him.

"Carlotta, we have a lot to talk about," Raziel said. "You have come to a big turning-point."

"How?"

"You think you want your husband back—but you love him. Nobody in all time could say otherwise than that."

"Yes. I love him."

"The big question is—do you love him for his good or do you love him for you?"

"For him. Of course, for him."

"You want him to be the world's greatest insurance salesman. Is that right?"

"Yes."

"I don't think he wants to be that."

"Men don't want to do a lot of things, Mr. Raziel. But there are such things as duty and character and purpose."

"You know something? Believe me, from my point of view—well, from my point of view it is over for you people very quick. Click. Bye-bye. Gone. Do you understand?"

"In a way."

"In all of what you call time, and I mean almost from the beginning, excepting perhaps Enoch and maybe Ezekiel, you are the only lung fish to have what it takes. And for what it takes, none of us will ever forget that you are the only lung fish who ever took it with her. It will never happen again. So I know you understand me. Duty? Very nice. But it has to be each one to his own duty. Character is something you inherit or absorb from a kind of environment or force on yourself through habituation, but it certainly isn't something that a man can be handed by his wife no matter how nice a girl she is. Purpose—purpose is not only a dream, but it is the very best dream. You want to know where your husband is right now, Carlotta?"

"With all my heart."

"He's on a luxurious ship. It wasn't his doing.

It wasn't our doing. The ship will go around Cape Horn, then into the South Pacific. They are going to leave him on a small, beautiful island stocked with lovely native girls, warehoused with prime steaks and beer and TV cassettes of the best old movies, where he will have a chicken ranch and a nice house with box-spring mattresses and indoor plumbing."

"That has always been Gene's ambition!" she exclaimed.

"Yes. *That* is Gene's ambition."

"But—how did he get it? How did it happen?"

"He got himself into a situation—or *we* got him into a situation and—aaaaah, it isn't important. What is important is that it just happens that what he got out of it is also his purpose. It is what he has always dreamed about and now he has it. And he doesn't have to make the very hard moral and emotional decision whether he must stay with you or go with Doris. He doesn't have to practice law for his dead uncle. He doesn't have to try to become the world's greatest insurance salesman and, what's more, because the basis for all guilt has been taken away from him, he doesn't have to worry about fooling around with fourteen or twenty beautiful women in the same week, or even at the same time. He has attained his real dream purpose."

"It is a purpose without a purpose!" Carlotta said hotly. "It is a small boy's purpose, it isn't for a man!"

"Who is to say? He wanted it, maybe he's stuck with it, but he has it. The point is: do you love him, Carlotta? Or do you want to take that away from him?"

She took her face in both of her hands. She wept. Raziel was reminded that she was human. "It is just that I don't see how I can live without him," she sobbed.

"I can help you there. We have an offer. Take your time about deciding. No hurry. Weep all you want. But if you decide you love him, I have something to take the bitterness away."

She looked up at him.

"You are a natural oligarch, Carlotta. You can develop into a top manager in the universal community.

We haven't taken a lung fish on the staff since Enoch. I don't mean you can ever become an angel, but there is a consultancy open for you and we really need new, sound oligarchic minds if the firmament is expected to show any growth potential—and you should see *my* quotas already! Our work here is finished. We'll be going back shortly and we'd like you to come with us. We can offer you immortality and a chance to bring your talents to bear on a really wide field of operations. You can be the most liberated woman who ever was."

"I can have anything except Gene?"

Raziel shrugged. "You can have Gene. Nobody is forcing you. You can take him and make him into a three-hundred-thousand-dollar-a-year man. But—if you make him take that, he must lose what he thinks he wants."

"I'll go with you," Carlotta said.

Fourteen

The Joint(⚐) Commission for the Evaluation of Sin wound up its convention. N'Zuriel Yhwh took the valedictory speech. "This here has been a very, very successful convention," he orated, "and we have found out a terrific amount about the central problem—namely money—and its effect on the lung fish. I know, and you know, that when our Bill Drafting Commission completes its examination of the magnificent White Paper filed by the Saxe-Coburg Combined Missions, we are going to have a grand, completely new moral code for these lung fish and a new set of sins, practical and easy for them to commit within the scope of the temptations which they have developed independent of our efforts.

"I was right before and I am right again—money is the root cause of their moral discrepancies. What we have found out in this historic session will assure, for many, *many* lung fish lifetimes to come, that both the Lower and the Upper Houses will get their fair share of souls, one of the major goals, of course, of all of our studies, and not just a hot, uncomfortable, overcrowded Hell when the Republicans get in, and a jammed, inconvenient, overburdened Heaven when Labour is in power, starting their endless wars and sending excess souls in before their time to overcrowd everything. I thank all of you for doing such magnificent work here. God bless! Zayn gezunt." He sat down. There was tumultous applause. It went on and on and on and, as N'Zuriel Yhwh beamed under it, Dagon, seated directly beside him, said, "But what is money?"

"How do I know?" N'Zuriel Yhwh said. "I haven't read the report."

o

At the Popina Matsoukis, Zeus presided over the getaway banquet, which the conventioneers would remember for many weeks to come, while Doris was packing uptown for her romantic trip to Greece. Zeus gloried in the knowledge that, in a matter of hours, he would have this incomparable woman at his side forevermore—or at least for as long as Athena could figure out how to keep to Hera doped up in the French Hospital—maybe sixty or eighty years. He was in love! He was the happiest man in the world!

"Who is the little blonde at Table number three?" he whispered to Hermes, who was seated beside him on the dais.

"She's new."

"But what's her name?"

"She's a granddaughter of mine, as a matter of fact."

"Everybody is related to everybody here."

"You remember when Odysseus took that long trip?"

"Yes."

"Well, his wife and I had a thing."

"Penelope?"

"That's the one. A terrific girl. A marvelous sport and a good dancer. But she was careless and we had a boy named Pan."

"The musician?"

"Yes."

"A very good musician."

"Thank you, Pop. I really should keep in touch with the boy more. Anyway, Pan got involved with Echo. Remember little Echo?"

Zeus nodded absentmindedly, staring at the little blonde at Table number three.

"And this blond kid is theirs. Her name is Iambe. Besides that terrific little body she has a marvelous sense of humor."

"Will she be on the Olympic flight tonight?"

298

"No. She goes out on the excursion flight tomorrow afternoon."

"Switch her," Zeus said. He got to to his feet smiling. He tapped on a crystal glass with a spoon to get everyone's attention.

"Well," he said to all of them, "all good things have to come to an end. I think you all did really good work here, especially with the retsina—eight thousand four hundred and twelve cases and a couple of bottles—and even if you didn't get a lot out of it on a political basis—as I think it is possible a lot of you didn't—it was very worthwhile for all of us to get together again to renew old acquaintances and to make new ones." He winked at Iambe lewdly, confusing her.

"I have had a couple of very good meetings with Spiro and he has agreed to make a comeback. If that comeback is successful—with our help, that is—and he goes straight into the White House, then we will make the big move here—a beautiful big new country with no substantial religions to offer us any competition whatsoever—and we will be making our own comeback in a great, big way. I mean everybody at this convention today will get some kind of shrine—big or small, outdoor or indoor; a crossroads shrine or a big-city temple—so, to the tune of "Happy Days Are Here Again," I say to each and every one of you: enjoy yourselves, have a *great* time, and have a good flight home." He winked even more lewdly at Iambe again, and this time she wasn't confused at all. "And toppa the maaarnin' tew yiz all," he said and sat down.

There was a profound applause which lasted through 318 bottles of retsina and four cases of Metaxas cognac. A voice from the back of the room yelled out, "Hey, Zeus! Did the Opposition people ever find out what is money?"

Zeus got to his feet, beaming. "A good question and I'm glad you asked me," he said. "That is the easiest thing in the world to define. Money is everybody's pocket mirror."

Fifteen

Between Christmas 1975 and New Year's Day, six months after sailing out of New York for the South Pacific, on the day he had screwed his forty-second different Polynesian girl, as he was drinking his 919th can of chilled Mexican beer, as the stench of the roosting chickens drifted across the yard to the porch, which had to be heavily screened to keep out the carnivorous mosquitoes, after he had seen the Richard Dix-Esther Ralston cassette for the ninth time, when he could no longer bear to think of chewing a beef steak, as he played the 13,462nd hand of gin rummy with the long-unwashed, unshaven Herbert "Little Pasquale" Ganglia, who had gained seventy-one pounds, Eugene Quebaro said, "If you give me an argument, Herbert, I'll break your fucking neck."

"Give you an *argument?*" Herbert said. "Are you crazy? I think I got a heart condition. All this sex in all this heat! Don't they ever think of anything else? And they always yell I got sand on it. Nine dollars for a one-pound box of pasta, fah crissake. And you know how Mukumoa makes pasta? She grinds it! You hear? She grinds the pasta. Pasta! You know what I'm gunna do, I get back to New York? I'm gunna head straight for the pay terlets near the barbershop on the ground floor of the Waldorf and I am gunna sit there maybe a month. Indoor terlets, they said. Indoor, my ass. Them dames had the goddam thing jammed wit' pork chops and cornflakes boxes five days after we got here. An' where is *The New York Times Book of Home Repairs?* Omaloeelahoa dropped it inna terlet. I got mosquito bites on my ass that are five months old. And you know what? I am never, never gunna eat chicken again. I hate chickens. They stink, they are

300

stupid, they are noisy and they are monotonous—I mean they all look the same."

"Herbert?"

"What?"

"Who sent me here?"

"Some rich Municipal Court judge name of Joe V. Zeuss."

"Why?"

"He was havin' a thing wit' your wife. He wanted a clear field. I just don't know anymore. I mean I—really—don't—know. I used to love beer. I mean *love* it, Gene. My wife used to call me a slob the way I used to be able to swill beer and most of all, of all the great beers inna world, I used to love Czech beer and Mexican beer. Now I see a can of Czech beer I wanna puke. It finishes me."

"My wife Doris—or my wife Carlotta?" Gene asked incredulously.

"Your wife. Doris. The gorgeous brunette. And sometimes I think I am draggin' my entire lower intestine along the sand behind me. But—what? What was you gunna ask me something? I can't keep anything but cards in my head anymore."

"I wanted to say I miss Carlotta," Gene said. "I can't stand it without Carlotta anymore. I want to go home."

o

They flew Qantas out of Tahiti to Nassau. They switched to Eastern into New York.

Miss Pimbernel had checked out of the Piedmont Hotel a long time before. Sometime last summer, the Assistant Manager said. Gene's office had been taken over by a German literary representative named Relleh, with a white beard. He couldn't understand Gene because Gene only spoke English.

Nobody anywhere knew anything about Carlotta. Miss Kehoe was gone from the hospital. Doris was gone. He thought Doris might know about Carlotta, but Mrs. Lesion said Doris had remarried and was living in Greece.

Gene went to Stamford to look for Carlotta.

There was a FOR SALE sign up in front of the house at 2535 Long Ridge Road. The front door was open. Gene went in. He wandered into the bedroom and lay down on the bed he knew so well. He couldn't figure out how he'd ever get himself straightened out again. That was what Carlotta did. She figured things like that out. Off in the distance he could hear the front doorbell ring. He decided to ignore it. What the hell. But it kept ringing and he couldn't ignore it. He made his way out to the front of the house and opened the door.

Carlotta was standing there, holding the FOR SALE sign. Wonderful Carlotta, his darling Carlotta was standing there. He grabbed her. She kissed him. Then she began to talk, her green eyes looking straight into his eyes. "On the way in I set up an appointment with Dr. Hanly, the executive vice-president in charge of national sales, and I had a preliminary talk with the Surrogate about your uncle's estate. He understands. Everything's okay. After all, you were only on holiday for a few months, right? The fat German guy with the white beard is only in 10 East 49th on a desk space deal so we'll get the office back in a flash and, let me tell you something, Gene, you are going to be the biggest insurance-handling lawyer this country has ever seen and, mark my words, within five years you are going to be a nice, steady five-hundred-thousand-dollar-a-year man."

She buried her face in his chest. He held her closely. They stayed, clinging to each other, forever.